. . . *from The Stone Dragon*

An awful knowingness entwined Glimmer. Like the tightening coils of a constricting serpent, an intuitive knowingness encircled him until all doubt left, like breath crushed within muscled coils.

"Ye both'll have much t' talk about," Cabbage-pants had said; *". . . 'tween you and the hearthstone,"* he had said.

Placing his mug carefully upon the flagstones, Glimmer slowly stood, strode with heavy deliberateness to that legacy of when the tower had stood alone, strode to the ancient, reinforced door that connected the kitchen with the house's communal room. Opening the door, he stepped into the large room, empty and dusty from disuse, his footsteps echoing.

He turned and faced the room's hearth, his eyes without surprise taking in the sight of a lively fire crackling in the firepit, a fire of dancing and glowing light vibrant with energy, and all this manifesting from a meager collection of sticks and branches bunched upon the firestones. Light rippling upon the mantelpiece, light drawing arabesques upon Glimmer's arms, light reflecting off stone—and then one stone high upon the stonework above the firepit—a single, oval obsidian stone captured light . . . and blinked.

The Stone Dragon

Tom Kepler

N
Cold Station
Naka
Cliffs of Kergan
Biska
The Key
Lookout
Lock Bay
Agate
Knight's Landing
(Slag) Hills of Eyre
Laurel
Gaff
Selkien Sea
Plenty
Bluestem Flats
Sea of Grass
Mato
Delta
Seal Rock
Sea Marshes (Ma-Adan)
Colima Calderon
Lavan Labyrinth
Taiga
Richland
River of Pearls
Harbinger
Wheatland
Black Buttes
Valley of Gold
Barl
Tween River
Blue's Crossing
Pichl
Lower Ford
River Quill
Dragon's Chin Escarpment

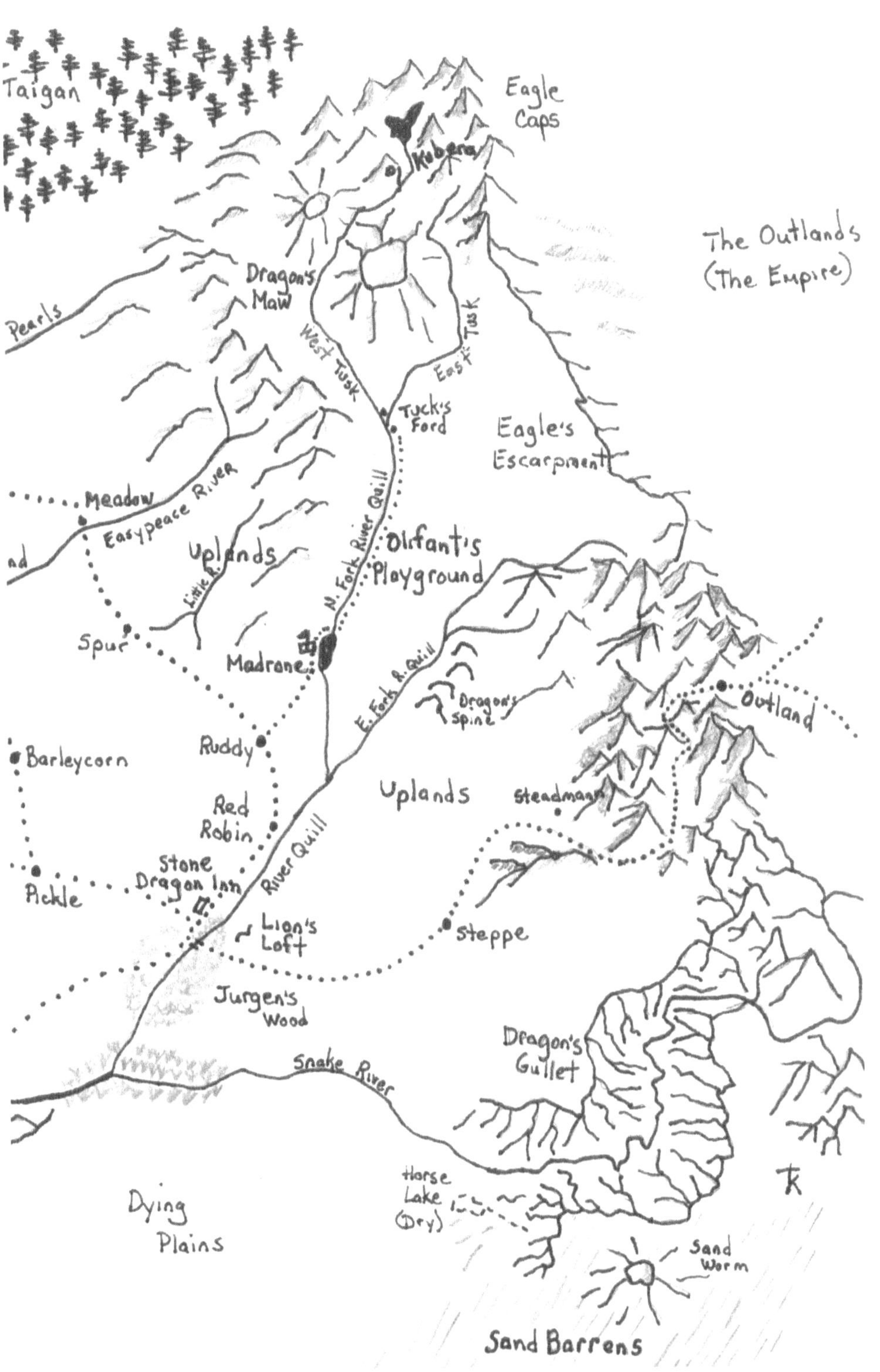

Taigan
Eagle Caps
The Outlands
(The Empire)
Pearls
Dragon's Maw
West Tusk
East Tusk
Kibera
Tuck's Ford
Eagle's Escarpment
Meadow
Easypeace River
N. Fork River Quill
Uplands
Olifant's Playground
nd
Little R.
Spur
Madrone
E. Fork R. Quill
Dragon's Spine
Outland
Barleycorn
Ruddy
Uplands
Steadman
Red Robin
River Quill
Pickle
Stone Dragon Inn
Lion's Loft
Steppe
Jurgen's Wood
Snake River
Dragon's Gullet
Horse Lake (Dry)
Dying Plains
Sand Worm
Sand Barrens

Published by Wise Moon Books
2130 Emerald Lane
Fairfield, Iowa 52556

Tom Kepler Writing: www.tomkeplerswritingblog.com

Facebook Page: www.facebook.com/TomKeplerWriting

This is a work of fiction. Names, characters, places, and incidents are the product of the author's imagination. Any resemblance to actual persons, living or dead, or actual events is purely coincidental.

ISBN 978-0-9842734-2-3

Special thanks to Allen Cobb, my technical consultant and friend, and thanks to Carol Chesnutt for her close reading and comments. And appreciation always to my wife Sandy, who kept reminding me that this would be a good project to finish.

About Photographer Suzanne Bonnefond

Cover images copyright by French photographer Suzanne Bonnefond, used with permission. The cover images are of medieval ruins, a monastery for nuns created in 1260 and destroyed around 1790. View her work at Flickr: **http://www.flickr.com/photos/sarvadon**. To contact her or to purchase photos, email **axzpro@yahoo.fr**.

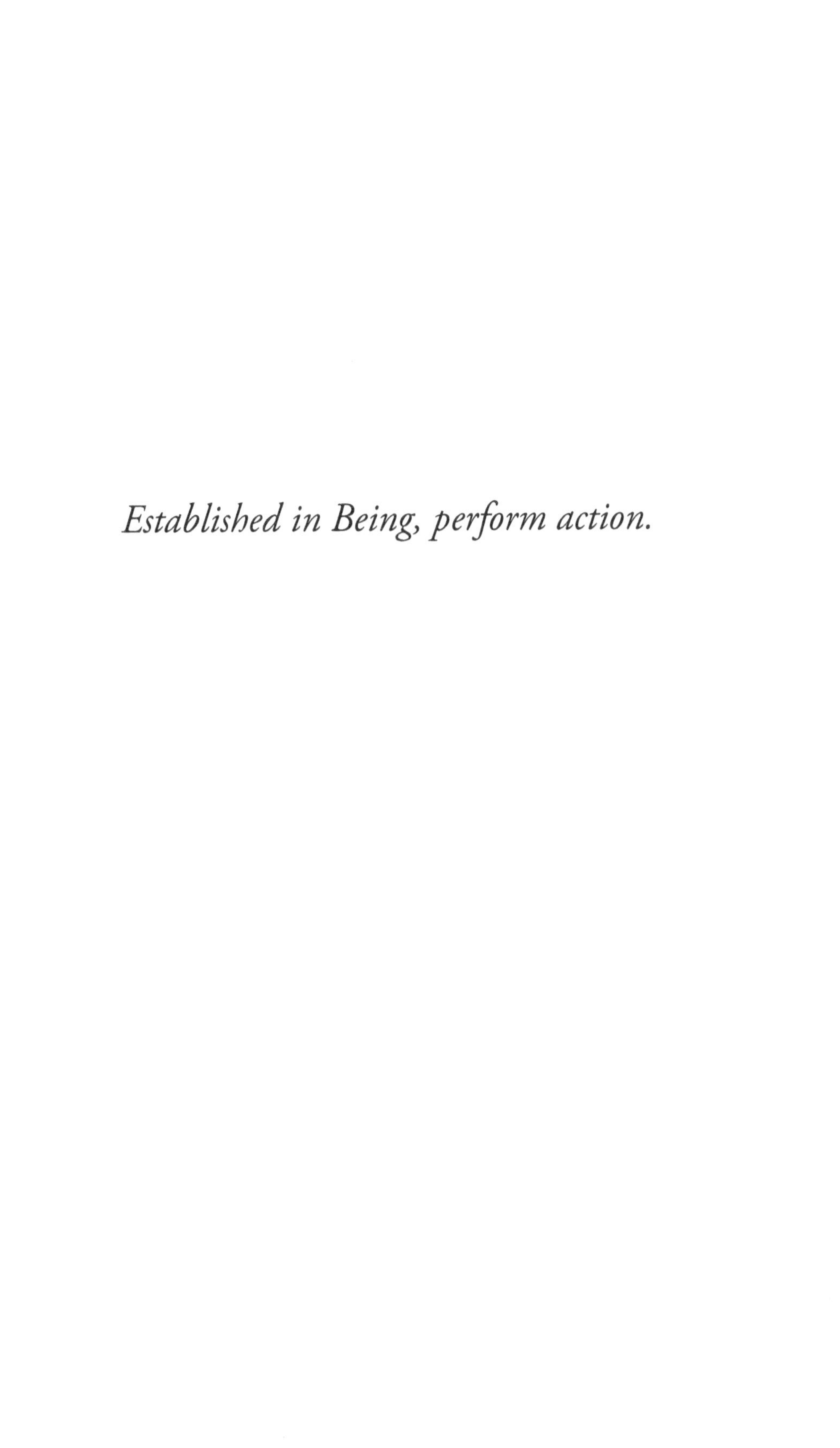

Established in Being, perform action.

Table of Contents

Chapter 1

❧

Sun blazed bright fire, and wings flamed in the silent void. And if wings, why not sinew and tendon, why not muscles to stretch and pull fire on its flight through space?

Scales of fire flexed beneath his body, and he heard the flap of wings, a sound like flame guttered by wind. He felt the surge upward and then the downward beat. Like a crown or halo, wings of light curved before him into the empty darkness—wings, and then a burning length of serpentine neck and triangular head rising to balance the stroke of wings. The viper's head turned, eyes like coals burning into his.

Breaking the fiery gaze, he traced the flaming line of the dragon's neck to his own body and saw fire astride fire. The flaming dragon he rode stooped like a raptor to the world below. One mass of land grew as flight narrowed to a destination, a land bordered by sea to the west and tall, white-capped mountains to the east.

His face grimaced as he approached the land. He could feel the pain that lay below the clouds. Fear distorted his mouth to a searing scream, but the vision tempered, darkened at the edges to indistinct shadows reflected on a convex surface. The perspective widened until vision was fringed with dark patterns of geometric regularity: black feathers surrounding a raven's eye. The world existed as he had dreamed it: a world dreamt through a raven's eye, a dream that shattered with a raucous caw.

Spreading its wings slightly, a raven shook itself and then flapped into the sky, wings rising and falling, head bobbing to the beat of its wings. It circled a young man who had risen shakily to his feet, unsteady, disoriented by the bird's cry.

Always this daydream, Glimmer thought, *but never in such detail or duration, only fragments, elusive bits of fire and flight.*

The raven circled as the young man shifted his awareness from the dragon of his dreaming to the bird flying the sky. He watched it fly full circle and land again on the grey stone of a garden wall. He stared at the obsidian eye, the bird's head cocked and steady. Then he shook himself, his eyes taking in the summer light falling warm upon a vegetable garden. The garden space was contained by grey walls of fieldstone, the north side of the square being the grey stones of a country manor. The garden lay green upon the soil, vegetables flowering and fountains of green leaves lifting toward the sky. Beyond and to the south and east, the land dropped in soft shoulders of pasture to a slender river that edged the base of the hill.

The daydream paled in the glare of the sun, and the young man turned back to his work with a shrug. Day was nearing noon, and it was difficult to determine which was louder, Glimmer's grumbles and sighs at the early summer heat or the hungry complaining of his stomach. Flaxen hair framing his face, he squinted at the sun and glowered, wiping sweat from his flushed cheeks with a sleeve of roughly woven linen.

One might as well be a turnip, he thought, a*s to be pulling weeds in a heat not even broken by the faintest breeze. Peas and carrots and cabbage!* he thought—but the sun-warmed earth in his hands was too exquisite to be overshadowed by the willful ways of weeds.

A smile broke Glimmer's thoughts. He liked this garden, after all. He liked this stone-walled sanctuary, this humid soil in his hands, these rows of vegetables neatly formed, peas primly trellised, cabbages like buried rings set with pale green gems of lapped leaves. And all by his hand, Glimmer's . . . apprentice magician. Glimmer, abruptly wiping his cheek with a sleeve again, scowled at the thought. The only magic here was magic made by sweat and busy hands, all the magic he could manage.

Glimmer turned to reach for his hand mattock and saw it twenty feet away at the head of the cabbage row. He surveyed the garden and realized, lost in his dreams, he had weeded more than he had expected. Starting early morning with the potatoes, although they had needed surprisingly little attention, he had weeded beans, parsnips, carrots, turnips, and what was left of the peas, methodically traveling the rows, scooting along, diligent enough to satisfy even a master of gardens. With never any doubt as to the task before him, Glimmer had worked with an easy energy, happily lost in the rhythm. Very little mind was needed to pull weeds, after all, especially as the plants matured—just the ability to tell vegetable from weed, the ability to pull weed and pat the warm soil flat. The stone walls, chest high, cupped the silent air, the rich earth-smells, the green magic of the growing plants.

If only I weren't a mismatched apprentice—an odd shoe nailed to a wayward horse, Glimmer thought, his mouth tightening in old habit. *Not a gardener's apprentice, nor a cook's apprentice, nor a miller's apprentice. An apprentice of nothing, that's what I am,* Glimmer thought with disgust.

He levered himself up to fetch the mattock for a nettle sprouting among the cabbages ahead. *A magician's apprentice with no magic at all. An apprentice with a mage of a master who doesn't mind a little time wasted—as long as it isn't his time. A master never around, who doesn't practice magic anyway, much less teach it.*

Feeling sorry for himself, Glimmer was, and then a graveled voice interrupted his thoughts: "No need to sour th' soil with iron when I can do the job just as well, if ye don't mind my sayin'."

Glimmer turned at the sound of the voice but saw no one—the garden as neat as always, filled with silently growing plants bathed in late morning sunlight. Then a cabbage tilted one way, tipped the other, and stood—not a cabbage at all, but a small, bow-legged, pot-bellied figure of a man with skin as mottled as all the shades of the earth, thick, lank hair the color of cabbage roots clumped with soil—a garden gnome. Shirtless and beardless (and Glimmer had thought that all gnomes had beards), the gnome wore a pair of trousers that appeared to have been tailored from cabbage leaves cured to the consistency and color of bleached leather. The trousers were so loosely and unevenly sewn, however, that the gnome's lower body seemed wrapped in swaddling bands like an untrained infant's.

His eyes as dark and bright as sunflower seeds rich with oil, the gnome continued, "I can get that nettle for ye," gesturing down the cabbage row. "No need to stick yer hands with nettles, now is there?" and with that the gnome reached into the soil up to his elbow with a movement that caused Glimmer's vision to blur, reached just as easily into earth as one would reach into pond water to pick up a stone sparkling below. The gnome set his heels to the earth and pulled, leaning back with a grunt, the nettle shaking free, roots focusing in a spray of soil. He tottered at the sudden release of the roots and then steadied himself, a smug look upon his face. "I'll just toss this in th' compost heap, Glimmer, and finish up easy on th' way."

The gnome's words were shouted back, as familiar as you please, as he ambled his bow-legged, confident way down the cabbage row. "Now don't worry about th' nettles and *me*. No nettles can hurt *my* thick ol' skin." The only thought that popped into the young man's mind was that he had imagined magical creatures like gnomes to be more soft-spoken, not as loud as a field hand at a wrestling match.

The gnome hummed to himself as he sauntered down the garden row, his left hand balancing the nettle on his shoulder, garden weeds in the cabbage row leaning their lanky stems toward the gnome as if he were a lodestone and they were iron. Weeds leapt from the soil, nestling into the crook of the gnome's right arm, forming a blanket of luxuriant green. The gnome laughed as a choker vine flew from the soil, wrapping itself around his neck. "Ornery little rascals," he chortled.

Then, nodding to the young apprentice again, the gnome's pebble-round eyes squinted up at the sun, adding even more wrinkles to his leathery face. "And I worked with th' 'taters a bit for ye, Master Glimmer, only don't spread it 'round too much, me being cabbage gnome an' all." The gnome grunted and actually looked furtively over both shoulders as he straightened with his load again. He nodded knowingly. "Y'coulda started with th' cabbages, y'know. Didn't have to leave 'em till last, as ye did. A gesture of respect, ye might say. Always start with highest first."

"How do you know my name?" Glimmer blurted out, finally finding his voice.

"Yer name an' ways is known by me an' others of my kind," the gnome replied, turning and bowing, bobbling his load of weeds.

Bitterness rose in the young man as he spilled out, "I'll just bet you know my name. *Not a Glimmer of Magic*, not a stinking glimmer of magic, that's what they call me, but that's not calling me by name; that's name-calling."

"Say what ye will, but where there's gleam there's gold, so th' sayin' goes."

"I thought it was 'All that glitters isn't gold,'" Glimmer retorted.

"Glimmer, gleam, glitter—it's not name but person that makes th' worth."

With that, Glimmer's vision blurred again as the knee-high gnome walked straight into the compost heap as if it were a curtained doorway. The gnome disappeared, leaving the nettle and weeds lying atop the heap of rotting herbage. Then a muffled voice drifted back, "A good day fer magic, ain't it, though?" The gnome's head appeared again, topped by a wig of green weeds. "Hey, you!" the gnome shouted, the volume so great that the young man started. "Like that better? Th' fact that yer *seein'* me must count as at least a *glimmer* o' magic, hm? An' where there's glimmer, there's gold."

Then the stone-walled garden stilled to a tableau of silence. Glimmer drew one deep breath, shifting his weight from one foot to the other; he drew another deep breath, waiting for the gnome to reappear, but the enclosed garden, its weeded rows straight and freshly cultivated, was silent.

A magical being, Glimmer thought to himself in bemused shock. *A garden gnome! No wonder the weeds seemed so few!* He could make neither heads nor tails of it, having never seen nor spoken to anything magical. But the garden was weeded and his work more than done, so with an air of practicality, young Glimmer let himself out the garden gate. *It was just a gnome, after all, not like a dragon or anything.*

As he crossed the road and descended the soft shoulder of the hill to the river, there to cool and clean himself before eating his midday meal, the young man did not notice, bright as black obsidian chips, a gnome's eyes solemnly following his steps, nor did he notice the raven leap into the sky, black flight following his path like a second shadow.

Chapter 2

"Contrarie to common beliefe magicians do not existe, only magick."

The Philosophie of Magick

"Dreme magick is the most dangerous of magicks because it is the most difficult to control."

Confessions of a Dreme Mage

☙

Glimmer leaned the ladder against the wall of his master's stone tower. *The perfect house for a magician,* he thought . . . *built all of stone, cold in the summer, colder in the winter. No wonder he doesn't spend much time here.*

The country manor consisted of a stone tower, the original edifice, two stories in height. Glimmer's master called the second floor his study, but the locals called it "the magician's lair," somewhat presumptuous, Glimmer felt, since his master spent little time in it, and also since his master was hardly a magician. The kitchen and Glimmer's living quarters were on the ground floor. The tower's architecture contained no underground rooms, or "dungeons," as some speculation had it.

In times past, a large, two-story addition to the tower, also composed of fieldstone, had been built by an order of the Brothers of Hospitality. Since Glimmer had never been able to find anything out about the Brothers and their stay in the house, he assumed the Brothers' stay had not been very hospitable. The upstairs of the addition had been two large rooms, a dormitory for the brothers and a room for guests, Glimmer assumed. The ground floor had functioned as a communal dining and work area.

A country squire had then acquired the house, constructed living quarters upstairs, and made a go at farming. However, either the land surrounding the manor had been too hilly and woodsy to sustain the country squire and his aspirations, or the aspirations of the squire had not equaled the demands of the land. Whichever the case, the squire had returned after a few years to the safe haven of family estates along the coast at Knight's Landing, leaving the manor unmanned, as it were.

Eventually, a mage had been given the manor as payment for his interactions with the local villages. The unnamed and forgotten mage had left for better prospects, and the manor had been abandoned for years before the coming of Glimmer's master.

Glimmer mounted a rough-hewn ladder leaning against the tower's north face, careful of splinters even though the rungs had been worn smooth from use. Daub the window casements to keep out summer hornets and winter winds. *And this one needs it,* Glimmer thought, surveying the wooden frame containing pale blue squares of leaded glass seated in the tower wall. It was almost ready to fall out, if not for the chocks, so much mortar had sifted away with the seasons. That was when a thought occurred to Glimmer, something he had never considered before.

He could remove the whole window, carry it down the ladder, set it on the ground, and then climb through the hole the window occupied. "That's how to get into the study without invoking the spell," he said aloud, the thought was so clear.

Glimmer remembered the last (and only) time he had been in his master's study. It had been five years ago when he was twelve years old, his first day as apprentice to Mage Alma-Ata.

His mage, a lean man with informal manners, wore the clothes of the local farmers. *No one would know him from an apple farmer with an orchard on a hillside or a wheat farmer from the valley,* Glimmer had thought as he had followed the nimble old man up the stone steps to the second floor of the stone tower.

"Now that you are an apprentice, I suppose you would like to see some magic," Mage Alma-Ata had said as they reached one of three wooden doors on the landing. "And to satisfy you, we will use a spell already in place." The mage had turned to his apprentice and added ingenuously, "To tell the truth, we're going to see if the spell actually works by what happens to you." Even the mage's smile had not stopped Glimmer's heart leaping in his twelve-year-old chest.

The mage had unlocked the door with a large iron key and then had pushed the door open, the hinges squeaking as if unused to such activity. With an elegant, friendly gesture, Alma-Ata had invited Glimmer into the room.

"This is my study, my library," the mage had said, gesturing to the shelves and tables filled with dusty leather-bound books and fragile paper scrolls. He had added with an upward turn of his mouth, "I don't use it much." The mage had paused, surveying the room, and then continued. "Hence, the spell, my boy . . . to keep out the over-curious, the greedy, and those desiring power over others."

Alma-Ata had pursed his lips. "Actually, the first task I am assigning you as my apprentice is to dust this room." These words had been followed by a silent pause and then a violent sneeze. "As I said," the mage had continued after blowing his nose loudly, "I don't use this room much. You see, knowledge needs to be here," he had tapped his temple with his forefinger, "and not just in books. But we should make this room more presentable, in case I have a scholar visit me . . . or in case I need to find a book for you to read some day. I have been told that the grandfather where you lived taught you your letters."

Mage Alma-Ata had smiled down at Glimmer. "Who knows when you may get a book, hmmm? Do you know your letters? Can you read?"

"Yes, sire," Glimmer had replied, although he was somewhat confused by the mage's manner. *The mage might as well be a miller or a grower of apples,* he'd thought. *Mages should be more . . . magnificent.*

Almost as if he were reading Glimmer's mind, Alma-Ata had added as he absent-mindedly tucked his jerkin to fit more smoothly beneath his belt, "I suppose you'd like to see some magic?" The mage's expression became mischievous. "Perhaps I should make the table sprout green leaves . . . or perhaps light the candles with a flick of my hand."

Alma-Ata had scanned the room, colored light filtering from the stained-glass windows, colored squares of light warming the dim interior, the east window an elongated rectangle of amber falling on the wooden beams of the floor, books and specimen cases beneath the windows in shadows. "No, I think there is enough light for cleaning . . . so maybe a dragon, hm?" Glimmer had gazed up with round eyes at the mage's suddenly serious face. "Dragons are nothing to trifle with, though. Summon a dragon to satisfy a boy's curiosity? No . . . large magic only for a large need."

The mage had lifted a stack of faded parchment from a stool fronting a writing table in the center of the room, dusting the seat idly with a sleeve. "I'll tell you what, boy," his tone now as focused as his gaze. "A magician," Alma-Ata had spoken slowly, "could possess any book in this room that he desired. Do you know why?"

As the mage had bent down, his face closer to Glimmer's, his eyes locked upon the boy's eyes, Alma-Ata had whispered, "Because a magician would know which books were his; a true magician would desire only books that he deserved." The mage had straightened and turned to gaze at the stacks of manuscripts and books that surrounded them.

"I'll tell you what—let's have a test. You may have any book in this library that is yours, but—" the mage, laying a skinny forefinger against his bony nose, had turned back to regard the boy "—if you take a book you should not have . . . well, some might call that stealing." With those words and a lingering gaze from beneath bushy, grey eyebrows, Alma-Ata had silently handed Glimmer a dusting rag and strode from the room.

Glimmer gazed through the north window from his perch on the ladder. He thought that he could see *the book* through the distorted blue of the ancient glass pane in the tower's north window; he thought he could see the one that had found its way into his pocket five years ago, a slim volume bound in leather, plain and unadorned, a small book, one that could lie flat against the thigh, tucked down the breeches. Yes, that *might* be the volume he had possessed once for a brief time. Glimmer began to scrape the powdery mortar away from the window frame, his breath quickening with excitement.

Five years ago, Glimmer had dusted the books on the shelves of his master's study. He had dusted the piles of manuscripts, careful not to disturb the sheaves of loose sheets of handwritten paper. Finding a broom, he had swept the dusty planked floor, progressing to the stone landing outside the study and to the stone steps connecting the first and second floors. He had turned at the study's entry and surveyed the room.

Done, his twelve-year-old mind had decided. The silent majesty of the room had enthralled Glimmer, the motionless books and parchments of the mages waiting for eyes to read, for a mind to connect with words and receive knowledge.

Glimmer had stepped back into the study, leaning the broom against the stone wall, and had turned to the books, reading the titles, ink on leather or silken cloth, or cramped script on curling, fragile paper—all this dyed by the blue, amber, and green glass of the windows set in the round stone tower—small, leaded squares of colored glass comprising each window: north, east, and west.

Something small, his mind had whispered: *something small and not so important . . . or easily missed. Something easy to tuck away.* And he had found just such a volume.

Or perhaps the volume found me, crossed Glimmer's mind as he finished whisking away the last of the mortar. Now the window was held in the opening by three wooden wedges, two on the sides and one at the bottom.

The book Glimmer had discovered five years ago was a handwritten journal, bound in plain, undyed leather, the paper hand-stitched into a simple and unadorned book. On the front cover in black ink were printed the words *Confessions of a Dreme Mage.* He had opened the volume to a random page and had read: *Safety lies only in silent witness.*

I can read this, he had thought, pleased with himself, *and the mage wants me to read. Otherwise, why leave me with the books?*

And Glimmer on the ladder watched the memory of himself slip the book inside his breeches flush with the skin—leather to skin, lie to truth—watched his younger self stride from the room.

Onto the cold grey of the stone landing and quickly down the worn stone steps, young Glimmer had progressed, and with that progression, the air had cooled and he had felt the chill sheen of sweat as his body, warm from exertion or excitement, had met the quiet, chill stillness of the tower's rough stone. His steps had echoed as he spiraled downward to the ground floor, and the echoes spoke to him, whispering his innermost thoughts.

It is not yours. When your master wishes you to have the words, he will deliver them to you. On the first day of your apprenticeship, you steal. Be true and all will be well. This is a test your master has given you, and you have failed.

Glimmer's breath had rasped in his throat like a sob as he'd stopped his descent and sagged against the stone wall. The inner well of the stairs was dim, flecks of dust floating in the diffuse light of the well. The words had beat at him as his heart had beat within, the cells of his body leaning to the truth like plant to sun.

Nowhere to go, you have nowhere. The mage chose you, and what are you choosing?

Desire had risen in Glimmer not to just return the volume to its place in the mage's library but rather to confess his actions, to tell the magician what he had done. The desire to place the thin sheave of pages in the mage's slender, labor-roughened hands had consumed Glimmer.

"Mage Alma-Ata?" he'd shouted. "Master, where are you?" he'd cried, his face wet with tears and voice ragged with emotion.

Only silence had met his frantic searching as he had descended the stairs to the kitchen. Out the east door and to his right, a rush along the crushed stone pathway fringing the straight length of the building connected to the tower, Glimmer had turned into the east entrance of the kitchen garden at the south end of the building: stone and stone, building and fence, and on a stone bench warming himself in the sun had sat the mage, his head nodding like a flower caressed by wind. The young man had stopped abruptly, caught by the absolute silence that had seemed to surround the old man sitting on the bench, the old mage who seemed to be so perfectly still, doing nothing.

Then Glimmer had thrown himself at his master's feet, hugging the old man's legs. "I took the book and I am sorry. Please forgive me!" Glimmer had stared up into the old man's eyes. "I told myself that the book was mine, but deep inside I knew it wasn't."

Then Glimmer had reached past his belt and pulled the slender book from hiding, placing the volume in his master's hands. The sun had suddenly seemed brighter, the day lighter. Glimmer had smiled as the burden was lifted from him; he had smiled, content to place his head upon the mage's lap. The mage had shifted the book to one hand and then had placed the leather-covered pages upon the bench. Then the mage's hand had absently smoothed Glimmer's tousled hair that had glowed like pale morning sunlight.

"So now you know magic," the mage had murmured. When Glimmer had raised his head to see his master's face, Alma-Ata had kindly gazed back. "You kept the book only minutes."

Alma-Ata had smiled softly at Glimmer's puzzled look. "A self-centered boy would have kept the book longer, perhaps even for the night, would have read some of the book, absorbing the words like seeds tossed to infertile soil."

The mage, raising his faded, blue eyes to the horizon, had stroked Glimmer's hair again. "A truly evil, powerful mage would have kept the book, reading and studying it, truths not belonging to him curling within like encysted parasites, the book eating at him. Over time he would learn to enjoy the sensation, would come to define himself as that sensation."

Shaking himself slightly, Alma-Ata had finished, "Well, enough of that. You are not that person, my thief-of-one-minute. Water runs swiftly down a straight channel."

Glimmer had sat up, cross-legged before his master. "I don't understand. You said *magic*? What magic?"

"The magic that returned my book to me."

"There was no magic." Glimmer had brushed his hair away from his eyes. "I did a wrong thing and told you."

"And you think that is not magic?" the mage had responded, standing now, tall and straight before Glimmer. An ambiguous smile on his face, Alma-Ata had reached down to touch Glimmer's head. "At least we know the spell works."

Glimmer had listened to the mage's words, confused in his heart. *Magic?* he'd wondered. Of his own choosing he had returned the book. Where was the magic in that?

"Now go to the kitchen and find something to eat," Alma-Ata had advised. "After all your work, a growing boy like you needs sustenance."

The mage had followed the retreating boy's frame with thoughtful eyes, and then reached to the bench, picking up the book and reading its cover. He pursed his lips, breathing in a sudden breath.

This book, the mage had wondered. *Why, of all the tomes, had the boy chosen this one?*

A coldness had entered Alma-Ata, even in the heat of the summer's day. His shoulders had slumped as if from a heavy weight, and then his spine had stiffened, straightened. The old man returned to his magic, his only safe haven, and sat quietly—breathing out, breathing in, nothing more.

Glimmer stood upon the ladder rung, staring through the pale blue stain of the glass at the room below, books and papers lying random and loose, an unfurled map on the scarred table. He pulled a trowel from his belt and pried the bottom wedge from between the frame and stone; then he removed the wedges from the sides of the frame, careful not to allow the window to tilt and fall to the ground.

If a pane cracks or a rectangle of glass breaks free from its leading, will I evoke the spell, Glimmer wondered, *or is there really a spell at all?* Maybe Alma-Ata had just amused himself by playing with the mind of a twelve year old.

Nonetheless, Glimmer gingerly eased the frame, cradling the latticed window sash from its blank-eyed rectangle on the curving north wall of the tower. He lowered himself carefully down the rungs, sliding the frame on the angled ladder above him until he reached the ground. Then he leaned the frame with its glass against the stone wall, making sure the glass was stable and would not tip and shatter.

As Glimmer gazed upward at the hollow socket in the tower wall, he placed a hand upon the ladder rung at chest height and then remounted the ladder, step by step, gaining the stone-grey empty eye at last. Turning on the ladder so he was facing outward, he surveyed the land about him. Nothing moved; no one interrupted the solitude. Facing north, before him was a meadow dotted with maple, oak, and apple trees, the young apple trees encircled with fences of woven saplings to keep away the deer. To his right, a road ran a parallel course with the river past the house, the river flowing south and west, out of Glimmer's sight, to the sea. The land due north rose in gradual undulations, and in the near distance lay the green upland foothills that rose to distant mountains.

With one last furtive glance, Glimmer slithered through the opening like a worm entering a fallen apple. He dropped to the floor and froze, his breath quick with excitement, closing his eyes and casting his attention within, waiting for an emotion to rise, a desire to cast himself back out the window and confess his intentions to anyone, everyone. His heart beat; he breathed in, exhaling slowly through his nose.

Maybe, he thought, *I have to actually take a book, to leave the room with it.*

And at that moment, Glimmer realized it wasn't any book that he was considering but rather *the book*, the one he had chosen five years ago, the thin hand-written journal by the dream mage.

Rising from his crouch on the floor below the window, he followed the wall of the study to the bookshelf from which he had taken the journal five years earlier. Was the thin volume he had seen from the window the book by the dream mage? Had Alma-Ata returned the book to its original spot, or had he hidden it to keep it from curious eyes? There, lying on the bookshelf as he had seen it from the window, not tucked in among the other volumes but on the lip of the shelf which fronted the books, lay the volume, its plain leather cover a warm brown in contrast to the time-stained wooden shelves. Written on the cover of the book in an economical hand was the title. Glimmer reached out and picked up the book. It was smaller, even thinner and less substantial than he had remembered.

As he held the book in his hand, he felt no strangeness in his chest, no upsurge of emotions, no guilt. He slipped the book beneath his belt and hoisted himself onto the window sill. Sitting with his legs dangling out the window, Glimmer still felt no remorse, no compulsion to cry out in confession. He turned and placed his feet upon the rungs, now half in and half out of the window opening, the book still tucked beneath his belt, the book now outside the building by a finger's length. Placing one hand on the book, ready to flip it through the window at the slightest twinge of regret, Glimmer descended one step on the ladder. Feeling nothing, he slowly descended step by cautious step to the ground.

He had done it. His emotions somersaulted in turns of glee and—not remorse—caution. *I may not have a glimmer of magic,* he thought, *and I may have a master who likes me only for my strong back, but I've got the book. I've thought of something he didn't think of, and how I will enjoy telling him of it when I see him again,* he thought, for he had never considered taking the book and keeping its taking a secret from his master.

Glimmer turned to peer up at the window opening. He would not replace the window yet.

No, not just yet. I will read for a time, and if I begin to feel anything, then I'll scramble up the ladder and return the book. Or perhaps I should climb the ladder now and read the book in the study? I could take a handful of crumbled mortar and toss it onto the floor beneath the window. I could say that I'd wished to clean the floor before sealing the window back into the opening. Mix some mortar first . . . no, if it dries, there would be the explaining of that. All the materials are ready, just climb the ladder and slide to the floor, open the book and read . . .

Following his thoughts, Glimmer found himself on the floor before the bookshelf. *Is this,* he thought, *part of the magic? I feel outside myself, watching myself.*

He scooted to the end of the bookcase and leaned against a stone pillar rising through the wooden floor to support the beams and the roof. A sharp angle of rock gouged his back, and Glimmer shifted again. Then he opened the book and read.

"Dreme magick is the most dangerous of magicks because it is the most difficult to control. What is a dreme but a phantom of waking, a phantasm that can walk the halls of night and conjure walls to fleshe and fleshe to walls? One is not apprenticed to dreme magery but born to it. One *dremes* with intente deep within the interstices of one's being, and then the dreme *becomes*. It is in this *becoming* that the danger lies, to dip into the mouthe of the springe from which nature arises to nourish one's dremes. One must not seeke to do; rather, one must humbly do what needes to be done. Safety lies only in silent witness. Nature acts and one witnesses and celebrates its splendore."

Glimmer shifted again, quickly leafing through the scant pages of the journal. *No spells,* he thought, disappointed. *It's just a lot of talk. But what does it mean?* He settled more comfortably against the stone pillar, against its safe and secure solidity.

Am I born to dream magery? he asked himself. *How does one dream with deep intent yet not seek, only humbly witness?* The phantom of his thoughts wandered more deeply the corridors of his mind, wandered the stone-lined hallways and stairwells of the magician's lair. He closed his eyes, safe within his master's den. His heart eased. He had learned no spells and practiced no magic; he had done nothing, really, just read a book—and a rather boring one at that. Worked hard all day, he had, and the room was cool and peaceful after all the excitement. Glimmer's eyes grew heavy, his breathing deepened, and then he slept.

Chapter 3

"With minde absolutely awake, one dremes without fear."
Confessions of a Dreme Mage

❧

Glimmer awoke to the awareness that he had been sleeping deeply, so soundly and restfully that even the hardness of the floor had not disturbed his slumber. Stretching and opening his eyes, he saw that he had slept through the afternoon, an early moon now rising on the horizon. He sat up, admiring the moon's wan light, a cool streaming through glass-paned doors which led to the north balcony. That the doors and balcony had not existed when Glimmer had dozed off was of no importance. They existed now. He felt a vitality flowing through him, a vibrant coursing energy. How deep his sleep must have been! How alive he felt! How beautiful was this study, so full of light, even by moonlight!

Standing, Glimmer strode through beams of moonlight to the glow of the doors and opened them. The rich scents of the warm spring season flowed into the room with the moonlight, scents of plants in blossom, of crop pollen and rainwater. The earth whispered promises of bud and birth, of possibilities, potentialities. So many and marvelous! Earth pressed its seeds into his hands; *grow these as you will,* it whispered in a breath of wind, *and take joy in the growing.*

Fireflies flickered in the grasses below as Glimmer strode to the balcony's edge, his hands caressing the smooth texture of the marble balustrade. Constellations of fireflies below and constellations of stars above: microcosm and macrocosm, the same fire burned in each. Glimmer breathed deeply, let the breath escape his lungs. Breath or breeze, it was all the same: all was one. He raised his hands before him, raised them to the sky and felt an energy flowing within them, blood of existence; closed his eyes, at one with all that surrounded him, each mote of matter the same life force that surged the life-blood of his body.

Exaltation, a physical vibration, flowed from him like light: energy emanating from his hands, rivers flowing to merge with the ocean of the sky. Filled with silent laughter, Glimmer reached out to touch the stars, grew huge in his joy and stepped from the moon-drenched marble of the balcony to the goat-cropped meadow below. He turned and touched the smooth stone walls of the tower, white-veined stone no different than his flesh, reached to the stars and stood taller than the tower, a self-contained massif of power and portent now gazing upon trees smaller than his knees, their rounded tops a rabble of shrubs to his majesty. Like an oak he grew, hard-grained sinews reaching to sky, ecstasy flowing from his fingers, his eyes shining with starlight.

The moon glowed in the sky and flowed its drifting course. *I could sail the moon,* thought Glimmer, *fill sails with cosmic wind and hands with stars. They would be an icy fire, and I would drink their crystal waters and burn with the cold purity of that light. Oh, stars! Oh, my brothers and sisters! Let me burn to nothing and be as you!*

He swayed in his vision, and when he brushed an ancient apple tree with his giant's calf, the tree burst into flame. Glimmer praised its light, reveled in the warm caress of leaves and branches burning, but watching the flames falter and then subside, felt a sadness. Too transitory was its light, not the ancient radiance of the stars.

I shall sift the sky for the souls of stars, he thought, *the fire that does not burn, the wings of light which fly the firmament.* And he reached his arms wide and wider, opening his palms to capture light. Three stars shot the sky—north, west, and east, flaring and fading to darkness. Glimmer filled himself with energy; it flowed to him. He glowed and grew. Tilting back his head, he inhaled the breath of the stars and opened his eyes, his gaze penetrating sky above, clouds about his shoulders like a mantle.

A single star glimmered in the sky, brighter than the other stars: yes, a glimmer, a flicker, a sparkle, a movement, an expansion of winged light. *Let me touch it; let me drink its light.* A silence settled, the crackling flames of the apple tree fading, limbs black and burned beneath him. Wind faltered to calm; clouds drifted, aimless as sullen fog. The burning star expanded, white light with laving coruscations the colors of dawn. It grew, and now Glimmer could see a rhythmic pattern to the light, light swimming darkness—no, light winging darkness, wings of light and not star but form, the body of the angel of a star, wings like dawn.

Oh, angel of stars, he sang, *shine more brightly and deliver unto me your soul;* and the star obeyed, and flight became the pitching dive of a raptor, and the flaming light of the angel became curling flames of breath, the body of light lucent scales, an immense serpentine swimming: fire-breather, worm sleeping in the mother of fire till woken!

Oh, apple-cheeked dream mage, your soul of stars, your angel of light, your dragon cometh! Find your freedom in my flames, and burn in the bliss of my fire!

Wings spread and spanned the world, tucked as the dragon dropped like molten stone, its body a serpentine sun hurtling down upon the young man, scales aglimmer, mouth an open, fiery maelstrom, flames curling and spitting.

Glimmer's heart cooled and blackened as the dragon hurtled downward, far distant yet still immense. The dreamer's fingertips, still outstretched from the ecstasy of his vision, felt the promise of fire. He shrank back, ducking below scattered clouds which had crowned his head. His hands to his face, he cringed, crouching and shrinking, smaller and smaller, elation dissipating like smoke, spent and acrid. Foolish mage-boy, an inner voice keened, dream and die! But then he thought, *Who dies with me? The trees and animals, the green grasses and garden? Which village and which farmstead?*

Standing now back on the dream-balcony of white marble, Glimmer turned, clutching his blackened hands to his chest, his hair singeing, curling like leaves sucked to flame. Into the tower he staggered, his lungs burning with cosmic fire. Before the bookcase, a crumpled form lay in well-used, rustic clothes—himself, he realized in awe, his sleeping form. Grey ashes settled on white marble, world collapsed to waking, yet still the crumpled form of Glimmer the apprentice lay before the standing dream-form of Glimmer the mage, lay upon a floor of rough wooden planks worn to smoothness by countless footsteps. The glamour of the dream dissipated to walls of plain grey fieldstone, the curved walls of the tower, his mage's study, the north window a rectangle of late-afternoon sky, cloudless and serene; yet Glimmer the mage could still feel the heat and pain approaching, could see through the roof as if it were a transparent pane of glass, could see the lethal bolt of serpentine fire descending upon the stone of the silent house beneath the dream-darkness of a night sky.

Oh, the silent, safe, solidity of stone! his heart moaned. Even stones will slag, will sag and ooze like so much basaltic pitch spit from earth. The dream-mage cast himself upon the sleeping form of the apprentice-mage, providing his burning body to shield the sleeping form.

One raw hand clawed the stone pillar next to the bookcase: so cool the stone, so much calmness and safety in stone. *Safety in stone! Safety of stone!* the young apprentice thought, sitting up, the mage now no more than incense in the dim interior of the study, but Glimmer could still feel the descent of the dragon, the awful, terrific weight of it descending upon the stone house, upon the meadow and its fruit trees, upon the river sparkling among its stones and the valley nestled among foothills, green and golden.

Safety of stone! thought Glimmer, stone the color of dragon skin, scaled armor of the earth. *Dragon to stone! Dragon in stone, the carved safety of stone,* his mind chanted in a litany of desperation and fear, and the world whorled, his wits a dust-devil in a dervish dream.

Glimmer awoke to the plain grey stone of waking state, awoke to wipe his face of tears with hands no longer ravaged by fire, brushed back blonde hair fire-like only by its faint, reddish tinge. He gasped a stone-cooled draught of air and shuddered in the silence, drew in another breath and opened his eyes. The thin volume of dream magic lay on the floor beside him, and he edged from it as from a threatening snake. Through the window, a meadow lark called out its jubilant song. A dragonfly landed on the stone of the window ledge, its thousand eyes evaluating the young man.

A nightmare, Glimmer thought, remembering every piece of it. *The nightmare! Or is it a daymare, since I dreamt by daylight?* No, no, too dark a vision to place beneath the sun. Burning flames of sun! He staggered to his feet, picking up the book and tossing it to the shelf where he had found it, adjusting it with a desperate jab of a finger to its original position. Turning to the north, he heaved himself to the hollow eye of the window, shooed off the dragonfly, and slithered through to the ladder and down to the green grass of the earth. Leaning against the rough wall, he dumbly gazed into the silent blue of the sky, his hands abstractedly fondling tufts of grass, cool and succulent. *The nightmare,* he breathed, *but still just a nightmare,* his body seeking reason for releasing the terror—a dream more real than real. He shuddered.

Then his eyes focused on the masonry tools, the mortar and water before him. Frantic with energy, Glimmer rose, grabbed the latticed frame of glass, tools tucked within pockets and belt, and mounted the ladder, sliding the window before him. He chocked the window into its space and then, descending the ladder, mixed mortar and sealed the window from winter winds—*and your own meddling,* his mind whispered. Collecting his tools, he rounded the tower to the west side of the house to the tool shed and stable.

Before him lay the waste of an ancient apple tree, its limbs contorted in the rigor of its burning. The acrid stench of charred life mingled with the fragrant incense of apple wood. An ancient life was dead, a few black, burned apples still dangling from the branches. His limbs moving with the woodenness of a puppet, his mind numbed by the blackened branches of the tree, Glimmer walked past the tree to the wattle shed, returning the tools to their shelf, carefully closing the door, and then returning to the north face of the tower. There he tipped the ladder from wall to ground, hefted it in the middle, adjusting his hands to balance the weight, and returned it to its place among the rafters of the stable.

Casting himself onto a puncheon bench beside the stable door, the mellow afternoon light warmed the stable wall, yet Glimmer sat on the side of shadow. He felt the chill of winter in his bones, felt the fear of dragon in his blood, felt sadness for the loss of the apple, its fruit so crisp and sweet, its branches so welcoming. He felt wonder that the dream had been true—and wondered what it meant that he could sleep and dream and destroy. He stood and rounded the tower again to gain the east side of the house and its entrance. Something liquid would be good, he thought, tea and then a swim in the cold clarity of the river—tea, a swim, and then sleep. He was so tired.

As Glimmer entered the kitchen, a thought occurred: to sleep but then to dream! How could he ever sleep again? It wasn't safe to sleep. Then he remembered: *safety in stone!* Those words, so powerful—but what could they mean, what could be true?

"Thought y' might like some tea," a gravelly voice stated as Glimmer entered the dimness of the kitchen. Looking down, on the hearthstones he saw a small man-like form no taller than his knee, skin mottled in shades of earth, thick, lank hair the pale color of cabbage.

"Have a seat, if it pleases ye," the gnome said even as Glimmer sank to the hearthstones in shock, his mind beyond surprise but so tired and drained. "Magic has a way about it, that it does, and sometimes th' best thing is an earth gift, so it's a tonic I've fixed for ye." The gnome lifted a cup to Glimmer's hand, a gesture simultaneously gracious and ingratiating. "Red cabbage tea with a touch of balm. It'll invig'grate yer blood and calm yer nerves."

Glimmer sipped the tea and grimaced.

"Yessire," the gnome chortled, rocking on the hearthstones with glee. "It'll do the trick."

"Had enough tricks," Glimmer muttered but took another sip. The homey taste of cabbage did settle his nerves if not his stomach as the gnome acknowledged, "A bit o' honey would've helped, but there was none t' be found."

Glimmer watched as the gnome gazed, dreamy-eyed, into the crackling fire, and then the young man said, "I know *what* you are—a gnome—but *who* are you and why are you here? Why are you doing this? You know my name, but . . ." Glimmer felt his fear and fought it back with anger that focused on the gnome.

"Thank ye for askin'," the gnome replied with a gracious tug of his forelock. "Ye were sum'mat surprised this mornin', so I didn't spend more time than needed." The gnome cocked his ankle upon his knee and looked up at Glimmer, mischief in his eyes.

"First, there's not much use in just sayin' *gnomes*, no more than there's just sayin' *trees* or *animals*. Oh, ye can say it, but to what point? Ye see before ye a *cabbage gnome*, Cabbage-pants of the cabbage gnomes, at y'r service." Cabbage-pants bowed at the waist with a flourish of his hands, almost unbalancing himself and toppling from the hearthstones before the fire. "Whoa, easy now!" he admonished himself. "Fire's getting' to th' head!"

Then he continued, "We cabbage gnomes, as I said, are th' royalty of gnomes. Of course, there are other, lesser opin'ons, but ours prevail—in my opin'on. We protect what's ours, perhaps ye've heard. 'Don't tread me cabbage, an' I willn't be savage,' ye might say," the gnome observed, chuckling to himself at his cleverness.

Silence lapsed as Glimmer was at a loss of what to say. Calling him *Count Cabbage-pants* seemed excessive. "I didn't know gnomes used fire," he finally commented, something to say.

"Leave off wi' ye," scoffed the gnome with a snicker. "Afraid o' a little fire—and especially now, with all that's here an' 'appened! Leave off pullin' m' leg! What, only eat th' cabbage raw? Now mind me, I've got nothin' again' plain ol' cabbage—there's yer slaw and yer salad and yer picklin' . . . but give up boiled cabbage?" Cabbage-pants stirred the fire with a smoldering branch and sipped his cabbage tea, lost for the moment in memories delicious. "Give up yer cabbage pie? Bubblin' cabbage? Stuffed cabbage rolls?" He shook himself at the thought. "O' course, you *would* be askin' about the fire, considerin' everything."

"What's that supposed to mean?"

Cabbage-pants winked at Glimmer's words. "Right, right. We'll just keep it 'tween you, me, an' the garden gate. A'right, I don't mean a thing, nosire, not a thing. Or should I asaid ''tween you and the hearthstone'?" the gnome said with a wink. "Ye both'll have much t' talk about, an' I'll be leavin' yer to't," and with those words and a simple bow, the garden gnome Cabbage-pants, his diaper-breeches low on his hips like those of a toddler, left the kitchen and house, turning right and heading for the garden, Glimmer supposed.

The silence of the kitchen and its ancient darkness suddenly seemed oppressive to Glimmer. The magic of the gnome seemed almost normal, homey, in comparison to Glimmer's dream of fire incarnate. *But,* he thought, *the apple tree stands outside,* a charred skeleton, that beautiful old friend climbed so often, which had given its sweet yet tart fruit.

Back and again returned the image of the dragon's gleaming eyes, its wings widespread, scales glowing like gold and silver fresh-born from the primal forges of the earth. The wide maw of the mouth, teeth to tear and tongue to taste his blood! Not dream magic, no—rather the magic of nightmares. And how did that nightmare connect with his daydream of riding a flaming dragon? Glimmer stared blankly into the fire, weariness heavy on his shoulders.

There was nothing nightmarish about the kitchen, though; the solid-ity of its rounded walls of stone, the worn, blackened fireplace and hearth were reassuring images to Glimmer's mind. He leaned against the stone mantel of the fireplace, sipped his tea and grimaced again at its flavor . . . *definitely an acquired taste,* he thought absent-mindedly. The stones had absorbed the warmth of the fire, and tendrils of warmth massaged the tenseness of Glimmer's muscles. He half-closed his eyes, languidly perusing the room, its rounded tower wall like the muscled roundness of some huge creature's shoulders. He idly mused on Cabbage-pants' words, considering the fire and hearth in the communal room on the other side of the stone against which he leaned. He remembered the grey fieldstone set in a smooth and regular pattern, like a snake's scales, and on the stone arch above the firepit, one stone, an oval darkness more polished than the other stones, almost glass-like, like an eye . . .

An awful knowingness entwined Glimmer. Like the tightening coils of a constricting serpent, an intuitive knowingness encircled him until all doubt left, like breath crushed within muscled coils.

"Ye both'll have much t' talk about," Cabbage-pants had said; "*. . . 'tween you and the hearthstone,"* he had said.

Placing his mug carefully upon the flagstones, Glimmer slowly stood, strode with heavy deliberateness to that legacy of when the tower had stood alone, strode to the ancient, reinforced door that connected the kitchen with the house's communal room. Opening the door, he stepped into the large room, empty and dusty from disuse, his footsteps echoing.

He turned and faced the room's hearth, his eyes without surprise tak-ing in the sight of a lively fire crackling in the firepit, a fire of dancing and glowing light vibrant with energy, and all this manifesting from a meager collection of sticks and branches bunched upon the firestones. Light rip-pling upon the mantelpiece, light drawing arabesques upon Glimmer's arms, light reflecting off stone—and then one stone high upon the stone-work above the firepit—a single, oval obsidian stone captured light . . . and blinked.

Glimmer started back a step and then steadied himself, gazing at an eye the size of a platter that scrutinized him from the stone mantel. Now Glimmer could see how stone was shaped in the suggestion of brow above the eye, and to the right and left of the firepit, he could see stone patterned to suggest a jaw.

Already knowing, Glimmer spoke in a raw whisper into silence the question that embodied his fears. "What are you?"

That which you summoned, reverberated upon his consciousness.

"And what is that?"

That which you perceive.

The fire flickered, tongues of flame tasting the air, reaching toward Glimmer. He could feel heat emanating from the fire, heat seeming to emanate even from the stone walls.

"Are you made of stone now?"

Rather the stone is made of me.

"Am I safe? Can you hurt me?" Glimmer asked, advancing one step closer to the hearth. "Am I in danger?"

It seemed to Glimmer that an emotion flickered, a harsh expression of light and shadow upon the stonework.

Fear and danger are the children of duality. You perceive danger; therefore, I am dangerous.

"But am I in danger?"

In danger from your own folly . . . indubitably.

Glimmer advanced to the fireplace and put his hand flat to the stones. The grey rock was cool, and yet beneath the coolness was a deeper warmth. He closed his eyes and felt energy radiating from the stones, just as in night he had felt sun-warmed stones still radiating heat. "Can you get out?"

And get you? As I said, I am not of stone; stone is of me.

"What does that mean?"

Stone remembers its greater self. You speak of danger. There exists no danger here. Death comes only at your bidding.

"I didn't command you to kill." Glimmer remembered the blackened branches of the ancient apple tree in the meadow next to the house. "I didn't command you to burn the tree."

You summoned me, mage-child, you and your nightmare of fire and death. The death of this day rests upon the stones of your hearth, not mine.

"And what now?"

I am the dream, young mage; you are the nightmare. The obsidian eye gleamed with crystalline light, talon-sharp. *You conjure destruction so easily. Show me how easily you conjure life. Then call yourself "mage."*

With those words the fire extinguished with not even a sour curl of smoke lingering. Glimmer touched the hearthstones in front of the firepit and found them cool, as cold as bedrock beneath soil and home. Passing back through the doorway to the kitchen, he pushed the door closed with both hands, hearing the muffled echo of its closing, feeling it through his hands, through his entire body, the quarry stone of the floor echoing with his desire to push away his memories, his nightmares, to again merely be Not a Glimmer of Magic working in the garden, alone and neglected, at peace with his petty miseries.

Chapter 4

"Two magicks existe: the magick of Being and the magick of
Contriving."
Treatise on the Two Natures of Magick

ॐ

Glimmer crossed the kitchen to the darkness of the pantry, entered and
threw himself on the rumpled blanket on his pallet, his living quarters
in this abandoned excuse for a home. When Glimmer had been twelve
years of age, Alma-Ata had found him in the only inn in Wheatland, a
small inn run by a family with just-born twins and a passel of older children, and no longer needing the extra hands of an orphan boy. Glimmer
had not even known Alma-Ata was a mage then, had been too young to
recognize the gratitude and respect in the eyes of those around him; he
just had seen an old man in commoner clothes gazing into his eyes and
asking if Glimmer had wanted to come and live with him.

Glimmer didn't have a name then, not even a nickname, had mostly
been called *the boy*, and sometimes words associated with fire because of
his temper and the faint red tint of his hair: *th' ember* or *th' kindlin'* and,
of course, no one with reddish hair, even the faintest blush, could ever
escape *carrot-top*; the appellations were never considered names, though,
never spoken or received with a sense of ownership. "Where's the boy?"
had always been the question. Glimmer remembered the mother calling
him a little mouse once when she had ruffled his hair and given him a
gentle squeeze, one cherished moment in his life.

Glimmer had also been *boy* to Alma-Ata, more often *son* or *apprentice*,
but the mage had not used them as names, more as designations until a
name was found. Alma-Ata had simply spoken to Glimmer, addressing

his sentences to the boy, his eyes full upon Glimmer from beneath his bushy brows. It had been enough, at least when Glimmer was younger.

Then one day Alma-Ata had been visited by another mage, one riding up to the stone house on a sleek black horse liveried with silver-studded tack, the mage's apprentice on a smaller chestnut. So grand had the mage and apprentice looked on their prancing horses, the mage's midnight cape billowing as the stallion danced on the road which skirted the garden fence, the apprentice sitting his horse quietly at the road's outer fringe.

"I am seeking the mage who resides here," the caped mage had demanded, his horse nervous beneath him. His eyes had glittered above a beard as severe as an axe blade.

Their faces sweaty and hands dirty from the work of the day, Alma-Ata and Glimmer, who then was tall enough in height to reach Alma-Ata's lean shoulder, had stood behind the stone fence which reached Alma-Ata's chest. Beside Glimmer stood simple-minded Wilim from the village, always delighting in any and every new novelty. Wilim's eyes and mouth were circles of wonder, and Glimmer had thought that even Alma-Ata must be impressed by the mage's finery, the mage's imperial manner.

"Perhaps you seek me," Alma-Ata had replied quietly.

"You?" the mage exclaimed, and then he had spat. "I feel only feeble power from you, old man, and from the boy next to you not a glimmer of magic."

"You mean for working spells?" Alma-Ata had asked, shrugging his shoulders and extending his hands in seeming confusion; and as he extended one hand, a mourning dove had flown over and soiled Alma-Ata's open palm. Alma-Ata had gazed in surprise at his dirtied hand and then calmly wiped the lime onto the rough stones of the garden fence. Then he had smiled a wry smile at the bird, an ambivalent thanks. "Magic always surprises me," Alma-Ata had suggested.

From across the road the apprentice had snickered, and the stallion of the mage had danced nervously. "I'm wasting my time here," the mage had uttered, turning his horse without another word and galloping down the road. The apprentice had cast one last sneer—it seemed to Glimmer that it was specifically at him—and then galloped down the road in pursuit of his master. The dust of the departing apprentice and mage had settled in silence, Glimmer cringing in embarrassment for himself and his master.

Alma-Ata had smiled a thin smile and commented, "Well, that went well."

Simple-minded Wilim had remembered only one thing from the experience, and that was the name the traveling mage had inflicted upon the boy; thus, Alma-Ata's apprentice had been given a name, "Not a Glimmer of Magic," one more cruel than even the ubiquitous "Hey, you."

The foreign mage and apprentice had ridden off erect and proud beneath the brilliant afternoon sun, Wilim had snickered and cackled, and Alma-Ata had said nothing beyond his original words. The mage had simply watched the travelers to the bend of the road, and when they had disappeared, had returned to his garden work. Glimmer had thought that there had been an extra slump to the mage's carriage but had not been sure. The work had been hard and the day long; no wonder the young boy's thoughts had drifted in envy to such fine clothes and noble horses! How could anyone not desire such glory?

Glimmer lay upon his pallet of blankets staring at the stone walls, his eyes searching for the eyes of a dragon. His mind was numb with the magic of dreams and dragons. His memories of that day long past when he had met the foreign mage and apprentice came to him like old and cherished friends. Anything was better than dragonfire and death, even memories of humiliation and neglect.

Why Alma-Ata had taken him as apprentice he could not understand. The more Glimmer had matured, the less the mage had stayed at the stone house. Glimmer didn't understand it; Alma-Ata spent as little time with him as possible. Perhaps the wizard felt it had been a mistake in taking Glimmer on as an apprentice. After all, what mage would want an apprentice without a glimmer of magic?

But I do have magic, Glimmer thought. *I have proven that today. What will Alma-Ata do, though, when he discovers what I have done? Will he still teach me, or will he drive me out of the house with a stick across my back? Will wizards consider me dangerous and lay spells upon me as has happened in legend to other dream mages? Shall I become as Wilim, a simple-minded fool?*

And what shall I do now? Glimmer considered. *Should I sleep . . . and dream? Should I lie here in my hole in the wall in my tangle of blankets which top these bundled rushes and dream? Shall something else burn because of my dreams? But I didn't burn the tree; I didn't kill. You can't trust anything a dragon says; that's what the stories all say. It didn't even admit it was a dragon,* Glimmer realized. *It may never come back; maybe it was never really there.*

As Glimmer drifted with the current of his fatigue, his thoughts thinned to tattered abstractions. Emotions faded like the last colors of sunset bluing into starlight. Glimmer's breathing deepened, and he slept.

The night sky was so beautiful, the infinite dark of space sowed with seeds of light. The stars glowed their fires, and darkness flowed an endless sea. Light was a tangible essence; a connectedness existed, a unity. The dark roil of night between the stars was not static, was not inert. *The dead of space* was a remarkable misrepresentation. Glimmer could feel its potential, the possibility of its becoming; and in the shining joy of the stars, he could feel the pulse of light settling to silence. Each was in the other, dynamic silence and silent dynamism. Closing his eyes, he could still sense the radiance and the darkness that defined the radiance. He could feel the ebb and flow of the entire starlit sky, the electric hum of existence creating itself, space and matter. One becomes the other; one *is* the other. Like a phoenix, sky burned in its own fires and then rose again from the charred blackness.

Glimmer raised his hands to the sky, his eyes still closed as the pure joy of existence coursed through him. It was such bliss to be! Such bliss to experience clear to the clove of existence and then to identify that the clay from which the world was formed was the clay of one's own flesh! Opening his eyes, he saw his arms silhouetted against the starry sky, and he saw them not as opaque shadow but also as light and space, form and ether. Why, he was mostly space, mostly nothingness, mostly space defining pinpricks of minute stars. He surveyed the rest of his body and saw himself as he truly was, a cosmos of starlight and infinite space contained within and containing his consciousness. He laughed in joy, and the stars of his lungs swirled in constellations of breath.

Stars and space curving, Glimmer turned to the tide of the stars, and before him stood the charred blackness of the apple tree, its bare branches swallowing the light of the stars. Too unbecoming! Too much the silencing of joyous, singing radiance! *He says that this is my doing,* Glimmer thought. *He says that this is my death, not his.* But it was not death—no, death was the wrong word. It was silent now; it was *unbecoming.* One foot rests upon the earth so that the other can step ahead. There is a rhythm, and each has its time. This beautiful tree, though . . . Was its time to *unbecome* come rightly? The blackness of the tree sang its darkling song, and Glimmer bowed his head to its silent lyrics.

He opened his eyes wide, willing himself not to shut out the charred nakedness of the tree. *He would remember!* And then at the base of the trunk where the roots heaved the earth, Glimmer saw a glimmer of light, a cluster of pale stars in the shadow of the husk of the tree. It lived! Life lingered within ancient trunk beneath the seared bark and heat-twisted branches. He knelt before the trunk and pressed his hands to the blackened surface. His hands met the pale constellation of apple-stars, and they merged, the pale stars brightening, their energy sustained and strengthened.

He stood in eager hope and stepped to the tree, stepped inside the burned trunk as if he were stepping into a showering waterfall, only this a showering of stars. Matter and space commingled, each recognizing it was the other. Light glowed and spread through his arms and through his legs, up the branching apple tree, down to the finest roots. Light flowed, expanded, forgiveness from the apple asked and given. Bark curled like new flesh, buds burst to blossom and leaves greened. Round, hard kernels of apple greened and then blushed to fruition.

Glimmer knew the patient years of the tree, knew them ringed in the starry rind of his own flesh. He bowed and stepped back and was outside the tree and then asked the blackened grasses to grow, to green the blackened ring round the tree. The grasses listened and responded, affirming the starlight within themselves. Bowing to the tree, to the grasses, to the sky, to all things within the wholeness, Glimmer wept with joy, so thankful to be a part of the beauty, for a moment to have *been* the beauty.

He awoke as naked as a newborn baby, lying in lush grasses beneath an apple tree, chilled in the pale light of dawn. *Am I still dreaming?* he asked himself, lying on his back, his eyes focusing on the colors above him: greens and shades of bark, brown and grey, the red globes of fruit, all backlit by the cloudless blue of the sky. He shivered, realized his nakedness, and looked about him for unwanted eyes. He was alone, of course, or . . . not alone, he thought, conjuring up memories of friendly gnome and haughty dragon.

Jumping to his feet, he reached up and picked one and then another ripe apple. One in each hand, he strode to the stone house, rounded the edifice and entered the kitchen through the door which gaped ajar. Setting one apple on the scarred kitchen table, Glimmer heaved the door to the communal room open and, without losing momentum, placed the second apple upon the stone mantel of the fireplace and then left, closing the door behind. Entering his sleeping area in the kitchen pantry, he saw his bedding straightened, his clothing folded neatly in a pile, and topping the pile a leaf wrapped into a packet, secured with a twig.

Why, the young man wondered, *did I awake beneath the tree and not in my own bed? Why was I without clothes? Did I sleepwalk?* The lack of consistency between the two acts of dream magery tightened his gut with fear. *Nothing will ever be as you expect it,* he thought. With shaking hands, he opened the packet, sniffed, then grunted in recognition. *Cabbage tea.*

Glimmer was sitting on the bench beside the kitchen door, sipping his cabbage tea with the deliberateness of a man taking medicine when he saw a figure approaching along the road from the north. He recognized Alma-Ata from the man's gait. For a mage so unmagical, he perused, Alma-Ata seemed to have a sense of timing that was too keenly honed to be coincidental. A magical sense of timing? *Too bad,* Glimmer thought, *it's so useless.* He took a large swig of tea, grimaced, and waited without further movement—other than a stubborn jutting of his jaw—until his master made his way up to boy and bench.

Alma-Ata sat down upon the bench, his wiry frame finding a comfortable spot for his back against the stones. He grasped Glimmer's cup of tea, brought the cup to his lips and sipped. Lifting the cup to his nose and sniffing suspiciously, Alma-Ata grunted to himself and sipped the tea again. Then, closing his eyes to the early morning sun, he handed the cup back. Neither mage nor apprentice had yet said a word. Silence stretched, Alma-Ata resting and warming in the thin rays of the morning sun, Glimmer willing himself to stillness, determined not to be the first to speak.

Alma-Ata sat beside his apprentice. *Silence to silence,* the elder mage thought, yet he could feel the tension beneath Glimmer's silence. The mage sat, let the silence within himself unwind, extend, flow outward until even the silence within himself disappeared to that stillness beyond nothingness. Finally, Alma-Ata turned his head to his apprentice and opened one pale blue eye. "So, young one, what news from the stone house?"

Glimmer started at the mage's particular choice of words, and then gratefully grabbed his chance to move and speak (*having barely won,* he thought), replying, "Is anything ever different here?"

"A good question, one best answered by you, since you are the one who's been here."

Alma-Ata faced straight ahead, tilting his face to the sun. He seemed content to just sit in the light, waiting for some response, waiting for something to happen.

He'll send me down the road, Glimmer thought, *if I tell him what I've done. He's not really a mage anyway; all he does is help farmers grow apples—which he's really good at,* he conceded. *We've got the best apple orchards anywhere.*

"I'd better check the garden and see what needs to be done," Glimmer said, standing. He waited for the mage to respond, to stand with him.

Without opening his eyes, the mage responded, "And pick our old friend, the apple. That's the reason I came . . . or one of them, anyway," he added, cracking one eye to squint at Glimmer. "The apples seem to have ripened early this year. Well, check the garden and then meet me at the tree. I'll gather ladder and baskets from the shed." Alma-Ata stood stiffly as if he were fatigued, and then he added a parting comment as he nodded to Glimmer: "Never pick until the fruit is ripe. I came to determine the quality of the fruit."

Glimmer walked to the south end of the stone house and entered the garden via the east gate. He grabbed a hoe and cultivated the soil around the cabbages, leaned on the implement and hoped for the gnome to appear. The sound of hoe cutting the soil was the only break in the silence of the morning. Glimmer puttered, his mind vacillating between numbness and turmoil. What should he tell his master? Either Alma-Ata already knew the situation, or he couldn't know it, had no ability to know or understand. In the first possibility, Alma-Ata would have a world of words to inflict upon Glimmer; in the second, would he even believe what Glimmer said? Would he feel Glimmer was making something up to impress him, something the mage could have no way of validating?

Disgusted with himself and his dithering, Glimmer finally leaned the hoe against the stone wall and marched the length of the house to confront (or confess to) his master. As he rounded the tower, he saw Alma-Ata, his arms full of woven baskets, emerging from the wattle shed. It was the apple tree, though, that riveted Glimmer's attention—full-leafed and full-fruited. Seeing again the tree that he had feared to gaze upon cast him into a storm of conflicting emotion. Yes, he had plucked two apples from the tree, but he hadn't stood back and taken in the entire tree, not in the chilled, naked state in which he had awoken. He saw now no indication of fire marring the beauty of the apple tree's fruitful bounty: apples red, striped with shades of green and yellow and pink, apples full and promising the mouth their tangy-sweet juice.

"This tree is usually always a little later than others of this summer variety because of its position to the house, if you remember, young apple mage," Alma-Ata chattered. "I always think these apples taste somewhat sharper because they are slower to ripen. Tart and crisp even for a summer apple. Late-early apples, if you follow me. Later than its fellows, that is, but still of the early summer variety. Let's see how they taste this year. It'll be good to get them in now, 'fore they drop or the sugar wasps get them." As Glimmer crossed the grassy swath to the tree's base, the mage added, "You climb and I'll catch, as always."

Glimmer reached up and touched the healthy bark of the apple tree, almost a caress; he reached for the limb above and lifted his foot to the lowest crotch of the tree, boosting himself up and then higher, crotch and limb to crotch and limb. "That's it," encouraged Alma-Ata. "Now toss me the apples, son," and the two slipped into their harvest routine.

It didn't matter to Glimmer that the urge to tell his master all that had happened had lost its momentum. The repetition of pick and drop, pick and drop, allowed him to stop thinking, to escape the worry of possibilities that swirled through his mind. He would rather be doing something, anything, than have to consider the consequences of his recent actions, and picking the apple tree was a very good something to do. The highest branches of the tree were picked by leaning the ladder against the tree, Alma-Ata below, braced against the boy's weight as Glimmer climbed the ladder, the healthy limbs of the tree easily supporting his weight. He carried a cloth sack for these apples, since the mage was occupied with the ladder. The lower branches they picked from the ground, filling basket after basket until the tree was finally bare but for a last few apples difficult to reach.

"And what shall we do with those?" Alma-Ata asked, and Glimmer replied the ritual response: "Leave 'em for birds and critters."

"Right you are, Glimmer. The tree belongs to all."

How, Glimmer worried, *can Alma-Ata not know, not feel what has happened to the tree?* Even to Glimmer it seemed that the tree with its fruit was somehow different, somehow drenched in its own magic.

Alma-Ata and Glimmer carried the woven baskets of apples to the entrance of the root cellar. There they sorted through the baskets, removing the bruised fruit, which would not keep. The baskets of unbruised fruit they stored in the root cellar to sit for a couple of weeks so that the skins would soften. Later they would be pressed and used to make apple cider.

After washing and cleaning the apple press and a couple of crocks, the mage and apprentice mashed and squeezed the apples not excessively bruised or rotting, pressing the apples for their juice. The juice was poured into the crocks and stoppered, to be drunk fresh rather than preserved as cider. Juice left unattended would eventually ferment to vinegar, useful in its own right. Glimmer enjoyed the coolness of the root cellar, herbs and onions hanging in bundles from the ceiling, root vegetables packed in clean, dry straw and sand, sun-dried vegetables in clay urns. There was an abiding peace for him in the cellar, a reassurance of food enough for the cold winter months.

As with every year, the first juice was set aside, poured into a crystal glass kept in Alma-Ata's study. After the pressing was completed, the mage washed and dressed in his best jerkin and breeches, combed his hair and scanty goatee. He held the glass of clear apple juice and left the stone house, walking to the apple tree with ceremonious steps. Alma-Ata lifted the glass to the sun, and the crystal glowed with amber fire. He turned then to the tree and poured a small portion of juice onto the earth at the base of the tree, speaking a blessing as he did so.

Amber blood, your nectar sweet,
May we sustain you.
In this sweet taste our lives do meet,
For this we thank you.

Then Alma-Ata, sipping from the glass, turned and offered the glass to Glimmer. Glimmer raised the glass to the tree, sipped of the nectar, the sweet juice strange to his throat. He remembered the charred skeleton of the tree, remembered his dream and the healing. Unplanned words slipped from his heart.

"In all the world," he murmured, "you are my brother." Alma-Ata's eyebrows rose at Glimmer's words, and then the elder mage bowed his head, first to the apple tree and then to Glimmer.

Finishing the glass, the two men returned, side by side, to the kitchen. As they walked, the mage said to his apprentice, "I had the thought. Perhaps you should choose a name for yourself; perhaps *Glimmer* is—"

The words of Cabbage-pants, "It's not name but person that makes th' worth," scrolled his mind, and Glimmer did something he rarely did; he interrupted his master. "I'll keep my name. I'll just have to find the gold." They walked in silence back to the kitchen, a thoughtful look on the mage's face.

The sun was well past its zenith and was closing on the evening horizon. The east side of the house was now in shadow, the summer air was cooling, yet the world still retained a pleasant warmth. Alma-Ata fondly gripped Glimmer by the arm, turning him to face the mage.

"Come, let's do something together. Let's share the rest of this day." Glimmer wondered if now, finally, his master was going to teach him some magic, to grant him some ancient spellcraft. "I think I'll change, and then we can wash our clothes together at the river. With all my traveling, I hardly have any clean clothes to wear." He released the apprentice and directed him toward the kitchen pantry, Glimmer's abode. "Go get your things, and I'll meet you at the washing rock." Glimmer's hopes sank to disappointment: dirty laundry in stagnant water.

Quickly bundling his soiled clothes, Glimmer left the stone house in a rush of emotion and dangling apparel and was first to the washing stone, a flat slab of stone a foot above the flow of the stream, cleaned by the high waters of spring storms. He dumped his clothing where the stone edged the river, plopped himself onto the rock, dipped a soiled shirt into the water, and then worked the fabric on the stone, dipping it occasionally in the water. Wringing the shirt savagely free of water, he placed the twisted bundle of clothing beside his soiled clothes and then reached for the breeches he had worn the day before while weeding the garden. After he had dunked the breeches, he pulled their dripping mass from the river and stared at them. Just yesterday Not a Glimmer of Magic had worn these breeches, and now Not a Glimmer of Magic was gone and what remained was too dazzling, was too much for Glimmer to bear alone.

I'll tell my master everything, Glimmer thought. *Better to be outcast than insane.*

Footsteps rustled on the path behind Glimmer as Alma-Ata, dressed again in everyday clothing, reached the washing rock. The mage pushed his entire armful of laundry beneath the water and then scrambled to retrieve an escaped stocking, almost tipping into the river. Splashing the wet clothing onto the stone, he squatted and began scrubbing a shirt. "I walked thirty miles yesterday to reach the house today. Slept the night in Jurgen's Wood warm in a bundle of leaves."

Alma-Ata rocked back on his heels, balanced as he looked to the leaf-patterned sky. He breathed in deeply, taking in the green growing and the liquid, flowing essence of the afternoon. "Ah! Life sings in this place," he sighed, breathing out his pleasure. He rinsed his shirt, wrung it, and began on his stockings, rubbing the two together vigorously. Fingering a hole in the heel of one, he muttered to himself. Glimmer continued to methodically pound and strangle his clothing into cleanliness. The mage chuckled as he observed Glimmer. "Best be careful who sees you at your washing. I'm liable to get offers to hire you out as a washboy . . . or an assassin, with all that enthusiasm."

He chuckled to himself but Glimmer glowered darkly, thinking, *Alma-Ata doesn't teach me anything, gives me nothing.*

"There's something you need to learn," the mage addressed Glimmer, even though Alma-Ata's eyes remained upon his wash. Glimmer jerked his head up to stare at the mage, shocked at the proximity of the mage's words to his own secret thoughts. "The problem is," the mage continued,

"I can't teach you."

"You won't be my teacher anymore?" Glimmer stammered, his anger evaporating, thinking, *Does he already know? Is that why he came today?*

"Oh, don't worry. You're not going to get out of your responsibilities that easily." Alma-Ata dunked his stockings again, this time one slipping into the current. As the stocking curled away in the water, a plop from the river bank and a brown head and shell marked a swimming turtle. The stocking caught against the turtle's shell, and as the turtle swam past the washing stone, the mage snagged the stocking, wrung it and placed it beside its mate. Plunging his arms elbow deep into the stream and submersing his traveling breeches, he continued without pause. "You need to gain a particular perspective of the world. The trouble is, even though I can glimpse what you need, I can't teach you. In fact, no one now in the world can, yet you must experience this—even if only a taste. Those who once taught this have been gone for about three hundred years."

Alma-Ata pulled the soaking breeches from the stream and let them fall with a splat onto the washing rock. He began to rub at the pants, concentrating on the knee and seat fabric. Glimmer's curiosity moved him from his dark mood.

"Then how am I to learn? Who will teach me? And why do I need to learn this—whatever it is?"

"To answer your first two questions: I have no idea. As to the third, all I know is that you need what all seek, even without knowing." The mage paused in his speaking and slapped the breeches against the washing stone. "What I am going to do is to prepare the soil, so to speak."

"What? I don't understand."

"Come now, young gardener. We have no seed, but still we can prepare the soil."

"But you said there is no one who can teach me, has not been for three hundred years."

"That's right."

"How will I learn? And what is it I need to learn?"

Alma-Ata smiled. "I don't know. Perhaps I am wrong. Perhaps there is someone, some ascetic deep in the mountains or in a cave or beneath the widespread arms of a giant tree or—" he slapped the stone they sat upon "—perhaps sitting, still and silent within himself, upon a stone on the escarpment above the Outlands. I don't know. And as to what you need to learn—why, the secret of life, of course." The mage laughed at the expression on Glimmer's face.

"Oh, *that*—" the young man said. Glimmer finished wringing his last piece of laundry and heaped the tightly wrung clothing upon his others like a miniature stack of firewood. "Then how is that possibility going to happen?"

"Lose a stocking, find a turtle." The mage smiled mischievously. "I don't know *how* it is going to happen, but I do know how we are going to *encourage* it to happen."

"And how is that?"

"We're going to turn our stone house into an inn," the mage replied with a smile. "I've heard rumors—gnome gossip, you might say—about the magic that's come. Perhaps you will want to talk about that," Alma-Ata included as an aside. "Build a chair, and a guest will fill it," he said, quoting a peasant's saying. He paused for a moment, considering. "Although it's odd . . ." he continued, tapping an index finger thoughtfully on the grey slab of stone. He fell silent, regarding Glimmer thoughtfully. "I came, but I cannot place my finger on the cause." He chuckled, "Of course, I never could."

The mage lapsed again into thoughtful silence. "Let me tell you a story," he finally said. "Actually," he confessed, "I've never told this to anyone else. It's not a secret—don't get your hopes up—I've just never felt the need." He leaned back on an elbow and gazed up at the tree-woven sky.

"When I was a young apprentice mage, another mage came to visit my master. This visiting mage had an apprentice about my age, perhaps a little younger, even. While our masters chatted, we played outside beneath an old oak. The boy was actually quite magically gifted, in a limited sort of way. He was telekinetic. Do you know what that means?"

"He moved objects with his mind."

Alma-Ata nodded and continued. "We were playing marbles, and he kept winning—and mind you, now, I was very good at marbles. Then the boy confessed—he was too proud to hold it back—he was aiming with his mind and not just with his hand."

The mage sat up and began acting out the story as he continued the telling. Glimmer stared at the movements of the mage's hands, imagining two small boys together, playing.

"The boy began moving the marbles by pointing his finger, forming letters and having the marbles slide and dance and leap. It was really quite remarkable. And then the boy said, 'Now, you do it,' and, of course, I couldn't. It was not my magic."

Glimmer now looked from the mage's hands to the lined and deeply tanned face. "It was not my magic," the mage repeated, as much to himself as to his apprentice, then returned to the story. "'Now you do something,' the boy repeated, gesturing to the marbles. He wasn't being mean. Actually, it was a reasonable request . . . but I had no talent, no spells to show off with."

Alma-Ata stopped speaking, a strange, poignant expression upon his face.

"So what did you do? What did you say?" Glimmer prompted.

"Nothing," the mage responded. "I said and did nothing."

"And what did the other apprentice do? Laugh?"

"No, we just stood there for a moment, both of us just waiting, you might say, when a red squirrel came scrabbling down the oak, took a marble in its mouth and moved it next to another. Then it moved another." Alma-Ata laughed, remembering. "We were both half-scared, it was so sudden and so close. And then another squirrel came and began to move acorns, and then a jay flew down with twigs, its mate joining, and then two juvenile jays bumbled in, all with something in their mouths— a family affair," the mage laughed again. "They formed a circle with lines radiating from it, a picture of the sun, and for those rays pointing at me, they made arrow tips at the end of the rays."

The mage gestured at the stone they sat upon, remembering.

"And then what?" Glimmer asked. "How did you do that? He must have been impressed."

"That's what the other apprentice asked: 'How did you do that?' And I said, 'I didn't do anything,' and then he asked, 'Then how did you make them do that?' to which I replied, 'I didn't make them do anything; they just did it for me.'"

"They just did it for you?"

"Yes, and the other apprentice didn't understand; I'm not sure that I did then . . . or even now." The mage turned to his apprentice and looked deeply into his eyes. "You see, I am a Mage That Gathers. I have no magic, yet magic happens around me."

"I don't understand."

"I mean I have no spells or talents to catch up my stocking when it goes floating down the current. A turtle brings it back—or I jump in and swim for it. A Gatherer is very rare . . . and rarely understood, sometimes even by himself."

"So you don't do anything?" Glimmer asked slowly. "You're not in control?"

"It seems not to be a matter of what I do, more who I am. I live my life, go through my ordinary day, and magic happens; it just *happens* around me, gathers around me. As I gathered you, for reasons I did not know. You just came to me, and I still don't know the whole of it."

"You mean I am your apprentice—by chance? Just a quirk of fate?"

"Ah!" Alma-Ata quietly exclaimed. "Everyone, *everything*, to some degree, at the deepest level of life, *sits and waits*. Perhaps *witnesses* is a better word. Do we create the world? Do we live in the world? Do we create the world and then live in it?" The man placed a hand on Glimmer's shoulder. "You are my apprentice. Time will tell us what that means."

A sense of fate overcame Glimmer. *He cannot help me,* he thought, *yet I must ask his help. There is no one else.* His throat tightening with trepidation, Glimmer confessed to his master, "There are some things that I must tell you." He looked up from the running water into the pale eyes of the mage. "It's my fault."

Alma-Ata merely raised his eyebrows.

"I figured out how to get past the magic of your study. I didn't pick the door's lock; I didn't break a window. I'm not confessing to you now out of compulsion. I was mortaring the window, sealing it for the winter as you asked, and I realized that I could take out the entire window frame, thus by-passing your spell to ward off thieves . . . and over-curious apprentices."

Alma-Ata remained a silent statue as the apprentice spoke. Glimmer lowered his eyes to the grey stone before him and continued telling the story of his entering and reading, continuing the story on through the dreams of dragon and tree. He finished with, "Oh, and I met a gnome—Cabbage-pants."

"Ah," nodded the mage with a slight smile, "as I suspected from the tea." Glimmer smiled ruefully.

Alma-Ata tapped his fingertips together thoughtfully. "First," he declared, "you did not out-clever the magic. The magic exists not just in the windows and door, but in the walls, indeed, in the very air of the room and even in the air across the mountains. And it was not my magic spell. I know no spells; magic just gathered, focused. Also, the book you read belongs to you. If the book were not yours, you would have met me on the road as I approached, confessing to me that you had entered the study and read it."

"How can a spell for your study exist across the mountains? How can it exist if it is not created?" Glimmer asked.

"What do you mean by *across* or *exist?*" The mage shook his head in exasperation. "Don't distract me with excellent questions. Not a Glimmer of Magic, that is why no one felt the presence of magic within you. Magic dreams while you wake and wakes while you *dream.*"

"Then why could I talk to . . . whatever . . . is in the stone of the house when I was awake?"

"The . . . presence . . . is both the agent and essence of your dreaming." Alma-Ata's eyes suddenly focused. "You have to understand," he said, fiercely grabbing both arms of his apprentice. "You did not dream a spell; you created a dream. You say you dreamed of a flying dragon, but I feel you have not ensorcelled the dragon. You called and it came."

"Can you speak to it?"

"Why should it speak to me? I did not conjure it."

"But can you watch while I talk to it?"

"I would see whatever it chose for me to see . . . or see nothing at all."

"But I can see and hear it. Why not you?" Glimmer asked. He felt fearful tears welling up from within and was ashamed.

"We share this waking but not our dreaming. And I do not claim to know whether I would see it or not. Magic *happens* around me: I do no shaping and claim no ownership."

The mage released Glimmer's arms and sat back on the washing stone, not minding its wet surface. "Dream mages are very rare," he said. "Perhaps that is best for the world. You have heard of the Slag Hills of

Eyre?" Glimmer nodded. "The Glass Towers of Raiano?" Glimmer nodded again. "The Ghost of Gelfandland?" As the apprentice nodded again, Alma-Ata continued, "All dream magery. All twisted from the tortured souls of dream mages. Dream magery is the most dangerous of magics," Alma-Ata finished. "Equally dangerous for the mage and the world. You have dreamt twice, and both times without catastrophe . . . at least so it appears." He lapsed into silence again.

"So what must I do? Never sleep again?"

"No! No, you must not do that. You must not twist your mind, not even with lack of sleep." The mage paused again, considering. "The ancient texts tell us there is an awareness that is not waking, dreaming, or sleeping—but is the basis, the source. Perhaps that will be the bedrock of your salvation . . . the salvation of us all."

The mage smiled as he levered himself to his feet, holding his hand out to Glimmer. As he pulled Glimmer to his feet and they stooped to pick up their laundry, Alma-Ata added, smiling, "We are all supposed to live this ultimate reality; it is our lost birthright. At least that's what Mage DeVasier said three hundred years ago. It's just more true for you, apprentice dream mage, than for anybody else. For you it's not the secret of your life; it's the salvation of your life."

They walked back to the stone house, laundry in their arms. "No, you mustn't worry about sleeping. Let me explain it this way. Think of your five senses as horses hitched to a wagon. The reins all flow back from the horses to the wagonmaster. If the wagonmaster falls from the wagon, then who will lead the horses?"

As they skirted the garden, the gnome Cabbage-pants, wearing new breeches of cabbage leather roughly sewn with wide stitches, stood idly amidst the cabbages, singing to himself and fussing with the cabbage heads. "Mage," he murmured, tugging at his forelock. The gnome ignored the apprentice except for a quick wink as the mage looked fore again. Over his shoulder, Alma-Ata added, "Glimmer's told all, so you don't have to pretend . . . although even if I hadn't been told"—the mage smiled—"the tea would have tipped me off."

"Yessire," the gnome affirmed, then shouted to Glimmer, "Ye look a little pale. I'll bring ye a packet o' cabbage an' St. James Wort. That'll fix ye."

"That particular concoction is a good one, but I suggest you stay away from his purgatives," the mage murmured to his apprentice. "Being of the earth, gnome purgatives are somewhat . . . hm, tectonic."

"I'm getting a picture in my mind. And why does he always shout at me?"

The mage laughed. "He wants to make sure you understand him. Now," the mage continued, "we will have Bega and her daughter Elesia come to help at the inn, and also Wilim, for a start, anyway. I believe they will be willing." Alma-Ata looked at the young man walking beside him, now almost exactly his height. "You've grown, Glimmer. You will be in charge."

"As if anyone's in charge of Bega. Besides, I don't know anything about innkeeping."

"Oh, this isn't the Outlands, you know. An inn with a clean bed, a hearty meal, a warm fire should do it. And you're right: a wise leader listens, and I'm sure Bega will tell you what is needed."

"Nobody travels this road."

"No one more than we'll need, I suspect."

"Will this work?" Glimmer asked as they reached the kitchen door.

"At worst, we will all die a terrible death and our land will be cast into a long reign of dark fire and despair," the mage replied with a wry smile. "But that's not what you would dream, is it?"

"No, I would not wish that. Master, would you come to the hearth with me, to see the dragon?"

"It is not my path, young apprentice. I did not dream this dream . . . but I will come."

Glimmer muscled back the ancient door that separated the tower kitchen and the communal room, and then Glimmer and Alma-Ata stood before the fireplace, an anemic weed of a fire sputtering from a few twigs and branches. The apple rested, full and ruddy, on the grey stone mantel. Shadows dulled the gleam of obsidian surrounded by fieldstone. Dust and disuse characterized the fireplace and the entire room: scattered tables and benches, candelabrum, the floor frosted with dust and scattered patches of straw and leaves.

"Just the fire," Glimmer said. "Everything else is normal."

"A gesture . . . as was your apple."

"Can I command him to come?"

"I believe you could, but to what purpose? Cooperation is best. Call it *dragon*, but this is no animal you have summoned, no beast." The fire flared, and one branch burned through and tumbled into the coals, quickening the flames. "You must rest," Alma-Ata continued, "rest, and avoid anger and strain and inner turmoil. Dream magery, as in all magic, involves attention and intent arising from awareness. One can sleep and dream without danger, but *you* must not be overshadowed by the events of your life. That is all you can do for now. So say good-bye to your *draco*, and I will meet you in the upstairs tower." With that, Alma-Ata turned without another glance at the hearth and left the room.

Glimmer stood before the fireplace in the silent room and considered its inanimate façade. He then picked up the apple sitting on the mantle. As he stepped and turned to leave, the obsidian of the fireplace gained life and stared at him. Glimmer said nothing, having nothing to say, simply stared back at the baleful, black hardness of the eye. His attention fell to the flames which sputtered in the firepit, fire prolonged in unnatural life beyond its meager means. He then turned silently and left the room, closing the door behind.

In the kitchen, Cabbage-pants squatted before the fire, tending to a boiling pot hanging by a hook and to a frying pan balanced above the coals on an iron trivet. "Yon iron will give't a bitter tang, but it's a col-cannon for us tonight, young master. First, ye boil th' potatoes, an' then mash 'em. Simmer yer cabbage an' onion in th' skillet wi' a bit of salt an' pepper. Just a'fore servin' I'll mix 'em together, an' a fine stick t' yer ribs meal will't be." The gnome's description faded as Glimmer crossed the room and mounted the stone stairs to the upper landing, the young man wrapped in his own muse, unaware of the gnome's recipe ramblings, unaware of sharp black eyes upon his back, eyes both considering and considerate.

At the landing Glimmer found the door to the mage's study open, along with the doors to the other two rooms on the second story of the stone house's tower. At the sound of footsteps, Alma-Ata came to the door of the study and motioned the apprentice inside.

"I'll give Bega and Elesia my sleeping quarters and you the room next door; I will use my study. I do not think you will thank me for your new quarters. The kitchen is warmer and lighter, but it will be too busy now.

Your current quarters will become a pantry once again." The mage fussed with his sleeping pallet which he had dragged to one corner of the study. "Wilim will sleep in the shed, which will once again become a stable with some reminding." He smiled. "You and Wilim will remind it."

"How long will you stay?"

"I will leave after we eat." Alma-Ata paused in his labors and focused his attention on his apprentice. "Glimmer, this is a most serious situation. We must not dally."

The mage seemed out of sorts and out of breath. *Is he worried,* Glimmer wondered, *or is he scared?* He had never seen the mage so restless or in such a hurry. *Almost frantic,* he thought. A chill coursed through him at the thought. Anxiety flowed though his body, leaching its way through him and into the timbers beneath his feet. *I am still alive. I survived the dragon and saved the tree. Alma-Ata says intention in dream magic is a key. I will use that key to lock myself safely away, a room of stone, sunlight falling in a silent beam from window to floor. If the dragon cannot reach me, then how can I not be safe?*

The mage stuffed fresh garments into a shoulder sack and then headed for the door. He threw up one gaunt arm, halting himself. "One book, apprentice, before we leave. Choose a book." Without thought, Glimmer pocketed the slim volume on dream magic. The mage grunted in response. "That volume contains no recipes for your magic, apprentice— only travelogues to ever-changing landscapes."

As they exited, Alma-Ata locked the door to the study behind him. Inhaling deeply, the mage exclaimed, "Ah! I smell cabbage for dinner."

"And potatoes."

When the two entered the kitchen, the gnome happily mixed the sautéed cabbage and onions with mashed potatoes, chattering all the while. The two men shared their supper, regaled the while with recipes of cabbage with brine, with vinegar—cabbage boiled, baked, stuffed, and raw. As they finished, Alma-Ata sat at ease on one bench by himself, his eyes thoughtfully on the gnome. Cabbage-pants and Glimmer shared the other, the gnome's plate resting on the bench because the table was too high. Scraping his plate clean, the gnome hopped from the bench and poured tea into three mugs.

"Cabbage and chamomile tea," he said as the offered a mug to master and apprentice. Cabbage-pants, holding his mug with both hands, knowingly sniffed his mug. "Now, th' cabbage'll be good for th' digestion, cleans th' bowels, 'liminates gas. An' th' chamomile, of course, helps with th' sleep. A perfect balance: sleep like a babe and wake in th' mornin' to th' body's nat'rl urges."

Glimmer waited until he saw the mage sip the tea before sampling it himself. Perhaps, he thought, this was one of the purgatives Alma-Ata had warned him about. The flavor seemed, though, just what one would expect in a blend of cabbage and chamomile. Supper had been better than the thin soup he would have managed, he had to admit.

After supper, Alma-Ata wasted no time before leaving. His hand on Glimmer's shoulder, he repeated his advice for the apprentice: rest, straightforward work, friendly relations, and good food. Then he must wait. Wait how long? *Silly question* was the response.

Again, Glimmer wondered whether the mage's manner was prompted by affection or anxiety, whether Alma-Ata was attempting to quickly initiate action to aid him or simply moving as quickly as possible to place himself a safe distance from the problem. Glimmer resented his master's leaving, wanted his master's unmagical presence.

"First, I'm off to Ruddy to see Bega. I'll spend the night there and then on to Spur. You'll have to find Wilim yourself."

Soon the mage was striding down the road to be lost in twilight: Gatherer of Magic, One Who Waits—One Who Witnesses, magic incarnated within the body of a man born to action. Alma-Ata strode down the road, wishing, needing to do *something*, fated by his magic to wait for the moment to magically *not* do anything.

And once again Glimmer was alone, Alma-Ata turning a corner and gone. True, there was the gnome—and that which Glimmer had summoned—but that was company of interminable recipes and basilisk obsidian eyes. The apprentice didn't even say good night or thank the gnome for dinner as he pulled his pallet, blankets, and meager possessions from the kitchen pantry and packed them upstairs to his new quarters. Dumping them on the floor outside the room, Glimmer returned to the kitchen for a candle.

"Thank you for the meal," he at last managed.

"Don't ya be worryin' about *me*," the gnome replied, hitching his breeches. "Ye've enough on yer mind," and Glimmer ascended the stairs, his thoughts already darkly turned.

How, he wondered, *can I keep myself calm and positive? That's like promising to wake up with a bounce in my step. How can I keep in good relations with those around me, come up with a list of ten good things to say about cabbage? And I'm supposed to sleep well tonight because I've had such a good day? Alma-Ata probably took off because he's scared of sleeping here tonight, afraid he might not live through the night, afraid he might awake to a living nightmare.*

The candle guttered, tipped in its holder. Righting the candle, Glimmer decided to sleep on the landing and not move into the room given him until after he had cleaned it on the morrow. Having decided his course of action, he straightened his sleeping pallet, arranged his blankets, and stood, staring at the arrangement, reluctant to take the next step and settle to it.

As he stood before the pallet, staring and lost between thoughts, a gruff voice spoke from behind. "I thought ya might be needin' this," the gnome stated, offering up a small, rectangular bundle of cloth to him.

"What is it?"

"A pillow sachet," the gnome responded.

"Cabbage helps you sleep?"

"Nay, lad, it's too invigoratin' for that. Don't be kiddin' a kidder. Mostly this be sweet, dried grasses an' herbs—chamomile an' lavender, though I *did* add a little red cabbage for gen'ral principles, ya might say." With a nod, the gnome descended the stairs, hopping down from step to step.

Touched by the gnome's generosity, Glimmer tossed the sachet next to his pillow. He sat down on his pallet, deciding that he would skip changing into his sleeping gown. He snuggled into his blankets, settled his head, and breathed deeply the sachet's aroma.

He wondered, *What is magic? When a magical being gives you a sachet of herbs, is that sachet magical? Is that sachet different than an identical one given by just anyone?* The mage had talked about dream magic and the importance of one's intent. Could the same be true of something as insignificant as a sachet? Was the magic not the gift but the intent of the giver? Glimmer nested his head more comfortably to his pillow, his thoughts slurring with sleep.

Crickets chirred and myriad fireflies flickered in the meadow across the river from the washing stone, night sky speckled with stars which haloed the country manor. In the meadow's center, silhouetted and unmoving as stone, the dragon curled upon night-blackened leaves of grass. Glimmer lifted his head from the washing stone—no, from the sachet which pillowed his head from the hardness of stone.

Come to me this good evening, the dragon said, its voice like a lullaby in the young mage's mind.

"You invite me?" the dream mage asked.

You dream me, the dragon replied in tones rich and soothing.

Glimmer walked a short distance upstream to stepping-stones and crossed to the meadow. He approached a dragon that was no longer immense and horrible, its head resting upon a foreleg, its eyes two obsidian stones that captured and magnified the starlight.

Come and sleep, the dragon offered. *Rest yourself against me.*

Glimmer approached, feeling no fear. "Aren't you my nightmare?"

I am the dragon in your dream.

"Then you are a dragon?"

As convenient a word as any . . . better than most, actually.

Glimmer sat within the nest created by the curl of the dragon's legs. The scales of its belly were soft, as soft and warm as lamb's wool, and Glimmer lay back against the scaled hide, feeling the purring rumble of the dragon's breathing. Fireflies and crickets and the spinning lattice-work of the stars, blankets warm as hearthstones, fragrant grasses and the perfume of lavender, the soothing balm of chamomile. Glimmer closed his eyes.

Words drifted through the winds of his mind. *Sleep, young apprentice mage, and I shall watch the night.*

Chapter 5

"Puritie is wet nurse to Opportunitie."
"Candlefyre does not die but simplie ceases to flayme."
108 Aphorisms of Mage De Vasier

•

Glimmer awoke nestled in his blankets, breathing the fragrance of lavender and chamomile. He sighed out an exhausted breath and cracked one blear eye at the grey shadowed stone of the walls. He remembered the peace of the meadow and the secure warmth of the dragon's protection. It was distant, a dream at the beginning of his sleep, and it felt as if that dream must have drifted into a long passage of dreamless slumber. He stirred in his blankets, stretching his limbs and yawning. *Was I dreaming magic,* he wondered, *or was I just dreaming?*

Sitting up abruptly, he shook the last sleep from his mind and resolved today to confront the dragon, for he truly believed now that *dragon* was what was best to call his conjuration. Already smelling the faint kitchen-scent of cooked cabbage, he stood and descended the stone steps. On the table sat a bowl of porridge. Glimmer sniffed it and shook his head at the faint suggestion of cabbage. A mug of tea sat beside the bowl, and beside both rested a wooden spoon. Not even bothering to sip the tea to sample it, he gulped a healthy swig, assuming the gnome had no immediate plans to purge him. Hungering for some honey, he ate his porridge and snorted to himself at the unannounced thought of what midday dinner would bring to the table.

He left the kitchen to wash: *Best to go to battle at my best,* he thought. *And why should I think of this as battle?* he wondered as he returned to the kitchen and swung open the weathered door leading to the communal room. Last night's dream had been a good one, peaceful and unassuming. The dragon had not threatened or demanded or dominated the dream. *So what's bothering me?* He continued to push his thinking, poking into places that hurt. *The dragon is so sure of itself,* Glimmer finally realized—*so poised, so centered, so self-sufficient. It is immeasurably stronger than I am,* he admitted, *and that scares me.*

The communal room was the largest room in the stone house. Upstairs had been converted to smaller sleeping rooms, and the stone tower was cozy, compared to the dimensions of the larger room. He turned on an impulse and began to circle the room, following the walls. The north face of the room consisted of grey, mortared stone—the old tower wall to which the sleeping rooms above and communal room below had been added. He toured the room in a clockwise direction, seeing the room with new eyes. The east wall included a series of windows with shutters, the windows providing a latticed view of the dawn, the road skirting the house, a partial view of the stone bridge crossing the river, and the beginning of the easy slope of land past the bridge as the river flowed south and west, fringed by trees.

Far off to the east, though, grasslands rose at a gradual incline, extending to cloud-like mountains, the Eagle Talons, at the ragged edge of the world. The south wall boasted a large panel of windows that allowed the distant view of Jurgen's Wood to the southeast and a closer view of a stone bridge that crossed the river. The garden, enclosed by its stone fence, was the glory of the southern exposure. Glimmer could imagine the Brothers of Hospitality working the garden, their guests sitting at the tables, eating at their leisure, entertained and soothed by the patient work of the brothers. In the distance from the southern windows, the Sea Fens, a vast expanse of rushes and water, extended to the hazy horizon.

The west side of the room provided a view of sunset and stable-shed, grassland and distant cultivated field, the ribbon of the road winding on to Pickle and to the breadbasket farms of the land. Beyond the faded haze of the horizon was the moist, salty air of the sea. A storm blowing in from the southwest could sometimes bring the briny tang of sea and wheeling seagulls that would gorge themselves on grasshoppers and crickets. The windows in winter could also offer chill to the body, and tapestries and shutters were used when cold iced the land.

As he completed the circuit of the room and squared the northwest corner, Glimmer righted an overturned rocking chair and carried it to the fireplace. Dusting it with his sleeve, he sat and rocked, willing his muscles to relax. The ancient joints of the rocking chair creaked with the unexpected activity, *or with anticipation, perhaps,* Glimmer mused. Truth was, he didn't know what to do and was more than willing to accept his mage's advice for calm and quiet. The firepit was cold and dark this morning, its soot-blackened interior soaking up light from the room's windows. *Why was there no fire this morning?*

Then he asked aloud, "Why isn't there a fire?" and then wondered if the gnome had been the one to light the hearth fire the other times, after all. Then he remembered the sudden extinguishing of the fire when he had last been in the room. "Dragon! I am asking why no fire," Glimmer said again, and the charred twigs in the firepit suddenly burst into energetic flame, as energetic as a well-laid fire of three times its size.

Gazing at the flames, his breath quickening, Glimmer swallowed and wondered what to say next.

"Was my dream last night magic or just a normal dream?" he finally asked.

Define "normal," or for that matter, define "magic." And while you are at it, apprentice, you can define "last night" or "dream" or even the concept "just."

"You really like word games, don't you," Glimmer replied. "Saying something in a way that means nothing."

Believe me—you do the same, only out of ignorance, whereas I seek clarity.

"Why don't you just—if you'll allow me to use the word—answer the question?"

An obsidian eye now matched Glimmer's gaze. He could feel the slight shifting of muscles within the building's walls—not feel with the sense of touch because the building experienced no tremors, but feel with his emotions, with some subtle sense as one feels one's own blood coursing through veins.

"I want to know what happened last night." Glimmer paused, leaning his head to the back of the rocking chair, closing his eyes and remembering. "I liked it—what happened, what I dreamed . . . whatever."

Glimmer heard a mental sigh. *You dreamed, and what you dreamed was true to your dream.*

"But not to my waking."

Where did you awaken?

The young man nodded slowly. "And you protected me . . . watched over me."

To be concise: yes.

"Why?"

Because you greened the apple tree.

The apple tree, picking the fruit and storing and juicing the apples was a sweet memory in Glimmer's mind. "Do you know everything I think?" Glimmer asked abruptly. "I don't want you in my head, rooting around."

Hogs root, young apprentice.

"You know what I mean."

When, no matter how truthfully I speak, you will in all honesty misapprehend, it is best to attend to meaning word by word.

Glimmer shouted, "I don't know what you mean half the time!"

You don't *know what you mean half the time, which, considering your last words, implies that you understand nothing. Well done, young dreamer. Now you begin to apprehend.*

"Are you mine to command?" the young dream mage suddenly asked. *Perhaps he wants to deliberately confuse me,* Glimmer considered. Glimmer could not command if confused, could not stand his own ground if off balance.

Thus we circle the room again. "Are" is a conjugate of "is"; do you doubt that I exist? And do you really wish to pursue the duality of "you" and "I," "mine" and "yours"? Only then can we begin to consider the potentialities . . . and responsibilities . . . of the state of being inherent in "is."

"You know more grammar than my tutor."

To know name is to know form.

Sitting forward in the rocking chair, Glimmer locked eyes with the fixed stone eye of the fireplace. "I will call you dragon. Last night in my dream, you agreed to that name. Do you agree now in waking?" The eye replied with a stony blink, the obsidian momentarily obscured by a stone-grey shadow. "My mage called you *draco*." No response. "And you will do what I ask you to do?"

I am not a dog wagging my tail, playing fetch the stick.

"I am not your master?" the apprentice asked, his heart suddenly pounding at his audacity.

The fire flared in its pit. *"Dragon in stone," you commanded, and in stone I am. Do not ask me to perform tricks: you might find my "roll over" and "bark" somewhat discomfiting.*

The fire cast light but no heat, cast a cold light, an illumination of winter and slow, cold death beneath frozen sun.

"Then what good are you?"

I am the dream; you are the nightmare. It is through your eyes that you shall perceive my good . . . or my evil. My best . . . or my worst. Young child-mage, world is as you are.

With these words, the eye died to obsidian stone and fire extinguished to black soot and ash. Glimmer stood and left the room, shutting the door securely behind him. He suddenly thought to clean his sleeping room, to order his few belongings, to give sense to his living. He gulped a mouthful of cold cabbage tea and gave himself to doing something he could understand.

The tower room Alma-Ata had assigned Glimmer was a storage room—or page's room—by design, but had been unused during Alma-Ata's years of residence. The mage had lived alone for many years before Glimmer, and for most of those years had traveled his circuit of villages, farms, and orchards, the stone house only one more stop among many. Glimmer actually knew little about the mage. He did not know how long the mage had been in residence in the stone house; he did not know how old the mage was or where the mage had been before he had come to the land between the mountains and the sea. Glimmer realized that he knew more about the lives of the ancient mages that he had studied with his tutor than he knew about Alma-Ata. He knew more about his tutor, although that was still little enough. The story that the mage had told him about playing marbles with the apprentice when Alma-Ata was young was the first time that his master had ever spoken of such things. The man was not secretive, as some mages were, Glimmer thought. It was more that the mage was always more interested in the present and its needs. Speculation didn't occupy Alma-Ata's time.

At least with me, Glimmer thought. *Perhaps he's totally different with others. Perhaps magicians are different around those who have magic and those who don't.* Glimmer felt uncomfortable, realizing how little he knew his master, yet how much could he know of his master when he still knew so little about himself?

Glimmer considered his life and master as he cleaned his new sleeping quarters, a dark stone room large enough for a sleeping pallet and an equal space beside it, a dark room with no windows, bats hanging from the ceiling joists near the curved outer stone wall, a ray of daylight leaking in from a small crevice. If not a storage room, then this was a room whose door should always be open, its occupant always hearkening to lord's beck and call. By candlelight Glimmer emptied the room of several old wooden boxes, a broken chair, and a mouse-eaten rag of an undershirt. Then he swept the room, walls included, as high as he could reach. Lastly, he mopped the room, and by the time he was finished, he was glad the room was not larger. The room smelled of wet stone, vinegar, and wood, and probably would take forever for the dankness to dry. As the wooden floor slowly dried, he removed the scrabble of the room to the cobblestones outside the kitchen door for later inspection.

Two squared stones and an old board provided Glimmer a place in the room for his modest treasures: a robin's nest from the apple tree, an ancient arrowhead chipped from flint, a mortar and pestle given to him by Alma-Ata, a book-sized wooden box housing a few coins and pretty stones. Into this Glimmer carefully placed the book he had chosen from the mage's library: *Confessions of a Dreme Mage.* Closing the box's lid, he patted it thoughtfully before continuing with his organizing. Beneath the board and stone assembly, he slipped a basket containing his clothes. From a hook cemented into the wall's mortar hung Glimmer's only cloak.

With that, he stepped back and scrutinized the room lit by flickering candlelight. *Still room for a brazier on the coldest nights,* he surmised, although on those nights he would probably sleep next to the kitchen fire. He could leave the door open, he thought, and heat does rise, although the cold stone would soon drink any rising heat. Glimmer was not sad to abandon his pantry-hole in the kitchen, though. It was as if he were leaving his childhood.

This room had perhaps once housed a squire's page who had kept his door open, awaiting his master's call. Not for Glimmer, though. His master was off, always something with the apples, leaving the apprentice to make his own way as best he could. Bitterness rose and Glimmer left the room to wash and eat, for the sun was now setting on this day of broom and mop. That night he slept on his pallet on the landing again, the damp mustiness of his new quarters being no fit place to sleep for one who wished to avoid unpleasant dreams.

The next morning, sunlight brightened Glimmer's perspective. He sat on the wooden bench beside the kitchen entrance and enjoyed the warmth and the sharp smells of the fertile land. He had slept without dream, or at least remembered none. Sun was almost to zenith, and Glimmer surveyed the detritus remaining from yesterday's cleaning. He removed a broken chair to the shed; perhaps it could be salvaged or used for parts for repairing other chairs. The trash, being dust, straw and such, he dumped on the compost heap. He liked the idea of taking what was considered useless and providing a use for it once again.

Returning to the cobblestoned area fronting the kitchen, Glimmer wrestled the cube-shaped wooden box to the front of the bench. Using a bar, he pried lid from box and discovered glazed earthenware dishes. *This will be useful,* he thought, wondering at the history which had led the dishes to be stored in the room where he now slept. *Are they from the Brothers of Hospitality, something the country squire couldn't fit to a departing wagon, or*—although he couldn't imagine the what and why—*are they some gift to Alma-Ata for past magic?*

The next box was of a narrow, rectangular shape. It proved more interesting, yielding a sword and dirk, leather scabbards and belt, and a light hauberk of leather scale armor and mailed coif formed from copper rings. Glimmer pulled the sword from its scabbard, producing a faint leathern whisper. The sword was an unadorned blade of earth color; *gold,* he thought, and then realized the metal was tarnished copper. The blade was leaf-shaped, tapering to a thinner point. The wooden hilt was wrapped with a tightly woven cloth—silk, he guessed, although he had seen the fabric only once before. He cut the air with the blade and felt its balance, not a long blade—copper could not be worked to an extended length or it would become brittle—yet powerful and agile to his young arm. Although Glimmer knew little about weaponry, he realized the sword and armor must be ancient, steel having long replaced copper and bronze.

Glimmer's reverie was interrupted by a sound from the road. A small handcart with wooden wheels squeaked along the road to the stone house, protesting its progress even with the slight downward slope of the land. The cart was too small to be pulled by a horse, by a donkey perhaps, but the cart had been equipped with a crosspiece of wood fronting the cart shafts which allowed a person to stand within the shafts and push the cart. Pushing the cart was Bega, a freewoman Glimmer had met a few times over the years, the strongest woman he had ever seen. Bega could stand and look more than most men straight in the eye, and this was exactly what she did. Much of Bega's work was considered a man's, but she had made it her work. She could use the tools of kitchen and home, the tools of the field, and the tools of warfare equally well, or so it was said, anyway.

Glimmer remembered one story told of Bega about when she had worked in a tavern hoisting mugs to thirsty patrons, and what had happened one especially hot mid-summer. Bega was in the habit of toting her own broom to work and back, a large broom that "fit her hands better," as she explained. One evening, two reveling travelers were seen following Bega out the tavern door as she left for home. Later that evening, they staggered into the tavern, ashen-faced except for the bloody bruises and welts upon their heads. They had been waylaid by thieves, the men claimed, but one old man had later observed that the marks could easily have been produced by a stout length of hardwood—a two-inch broom handle, for instance. Bega had remained silent about the affair during the following days, continuing her own way, being the kind of woman who did her own house-cleaning, as one village woman smugly said.

Bega wore a grey dress of linen, broidered blue at hem and sleeve. Her hair she tied back, but it was so thick and curly it constantly threatened to escape and frame her face with a mare's nest of lively tangle. She pushed the cart easily, the road not muddy and the slope sufficient for gravity to lend a hand, even though the cart was full of goods and also carrying a passenger, a young woman somewhat older than Glimmer. Whereas Bega was strong and athletic, auburn hair streaked with grey, the young woman was pale and blonde, slender and delicate as a reed. Elesia she was named, Bega's daughter. Although little was known of Bega's history, other than what work she was capable of doing, even less known of her daughter.

Reaching the road fronting the kitchen door, Bega turned the cart onto the cobblestones and tipped the shafts to the ground. She straightened, stretching her back and dusting her hands as Elesia, stumbling slightly, slipped from the cart onto the ground. As she gained her balance, Glimmer could see her shoes, one sole thicker than the other to compensate for the shortness of her left leg, a mischance of birth which limited the young woman's mobility. She could walk but would tire over-quickly; she could run but with a precarious, rocking gait.

Both mother and daughter smiled at Glimmer as Bega declared, "Well, we've come as your master requested, straightaway and with no fuss, although Alma-Ata made one. We left within the hour, packed and gone and good riddance to the innkeeper at Ruddy. And now we're to open an inn and to run it with your help, young apprentice?"

Glimmer considered the woman's words: "left within the hour" must mean she had been traveling more than all night and into the day, yet she did not seem overly tired. Had Alma-Ata been that persuasive, or had her desire to leave Ruddy been that great?

Bega was advancing to the door, already intent on the business ahead when she spied sword and armor. "What's this? Intend to defend th' inn from vandals? Ancient vandals?" she added, taking a closer look at the bundle.

"I just found them in the box when I was moving into my new quarters."

"From the glint in yer eyes, I suppose I'll have to teach you how t' use them. I've seen that look often enough. It'll most likely bring you trouble—and, most likely, you won't listen to sense. Lord knows your master won't be able—or willing—to teach you t' stick pigs."

With that she swept into the house, Glimmer and Elesia trailing behind, for a quick tour, Bega leading the way with Glimmer identifying rooms that the woman entered with no regard to privacy.

"Empty rooms need t' be filled," she proclaimed. "It keeps th' secrets walkin' soft an polite." Glimmer reasoned to himself that there was not much secret about Bega.

The two women were soon busy in the tower, washing the room next to Glimmer's. "I don't see the rush, though, an' I'll bet yer master traveled all night an' more to catch me up early." Glimmer was soon sent on his way to Jurgen's Wood to convince Wilim to join the enterprise. By the time they returned to the stone house, sun was edging toward horizon and Wilim was wondering what they would be eating for supper.

"Stew and hot bread, I'll just bet," he declared. "No, I mean stew an' hot bread an' honey. Yea, that's right, an' mebbe some pie! What kinda pie yer think, Glimmer?" the man asked, Wilim's eyes round and innocent with sincerity.

Wilim's hunger proved more creative than the house's means, though, and cold cuts were a brief interruption in a whirlwind of activity, Bega providing the energy and direction. As they sat at the table in the kitchen, a silence descended on the stone house, a silence accentuated by the faint sound of chewing and occasional pop and crackle of the fire.

Glimmer stared absently at the flames when Bega interrupted his thoughts. "What kinda wood ya burnin'? Th' fire seems lively fer such a small bit o' wood."

"Yeah, it does that," Glimmer moodily replied. "I've asked it why—"

"An' what's the answer?" Bega asked, amused.

"*Fire burns from within,*" he responded. The woman stirred on the bench, staring more closely at the fire, remembering that she sat at the table of a magician, and as she ate the bread, she wondered at the cost of the meal.

Beneath the faint light of a new moon, Glimmer found his way later to the river to bathe before sleeping. Exhausted yet satisfied with the activities of the day, he washed the dust and dirt from his body, finding himself soothed by the lack of human sound. He realized how accustomed he had become to being alone, to pacing his day to a slower horse. Now he felt he was riding a galloping runaway, holding to it by its mane, his legs clasped to the barrel. It was a heady experience, such a turnaround in his life, but he was not sure of his destination and felt more that he was riding to ruin than riches.

He finished washing and stared across the stream at the meadow, a pale, shadowed openness within the darker circle of tree canopy. No dragon shape rested like a huge statue in the meadow; no grass lay crushed from a night's length of magical sleep. What was true and real for dreaming was not true for waking. But wasn't that the whole point, for magic to influence the world around? A dream mage could influence the world, though; he had already done that. *And don't forget the Slag Hills of Eyre and the Ghost of Gelfandland,* he reminded himself. Other dream mages had influenced the world—or, at least, legend had it. Some dream magic manifested in the waking world, and some dream magic did not. And there seemed to be no reliable signs while dreaming to predict the effects of any dream.

"Dreme magick is the most dangerous of magicks because it is the most difficult to control," his book read, and Glimmer could see the truth of it. What he hoped was that Bega would find so much for him to do that he'd have no time to worry during the day and no energy to dream during the night.

Glimmer turned and made his way up the path to the kitchen. Silence greeted his return. He must have been gone longer than he thought. Certain that his day would begin early tomorrow and continue long, he climbed the stairs. When he gained the landing, only the door to his room remained open, the door of mother and daughter already closed. He entered his room, closed the door, and placed the candle he had lit from the kitchen fire onto his makeshift nightstand. His master had been right: hard work did ease. Glimmer certainly had no desire or intent to perform dream magic. He would need no magic to fall asleep and rest the night away.

The stone walls seemed to breathe deep rhythms of sleep around him as he drifted. There was no need of a meadow to ease his sleep. There was no need of stupefying work to dull his sleeping to black inertia. He was protected, not by dragon talon but by dragon intent. He did not understand but felt the truth of it. He did not fully know what the dragon was or why all these people had come into his life, but he felt a deep ease, a confidence that he could and would be successful—even if he did not clearly comprehend his goal. The arrow had been released and would find its target.

Glimmer envisioned himself sleeping on the second floor of the stone tower, above the earth as if in the grandfather of trees or as if standing on a bluff, empty space before him. He was not sleeping on his pallet or on wooden planks that bridged the stone hollowness of the tower; he slept on air, floated in space, his head pillowed upon pliant mists. Would he drift if wind brushed shoulders with him? Would he drift like a babe in a basket cast adrift down an ancient river? Would wind babble in the eaves as water babbled in a stony brook?

The stone tower, like the apple tree in his dream, grew luminescent, points of matter somersaulting amid the glowing ether of space. Glimmer slept in a nest of blankets couched in space, unaware of somersaulting constellations and celestial visions—unaware but not alone. Bega and Elesia and Wilim were with him, gliding on wings of wind; and others were approaching, unnamed stars approaching like boats rowing the cosmic sea. They drifted, slowly orbiting the warm hearth of the stone house while stars spun night upon its axis. Glimmer slept and dreamed he was no longer alone. He stirred in his sleep, innocent in his luminescence, pillowing his head on lavender and chamomile. No watching or waiting or wondering existed, only the succulent lotus of sleep.

He awoke in a strange room familiar only in its silence. Neither memories nor dreams lay tucked within his mind. He sat up, filled with sudden purpose: he would not be rousted like a slacker from his bed by freewoman Bega, or even more ignominiously, her daughter Elesia. He stood, dressed, opened his door and descended to the kitchen. This morning, Cabbage-pants did not greet him nor did oatmeal cooked in cabbage broth await him at the table. He was first up at first light and knew his course of action before the others arose. He opened the door to the common room and turned to face the fire and beard the dragon.

A cheery fire cracked and popped within the firepit as if wood particularly heavy with resin had been used. The obsidian eye gleamed with awareness, the shadow of brow raised as if in curiosity or amusement. Glimmer faced the fire, balanced upon legs slightly spread—if not a belligerent at least a forceful stance.

"I suppose you know what's going on," he stated without preamble.

Yes.

Some of the starch left the young man's carriage as he admitted, "Then I suppose you know more than me."

Suppose?

"Why is it you twist everything I say?"

The worm turns in the apple of its own accord.

"If I want aphorisms, I'll read the Mage of DeVasier."

And I will explain the import.

"So you know more than me?"

So you always state the obvious?

"Look, why are you here?" Glimmer finally asked.

Because you summoned me and bound me to these stones, young master.

"Do you intend to hurt me or help me?"

That is your first reasonable question, the dragon replied, flames of fire flickering in agreement. *Ultimately, you help or hurt yourself. I assist you in your endeavors. Think of it in this manner, young mage. The flaming light of this fire will ease your reading no matter what you choose to read.*

Glimmer thought long on the stone dragon's answer. What was the dragon saying? If Glimmer did something dangerous or foolish, would the dragon help keep him safe or simply help him carry out his foolish, dangerous action? If he chose to read a spellbook that cursed whoever read it, would the dragon light the words and ease the reading, nothing more? If he attempted to assist a man being robbed by a bandit, how would the dragon help him? If he attempted to assist a man being robbed by ten bandits, how would the dragon help? Or would that be a foolish, dangerous action?

"You said the world is how we make it . . ."

Even before the making; world is as you are. It is structured within you and is your structure.

"Then I don't see how you can help—or as you said, *assist* me. I still have to choose, and I may choose well or no."

Now you begin to understand. Only you can choose your actions. I will assist you in bringing them to fruition. Let us consider a clear-cut situation. You fall through spring ice. You could choose to not extricate yourself and die, or you could choose to struggle clear of the water and live. In either case, I would assist.

"And how would you assist—in such a clear-cut example?"

There are many variables. Are others nearby? How thick is the ice? Is there current? At this time, I am confined to these stones, which establishes some parameters on my ability to act.

"So if you could leave the house, you could just swoop down and pick me up?"

That would lack finesse, but, yes, I could do that; however, you would first have to release me from these confines. Then I could choose to physically assist you.

Glimmer sat in the rocking chair and stared into the flames . . . and remembered flames eating at the apple tree, the dragon's eyes pools of fire, twin suns promising death, not nourishing warmth. *The dragon wants freedom. Can it be lying, or if it can't lie to me, can it assemble many small truths into a larger illusion to deceive me?*

"But if you were free, you could also choose not to help me. You could watch me drown."

I am not a dog-lizard come to save the little boy fallen into the river. I do not exist to save foolish boys from their peccadilloes.

"I still don't see how I can use you."

Use me? Better to use your Self.

Glimmer stood. "I just don't want to do something . . . foolhardy."

Half-right and half-wrong—only you will—

The fire extinguished with the sound of pots clattering in the kitchen. Glimmer walked to the connecting door and heaved. As the door creaked open, Bega turned from where she was bent over the kitchen hearth and exclaimed, "This house must have one of the best drawin' chimneys I've ever seen. The fire starts right up and stays lively with little smoke." She paused, one fist on her hip, staring affectionately at the fire. "There's no better way for a cook to start th' day than with a easy startin' fire. I've never seen anything like't." Bega raised her eyebrows and asked Glimmer, "And what're you doing first one up?"

"I guess I just woke up, that's all. I like the rocking chair in the common room."

"The one before the hearth?"

"Aye, it's a nice fit."

"If we had more, you could take it t' your room, but as 'tis, I wish we had one more so two guests could sit before th' fire and rock an' chat away th' winter chill. Travelers look forward t' such things while walkin' down cold, lonely roads." The woman poked her head into the pantry. "Why don't you wash outside an' then bring more wood? What we have here won't last long." (*Longer than you think,* Glimmer reckoned.) "I'll be making breakfast, and then it'll be a full day's work an' then some for us."

His face and hair wet and his arms full of firewood, Glimmer detoured to the garden before returning to the kitchen. There awaited the surprise of not only Cabbage-pants working the planting beds but three other gnomes, smaller and in a various of shades of coloration. Cabbage-pants waved to Glimmer and approached the garden wall, the other gnomes continuing to bend to their work.

"Who are these gnomes?"

"Ye've got yer turnip gnome," Cabbage-pants replied, indicating a pale, pot-bellied gnome whose head and hair sported a faint, purplish tinge, "and yer 'tater gnome," was added with a nod to a pudgy gnome of dark earthy coloration who was wading waist deep down the row of deep green potato plants, "and the feisty one's a pepper gnome," the gnome shouted up at Glimmer, and apprentice and gnome turned to watch a lanky gnome dancing around a pepper plant.

"What are they doing?"

"Why, workin' th' garden! What d' ya think?" the gnome said, cupping his hands to his mouth.

Glimmer sputtered in exasperation. Couldn't anyone figure out what he meant? "I mean why are they working in the garden? Or," he hurried to clarify, "why have they chosen to work here now. Or have they been here all along, and I just couldn't see them till now?"

"Oh, word has passed over th' years how things were a goin', but these here gnome-folk came 'cause they were *called*, ye might say."

"Called by you?"

"Nay, called by their patron plants, an' called mebbe by you. Ye've put th' magic back in th' place, that ye have."

"Does this mean you won't be cooking me cabbage breakfast from now on?"

The gnome flashed a glance toward the house and then stepped closer to the fence. "Just between you, me, an' th' gatepost," he said, lowering his volume somewhat, "some folks don't 'preciate cabbage as much as you an' me. Don't ye worry, though," he added. "I'll be findin' some manner t' meet all yer cabbage needs." The gnome chuckled to himself. "Yessire, don't you worry none about *that*."

With those words and a cautious glance to the house, the gnome waved a good bye and ambled back to his cabbage patch, muttering to himself. *No doubt cataloging cabbage recipes,* Glimmer thought.

One day of work grew to a week's work, and one week's work stretched to two. Floor and walls cleaned, tapestries beaten to rid the dust, windows washed with water and cider vinegar, tables and benches repaired, ticking replaced in mattresses—the stone house was transformed into a stone inn situated on a road little traveled, a refuge for weary travelers and wanderers.

And Alma-Ata was one dusty traveler who frequented the inn when he passed through on his circuit. The magician would stop at the inn to press apples for cider and to transact business with Bega. Then he would return days or weeks later to rack the cider, siphoning the liquid into new jugs to remove the sediment which affected the cider's shelf life. The jugs were stored in the cool root cellar to minimize the fermentation process. With careful attention, the apple juice would keep the year, slowly turning to cider. The apples from the land between sea and mountain were known for their mild flavor, lacking the sourness caused by too much acid.

The mage did not linger at the stone house when he visited but was always off and on his way within a few days. He praised Bega for her resourcefulness and raked Glimmer with thoughtful, penetrating eyes. As the season progressed, the group settled into a routine centering on using summer and fall to prepare for eventual winter. Bega continued her campaign of improving the inn's capacity to bed, feed, and please its guests. Guests were all they needed now. Most travelers had already established traveling habits and showed little desire to change them, though some didn't mind stopping on a hot afternoon to quench their thirst before continuing on.

"It will take a while for word to spread, and then travelers will come," the mage had said as they all sat around a table near the common room hearth. "A sign over the door," he added, nodding to the main door to the common room on the east wall. The door's recently painted exterior gleamed a bright green as it stood open and inviting. "A sign over the door would help. What shall we call the inn, young apprentice?"

"The Stone Dragon Inn," Glimmer responded without a moment's hesitation. None but Alma-Ata knew of the dragon residing in the stone, but the name was instantly approved.

"A name worthy of a song," whispered a bard who had stopped at the inn, accompanied by his apprentice. The bard had all but lost his voice through accident, the few words he had spoken not telling the whole story; but with his forthright manner, emphasized by his square-cut beard, he and his bright-eyed and smiling apprentice had been a welcome addition to the main meal of the day.

The apprentice, Jukka by name, picked up his lute and strummed an experimental chord.

> Walk far and long across the sand
> And linger where ye will-o.
> In better bed ye'll nev'r land
> Than Stone Dragon's fiery pillow!

The company clapped their hands in merriment, Bard Reis nodding his approval to his apprentice. Striking another chord on his lute, Jukka gazed challengingly to the others. Elesia, her face flushed and gaze full upon the young bard, began to sing, tremulously at first and then with growing confidence.

> With table full of food and drink
> And hearth to toast our health to,
> We sing and stand, our arms to link
> And dance Stone Dragon's jingle!

More clapping, and the flushed happiness of the revelers seemed to brighten the fire. Glimmer gazed into the flames, and did he see small dragons formed of flame dancing? Another provocative dance of Jukka's fingers across the lute, and then a voice added to the merriment from the open doorway.

> A dragon knows no earthly fear,
> Unless it be one thing-o.
> Untimely try to snatch and sear
> A cabbage gnome, we deem so!

With these words and to the laughter of the humans at the table, the gnome scampered back to his cabbages as if to check that they hadn't been crisped because of his verses.

So all see and hear the gnome, Glimmer thought. *Is it as Cabbage-pants says, that the magic of this place increases, or is it that these people see more deeply to the fabric of life? And if that is so, how much is due to my master's magic of Gathering?*

Ala-Ata then retired to his room to pack, leaving again soon, and the remaining company settled around the table and chatted in growing familiarity. Bard Reis sipped from a mug of cider, rolling the liquid in his mouth and trickling cider down his throat.

"My master came here to partake of the apple-elixir to heal his throat," explained the apprentice minstrel Jukka. As the elder bard nodded his agreement, the apprentice continued, "He felt coming to the elixir's source, Alma-Ata's own trees, would provide a more powerful effect."

"What do you mean?" Glimmer asked. "Cider's just cider, some better than others, I'll grant."

A silence moment ensued as Bega and Bard Reis exchanged glances, Elesia's eyes on blonde Jukka, and Wilim glancing with round-eyed incomprehension from one speaker to the other. Bega cleared her throat. "Ye mean ye don't know of yer master's repute?"

Now it was Glimmer's turn at confusion. Was Bega commenting on Alma-Ata's magic of Gathering, or was she referring to his second trade (*or should it be considered the first?* Glimmer wondered) of apple master to the local farmers. "I'm not sure I understand what you mean," Glimmer said in reply.

To Glimmer's surprise, the woman remarked, "I was born in th' Outlands," and the minstrel-bard added, "My feet also have traveled that road." The bard's voice was paper thin, and Glimmer leaned to him to better hear. The bard continued, his words fragile in the air as if the center of the sound had been pulled from them. "This cider, made by your master's own hand and from his own trees—it would sell for its weight in gold in the Outland kingdoms."

"As ye say," Bega said to Glimmer, "cider's just cider, some better than others, but yer master's cider is just th' *medium* fer th' magic, a place fer't to collect, ye might say." The woman paused, her gaze upon her daughter. "An' that magic *heals*. I wash my daughter's leg with 't every night," Bega admitted. Elesia sat, eyes downcast, as still as stone. "An' that magic's why we came here so of a sudden—that, an' th' innkeeper at Ruddy keeps a pig sty," she added, laughing. Wilim laughed loudly along with her, eager to be a part of the company, understanding nothing.

"Great is the magic of the natural world," whispered Bard Reis's voice, "and that magic siphons into Mage Alma-Ata's cider."

"I like th' taste, too, yep, it's good," Wilim said into the silence that followed the bard's whispered words.

Glimmer's mind whirled. *I've never been sick,* he thought, *since I've come to stay with Alma-Ata.*

Of course, he had never been sick much before—as least, as he remembered. A wider view of his master filled Glimmer's mind, yet still he wondered how this could be called his master's magic. In the south garden, the turnips would now grow great and glorious—not due to Glimmer's magic, surely, but due to the turnip gnome's magic—and the magic of the plants themselves—and the magic of the earth they grew in—the ripples of connectedness spread wider and wider. How could Glimmer take the credit for the gnomes who now graced the garden where, for so many years, Glimmer had toiled alone?

And what of his master? The young apprentice imagined apple orchards full of gnomes touching and talking to the trees, the green radiance of the earth lively in their hands and voices. Could Alma-Ata take credit for that? How much credit could the apothecary take when he mixed his tonics and tinctures? Alma-Ata himself had said that he did nothing, that magic gathered around him of its own accord with no intervention from the mage. There was more here than he understood, the young apprentice reckoned, yet he also had to be careful not to add more to it than there already was—no need to call the barnyard goose a swan of the lake.

Soon Alma-Ata was on his way again, first to Jurgen's Wood and then to the village of Pickle; and then on to the wide valley's grain-producing communities of Barleycorn, Wheatland, and Richland. Then it would be on to the port of Knight's Landing and by boat down the coast to Delta. Up the River Road to isolated farms and orchards the mage would travel, Ari's Farm and Ana Sayfa's Redstreaks, the Sea Fens to the south, a maze of waterways gradually extending from grassland river to sea; such were the starts and stops of Alma-Ata's circuit.

As Glimmer watched his mage's striding form diminish with distance, he wondered again why his master always left, why his master did not instruct or advise or at least remain for support. *He never has, though,* Glimmer had to admit. Perhaps it was as the stone dragon had said: Glimmer had to rely on himself. However, the dragon had also said that the apprentice could listen and learn before deciding a course of action. How could he listen to the wisdom of his master if his master was never around? How could he rely upon his mage's guidance if the only constant of his master's instruction was what he saw right now—the backside of Alma-Ata's shirt seeking the distant horizon?

Chapter 6

"A blade is for cutting."
108 Aphorisms of Mage DeVasier, the "Whetstone" sequence

చ

Bard Reiss and his apprentice left the day after Alma-Ata, having rested at the Stone Dragon Inn a day beyond their expectation.

"We're playing the smaller towns and entertaining at inns and even some of the larger farms," Reis explained in his rough whisper. "Jukka needs the seasoning . . . and we need shelter and sustenance."

"Until my master's voice heals," young Jukka explained. "Red Robin and Ruddy and on north to Spur and the like. I've never been this way. I will sing and master will play. Indeed," the apprentice said, "Master says that I am nearly ready to become a journeyman in my own right."

The young bard—although to Glimmer's mind Jukka was already a man, being a handful of years older than he—grandly looked down at the folk of the inn from the saddled prominence of his horse. As the minstrel and apprentice reined their horses to the road, Elesia stepped to Jukka's steed, holding onto the stirrup strap to stay the horse and rider. With eyes large and with all her dignity in delicate balance, she lifted her hands to the young minstrel and presented him with a gift.

"For you and your comfort," she murmured.

Jukka stared long into her eyes and then accepted the gift wrapped in white linen. Removing the linen, he held the gift in his hands, a pillow small enough to fit a saddlebag or bedroll, a pillow embroidered with lute and meadow lark, the bird's head lifted and throat swelling with song.

"It's stuffed with goose down and will ease your sleep on rocky earth and strange roads."

As he leaned down in his saddle to murmur to the young woman, the elder minstrel leaned in his turn to whisper to Bega, who stood nearby. "How many songs d'ye think that pillow will inspire? More than one, I'll wager." With a hoarse chuckle, he touched a spur to his horse and trotted north, calling over his shoulder for his apprentice. Apprentice followed master but not without a last look behind at the willowy blonde form of Elesia.

Summer advanced, and days lengthened in the routine of cleaning and mending, serving a meal to occasional traveler, providing an infrequent bed. The only diversion for Glimmer was his preoccupation with the copper armor and weaponry that he had found boxed in what was now his sleeping quarters. A man-of-arms, Alma-Ata had said, had left the box, a soldier who wished to hear sounds of silence rather than those of war. On his way to find seclusion among the anchorites of the Eagle's Escarpment, he had left the box, saying to the mage in parting, "If I ever come back for this, tell me you gave it away."

Glimmer began practicing with the sword, striking grim poses and thrusting with the blade or stabbing with the copper dirk that had accompanied the sword. He constructed blunt wooden swords and practiced swordsmanship with Wilim—to Wilim's everlasting delight.

"I'm a reg'lar soljer, I am," he would say to Glimmer as they practiced. "Better watch't or I'll knock y' on yer fanny." Wilim would chuckle to himself, his childish joy expanding at the thought of himself in armor. "No, I'm a knight, an' I don't mean th' sun's down," he'd ramble. "I'm a knight an' own a castle. Yea, that's it—I'm a king an' own four castles an' three horses, no, three castles an' four horses. Yea, that's it."

The sound of wooden swords striking would bring Bega to the kitchen door, where she would stand and glower. Finally she allowed if Glimmer were to hold a sword, he had better learn more than he could learn from practice with simple-minded Wilim. Parry and thrust, she taught, slash and stab. Footwork and balance, moves in sequence, engage and disengage. Glimmer improved to where he could easily overcome Wilim's artless enthusiasm.

Glimmer worked hard at innkeeping and played hard at soldiery, allowing himself to forget the hearth with its obsidian eye. Practice grew more vigorous, yet as day followed day, the sun began to beat with less vigor on the two men playing at war. Autumn browned leaves to the color of ancient copper swords.

One day as leaves dyed themselves russet, Cabbage-pants placed himself before Glimmer, who was lost in thought. Standing with legs widespread, the gnome was dressed in new fringed cabbage leggings, tasseled belt, and jerkin of tightly woven fabric a supple pale green: cabbage-cotton, the young man decided to call it. With his earth-colored eyes full upon the apprentice, the gnome spoke: "'Tis th' Gnome's Path for me. I ask ye formal to be my ally."

Glimmer's attention was captured by the gnome's words and tone. "Be your ally?" he asked. The young man was familiar with the gnome's comical ways but never forgot that the gnome was still a magical being, deserving of respect and caution. He had noticed, too, a change in the gnome; with the maturation of summer, the gnome had changed, his comments more complex, his wise eyes containing greater knowledge than recipes and crop reports. "I hope you know I am on your side—your ally—but I'm not sure I understand all of what you mean."

The gnome placed one fist on his hip; with his other hand, he pointed a pudgy finger at Glimmer, the perfect image of a dry, scholarly lecturer.

"Gnome ways are not th' ways o' men," he began. Cabbage-pants looked down his nose at the young magician, which was rather difficult since Glimmer was sitting on the bench outside the kitchen door and the gnome was actually looking up at him.

"Big folk like t' celebrate the beginnin' an' end o' things—lots o' happiness an' sadness—but gnomes," and the gnome touched his nose and winked, "gnomes celebrate the midpoints, the halfways, ye might say."

At Glimmer's blank look, Cabbage-pants continued. "Celebrate th' seasons in their fullness, not at the beginnin' or end. And," the gnome sagely nodded, "celebrate by th' dozen."

"By the dozen?"

Cabbage-pants sputtered in disbelief that the young man didn't understand. Dropping his caricature of a scholar, he stepped to the young man and patted his knee and spoke.

> Twelve moons together a year does make,
> An' twelve times twelve's called one *moon round.*

> Twelve rounds t' fullness does it take
> T' walk th' Gnome's Path an' then lie down.

"A gnome lives 144 years," a voice explained from the doorway. Glimmer turned his head to see Elesia leaning against the doorframe. "Twelve times twelve is the *twelfth round*, the span of a gnome's life."

"How do you know this?"

"It's a math riddle my mom taught me. And a gnome's birthdays are at the *cross-quarters*, each quarter of 144 years being 36 years in length. Gnome's have four birthdays: years eighteen, fifty-four, ninety, and 126 of the gnome's life."

Cabbage-pants spoke again in verse.

> Celebrate once each quarter the fullness o' life,
> An' follow th' Path to a place unknown.
> Like a snake that coils round joy an' strife,
> Th' Path ye walk is never alone.

"You're being invited to a birthday party, to be ally to Cabbage-pants and walk the Gnome's Path with him." Elesia, her eyes the pale blue clarity of the sky, stared silently at the young mage for a moment. "I'd do't if I were you."

"How does the riddle-song end?" Glimmer asked.

"As all riddles—with a mystery."

"And what's the mystery here?"

"If I could answer that, what would be the mystery?" Nodding to the gnome before retreating into the kitchen, the woman's last words came from shadows. "I'll tell you, though, I've never heard of a man following the Gnome's Path."

"Now mind ye, I'm not sayin' it's never happened. I'm just sayin' no one remembers it ever happenin', but that don't mean they're not agreeable. An' we all o' us gnomes agree that it prob'ly won't cause ye no injury, or at least nothin' permanent-like."

"Well, that's good to know," Glimmer responded. "And where is this Gnome's Path we're to walk?"

"It's not just one path—no, not at all," the gnome said, sitting next to Glimmer on the bench. "Some walk a garden's path, some walk a path through forest, and some even walk a path seen to no one but themselves. Nay, Gnome's Path isn't a *place* but a *manner*, ye might say."

"Then in what *manner* are we to walk?" the young mage asked, less apprehensive as the discussion drifted to gardens and forest paths.

"In a manner o' speakin', not upon a path at all."

"Thanks for clearing that up for me," Glimmer said, his misgivings returning.

He wished Alma-Ata and his advice were at hand. *Is that why my master is not here,* the young mage wondered, *so I'll learn to trust myself?* "It is not my magic," he heard his master saying. *It's not my magic either,* Glimmer thought. He thought about the words of the riddle: *like a snake that coils round joy an' strife.* That was his magic—as easy as walking a snake's back. *As easy as facing dragonfire,* he thought, and took a deep breath and let it out.

The gnome swung his legs back and forth, staring at the ground below as Glimmer sat beside him.

"Don't bother yerself. We'll be walking a road made by men—most way, at least."

"Where are we going?"

"Th' Dragon's Spine."

Glimmer's blinked at the words. Where had he heard them before? He had expected a walk in the garden or the fields nearby, a walk to the river or perhaps a walk to Jurgen's Wood. But the Dragon's Spine? "Is that a gnomish name for a plant that grows around here?"

"Nay, young mage, it's th' place o' th' glass rock. 'Tis known as th' Dragon's Spine, but—" Cabbage-pants added with a knowingness in his eyes as old as mountains worn to hills "—ye might know't better as the source o' th' dragon's eye." The gnome pointed to one of his bright, black eyes as he spoke, and Glimmer pictured the stone on the mantel in the common room, the stone as large as a plate focusing with magical awareness . . . and then blinking.

"Obsidian?" The word focused the geography of Glimmer's mind. "The Dragon's Spine's days from here, maybe a week or more," Glimmer complained, frightened again. "I've never been there."

"Aye, an' *there's* never been *here*." The gnome leaped to his feet, his eyes now even with Glimmer's. "That's th' point! Are ye with me?"

Glimmer's mind filled with the sudden desire to be rid of the stone house, to distance himself from hearthstones and baleful obsidian eyes and dancing fires. "Yes, we shall walk together!" he exclaimed, gratified by the leap of joy in the gnome's eyes. This was a chance to discover how closely his magic was linked to the house and dragon. Perhaps a few days' walk and he could be Not a Glimmer of Magic again. The young apprentice, lost to his whirl of thoughts, forgot the gnome who sat patiently at his side, as silent and still as a stone marking a roadway.

Cabbage-pants then quietly murmured Alma-Ata's words, "It is not my magic," and slipped from Glimmer's side. The young man sat alone on the bench as the sun traveled its path across the sky, and when he finally stood and entered the house, no one walked beside him.

The next morning's dawning was greeted with a sharp, "You are what!?" issuing from Bega's mouth.

Glimmer's mouth equaled the stubborn set of the woman's. "It's mage business," he responded, to which she made no reply but the down-turning of her mouth and an abstracted brushing of a strand of hair from her eyes.

Even Bega of the forthright manner recognized the futility of the response, "It's childish business!"

As she turned from the apprentice mage and returned to her bread-making, Glimmer exited the kitchen and set his bedroll on the bench next to the door. He then returned to his room and gathered the ancient arms and armor and exited through the kitchen, placing the mass upon the bench beside the bedroll. He slipped on coif and then hauberk, their weight settling upon him like a heavy hand. Buckling on sheathed sword and dirk by hangers and swordbelt, Glimmer stood in the morning sun, hauberk creaking in the silence.

"Bega told me yer goin'—just afore tellin' me to get out o' th' kitchen," Willim said as he hurriedly exited the tower's kitchen door. He wiped his nose with his sleeve and then took a full view of Glimmer, his lips pursing in appreciation, his eyebrows rising. "Whoo-ee, you sure look fine! Nobody's gonna mess with ye, or they'll get it, I c'n tell ye that. Ye've done th' same t' me a time or two." As he nodded his head enthusiastically, a pot clanged noisily upon hearthstone in the kitchen.

"Whatcha say we *du-el*," Willim whispered conspiratorially, savoring the word, "afore ye go? It doesn't have 't be a hard go, no 't don't. That's right, it'll be a warm-up. I'll be getting' ye ready fer action."

Wilim lifted the wooden swords leaning against the tower wall beside the bench and offered one to Glimmer. A final crash of metal on stone and then a whirlwind of skirt and wiry hair raged from the kitchen, grabbed the swords from Wilim, tossing one to Glimmer. "What d'ye think yer doin', young Glimmer? I'd as soon send Elesia out with a sword as ye."

"A man's got a right to protect himself."

"More have died protectin' themselves with a sword than've lived."

"You've used a sword and taught me what I know. You said I was getting pretty good." He held up his wooden sword and saluted the woman. "What, now you don't want me to use what you taught me?"

"I said lots o' things, an' no, I don't. An' why? Because I've finally learned what women wi' more wisdom knew all along: 'tis better to clean wi' broom than brand, and blades are best left to th' cutting o' bread."

With a shrill shout Bega attacked with her wooden sword, aiming a vicious stab to the young man's heart. He parried, dropping and twisting his sword from its salute, and the woman whirled, a cloud of skirt and a blur of wooden blade, bashing Glimmer a heavy blow across the his ribs. He staggered back and Bega closed, shoving with the flat of her blade against his chest and then slashing the shaft at his protected neck. Stepping back, Glimmer stumbled on the cobblestones and fell to his back, Bega suddenly above him, sword to his throat, her hair a dark, wild cloud framing her pale face.

"You surprised me!" he protested in indignation, attempting to regain his feet.

"An' yer *dead*," the woman replied, pushing him back with the dull point of the wooden sword. "Aye—surprised, or bigger, or better—any way you cut it, you're still dead." She squatted next to Glimmer's sprawl. "Ye're just bein' foolhardy," and Glimmer chilled at her choice of words, remembering his conversation with the dragon.

"I just don't want to do something . . . foolhardy," the young man had said, and the dragon had answered, *Half-right and half-wrong—only you will—* and then had disappeared with the clatter of a kitchen pan. But how could it be wrong to be safe, to avert danger?

"Then how should I *protect* myself?"

"What d'ye mean by *protect*? No home or family, an' th' gnome can look to himself." Bega stood and brushing her hair back. She tossed the wooden sword with a dull clatter upon the cobblestones. "Protect yersel'? What ye do is *run*, young apprentice! Who'll catch a rabbit such as ye?" She stared down at the young man on the cobbles, bruised in body and spirit. "But like most men, ye'll not avoid th' smell of death until ye've had yer nose rubbed in't."

She turned and walked in defeat to the kitchen, turning at the last to say, "I knew a man who died with sword in bloody hand to give his wife a chance t' run—when we could've run side by side. He was a fool, a brave an' lovely an' grand fool, he was." Her voice broke in a sob. "Now he's a fool dead an' gone long years. Don't be the fool," the woman pleaded, but the promise of being free of the stone house with the obsidian eye was hard upon Glimmer and, ignoring the round-eyed, dumbfounded wonder of Wilim, he stood to his feet.

Settling the weapons to his hips and slinging the bedroll to his back, Glimmer did not glance again at the house as he strode, prickly in his pride, across the cobblestones to the twin dirt tracks that fronted the inn. Turning north, he strode up the road, land gradually rising before him in the distance, the far mountains beyond like the mandible of some fey reptile, fangs sharp and dire in the morning light.

Days to travel, he was thinking, *more than a week.* Leave the river at Red Robin and continue on to the village of Ruddy, then off the road and onto the path that led to Madrone. Madrone lay upon the Olifant's Tear, a lake where the north fork of the River Quill widened. Cross the lake by ferry, march east across the grasslands of the Olifant's Playground, and somehow ford the east branch of the Quill. Across the river was the Dragon's Spine, a series of round upthrusts laced with obsidian. Days and days of travel.

He settled the bedroll more comfortably across his shoulders and did not look back until he had traveled far enough that the inn was hidden by trees. Then he turned and stared to the place he knew the inn to be amid the trees. How many parts the stalwart ally—and how many parts the fool?

How many days of travel? How long when he was traveling with a gnome no taller than his knee? A movement from the corner of his eye answered his question. Trotting beside the young man was a fox, a large, mature fox, its flaming red coat gleaming in contrast to the mottled, variegated earth tones of the gnome that rode upon its back. The fox trotted to Glimmer's side, its red tongue lolling, its gait easy.

Without a word, Glimmer followed as the fox continued up the road, ally and gnome setting off to travel the Gnome's Path. Silence can stretch to breaking, though, especially when one is young; and Glimmer finally asked, just to hear a voice, just to say something, anything, "Shouldn't we be singing a song or reciting a poem?" to which the gnome replied, "Go ahead if yer in th' mood."

The gnome stared ahead into the distance, easy with the fox's gait, studiously ignoring Glimmer's—*let's be honest,* the apprentice thought—homesickness. The morning was warming to afternoon, and the leather and mail were hot and chafing. Glimmer was no minstrel and knew no marching songs, and singing and poetry wasn't what he wanted, anyway. He was alone, deep in magic and outside the familiar company of man, accompanying a gnome who no longer seemed so child-like, so cute. The fantasy that Glimmer was the older, wiser brother to the gnome was no longer so easy for him to maintain. Glimmer began to pay more attention as he walked the foreign road; magic lay around the corner—and whatever else fate chose to place upon the path.

The road did not follow the river closely; the River Quill could be seen a long arrow's flight away, a cool, sparkling promise amid alders and cottonwoods that lined its course, but the land between was cut with sloughs and marshy sections. Too near the river was treacherous or, at best, a wet, mucky business. Glimmer sipped water from his leathern flask and strode and sweated through the increasing heat of the day. The gnome, silent beside him, continued to lead with eyes ahead, the footfalls of the fox barely rippling the silence.

Cheese and bread, garnered from the pantry, and water from the flask were the victuals of the journey as fox and gnome continued at an easy yet steady pace. The dusty ribbons of the wagon tracks rose and fell, twisting with the still-gentle slopes of the upland verge. Farms tracks diverged from the main road, cuts in the earth overgrown with weeds, little used. Going to village was a rare and wonderful event for families come from the farm. Harvest celebrations after the milling of wheat and barleycorn, bartering in open-air markets, such activities were rare breaks from the hard routine of the farm.

Autumn was in its glory, and little time was there for frivolities such as apple-bobbing and wrestling throws. The long summer's labor needed to be harvested and stored to last the cold months when the land was sleeping. The road was empty and the days were hot to those who labored hard. Glimmer sweat beneath his armor, chafing where hard metal and leather argued with skin and joint. He sweated, and the armor weighed upon him: fool he was to wear it and let it wear him to the ground. Fool he was to ally himself to the gnome and wander down the road in red armor beneath a red sun. Fool he was to read the book and dream of fire and wing and talon. Glimmer remembered then the look of joy in the gnome's eyes when he had agreed to accompany him on this path. He remembered his tutor, old in his letters and glad for a place to spend the winter, lecturing on a frozen day before the kitchen fire: "Magic exists and should neither be denied nor twisted." Straightening his shoulders and lengthening his stride, the young mage paced the fox; man to gnome, a steadfast ally he would be.

They continued on into midday and to the middle of the next day, passing through the village of Red Robin, their shadows bunched at their feet, passed by tavern and guildhall, the stone houses of merchants thatched with straw—a four-corners village if more than one street had ever crossed another. A few faces that happened to peer out windows saw a lone man of arms, tall and lanky, geared in aged copper and leather, a slender young man flanked by the regal presence of a fox. It was an odd sight, and one that caused some conversation over the next days in kitchen and field.

Outside the village, farm and cultivated field abutted one another for a time, rather than the more typical farm surrounded by wild land. Afternoon was advancing when the fox veered from the road to a small copse of trees at the foot of a hill. Glimmer stood in the road a moment. To the west of the road, a little-used track angled from the road, rounding the slight hill and disappearing. Climbing the hill in a dozen steps, Glimmer saw a small farm beyond the crest, the farm humble in size and unpretentious, yet the garden was green and well-tended and kine grazed contentedly in a pasture past the farmhouse. The house, built of stone and sod with grassed roof, opened its door to the rising sun. Flowers blossomed in beds below the two east windows, one to each side of the cottage entrance. *Neither poor nor rich, with roots deep in the earth,* he thought. He turned thoughtfully and crossed to road to the copse where the fox and rider had disappeared.

Beneath the shade of trees rustling their autumn leaves, Cabbage-pants sat with four other gnomes in a loose circle, the side nearest the road still open. As Glimmer approached, Cabbage-pants patted the earth at the open spot and said, "Sit, young sire."

The four gnomes sitting with Cabbage-pants stood as Glimmer sat, speaking in unison: "Wel-coome, Ally." One round-faced gnome with chestnut-brown hair, wearing a sleeveless sack of a dress woven from dried grasses said, "Eat and be strong," and another gnome dressed in a similar dress said, "Drink and never tire."

Bowing to their words from his place on the ground, Glimmer nibbled what tasted to be a nut and vegetable loaf, served on a large leaf. He then drank sweet water from a small cup cleverly folded from leaf. The food was mild and pleasant, and the water was sweet, both savory with earth flavors.

"These're th' gnomes of this copse," Cabbage-pants explained. "They help th' family 'cross th' way." Then he winked. "An' help themselves to th' vegetables." At this the other gnomes laughed in their high voices and clapped their hands.

"That sounds fair to me," the young man responded.

"Right 'tis," responded one bearded gnome with a sallow complexion and a long, thin nose. "We've asked th' rabbits to keep to th' meadows."

"This is Carrot," Cabbage-pants introduced, "and Holy Basil, Pea-sweet, and," he continued, looking to the one gnome who had not yet individually spoken, "Green Cabbage Talking." Glimmer bowed his head respectfully.

"Kin to you?" he asked Cabbage-pants.

"Closer to say 'of the same seed.'"

Gnomes and Glimmer ate in affable silence, the sweet water invigorating the young man and the meal nourishing him. He discreetly observed the gnomes of the copse, especially the women, having never seen female gnomes before.

As they finished their portions, discreet glances circled the group, and then Cabbage-pants said, "The mother-gnome Holy Basil wishes to speak."

"I was wondering about women gnomes," Glimmer said, somewhat awkward with the question. "You are the first I have met."

Holy Basil and Pea-sweet looked at one another in wonder. Pea-sweet said, "Usually mother-gnomes are the first man-children see." She smiled at Glimmer. "All young we love and protect."

"Hm, all young, yes . . ." Glimmer murmured, to which Holy Basil asked, her bright, black eyes turned alertly up to his, "Ye've a question?"

The young apprentice glanced at the gnomes sitting comfortably on the soft, green grass beneath the trees, feeling himself hot with sudden blush. "Well, er, ye see, gnomes are known, but little is said about the mother-gnomes and, er, gnome children." Glimmer took a sudden deep breath and blurted. "There is some speculation about . . . how gnomes have children," he finished in a sudden rush of words, feeling the beat of his heart as blood rushed to his face.

"How d' ye think!" sputtered Cabbage-pants as the other gnomes giggled and laughed with amusement.

"Well, there are some who say there are certain . . . toadstools . . . that grow up?" Glimmer ended lamely, his voice cracking with the question.

"Toadstools! What d' ye think we are?" sputtered Cabbage-pants to the hoots and gasping laughter of the other gnomes, Carrot chirping, "Better watch where we sit!"

"You are magical beings."

"Magical *beings*, right enough! Magical beings, not magical *fungi*." The laughter of the gnomes was without derision, though, and Glimmer felt its warmth and good humor, the joy of the gnomes to be sharing their meal and the moment with him. The mirth subsided to quieter good will, even Cabbage-pants' grumbles alternating with a good-humored upturning of his lips.

Then Holy Basil laid her tiny hand upon Glimmer's palm and looked deeply into his eyes. Glimmer thought of small plants, aromatic and green in a farmwife's carefully tended herb garden: basil, green and tender; dill, tall and leaning; lavender, purple blossoms and dark leaves; sage, furred leaves a pale green-grey. *As a child I saw no magic,* he thought, *had no mother, human or gnome.*

"You shall live and grow in wisdom," the mother-gnome said, including Cabbage-pants in her gaze, and then she chanted in a low, melodious voice.

> Earth silent, dragon flies.
> Water quickens, child cries.
> Pull weed, soil do harrow,
> Bloody deed where road is narrow.
> Gnome and quest, mage and dream,
> In wilderness wild do women keen.

Afternoon filled with silence as the chant ended. The young mage bowed respectfully as the copse-gnomes gathered themselves and silently departed. The travelers continued down the road, silence loud between the footfalls of man and fox. Glimmer thought about the words of the mother-gnome Holy Basil. Some were easy to understand, the part about the dragon and the part about gnome and mage. He did not understand nor did he like the references to crying, keening, and blood, though.

"And what did it mean?"

"Why just what she said," sputtered the gnome. "The quest'll be successful, assumin' we don't die."

"I was afraid it meant something like that," Glimmer replied.

"Don't worry yer head," the gnome replied. "The Gnome's Path can lead to many places."

"And what was all that about a quest?"

"All gnomes walk the Gnome's Path on their second cross quarter birthday, but longer walks 're sometimes called quests."

The road to Reddy was well-established but contained long stretches of grassy hills and ravines dotted with upland scrub oak, stretches of green devoid of any sign of man. Man's mark upon the land by plow or scythe would manifest over the horizon eventually, but Glimmer was uneasy in the solitude. He found himself glancing from side to side and over his shoulder, peering ahead and imagining shadows of movement.

Cabbage-pants spoke into the silence, his words slipping into a rhythm matching the fox's whispering footfalls, and Glimmer listened as they continued their way to the village of Ruddy.

"In th' time before gnomes worked with men, they lived wild in th' untouched land an' cared for't as children of men would care for a garden—now an' again—as't pleased them. Less talk an' less ceremony; more songs composed jus' o' th' sounds o' earth, water, an' sky.

"An' then men came, an' we came t' love th' beauty o' a garden an' orchard, that cabbages in a row had a beauty diff'rent than those wild. Not that all gnomes did this, mind ye. Many still live afield, but songs changed t' become more like those o' men, and t' understand th' words, some gnomes left their patches o' land and wandered to th' gardens."

The gnome had spoken more quietly as he had continued, more thoughtfully. Words spoken were interspersed with long periods of silence and footsteps. Afternoon cooled and shadows lengthened. Glimmer thought about the gnome's words and said, "And these long-wanderings came to be called quests by those who did not stray from garden or field?"

Cabbage-pants affirmed Glimmer's words with his silence. "And what have those wanderers learned?" Glimmer then asked.

The gnome placed his hand upon the head of the fox, and the travelers stopped, the gnome looking up into the young man's eyes. "That th' song th' wild gnomes sang has been lost in much of th' world."

"Other lands have lost their gnomes?"

"Nay, not lost." The gnome leaned to the side and scooped a handful of dirt from the road, letting the soil trickle through his fingers. Leaning again, he drew a line in the soil with his finger. "Ye c'n see the mark I left," he said, nodding to the line he had drawn, "but could ye see't if drawn in air? Nay, some men've made th' land too heavy, 'tis all that c'n be said."

The gnome urged the fox into motion again and then chanted with gravely voice as the travelers continued down the road.

> In land o' men stone is stacked;
> Tree is hewn by might of back.
> House o' fire t' melt th' stone
> From valley's belly, mountain's bone.
> Brick an' iron, brass an' tin:
> What dream o' green in land o' men?

"So men drain the land of its magic?"

"Too many men and o' th' wrong kind scatter magic, like wind can steal th' soil."

They continued walking as the day progressed, and it seemed to Glimmer that his footsteps were heavy in the air, weighted as they were with the accoutrements of war, uncushioned by prairie grasses because they walked upon raw scars of a road men had cut into the earth. Grass was heavy with seed, stems turning red and blonde. The bare branches of trees were interspersed with those still retaining leaves, green and golden. The land was in transition even as man and gnome traversed it. Earth abided, yet loss to one part was also loss to the whole.

Chapter 7

"A sharp blade for a clean cut."
"A blade forborne leaves no scar."
108 Aphorisms of Mage DeVasier, the "Whetstone" series

⌘

The sun was lowering in the sky and dusty miles lay behind them when Cabbage-pants led the way into Ruddy, two crafthouses and an inn surrounded by upland orchards of apple and pear. The farms were, in the way of the land between mountains and sea, self-sufficient in their diversity. Walk over the hill or across the dell from one farm to the next, and the mark of each farmer's calloused hands could be seen upon the fields and trees.

Glimmer marched with his armor draped across a shoulder, bedroll across his back and sword and dirk at his waist. He stopped before the inn, where a man, greasy apron failing to contain an ample belly, was sitting on a bench outside the door.

"Are you the innkeeper?"

The man eyed the young man before him, strawberry-blonde hair and a fox beside him, a soldier's gear on his shoulder and about his waist. "Aye," he replied, his eyes cautious as he wiped his mouth with his soiled apron. "C'n I be helpin' ye?"

"I'd like to leave this with you," Glimmer said, hefting hauberk and coif from his shoulder. "I'll pick it up later, or if Mage Alma-Ata comes, please give it to him."

"*Mage* Alma-Ata," the innkeeper commented as two men filled the doorway at the sound of the innkeeper's voice. "Mage of cider, maybe. He knows that for sure. An' a bother t' an 'onest innkeeper, that's fer sure, since he took me help. I feel no need t' help th' mage." Rubbing his hands together in a washing motion, the innkeeper asked, "An' who might ye be?"

"His apprentice."

As innkeeper and Glimmer had conversed, two men had gravitated from inside the inn to stand outside the open doorway, attracted by the conversation. "That'd make him just a little juice," one man commented with a chuckle. Glimmer could see the man was tall, even though the man slouched as he leaned against the doorframe.

"Mebbe we should squeeze him an' see," the other man laughed, in appearance similar to the first speaker, dark of hair and an unshaven angular face, only this man shorter in stature.

The innkeeper considered the fox beside the young man and reconsidered his words. "No reason not t' help ye, although I don't much like how Alma-Ata stole Bega an' her girl. Good worker, that Bega, but she took outa here 'fore sun an' me got up; left in a hour, she did. An' that left me short-handed."

Glimmer thought it likely that the man before him had never been overworked or, rather, worked over-hard in his life, but he said nothing. He could readily believe losing Bega would be a blow to any enterprise, and as for Bega's leaving before the man had awakened, Bega and Elesia could probably have left hours later and still accomplished the same.

"An' don't mind these," the innkeeper commented, pointing over his shoulder with a thumb to the two men framing the doorway. "They come from halfway t' th' Outlands an' back, they say, an' so don't have th' wit t' respect yer master."

"Watch yer own wit, innkeep," the shorter of the men retorted, "or we'll cut 't off for ye."

Handing the innkeeper the armor, Glimmer nodded his thanks and continued on his way, the fox beside him as docile as a hound. The appraising eyes of the taller outlander left the young man and surveyed the armor in the innkeeper's hands.

"Old," the keeper commented, hefting the armor and inspecting it. "Nobody uses this anymore."

"I seen th' likes o' this in th' empire. Rare and precious to th' right party," the shorter of the two men observed, his eyes squinting in appraisal.

"Right ye are, brother. We seen 't in a museum 'n Ostrand. Ev'rybody thought 't was grand, all polished an' ancient," the taller man considered. His eyes strayed back to the young man leaving town, sword in scabbard slapping his side.

"Want to leave the blades, too?" the innkeeper called out. Glimmer stopped and turned, the fox stopping beside him.

The shorter of the outlanders smiled ingratiatingly and asked, "C'n we see 'em?"

Glimmer hesitated and then pulled the blades from their scabbards, and they fit his hands so well, their balance so fine, their color so rich of hue in the dying sun that he said, "No, thanks, I'll keep these," sliding them back to scabbard and sheath.

As Glimmer continued on his way, the taller man, still leaning against the inn's doorway, said, "Them two blades was ev'n nicer than them in Ostrand." He nodded to his brother, and they turned inside and settled to their mugs with whispers and sips. None of the men at the inn had seen the gnome sitting the fox, and as Glimmer and the gnome continued down the road, Cabbage-pants stared back over his shoulder at the men from the Outlands, a stare of unequivocal understanding and acceptance. Time would pass and darkness fall, fortunes rise and fortunes fall . . .

And sun was a hammer beating his face—his face throbbing to the beating of the hammer, to the beating of his heart, to the throbbing of his head which still lay attached to his neck, Glimmer's body lying in an awkward sprawl across grass and stone.

The sun had already climbed the horizon, and it was noon the next day, sky bloated with painful fire, when Glimmer regained consciousness, alone and bloody, surrounded by a sea of grass. He touched his head, and his hand came away red. It was then that he became conscious of pain and dizziness, sun stabbing his eyes. Sky spun in a blue pattern as he lay back. After a time he could remember the night before—stars and sky and the sighing lull of wind in grass, the barking of a fox beneath the risen moon and the rush of boots bruising earth, the shine of naked blades.

Glimmer lay back, willing the whirling to stop, but the world wouldn't listen and continued its spin. Closing his eyes, he gripped the earth to still his dizziness, would have fallen if he had been standing, felt as though he were falling even though he lay on his back. He remembered the soft grasses beneath his blanket, the peace and wonder of bivouacking with the gnome and wild fox for companions. They had camped off the road but not far distant, where two hills, taller than most, stood side by side and the road ran a narrow thread between them. Glimmer had built a small hatful of fire and brewed cabbage tea, proud of his skill with flint and steel. Then the fox had barked sharply, and men had surged from the sea of grass, sword and knife in moonlight.

Without thought, as sword had descended upon him, Glimmer had raised his own sword, still sheathed, and countered the blow. The strength of the strike, all the man's weight on it, had numbed the young man's sword arm. The sword had dropped from his hand, and as the attacker's sword had risen again, silver steel in moonlight, a quick shadow had attacked the man's legs, the fox to Glimmer's aid! A yell of protest from the other attacker as another shadow, short and stout, had tripped the man up, and then both looming silhouettes, blades in hand, had rallied themselves again, turning to their sure target for thrust, slash, and stab. Words shouted into Glimmer's mind as he had ducked, steel whistling over his head; and he had remembered and heeded Bega's words, had run blindly from camp into the silver ocean of moonlit grass, over hill and away from camp, away from road, had run full speed until he was suddenly airborne, had run full tilt into space and crashed from the level prairie into a tiny dimple in the earth, disappeared and unconscious as his head met the rocky bottom.

The spin of the world slowed as Glimmer gripped two handfuls of prairie and held on tightly to slow the spinning so that he would not slide off the world and descend into darkness. Through squinting eyes he saw a cloudless sky, and at the edges of his vision, sky met prairie grasses, green pennants on a blue field. He groaned and rolled to his stomach, pushing himself to hands and knees. The ground before him was crushed by the hours he had lain upon it. Groaning again, he sat but could see only the grassy cup of prairie and the blue sky above. Silence surrounding him, Glimmer considered shouting, but sound could be heard by foe as well as friend. His lips were parched, and he wondered whether he could have managed more than a croak anyway.

As Glimmer sat, staring without focus, a dragonfly flew over the rim of the hollow and landed on the grass before him, bobbing on a stem ripening with seed. Beside the dragonfly flew three damselflies, two flanking the dragonfly left and right and one behind, their delicate bodies an almost translucent iridescence. The dragonfly's legs gripped the grass stem, and its wings beat once and stilled, beat again, the veined wings like a map stretched before Glimmer's eyes. He was amazed, even in his pain, that the insects had landed so near him, easily within the reach of his arm. He slowly reached out a hand, and the insects darted to the air and several feet away, keeping their formation as they landed again upon the seeding grass.

Glimmer stirred gingerly, but nausea or dizziness did not recur. Slightly higher than the damselflies, the dragonfly sat its grass stem like the grandfather of all insects, its segmented body, its eyes reflecting many colors. Glimmer edged closer, not wanting to be alone, even if insects were his only companions. Silence and blood-stained hands were too much to bear alone. As he settled, the insects rose again, circling him and then darting to the lip of the hollow and landing, dragonfly to the front, damselflies to the sides and behind. The young mage's mind stirred, curiosity and intuition overriding pain. *Magic,* he remem*bered, should not be denied.*

Raising himself cautiously to his feet, he approached the insects bobbing on the stems of grass, the gauze wings of the insects shifting patterns of iridescence. Slowly he raised his head, peered out, and saw a rippling sea of green and tan, prairie flowers like spent wreaths upon a green sea; but he saw no life other than dragonfly and damselfly. He stood and, wobbly in his gait, approached the insects; again they flew away, this time a dozen paces before landing and, it seemed to Glimmer, waiting.

The young mage followed the insects, and they continued their sport of fly and wait, their flight distance expanding until stops grew less frequent and the pace of travel increased. He followed them, stop and go, until they finally flew ahead and disappeared in the grasses. He advanced slowly and found himself on the lip of another depression in the prairie, this one deeper and larger, a shallow pond in its center, surrounded by reeds. A circle of gnomes sat next to the pond beneath a willow tree, the willow's fronds of branches sweeping the earth with the yellow leaves of fall. As Glimmer stared down at the gnomes half-hidden by the willow branches, the fox appeared beside him, rubbing against his leg once like a cat before descending to the hollow and lying down beneath the tree.

One gnome, Cabbage-pants, stood and smiled at Glimmer's arrival, but the other gnomes, also standing at the young man's appearance, faded up and out of the hollow, disappearing at the lip opposite the man. No deeper had they retired into grasses taller than their gnome-height, and then the gnomes squatted or sat or even stood—weaving grass stem, grass blade, a leaf, a flower stem—until they disappeared, as rooted to the prairie as plants of actual root and seed, all except one gnome who remained at the hollow's bottom beside Cabbage-pants.

As Glimmer descended into the hollow, he saw a dragonfly sitting on one shoulder of Cabbage-pants, two damselflies on the shoulders of the other gnome. The young apprentice sat heavily next to Cabbage-pants, who stood and gazed intently eye-to-eye into the young man's face, relief in the gnome's eyes. The third damselfly landed on Glimmer's shoulder as he settled. Glimmer, though, hardly noticed. He was thinking about the gnomes who had silently disappeared into the grasses at his arrival, gnomes wearing no more than loincloths of woven grass, gnomes whose skin had been mottled shades of tan and ivory-tinged-with-green, shades that blended with the grasses, gnomes into whose hair had been woven strands of grass and wildflower of different hue. They had seemed not so much small versions of men as incarnations of prairie, standing still and silent or moving in shimmering waves of green and gold, arms and leaves.

The gnome who had stayed behind sat within the depression, his eyes half-open or half-closed, his gaze half-focused on Glimmer or half-focused on the space that would remain after the young mage was gone. The gnome wore a loincloth as the other gnomes had. Hair to his waist was the color of dried grass and woven with plaits of prairie grasses, blonde and amber, red and green. His skin was a mottle of prairie colors, browns and tans and shades almost green. The gnome had that ageless appearance that grasses attain when dried by winter winds—bleached and brittle yet able to prevail against snow and wind.

"Wild gnomes?" the young mage whispered. At his words, dragonfly and damselflies took to the sky, flitting across the pond. Glimmer started, marking with greater clarity the damselfly that had rested upon his shoulder.

"Aye," muttered the Cabbage-pants. "No more int'rested in the doin' o' men than in a blackbird 'n its nest."

"Your seed-folk?"

"Nay, sky an' wind, these folks. Mine're people o' th' dells—a small step from dell t' garden, all fenced an' proper."

The young mage closed his eyes and let sun and silence heal him. How best to affirm the magic of this moment? He would wait: let magic gather, however much it would. *Heartbeat and heartbeat, thistle and down. Sky without wind, song without sound.* His mind wandered, his head ached, time without meaning, seasons and seeds. In his mind's eye, Glimmer saw his master, Alma-Ata, sitting on the bench outside the kitchen door of the stone house, just sitting, doing nothing, just *there*, waiting.

Glimmer opened his eyes and saw that Cabbage-pants had sat beside him. Before them sat the prairie gnome, and the young mage realized how alike Cabbage-pants and the ancient prairie gnome were, both as still as miniature outcroppings of sandstone sculpted by the elements, both alike not in outward appearances but in inner silences.

Extending a hand to the mage, as if it were the prairie itself speaking, the ancient one whispered, wind in grasses: "I place seed-joy within your hand," and onto Glimmer's palm the wrinkled hand of the gnome placed a single seed of grass.

In his mind, the young man formed words of appreciation, closing his fingers around the seed, but the old one had already risen, disappeared into the prairie grasses; gone were all the prairie gnomes, leaving Glimmer and garden gnome alone.

Glimmer cast his gaze about in the silence but saw no one, nothing but the eternal green and golden hues of the prairie. Opening his closed fist, he found his palm empty. Frantically, he dropped to his knees, searching the ground for the seed.

"Ye didn't drop it."

"Then where is it?"

A faint, gravelly chuckle. "In yer hand." At Glimmer's blank look, the gnome added, "Musta been good soil."

The gnome stood and looked to the east. "Let's c'llect yer gear an' find th' road; th' path's awaitin'." As Cabbage-pants mounted fox and led the young mage to the east, he said over his shoulder, no longer shouting, no longer the magical buffoon, "Fergit yer redmetal, the men from th' tavern took th' blades. Fox an' me, we watched from the grass."

"The men from the tavern?"

"Aye, th' two at th' door. Took yer lovelies back to the road and left." The gnome spat. "Outlanders, headin' over the mountains, needin' summat t' sell t' pay for their walk."

"Blood where the road narrows," Glimmer remembered.

"Aye, it narrows here a'tween yon two hills."

The fox led them to their camp of the night before, grasses trammeled and Glimmer's blanket still on the ground. The young man picked up his water flask and sipped a mouthful. He glanced uneasily left and right as he rolled and tied his blanket.

"Don't worry, those two're gone," the gnome volunteered. "Down th' road to Red Robin and on t' th' Stone Dragon, that's for sure." He laughed and then grew solumn. "What if they pack their plunder into the Dragon for th' night? What'll she do, ye think?"

Glimmer considered, remembering the flash of sword and knife in the moonlight. "Bega's no fool . . . and the inn has a way of taking care of its own, I think," yet the thought still gnawed at him.

The gnome chuckled. "Get their tails in a world o' trouble, they show up packin' yer lovelies," and Glimmer murmured sounds of agreement but walked in silence, suddenly ready to end the quest and return to the stone house beside the river.

Silence widened in ripples, washing against Glimmer's anguish as he considered the trouble slouching down the road toward the Stone Dragon Inn. Silence washed against the apprentice but did not wash the worry from him.

"Yer thinkin' what ye can do, how ye can use yer magic, ain't ye?" the gnome finally asked, the fox continuing down the track without even breaking stride.

"How can I not? They're in danger."

"Magic org'nizes its own way. Time t' stop thinkin' of yer magic as summat belongs t' *ye*; let it be."

"This danger was caused by me. How can I not do something about it?" Glimmer suddenly remembered the dragon's words: *Death comes only at your bidding.* Sickness welled up inside himself.

He could not escape one magic by following another, he realized, could not deny one magic by affirming another. *Who will take care of me?* a secret voice whispered, and he dreaded the hollow echoing silence within him.

Precious moments whispered through time, step by step, and then the gnome, his voice reassuring and certain, said, "I'll tell thee this, young apprentice mage: th' fastest way back is ahead. Ahead lies magic greater'n two louts with hungry swords." The gnome's voice rang with authority, and Glimmer remembered the ancient prairie gnome when he had spoken: *earth* speaking through the mouth of a magical being.

The country road had become a track when they had left Ruddy, a track through grasslands, a wide plane of earth that had tilted in an up-thrust of earth eons ago, forming the long, gradual climbing until earth leapt into sky at the Shield's edge, the escarpment that dropped its thousands of feet to the Outlands beyond. The track extended up the plain to Madrone, where the north branch of the river widened into a lake, the Olifant's Tear. At the east side of the lake was the sanctuary of the Sisters of Hospitality, where resided good women who had dedicated their lives to giving to others as the earth gave: giving sustenance and nourishment, shelter and safe harbor, without constraint or condition.

It was almost sunset when the travelers reached the lake, the air cooled by the water reviving the young man who was staggering from his wound and from lack of food. No farms had interrupted the trek up the plain, and Glimmer remembered a conversation with the old mage who had taught him his letters. "Olifants sported upon the Playground, times past," he had said. "Now mostly wind frolics with grass; folks live down in th' valley and leave the escarpment's bench to the wind."

The winds were gentle this day, and as the travelers skirted the lake, there rose before them stone walls covered with ivy, a road widened and lined with trees. Behind walls taller than a man's head jutted the heavy stone battlements of an ancient castle, slit-eyes staring cagily at all who passed. They followed the wall until they made the entrance to the south.

"This can't be the sanctuary of the Sisters of Hospitality!" Glimmer exclaimed in weary dismay, even the blue sky of summer dimmed by the drear of the building. "If it is, then hospitality must be under siege," and man and gnome advanced warily to the entrance.

"Food an' bed an' a look at yer wound're what ye need, and ye'll get that here from what ye've told me." The young man felt exhaustion lean upon his shoulders at the mention of food and rest.

He looked to the stone pillars, the wrought iron gate with spear-like bars rusting red, and the over-arching wrought iron filigree that loomed over the entrance. "Well, the sooner in, the sooner out." Before the gates a statue stood, grey and worn—a woman attired as a Sister, gesturing with cold hands, a gesture ambiguous to Glimmer, who could not tell whether the gesture was one of welcome or one discouraging entrance.

"I'll be waitin' out here," declared the gnome, gazing up and wrinkling his nose in distaste. "Too much cold metal. They ought t' be ashamed o' themselves. *Hospitality*, indeed!" With that, Cabbage-pants, followed by the fox, stomped across the road and into the woods, leaving Glimmer alone before the statue of a Sister of Hospitality who clearly felt kindliness was no laughing matter.

Glimmer advanced down a stone walkway bordered by severely pruned apple trees, a few puckered apples still on the uppermost branches. The grass beneath the trees precisely edged the stone walkway, lines of growth so exact they must have been measured. A sense of sterile orderliness dominated the environment, an exactitude of welcome precisely calculated, generosity and lovingkindness the product of analysis. As he approached the twin massive wooden doors to the sanctuary, Glimmer found their somber and forbidding bulk closed; even in the heat of summer they would remain closed, he surmised.

Opening one oaken door just enough to slip inside, Glimmer was met by two women covered by long, thickly woven gowns, their heads and necks covered in scarves of a wrap unique to their order. As one Sister pulled close the door, the other Sister gazed sharply at the young man and then gestured silently for him to follow. He was led across a large hall filled with tables to the entrance of the east wing of the building. Asking no questions, Glimmer followed the Sister silently as she hobbled down the hallway, an old woman, he realized, bent with age and years of service, although he found himself also hunched and weary as he followed the woman.

He was led to an infirmary, bottles of unguents and tinctures sitting on the shelves and bundles of herbs hanging from a drying rack. Motioned to sit on a hard cot covered by a linen sheet, soon another Sister, shorter than the first yet more vigorous, strode into the room.

"A head wound, she told me," were her words, and she brusquely twisted the young man's head to examine the wound. Grunting to herself, she asked, "How'd it happen?"

"I fell," Glimmer replied, reluctant to relate everything.

"Must be clumsier than you look," was the Sister's only comment as she efficiently cleaned the wound and applied an unguent that exuded a sweet, invigorating odor. A kinder look softened her eyes. "Keep it clean, and a good meal and a night's sleep will put you together again."

The Sister gestured for Glimmer to stand, and as she shooed him out the door, she asked, "Who'd you have the argument with?"

The young mage faltered for a step and then replied, "A rock."

"Hmph, must've been a hard rock to break th' head of someone your age," but Glimmer could see the jest and kind regard in her eyes and nodded his thanks as he left.

At the entranceway of the infirmary, he was met again by the aged Sister, who without a word hobbled back the way they had come, leading him to the central hall and a table where he was sat and fed a meal of bread, cheese, and stew, wholesome even if served in restrained silence. Two helpings later, he was escorted to a barracks on the second floor, assigned a bed, and left to himself. Another guest sat on his bed at the end of the barracks, separated from Glimmer by two cots, but the man displayed no interest in conversation, the gloom of the room not lightened by one window high on the stone wall, narrow and deep-set into thick stone. Full of stomach and evening falling, Glimmer was not much inclined to conversation himself. He lay back on the cot and covered himself with his blanket, little warmth to be found in the room.

Rest and complete the quest, he thought, his forehead tingling where unguent met torn flesh, his mind remembering naked steel in moonlight and a stone house next to a river, its doors open and inviting. *Trust the magic,* he repeated to himself, *trust the magic,* yet the words seemed impotent, lies and betrayal. He could do no more, though, could not go on without rest, could no longer deny the authority with which the gnome had spoken.

As dreams go, it was not a nightmare. Glimmer had suffered injury and terror, though, and violence collects its own payment from both body and soul. Perhaps it was the blow to the head; perhaps it was a fugue spawned by despair—despair at men who would slice a body's sack just to hear the sweet hiss of life's grain bleeding to the earth; perhaps it was the irony of such austere hospitality served within such bleak walls in the name of spiritual service. He dreamt a miasma of dreams, a coming and going of images, deep cuts of emotion which bled dry. The stone inn, shifting forms of two men demanding gold and silver with sharp words and sharper blades. Meadow and hearth and candles; hot wax spitting at cold eyes; tables and benches vining to grasp and trip. Wind sounding in the chimney a deep, subterranean roar while smoke and soot flared like giant, leathery wings. Men running, boots pounding like heartbeats, and Wilim and two women holding to one another as house settled back onto its bones, fire crackling in the pit. Glimmer dreamed yet remembered only fragments of dream . . . and none of the next.

The sounding of the breakfast bell awoke Glimmer, tangled in his blanket. His dry mouth he eased with water, and then he made his way downstairs to break his fast. Hospitality was served on time, and he had better be the grateful guest, he thought, or that first cup of refreshing water might well be splashed upon his sleeping face! Porridge in a bowl, a flask filled with water, a rough sandwich of bread and cheese to eat while on the road, and the young mage was on his way, head set much more firmly on his shoulders, albeit delicately balanced. Thanks to the unflinching hospitality of the Sisters, he left stronger of limb and purpose, with no smile on his face and a cold knot of worry in his stomach. At the main hall doors leading out of the sanctuary, Sister Superior of the Madrone sanctuary met the departing guests, her countenance a look of disciplined, besieged satisfaction.

Exiting the sanctuary proper, Glimmer continued on in the morning light along the stone walkway lined by apple trees, out the main gates, and onto the roadway. Standing before the entrance to the sanctuary grounds stood Cabbage-pants, wearing an enigmatic expression. Glimmer halted and felt his spirits rise at leaving the sanctuary. *Hospitality is a bitter tonic,* was all he could think. The gnome stared at Glimmer, an odd expression still on the gnome's face, an expression of neither buffoonery nor prophesy, and then Cabbage-pants raised his gaze to scrutinize the statue which fronted the entrance.

Glimmer's gaze followed that of the gnome's, and then he realized that the statue, which had consisted of one figure the day before, now consisted of three. He stepped beside the gnome, and now both stood before the statuary, staring at three people: two women and a man, captured in stone. The figure in the middle was that of a man, and that man was Glimmer, a wide, mischievous grin splitting his face. The woman to one side was the Superior of the Sisters, the woman who had overseen the morning's departing guests—only Sister Superior's stone image was carved sporting a secretive smile as she caressed Glimmer's back with one expressive hand. The other woman was a younger Sister, one Glimmer did not recall having seen, an impudent smile on her lips, her habit split to mid-thigh and revealing an expanse of leg.

"Young mage, p'haps we can talk o' this down th' road a piece as we go," the gnome commented. "It's a good mornin' for a walk, don't ye think?"

Without comment, Glimmer and the gnome turned and hurried down the road, the fox to one side of the man and the gnome to the other, both trotting to keep to the man's pace. At the corner of the sanctuary's stone fence, the gnome paused to seat himself upon the fox, increasing the speed of their leaving. Glimmer continued walking without pause. He did not remember dreaming the statue, did not remember the magic; but he did remember fragments of another dream, of knives and tendrils of fear. His magic was like throwing stones blindly into the night. Where they would land, to what good or ill, he had no idea.

What have I done? he asked himself but found no answer other than steady footsteps, each bringing him closer to journey's end, each step one closer to his return home. He tried to take solace in the fact that, even though he was progressing directly away from the stone inn, he was, according to the gnome, still taking the fastest path back home.

Boats on each bank of the river at the head of the lake were available for crossing the water, the travelers had been informed, and Glimmer rowed while fox and gnome peered over the boat's side.

"Int'restin'," the gnome commented at the splashing of the water and the easy quartering of the boat to the lake's diluted current.

"Do gnomes swim?" Glimmer asked, but the gnome's reply, "Like fish," seemed pale in conviction as the gnome's fingers tightly gripped the gunwale.

The fox sniffed at the water and then stepped to the bow of the rowboat, watching the grassy shore opposite steadily grow nearer. As the boat skidded onto sand, fox and gnome hopped out, Glimmer dragging the boat farther onto shore before they faced the expanse of grassland before them, a green expanse stroked by winds funneled between white-tipped mountains on the distant, blue horizon. In the nearer distance at the far edge of the grass, a series of low ridges, grey and black, met the prairie— the vertebrae of the Dragon's Spine.

"There lies th' dragon—an' what we've come to find," the gnome said but was silenced as Glimmer overrode with, "What we've come to find, say you?" and then dismissed the significance of words by striding into the grass, forging a direct line to their destination. Cabbage-pants, seated on the fox, had led the way throughout the journey, but now the young man broke a trail through the tall grasses, gnome on fox trotting behind. Glimmer feared dire events at the Stone Dragon Inn, danger already happened and nothing to do about it, danger not of his making, he believed. *How can I have any certainty, though, with my dreams unrestrained and even unremembered?* His stride lengthened as if to shorten the days left before he reached the inn again. *Days! Why not turn back now?* he thought, but knew the answer: no one was ever served well by magic incomplete.

All day the Spine thrust itself further out of the green flesh of the earth as the travelers strode the grassland, Glimmer now leading as if sleepwalking, silent and focused on the approaching rock formation. Still weakened by his head injury, he stumbled through tall grasses, uncertain of his path, both literal and figurative. Would his name be despised by future generations, the mage who had created some as yet unnamed chaos? Would he despise himself, having set in motion events leading to the injury of those now close to his heart? Step by step he continued, resolute yet unsteady in gait, trusting the gnome, trusting that the shortest path to the inn lay ahead, continuing to journey's end.

At the foot of the Dragon's Spine the grasslands were separated from rock by water, for in the lower valley the River Quill had branched, the upper arms of the river embracing each side of the valley and its grasslands. As the travelers reached the bank of the river and stood on the grassy shore, from the rocky shore opposite, a shout met them.

An old man hallooed the travelers. Dressed in a motley assortment of clothes consisting of skin, fabric, and woven grasses, a long beard stretching his already lean face, a man waved a disreputably woven straw hat while shielding his eyes from the afternoon sun with the other. A rowboat that had been hidden within a rocky inlet was launched, the old man displaying wiry strength in crossing the brisk current.

"I saw you crossing from my eagle's perch," he shouted over his shoulder, pointing with his eyes at a rocky promontory above as he oared across the water without pause. Driving the rowboat onto the grass and sand of the riverbank with a final heave of his shoulders, the man leapt from the boat and bowed with polished ease.

"Lahad, at your service. Do you seek passage across the water?" The man's cheeks were red from sun and exercise, and his eyes were bright with curiosity. Glimmer imagined a shopkeeper with nothing to sell meeting a customer with no means to buy and the lively conversation that would ensue—or perhaps he saw a man who had not spoken with another for considerable time. The man straightened, slapping the sun hat onto his head. Lahad wore a leather vest, roughly tanned, and linen breeches; for shoes he wore sandals constructed from grass and vine, tightly woven with an elegant mosaic pattern of varied hues. The man paused in polite silence, obviously awaiting introduction.

"I am Glimmer, apprentice to Mage Alma-Ata." At this the man's eyebrows rose. Glimmer was unsure whether or not to introduce the gnome; after all, what if Lahad could not see him? As the man pointedly appeared to be looking at the gnome, the apprentice continued, "And this is Cabbage-pants of the cabbage gnomes, walking the Gnome's Path on Gnome Quest, and I am his Ally." Lahad bowed politely to the gnome, his eyes beneath bushy eyebrows closely observing; and then the man turned his gaze to Glimmer's opposite side, where sat fox with tongue lolling. After a pause, Glimmer continued, "And this is Fox, companion on our quest," and the gnome finishing, "And friend of Alma-Ata," at which Glimmer's eyebrows rose. An equally elegant bow to the fox, and then gesturing to the rowboat, the man asked, "Shall we cross?"

Angling upstream, Lahad worked the current skillfully, oars creaking and an occasional grunt escaping him as oar blade bit to current. This branch of the river was shallower, the current swifter. As the boat passed the swiftest flow and eased into quieter water, the rower called over his shoulder for the travelers in the bow, "Alma-Ata is a man I know. I left him a box of family heirlooms when I tailored cloth for my new profession." He chuckled, gesturing to his motley. "Those who heed the screed of the soul are rather casual of style, at least here on the Dragon's Spine."

Gaining bank, Glimmer found his mind in turmoil. Coincidence or magic? Or was there such a thing as coincidence? "Sir Lahad," he murmured, "was it armor and weapons of copper you gave to my master for safekeeping? If so, I have lost them, lost them on this very journey."

"No man has fitted me with that title for many years; it seems a loose fit now." Completing a quick hitch to secure the craft, Lahad turned and scrutinized the young man before him, taking in scabbed forehead and strained, pale countenance. "Well, well, what goes around comes around, it seems." He straightened and reassured the young man before him. "I have preferred for many years to think of what you lost as no longer being mine. At any rate, I would guess that which you lost was more likely taken by force." Reading the emotion in Glimmer's face, he continued, "Should you ever again meet this man—or these men—you must thank them."

Water whispered from the riverbed, and wind soughed in the hard crevices of the cliffs flanking the river. The fox sniffed along a path among the boulders, and the gnome squatted, drawing a pattern in the sand.

His voice quiet with deliberate constraint, a question tightly controlled, Glimmer replied, "I seek to understand your words. For robbing me and attempting murder, and for acts I fear to those I have left behind, I should give thanks? Two men in the night with sword and knife brought cruel gifts!"

"They robbed you, sword and mail, and now you stand before me with open hands and open heart." The knight paused, searching for the right words. "A sword has two edges . . ."

"To attack and to defend. I would have defended."

"Aye, there is nothing wrong with defending oneself, or others, but if there is a better way, should one not choose it? You stand before me with open hands and open heart," the knight repeated. He removed his floppy hat of straw, revealing hair tied in a long grey strand. "Could you say as much if you had killed those who sought your death? Was the outcome so ill that you must begrudge not having whet your blade upon living flesh? Be glad you carry not the burden of death."

Confusion knit Glimmer's brow. The words of the man almost made sense, yet his heart protested. "The men still live to do harm."

"Or come to harm."

"I fear they travel even now to that moment with evil intent."

"And who can say how the world will deal with them?" The knight sat upon the sandy shore and placed his roughly woven hat on his head. A simple rustic he appeared to be, dressed in worn and humble clothing whose only elegance was that of utility, a face and manner that reminded Glimmer of his master. "I came to these hills," Lahad said quietly, "because I found myself becoming that which I hated." Lahad closed his eyes and then opened them, his eyes seeking not those of the young mage, seeking rather the current of the water, late afternoon sun gilding grassland. "With a sword we may win the battle but never the war."

The gnome had been squatting in silence, his back to the stone outcroppings at the water's edge. "I'm glad ye lost it, young master, even at th' cost of a bump on th' head. Even red metal brings some discomfit to them as me. Th' path o' blade an' blood is th' way to nightmare. A blessin', t'was. "

"More blessings like that, and you'd be blessing my bones," Glimmer commented, but the reference to nightmares chilled him.

The knight laughed. "Luckily for you, it was your head that was hit. Anything softer and you'd have been in serious trouble." After a pause, the man added, "Before battle, the knight must deny his doubt and place trust in arm and blade. You are apprentice to a mage and must deny your doubt and place trust in magic. Easier said than done, of course," Lahad ended with a bitter-sweet smile.

Standing, Lahad stretched and indicated a path leading upward. "So you come," he asked, addressing Cabbage-pants, "with this young man as your Ally? There has been a stir among the Silent Ones, and now I know the reason. Let us repair to my humble abode," he said with a wry smile, "a cave with a view. The gnomes will know that you have arrived," he added to Cabbage-pants, "but I suppose you know that." The knight made his way up the trail, Cabbage-pants and Glimmer following.

The knight's home consisted of a huge tabletop of stone capping one vertebrae of the Dragon's Spine, the overhang forming a vast porch so that the man possessed a veranda from which to view the surroundings to east, west, and south. On the east side of the hilltop a crevice opened to a small, dry cave where Lahad slept and kept his few possessions. Come winter, he would narrow the crevice with stacked stones and then cover the smaller opening with animal skins. Leading the travelers to the west "veranda," the sun was setting, its golden beauty bronzing the grasslands embraced by the twin branches of the river. Mountains rose beyond the river and meadows to a silence so profound it seemed to Glimmer a tangible thing, something he could reach out and touch.

Lahad led them to a sheltered place where they sat on simple mats of grass. As they sat facing the sunset, three gnomes appeared before them, their arrival so silent they could have suddenly materialized in the air. Swaths of cloth wrapping their loins, these gnomes had beards of yellow-white, not full and combed but scraggles of hair the color of winter grass. They were not prairie gnomes, though; they were more incarnations of air and space than the grassland below. An aura surrounded them, a graceful quality like wind dancing in the branches of trees. The center gnome gestured greeting, and Cabbage-pants stood, returning the gesture. Even though Cabbage-pants was dressed in leggings, jerkin, and tasseled belt, and the three silent gnomes were dressed in swaths of linen, Glimmer recognized first and foremost their similarity, their unity.

"You're not just a gnome, are you?" he said to Cabbage-pants.

"Even the simplest gnomes're still totally themselves," was the reply.

"But these who are silent recognized you, Cabbage-pants. You're different as they are different; you're like them."

"There was a time when I was silent," admitted the gnome, adding with a small smile, "an' it took a while getting' used t' talkin' again. Volume, y'know." He and the gnomes then bowed to the men and silently left them, disappearing, it seemed, into the setting sun.

"What are they going to do?"

"*Do?* The Silent Ones don't *do* much of anything."

"But Cabbage-pants came here for a purpose. The Gnome's Path led him here. This is his quest," Glimmer protested, images of flashing blades and the stone walls of the inn in his mind.

The knight sighed, his gaze extending into the distances above the plain. "The gnomes and I and a few other men share these hills, but we share them in silence. Oh, we speak some, communicate, but mostly we are alone. As for your gnome . . ." the man's voice thoughtfully trailed off into silence.

Curiosity prompted Glimmer to ask, "What do you do here?"

"That word again," the man responded. "We seek the Silence of the Saints."

"Then you practice the Silence?" Glimmer asked excitedly.

"We seek it. We men, at least. Gnomes have their own way and perhaps are born to it. Once the Silence was taught to men in as straightforward a manner as one would teach how to put knife to stone to whet the blade. Both stone and blade still exist, but the actual procedure . . ."

"And the gnomes?"

"Come from many clans, from many places. They are different from us, though. In many ways they are our teachers, although they are too different to teach us what they know. With them I believe they are born within the Silence, that they do not have to find it, although they can, perhaps, forget it."

"Their magic?"

"Call it that if you like." Lahad gestured to the river below. "The river makes its song. Would it be the same music if the waters were filled with the tramping feet of men and the hooves of animals? The gnomes who come here wish not to *find* the music, more to hear it untrammeled, you might say. They are different than we, the little people are."

"And you have found the Silence?"

The knight smiled a bitter-sweet smile. "Whispers of silence, perhaps."

"Mage Alma-Ata says he does nothing, yet magic gathers about him."

"I think your master is more interested in the Silence than in magic." As Glimmer pondered his words, the knight continued. "Have you ever heard of Gil-Lahad?"

"A warrior," Glimmer responded, "a mighty Outlands warrior and king—and with the same name you speak for yourself."

"Yes," Lahad commented drily. "A mage like Alma-Ata—one who Gathered a mighty army. But your mage is a good man, one who would rather gather apples than men."

Glimmer looked from the vista upon the wilderness—the vast expanse of untouched grassland of the escarpment, the mountains to the west and, he knew, if he circled the top of the hill and looked east and north, the white-capped mountains that the escarpment interrupted.

"How do you eat?" he asked.

"The Sisters of Hospitality meet our needs," replied the man, "albeit, they have fallen under some cloud of despair over time," Lahad added. "The Sisters help us men. Sometimes when the winter is most severe, I stay at the sanctuary for a time." He shook his head. "Less and less peace is to be found there."

"And the gnomes?"

"The gnomes go their own way."

"And what do you think Cabbage-pants and the other gnomes are doing now? We need to be on our way."

"Ah, that word again. Three time's the charm." Pursing his lips in thought, the knight responded, "I do not think they are *helping* Cabbage-pants *do* or *become* anything; no, they are not *doing* anything. I think they are . . . affirming or celebrating what he already is."

"And how long will that take? While they're celebrating . . . I need to—" but Lahad interrupted to answer his question with another. "What worries you so?" the knight of Silence asked.

The story arose from within the young man in its entirety, rose like a mountain storm sweeping down upon a valley, dark and tumultuous, roiling within itself. Never had he voiced all he had experienced, all he felt and feared. The storm of his emotions rained forth, a flashflood of narrative, illuminations sudden and stark like landscapes caught in lightning flash. As Glimmer spoke, the man composed himself, straightened, cross-legged upon his sitting mat, his eyes closed, becoming completely one-who-listens, not judging and analyzing but accepting and embracing. Tears streaked the cheeks of the apprentice as he spoke his story, no longer a matter of relating but more that of self-discovery, of confessional and purgation. To act without understanding, to choose without knowledge, to have more power than wisdom—how could good ever come of that? How could he be anything other than what he was, a young man holding the tiger by the tail, afraid to let go—and to not let go? How could he walk his path upon the broken bodies of others?

"I was once told a story by my tutor," the young man ended, "how when he had visited the sea, he had watched otters swimming with the waves, slipping down the waves as sea curled to shore. He had seen otters in similar antics on muddy riverbanks, sliding down a mud-slicked run to splash into the water, leaping and twisting for the sheer joy of it." He turned to the man sitting silently beside him. "That's what I want: not power, just the ability to safely . . . exist . . . within that power without drowning."

The knight slowly opened his eyes. "Who would not rather swim than drown?" Lahad reached out and patted Glimmer's hand. "I think you just want to be a kid, and who can blame you that?"

Any further comment was interrupted by the appearance of Cabbage-pants. *His name seems so childish, compared to the names of men,* Glimmer thought, staring at the magical being before him, knee-high and therefore at eye level as Glimmer sat cross-legged.

The western sky was ruddy, the mountains now in shadow across the plain. The gnome was backlit by sunset, the sun's burnished light a giant nimbus surrounding the gnome. *How*—the young apprentice thought—*could I have ever thought this being foolish and trivial?*

Sun was setting, yet the gnome would stand even in darkness as a child of the light. Night was approaching, and what dreams would come, shrouded in the tattered, black shawl of sleep? Whatever came, whatever beast slouched down from its bone-littered lair in search of blood and soul, Cabbage-pants, his skin now painted with patterns of earth and plant, with whorls and stars—whatever came, this gnome would stand as he always had, washed by flames of purity and innocence.

"Ally of mine," the gnome uttered, and the words hung in the air, magic in their portent. "The quest is completed; now Ally of ye am I." The gnome spoke with a quiet dignity without shouting or asides regarding recipes for cooking a certain vegetable. Glimmer uncertainly looked at the knight as silence lengthened. *What do I do now?* was the unasked question.

"You say you are now my Ally? Before you came to me, you were one of them, weren't you?" the apprentice asked, nodding to the silent gnomes flanking Cabbage-pants, gnomes established in silence so thick it covered them like pale dust turned golden by the setting sun.

"I am more than I speak . . . and all that I speak," the gnome responded. Glimmer considered the words in silence. "Best you consider, though, " the gnome continued, "who and what *you* are."

"Mage Alma-Ata told me my teachers would come. I am sorry that I did not realize you to be among them."

"I'm not yer teacher, apprentice," the gnome replied, slipping into a more comforting, familiar manner. "Ally to ye am I." Silence fell again, yet it was a comfortable silence built on trust and experience.

Into the silence, the gnome spoke again. "The Silent Ones gift ye this to drink. Ye are needed, here and now, elsewhere and ever." A small gourd the gnome extended to the apprentice, the dried exterior of the container glowing like gold in the setting rays of the sun. As the gnome offered the drink, Glimmer saw that the gnome's hands and arms were painted with plant dyes, painted with sun and river, wind and womb of earth.

> Upon th' mountain the sacred grinding stones stand.
> Prepare herbs, loosen their essence, pour forth sacred waters,
> An' sieve the green-tinted mixture through th' fleece.
> Drink of it an' know th' flow of a thousand streams.
> Drink an' may wisdom speed ye along auspicious paths.

As the sound of the gnome's chanting faded, the sound of Lahad rummaging in a leather bag broke the spell of the moment. The man said, "Before you drink, take this, and you also, gnome." The knight handed Glimmer and Cabbage-pants knives of wooden hasp and obsidian blade, the man's with a four-inch blade, flecked to sharpness greater than finest steel, and the gnome's, a miniature version of the man's, its blade no longer than an inch.

Looking at the mage, the knight said, "Something to show for your journey; you can say you came for these." He bowed and delivered the gifts. "Magic surrounds you, young mage. You dream; you are given gifts from those who walk in magic." He paused. "And I think you have something of your master about you. Don't you feel magic *gathering* about you?"

Slipping the sheath onto his belt, Glimmer said nothing, his mind in a whirl. He then drank from the gourd a liquid syrupy-bitter, its taste that of the rich blood of the earth, of the flavor of roots and harvest and water leeched through mineral-lush soil. Wiping his lips with his hand, he met the ancient eyes of the gnome, but no more words were spoken. Glimmer placed the gourd on the sandy floor of the knight's stone aerie, felt slumber visiting him with dizzying speed. He placed his head on a pillow of aromatic grasses, breathed deeply, vertigo overwhelming him. He breathed again and then fell face first into dark waters as substantial as stone.

He was dreaming, dreaming that he was dead or that he had never lived until this moment. He was walking down a trail, it seemed, guided by small hands gentle and insistent. He trusted, knew his path was sure, walked down and felt the swish of grasses against his breeches, heard the roaring of the wind, felt the pressure of world whirling him as he angled into its pressure. He walked along a path, down a hill and through grasses; pleasant it was except for the sensation of falling, of having no weight or perhaps no body. A woman weeping, sorrow like stone in her heart, one woman and more, bowed by grief insufferable, the keening of their voices a wind pushing at him. He followed the pressure, the sadness beseeching alleviation and consolation, followed the pressure of hands gentle and insistent through darkness rising to extinguish the ruddy blush of sunset.

Stone before him, stones cut from earth and stacked helter-skelter in patterns arrogant: disharmony and the keening of the hearts of women within, keening even as they slept; and even within the dreams of these innocents were dark and disturbing shadows probing at fissures, seeking frailty.

Glimmer stood before a sanctuary dark of stone and desire, felt stones dark with agony, even atrocity—*don't know what,* the mage thought, *don't need or want to know*—something old brought to focus by the placement of the stones, something magnified by their alignment, something malign sucking hospitality from Sisters and guests in a dark stream. *Whosoever built this, built wrong,* and that wrongness had grown over time, small doubts and petty angers increasing, stored in stone, angers building to avarice, guilt building to grief, malice building to madness and murder.

They have brought me here to fix this, the dream mage thought, *but I am not dreaming.* Gentle hands brought him, but dreaming would not undo earth-magic out of kilter. Hands must undo what hands contrived; action must counter action, earth demands it. Hands gentle and insistent led him to the building. *How can I pull this building down?* Gentle and insistent, hands led him to the building, through the entrance of the stone-walled fence, man high, and up to the cold, dark walls bleeding accumulated misery from tortured stones. He placed his hands to stone, wanting to shout the building empty and push the walls down, and his hands warmed the stone. His hands glowed and warmed the stone!

As if prairie itself were speaking, Glimmer remembered an ancient gnome whispering, wind in grasses: "I place seed-joy within your hand."

He touched the stone, running his fingers across rough surface and feeling the hard-grained suffering warming, dissipating beneath his touch. He painted stone with seed-joy, with the force that drives seed to germination, painted stone with his hands, joy flowing from palms and fingertips, the whorled patterns of his palms finding kinship with glowing veins of stone; his being balancing this poor pain of the earth, bones out of cant, rectifying ancient indignities laid upon innocent stone. He moved through space but not through time—no past, no present, no future—only becoming, only the fountainhead of possibility; yet not a solution but a postponement, not a healing but a bandage. His touch was an abeyance, not a rectification. Full accord could not be achieved with a touch—no, wrong construction required reconstruction; that which was built would have to be rebuilt.

The night was cold and the sky that deep clarity that precedes the dawning. Glimmer shivered and stood back, gentle hands pulling him away from the building, insistent and gentle. He could feel the light of the new day rising, its pristine light never before falling upon this newborn day dawning, and he did not want to leave, wanted something else, one more gift to lessen the burden stone never should have borne.

Yes! Let the innocent rays of the sun shine at first light into sanctuary to warm the heart; let it enter and wash the stones, light the faces of good Sisters with its radiant beginning! A small gift, a small dream for a smile to kindle a kind face. He asked and earth obliged, stones eager to obey. Gentle hands and innocent stone, tree-flesh and even iron wrought and rusting listened to designs in accord with the fiber of their being; sun broke the eastern mountains and advanced across the grassland, crossed river risen to lake and met stone stacked as tall as a man, found a gate to the east, a statuary of three smiling welcome, entered, purity of first-light, pale, evanescent, found a doorway open and inviting, entered, a welcomed guest, and accepted the hospitality of the Sisters, warmed flag-stones and the faces of the Sisters, eyes round with wonder at the beauty of a building aligned to greet the dawn, memories of the long night fading. Yes, a bandage and a beginning, dragonfly and damselflies, wings damask in the morning sun.

A dragonfly's wings, he thought, *and small hands gentle and insistent—* and would have raised his arms, his soul, and lost himself in the whirl of world expanding except for the insistent child-hands that guided and encouraged him now to walk at an easy pace, never mind the pressure of the wind or the spinning of the earth, never mind the happy faces like flowers in the windows—just follow gentle pressure guiding him home, for he knew that was his destination now, home and haven and safety like pillow and sleep and world at ease, *and why not,* he asked himself. *Why not?* The deepest gulf within is only a softer pillow, a greater knowledge that all is well and that mother is at home. Only he didn't know his mother, orphan that he was. *What do you mean by "mother"?* the dragon asked. *Mother resides within: within a body, within a time, within all things.* Gentle hands urged him to sit, to lie down, to cradle his head upon soft grasses, to sleep, to sleep, for waves of sea to settle to silent, infinite depths, for wave to become sea, for sea to become ocean.

Implicit within the ability to dream with magic is the potential to dream without magic, and implicit within the ability to dream without magic is the possibility of nightmare. And what parts memory and what parts fantasia compose the nightmare? Glimmer rose from the ocean of sleep to the memory of pain deep and prolonged, memory not his but gained in magic, magic not his but remembered in nightmare. Shaft of obsidian, a splinter rising from sullen rock long and black and needle sharp, the lance calling, compelling, commanding and wings obeying, stooping to the summons and then acquiescing to the pain as the stone lance pierces and heart bursts, yet magic sustains the pain, extends life-in-death to millennia, pain and madness, dragon heart and dream mage, ancient dream and ancient agony . . .

Glimmer awoke, sun rising in the east, his brow damp with dew and sweat. He breathed in a ragged breath and let it out, the memory that was not his and nightmare that was both lingering. He sat up and saw that he was alone, open sky extending before him to the west, but not the grasslands of the escarpment; no, he lay upon Lion's Loft, grass settling off the promontory to the valley below. In the distance, a line of trees and ribbon of road skirted the River Quill, far off a slate roof rising above the trees where bridge crossed the water. Glimmer's gaze flowed downhill to the stone inn, morning bathed in the lambent beams of dawn.

He let the bloodstained scales of memory and nightmare slough from his being. Gentle hands had sustained him and brought him here. It was dawn and a new day. He was home—sufficient unto the day.

Chapter 8

"A spelle written is no more than a recipe, words written upon parchment to guide the magickal actiones of the mage. Words are language, vibrations of sounde. These soundes are emanationes of minde; minde finding powere in awareness. Thus, one sayth that a written spelle is no more potente than the awareness that perceiveth. Magick is consciousness."

The Philosophie of Magick

⅓

The smells . . . yes . . . and the manner in which sound carried in the open air—before Glimmer had even opened his eyes, he had known that he was somewhere different, elsewhere and elsewhen. Dream was supplanted by day; such is the process of waking, even from nightmare.

The elbow on which he propped himself to survey his surroundings gave out, and he fell back to the bedewed grasses of Lion's Loft. *All that has happened,* he thought, *and yet nothing has changed.* He groaned, disoriented and weak, his head aching and his stomach cramping with hunger. He placed one hand over his heart yet felt no pain, his hand unstained by blood. High above, a hawk glided on outstretched wings. Far below, the inn sat at its bend in river and road, a faint wisp of smoke rising from the chimney.

Glimmer sat up again, holding his head and squeezing his eyes shut to push out the pain. Then he opened them and saw the sky, the grass, looked about him and saw the dark volcanic plug of stone, blown from volcano and weathered over the eons to become the Lion's Loft. One clump of grass moved. The young mage blinked, and Cabbage-pants sat at the bluff's edge, gazing into the haze to the Stone Dragon Inn below.

"Soon we'll be seein' if the cabbage in th' cellar is farin' well."

The night and the dream, or the lack of dream and the gentle hands—his hands and seed-joy flowing into stone—all were resurrected by the gnome's words.

"What do you mean the *cabbages*? What about the people?"

"Aye, o' course, though people have a way of takin' care of themselves. An' 'tis good t' see yer mind's workin' again."

Staggering to his feet, Glimmer scanned the slope for the quickest path off the promontory and onto the plain below. He had no weapons, he thought, and then his hand slapped the sheathed obsidian knife at this waist. He removed the blade and examined it, the obsidian blade a glassy luster of color, deep purple, green, and gold bands of color lapping the black sheen that predominated. Resheathing the blade, he began skirting the rocky crown of the bluff when he heard footsteps behind. Confused for a moment, he linked the footsteps to his memory of boots and blades in the night.

Glimmer turned to see before him a tall man, sturdy and strong, with deep brown hair framing a round face. The stranger cleared his throat as Glimmer backed away from the edge of the bluff which dropped a hundred feet to grassy slopes below. The man before Glimmer was not either of the men from the inn at Ruddy, the men who had followed and attacked him in his camp on the uplands.

Where, Glimmer wondered, *has this stranger come from? How . . . and why . . . has he come to this isolated spot?* No one ever came here except for the occasional shepherd and his flock. The man was dressed in black garb, cut to indicate freeman or tradesman status, the color and style suggesting an academic.

"My pardon, young sir, but . . ." and the man's speech faltered to silence. Then the man girded himself and spoke again. "Could you tell me where I am?"

Glimmer was taken aback, expecting the false friendliness of a thief or the condescension of a social superior demanding assistance. He gestured abstractly to the panorama before them. "Road and inn are below."

"I've been walking since dawn down to the valley. It's like nothing I've ever seen." The man, it appeared to Glimmer, was about twice the apprentice's age; his face expressed genuine bemusement. The man fixed

Glimmer with a sudden, unexpected piercing glance. "You're the first person I've met."

"What were you doing so far into the steppe?" Glimmer asked, still suspicious as the man advanced to bluff's edge.

"It's where I woke up this morning, but the oddity is that here, "the man gestured around him, "is not where I lay to sleep last night." The man looked around himself once again, at the mountains and prairie rising behind them and the oval of the valley before. "I lay down last night in the forests of the sadhus, beneath my master's hut of boughs, having sung the ancient hymns in praise of the mother of the moon."

A memory stirred within Glimmer, an old story told to him once by his tutor as they read about the ancient mages. "But you slept not upon the earth but in a tree, a giant spreading tree, your sleeping platform formed by limbs woven a few feet below the larger platform of your master's," the young apprentice finished for the man.

The man stared at Glimmer oddly. "How do you know this?"

"In a story I once heard." Suddenly the apprentice wondered if this scholar were playing some convoluted joke on him, or if the story were meant to confuse or amaze him for some unknown purpose. "And the tree covered a hectare. Your master's house-in-tree lay at the center. You had to wait till the moon rose and cast its slivers of light through the leaves so that you could find your way to a meadow to see the moon in her full radiance."

"Yes, yes!" the man exclaimed. "How do you know this? Are you a seer?"

"Rather a dreamer," Glimmer responded dryly. *Magic gathers around you,* Glimmer remembered a voice of Lahad saying.

"But how do you know these things?" the man asked. He sat down suddenly, awkwardly, upon the grass. "They happened just last night, and in a place nowhere similar to this."

"I, too, slept last night in a place far from here—days, not as far as the fabled land of the sadhus—yet woke up here, just minutes ago." Glimmer gestured to the chimney and its wisp of smoke below. "That is my home, one I fear besieged by men intent on violence. I go there now."

"You cannot leave—" erupted from the man.

"Perhaps what I cannot do is turn my back on you," was the reply.

"Why do you wish to keep me from leaving?"

"How could you know so much about me unless you did this to me, necromant?" the man reasoned, no longer with bemused expression, his eyes focused and wary.

"The events you related happened three hundred years ago," Glimmer responded in a harsh voice, stepping even farther away from the man. "They happened to Wald, the great Mage of DeVasier. It is one of the stories of his sojourn with his master, the Seer of Silence." Pointing his finger at the man, Glimmer shouted, "It is a common story, and what is your game! Why do you seek to gull me? I have something to do, and I have no time for knavery."

The man gestured, seeking to placate the young man's anger. "I seek to gull no one. I am Wald of the DeVasiers, the name you spoke, but I am not a great mage . . . I am a student, a disciple, and know nothing of this three hundred years of which you speak. I am mightily confused, is what I am." He suddenly looked down and chuckled to himself. "So that is what my master meant . . . perhaps . . ." Glimmer remained silent, not allowing himself to be pulled into the stranger's strange tale. Peering up at Glimmer, the man continued. "Let me try my turn at prophesying. Your master is a mage who Gathers, one who would teach but has nothing to give."

"Aye," Glimmer responded slowly, "that could be one way of sayin' it."

The man stared at Glimmer, his round face filling with awe. "So, you are indeed the one."

In turn, Glimmer found himself bemused by the man's words and tone. "I'm the only one out here, but don't think ye can get the best of me."

"No, no," the man protested. Then he laughed and added, embarrassment in his voice, "My pardon, sir, but I will use my master's words. You are the one, 'a fool destined for greatness or death.' Again, my pardon, but those were his words. You and your master are to be my first students."

"The First Ones," Glimmer murmured.

"This is also a story you have heard?"

The young mage was captured by the moment, too fantastic to be coincidence. "Once the mage was asked whether the great center of learning he established in DeVasier was the first place he had taught. Had the mage first taught the sadhus? Who were the first students he had saved from the wilderness of ignorance? And the mage replied, 'I was lost in time and place, and my first students saved me. I set their feet upon the path leading to knowledge, and they set my feet upon the road leading home to DeVasier.'"

The stranger stood and stared at the road below, one direction leading to the sea, the other to the mountains. "There is something that I must teach you, and then would you tell me which direction I should take?"

Glimmer remembered Alma-Ata saying a teacher would come, one who would teach that which no one in the world knew how to teach. Uncertainty tore at the young man: hurry to the inn and friends or follow the magic?

"The direction I must take is to my home and people to ensure their safety."

"Then that is my direction, for I must ensure your safety."

Magic added with gravely voice: "Let's go to th' inn, young mages. Let magic organize by its own design." The two mages locked eyes and then nodded, allowing magic to weave its greater design, trusting the truth resonating in the gnome's voice.

At their nod, the gnome turned and leaped off the bluff. Glimmer and Wald ran to the rocky edge, but grass stretched below in unbroken undulations lowering across the plain to the distant sea. The gnome was nowhere to be seen.

Trust the magic, Glimmer told himself. He thought of his master, Alma-Ata, and realized his master's life had been one of the mage walking a path, winds of magic swirling and billowing about him. Glimmer remembered more words to the story of the First Ones. In the ancient stories, the Mage of DeVasier had said: "I slept at the feet of my master, dreaming of a dragon that taught me to fly. I flew all the night and awoke in a strange place, the grass where I lay flattened as if by great weight, the ground where I lay still warm, although the night was chill."

Glimmer turned his eyes from the expanse of grass below back to young mage DeVasier, who then voiced Glimmer's thoughts: "We've looked, and I, at least, find no need to leap. I suggest we find a way down by foot."

As the two mages were skirting the promontory's edge to where it merged with a steep hill of grass dropping to the plains below, Cabbage-pants was stepping from the Gnome's Path onto the cobblestones before the inn. He moved with phlegmatic assurance from greater magic to lesser as matter-of-factly as he had stepped from rowboat to shore the day before. Perhaps more matter-of-factly, he might have admitted, if such doings were worthy of words. The Ally to the young mage shook his head, slipped his tiny obsidian knife from its sheath, and entered the main commons room to the Stone Dragon Inn.

Immaculate was the timing of his arrival and definitive were his actions. Afterwards, he left the battlefield to brew a cup of cabbage tea to celebrate the moment, finished except for the telling.

Mage and mage walked the lowering prairie, their pace quickened by Glimmer's concern. "You know where we're heading," Glimmer advised DeVasier as the younger mage steadily pulled away from the heavier man. "Who can catch a rabbit such as ye?" Bega had asked when gnome's quest had begun, and Glimmer now denied the fatigue of his sleepless night and dismissed until later the mystery of his unexplained appearance at Lion's Loft; he ignored the more deliberate gait of his new-found teacher and rabbited down the slope. He didn't consider what he would do if he arrived at the inn and had to place himself in harm's way. His legs ate the distance to the inn, and soon the young mage was at the door.

He entered to find Bega ministering to Wilim at the table before the common room's hearth. Wrapping white cloth around his head, she was muttering to herself and throwing dark glances to where two men lay, trussed upon the floor before the fireplace. Elesia entered from the kitchen with a steaming pot, and the gnome was nowhere to be found. All heads turned at Glimmer's entrance, the young mage quickly counting bodies. Steps outside announced the arrival of Wald DeVasier, breathing heavily but easily, one of the man's hands gripping a stout length of wood.

Into this tableau Glimmer breathed the words, "Where's the gnome? Is he all right?"

"Don't ye be worryin' about *me*," was the reply that drifted from the kitchen, followed soon after by the diminutive form of the gnome, an earthenware mug held in both his hands. The young mage didn't bother asking what was in it. "We're doin' just fine here, that we are, an' I'll be fixin' ye a hot bowl o' cabbage an' porridge t' break yer fast. But first have some tea." He trotted up to the mage and scrutinized him. "Red cabbage it is, an' I'm glad, peaked as ye look."

Glimmer accepted the tea; it was hot, at least, and the aroma of cabbage in the tea and the cabbagey taste of the porridge when the gnome later brought a steaming bowl did indeed relax him. *Home, sweet home,* he thought, sitting at table. The two trussed men, he saw, were indeed the same two from the inn at Ruddy. He sat at the table, tired yet exhilarated, all safe at home and a story to tell. Morning sunlight streamed through the eastern windows, and from the southern exposure, Cabbage-pants shouted to gnomes in the garden and then left the people in the commons room, off to join his own kind and to learn the garden news. *People do,* Glimmer thought, *have a way of taking care of themselves—especially when they are taken care of.*

They sat at the table before the fireplace, the trussed men on the floor silently glowering at their captors, faces welted and lips bloody. The others sat and stared at one another in silence: three tales—or even four, counting DeVasier—and where to begin? *Does one ask,* Glimmer wondered, *magic to explain itself?* It seemed Glimmer knew more about what had happened to DeVasier than he himself did, since Glimmer knew the ancient stories. And their journey, their Gnome Quest, seemed secondary to the reality of bandages, blood, and two men tied with rope with desperate plans in their eyes.

Bega, a frazzled expression on her face and hair only half contained with a single ribbon, finally demanded, "Somebody should start, an' it might as well be me." She stood and picked up her broom, its handle long and of unusual thickness—"a stave with straw," it had been called. She shook it at the men bound before the hearth and began, circuiting the bound men as she spoke, occasionally tapping one of the men with her broom, and several of her taps none too gentle.

The two men had arrived the evening before, one limping from a turned ankle, and both in sour moods. They had paid for a room, and accent and coin had identified them as Outlanders. Carrying a bundle wrapped in a dirty cloak, they had begun to ascend to their room when the turned ankle of the smaller man had given way.

"Jumpy they were," continued the woman, "an' the one fell against th' other, an' th' bundle fell, an' there it was, armor and swords. I give a yell an' asked how they got it, and they picked it up, the taller over there," Bega nodded to one of the men, his eyes glaring from a sweating face, "grabbin' for one o' the swords, for they had their weapons wrapped in th' cloth."

"An' I was outside, gettin' wood," Wilim continued, his first words. "I heard Bega shout, loud an' a bad shout." He looked at the woman. "Not like she usually yells at me, ya know? That's right, it was a bad shout, no louder than always, just meaner'n usu'l." Bega stared at the man as he spoke, an odd look upon her face—soft, amused, and something else. "I jus' ran at 'em, ran an' tossed th' wood right on 'em."

"That he did," the woman continued as the man beamed up at her. "An' got a sword hilt to the head for his trouble. Good for them they had no time fer more." She touched Wilim's head and then continued with the story. "I got my broom and commenced t' sweepin'. They had swords now, one steel an' one the copper, but I'd got in a coupla good licks, an' they was dazed, both."

Silent Elesia continued the story. "I came down the stairs at the noise and screamed. When they turned, I threw the candle at them an' hit him in the face," she said, indicating the taller man. Glimmer could see one red eye and red splotches on one cheek. "They broke for the kitchen door and ran into the pantry—must've thought it was the door out. Mother slammed the pantry shut, an' we've spent the night at the door, Mother with her broom."

"Yeah, an' me with th' pitchfork. I'll stick 'em like rotten pun'kins!" Wilim said, making jabbing motions at the trussed men. The larger groaned in disgust, closing his eyes.

"And so how did these men reach this state?" asked DeVasier, indicating the men lying on the floor, tied like sheaves of wheat awaiting the flail.

"Th' little man!" shouted Wilim. "We was sittin' an' sittin', and th' *gnome* came in th' door with th' wind blowin' like wolves." The man stood, so great was his excitement. He spoke, his voice rising and his arms waving. "Whoosh, an' in he came! An' 'nother whoosh! An' th' door t' th' pan'ry opens. An' whoosh! He's 'n there, that little knife'n his hand. An' he's dancin', whirlin' so fast it all got blurry!"

Wilim began dancing around the room, acting out the event until he wobbled in dizziness and Bega and Elesia sat him at the table's bench. "Ouch! Oooch!" he muttered to himself, Glimmer and DeVasier leaning to the man to hear his words. "An' then Bega jumps up when they come tumblin' out o' the pantry. And ye jus' gotta believe she gives'm th' what for! That's right, tha's right, I saw th' gnome, th' little guy with a big voice . . ." he murmured and braced his head with his hands as he slurred into silence.

"The gnome evidently pricked their legs and poked their bums—he called it 'a few well-placed bee kisses, if ya know what I mean.' Those two came stumblin' out of the pantry hole, blinkin' at the light an' one hand t' their arses—their faces a couple of big, sweet targets, so ye might say then th' broomstick gives 'em some kisses, snickery-snack," Bega added.

"An' rope we had at th' ready, an' any hand good with needle knows how t' tie a knot that won't come loose," finished Elesia, staring down at the men before them, helpless as flies swaddled by a spider.

"And what will happen to them now?" DeVasier asked into the silence that had fallen at the end of the tale. "To the sheriff?"

"We have none," Glimmer replied.

Wald shook his head in dismay. "Who protects you?"

"From what?"

The man gestured to the men trussed upon the floor. "Invaders, robbers and thieves, the lawless."

"We have little of that."

"Who governs you?"

"What governs a farmer? The seasons? The weather? What would a king tell him, 'Plant now,' when such a thing is common knowledge?"

"What do you call this place?"

"This is the Stone Dragon Inn. Up the road is Red Robin and Ruddy; down the road is Delta."

"No, what is this whole land called?"

"We know what ye mean," Bega intervened. "There is no kingdom with a name. It's just the land between the mountains an' th' sea."

"The mountains protect us east and north," Glimmer gestured. "The sea currents and the rocky shores protect us west, and desert protects us to the south."

"This is a magical place."

"This is a boring place, but," the young man considered, "I won't mind being bored for a while."

"And what will happen to them?" DeVasier asked again, indicating the two men before them.

"To Knight's Landing," Elesia said. She turned to her mother. "You said th' 'knights' like to play at bein' empire."

"That they do," mused the woman. "The lost dreams of days of old."

"And what will they do at this Knight's Landing?"

"These men're Outlanders. That's where the lost dream o' the knights of the Landing came from. Tell me, Outlanders, what would your empire, one of your thousand kingdoms do with ye?" When the men paled, she nodded, "Aye."

"What would they do in your kingdom, DeVasier?" Glimmer asked.

"An' Outland name and kingdom," Bega observed. "What're ye doing in these parts?" she asked the man.

"Seeking two students, one of whom I have found," the man replied, nodding at Glimmer.

"Magic'll give this inn a bad reputation," the woman muttered.

"And I have a suggestion. Let me take these men with me. They will become my students, too." He spoke to the men. "Better to fill your head with knowledge than lose your heads to ignorance."

"Yes, sire," said the taller, but Glimmer discerned a calculating look in his eyes.

"Let me see if I can add to the bad reputation of this inn," the young mage said. He stood and faced the two men on the floor before him. "You agree to what Mage DeVasier says, yet you plan to use violence at first opportunity. But what do you know of magic, you of the Outlands, where magic is the stuff of children's stories if I am told correctly."

Glimmer confronted the taller of the two men. "Tell me, why did you leave the pantry as you did?"

After an insolent moment, the man sullenly replied, "It warn't no cabbage, like th' idiot said, more like th' woman's words—though I'd call't hornets an' not bees."

"You saw no magic," Glimmer said, verifying the bound men's words. He turned to DeVasier. "They will kill you unless they believe."

DeVasier said, "I am a teacher, not a mage, whatever you say."

"What is the name of this inn?" Glimmer asked the men tied before him.

"Yer got a picture o' a dragon above th' door," offered the smaller man.

"The Stone Dragon Inn, as ye said," added the other.

"Violence in the Stone Dragon's inn," the young mage continued. "What do you think that means?" and the walls trembled at the words, and fire flared in the fireplace. Knowing that the dragon was with him, Glimmer pointed to the mantel of fieldstone, to the obsidian stone surrounded by grey, and the stone blinked, focused on the two men on the floor who had rolled to face the hearth. The eye stared down at the two men, the suggestion of eyebrow in the stone above, and the men quailed at the consequences inherent in that gaze.

"So, which will it be?" asked the young mage. "Knight's Landing and Outland justice or fealty to DeVasier . . . and keep the dragon happy?"

DeVasier faced the men, his countenance reflecting twin emotions, understanding and retribution. "The Outlands lie east of here, over the mountains, and also a land called DeVasier?"

"They," with a nod to those sitting beside DeVasier, "call it th' Outlands; we call it the Empire, but there ain't no empire no more, really," the man conceded. "As t' yer name . . . maybe I heard somethin' like't."

"*Draconia* was the ancient name of this land, long before my time," DeVasier mused, and then the mage turned to Glimmer, "which would be long, long before your time. *Land of Dragons*: some said named for volcanoes; some took a more literal view."

The teacher stood, filled with sudden energy. "I will teach you," he said, nodding to Glimmer, "and then we will be on our way," he finished, including the two bound men in his gaze.

"And what about my master, your second student, as you said?"

"We will let the magic organize itself, as the gnome said." DeVasier grinned. "That's worked pretty well so far."

Three days later, the smell of burning wood drifted through the trees, and the clinking of pots and pans provided a counterpoint to the faint susurrus of the river. Glimmer and Wald of DeVasier rounded the corner of the road, the stone bridge and stone house opening through the trees. The river lay beyond, and the bridge ahead and to the left as they approached, the stone house with its tower beckoning. Above the eastern doors to the common room hung a sign with the painting of a greyscaled dragon breathing fire. The teacher had completed his instruction of Glimmer, taken upon Lion's Loft, the place of their meeting.

At Lion's Loft the young dream mage had turned to the young Mage of DeVasier, and as the ancient stories of the First Student related, had asked, "What would you have me do?"

And the teacher had replied, "I would not have you *do* but rather *be*." With a gesture from the teacher, they had sat upon the ground, and dream mage was given the Silence of the Saints.

Later Glimmer was to ask, "How can something so profound be so simple?" to which his teacher had replied, "How can experiencing yourself seem strange? It is your birthright." Glimmer was to think again and again on those words. He felt as if he had been a king who had been living in a hovel outside castle walls simply because he did not know the castle belonged to him.

DeVasier now appeared more focused and assured. He had brushed his clothes, trimmed his beard and washed, and appeared to be in good spirits.

"I may have awakened in a strange place—and time—but at least I have my satchel and, therefore, my essentials." He placed his hand to his shirt spun of fine cloth. "Elesia pressed this. And now it is time for me to continue."

"Are you sure it wouldn't be better to wait here for my master?"

"No, I have a distance . . . and a time . . . to cross, and I wish to begin that journey."

"And you feel it is right to take the two men?"

The two men had been chained to the anvil in the wattle shed for the past three days. Both men remembered the obsidian dragon's eye and the words all had heard within themselves, albeit spoken to the men lying bound before the hearth: *Go with the man, and if in thirty days you still wish to kill him, you may do so without consequence from me.*

Wald DeVasier breathed deeply, considering, and then replied, "Yes, it seems some things are organized by forces greater than ourselves."

"How are you going to get back—the distance you can manage, but the three hundred years?"

"I don't know," admitted the DeVasier. "I've been thinking that if I begin walking to the *place*, the *time* might take care of itself." He shrugged with some humor. "That's my plan, anyway, such as it is."

Planning to walk the road to Steppe and then to continue on to Outland-at-the-Pass and across the mountains to fragmented empire, Wald DeVasier, the future (or, Glimmer asked himself, is it past?) Great Mage of DeVasier, left after the midday meal. They gathered at the cobblestones which flanked the east side of the inn: Glimmer, Bega, Elesia, and Wilim. DeVasier cut the bonds of the two men. Each was given a pack of provisions by Bega, and each turned and followed the man destined to be teacher and mage for a civilization, his future fate three hundred years in the past. Down the road they traveled to the bridge crossing the river; then they turned west, following the road until they were lost from sight in the trees.

After Wald of DeVasier was gone, escorted by two men glad to be shut of stone inns that lodged dragons, Bega gestured Glimmer to her side. "The man insisted on payin' in good coin, but look at the coin, young Glimmer!" She opened her palm and displayed a bright coin the size of a crocus flower. "I seen these when I worked the Outland pass. Outlander silver, Old Empire silver, hundreds o' years old—but look, not worn in the least, like new. Can ya imagine that?"

Although he felt no trepidation in confiding to Bega, Glimmer had felt a restraint in telling all things magic to a woman who mostly felt it was bad for business. His magic was so new, so little under his control, so unique to himself. He had spent so much time alone experiencing . . . not a glimmer of magic . . . that he was reluctant to discuss with others dream magery and the stone dragon. He did not relish being asked questions he could not answer, nor did he wish to make others uncomfortable, considering the magnitude of his ability and his tenuous control over it. Alma-Ata did seem to have established with Bega that Glimmer would sometimes need some time to attend to his apprenticeship, even though he had left his apprentice with few instructions and those vague at best. *Don't let yourself get upset* indeed was minimal instruction.

Evening supper was finished, and Glimmer had cleared the dishes. For the moment, the common room was empty, all others to their rooms or kitchen. The Stone Dragon Inn was a rather informal affair, one or two guests at ease, much more in the spirit of the word *guest* than *patron* or *lodger*. Guests would wander into the kitchen or even help with the meal or dishes. It was a touch of intimacy more that of an extended family dropping in to visit than paying customers. *If we ever were to have ten or a dozen or more lodgers,* Glimmer thought, *what would we do with ourselves?* But now he had a moment alone, some quiet before the dragon's fire. He smiled as the hearth assumed the fluidity, the suggestion of animation, which revealed the attention of the dragon.

It will be cold tonight. You should take a brazier of coals to your room.

Glimmer smiled at the homey concern of the dragon. "I'll be warm enough. The guests have even mentioned how warm their rooms are. Now, I wonder why that is."

Yes, but it would be good to take some warmth to your room, to have some fire, don't you think?

Glimmer thought perhaps cold wind would be blowing down the mountains and across the upland. "Can you tell what the weather's going to be? That's something useful you could do," which earned a blear eye from the dragon.

If this were a magical story, what would next happen is this: "And then the dragon spoke for the third time, 'Take a brazier of coals to your room this night, O young mage.' And outside an owl would hoot three times, a branch tap three times against glass, three dark horsemen ride to the inn door." Young mage, are you being deliberately obtuse, or did Bega bat your head with her staff today?

A pause, and during that pause, Glimmer blinked three times. As he opened his mouth to speak, Bega entered the room from the kitchen. She handed the young man a cloth and said, "Wipe the tables before you sleep."

"And I think tonight I'll take some coals to my room in the brazier for the chill."

"It's not that cold an'll probably weaken yer blood, but Alma-Ata told me t' give ye some freedom in foolish requests, so suit yourself. Just be sure t' rake yer own ashes, young apprentice."

Nodding to the hearth, Glimmer began to wipe the tables, making sure he missed no crumbs because, foolish requests or no, if he didn't do his work, he might well feel Bega's broom against his pate after all.

Finishing his task, Glimmer collected coals in a bronze brazier and carried it and a couple of knots of wood to his room. Setting the brazier on a flat stone, he once again felt awe at the subtle magic of fire in the stone house, that two knots of wood would burn all night and spread the fire's warmth, that even rooms with no fire would retain warmth . . . *like sleeping next to the belly of a dragon,* he thought.

He sat on the bed, readying himself for sleep, when the glow of the coals stirred and the miniature form of a dragon rose above the coals, a ruddy, golden presence of heat and light.

Sit beneath DeVasier's banyan tree for a time, young mage.

"I have already practiced my meditation."

Close your eyes again and experience the silence. It is time to be a dream mage.

Glimmer felt his hearth pound as the diminutive dragon floated lazily on zephyrs of heat. He sat cross-legged on his pallet and closed his eyes. He sank into the silence of himself, his heart calming and his breathing settling like waves merging with ocean depths. After some time he became aware again of breathing, aware of thoughts, aware that he had a body. He breathed a slow, deep breath and lay down on his pallet, giving body and mind the opportunity to ease into activity. He lay, easy in the moment, comfortable in the warmth emanating from burning embers. He drifted, at peace with himself and the world, into a deep sleep . . .

. . . And stars burned in the primal night. The meadow across the stream from the washing stone no longer acquiesced to the black-branched frosts of fall. The air was warm, and the stars glowed in the thick humidity of summer. Fireflies flickered their imitation of the stars, and crickets sawed their violin melodies.

Glimmer crossed the stream on stepping stones, stable moon-pale stones surrounded by the swirl of dark waters. The stone dragon lay on its belly in the grasses, its legs tucked beneath its torso, its neck and head lifted and still, no nest offered for sleep. Glimmer approached the dragon to stand before it, elevating his gaze to meet dragon's gaze.

What dream magery do you wish to perform? asked the dragon, words sounding in the mind as clearly as if the words had been spoken.

"Will I always need you to perform dream magic . . . or to do so safely?

Always is a long time, young mage. I will not speak in such absolutes. Tonight I am guiding and assisting. I am here—as you are—unless you would prefer I leave, responded the dragon, stirring slightly.

Glimmer breathed in the humid pollen of the night, catching a tendril of scent like that of a smithy's fire. "No, I don't mind you being here. What did you mean that it is time for me to be a dream mage?"

A mage—or at least the best—administer their craft with wholeness of vision, something of which you have a . . . growing glimmer . . . through your experience with what you call the Silence of the Saints.

"But I am dreaming, which is why I am speaking to you. Stone houses don't speak. Isn't the Silence deeper than waking, dreaming, and sleeping? Isn't it the basis?"

You are in your dream but not of it.

"And you?"

Dragons don't dream.

Lifting his hand before his eyes, Glimmer's hand became translucent, a glow freckled with points of matter. He was one; he was the other: he was the unifying wholeness of both. "So how do I perform dream magic now? Deliberately, I mean."

Ask yourself that question.

Glimmer paused, thinking, and then said, "Considering the nature of dreams, I think there are many ways to practice dream magic once I'm in the dream."

Then how will you proceed?

Glimmer sat on the grasses lush with summer, and the thought came to him of his master sitting on the puncheon bench beside the kitchen door, waiting. "Since I have no plan, no intentions, I'll close my eyes and wait. I'll think of all the possible things I can do, and then choose not to do them. My dream magic shall be to choose not to practice dream magic."

That would indeed exhibit the quality of discrimination.

Glimmer sat, his eyes closed, seeking to settle to an idea. Phantasmagoria of impressions, ideas, emotions, raced through his head. Opening his eyes, he scooted closer to the dragon, leaning his back against the dragon's foreleg. Above him, the stone-still body of the dragon blocked out the stars, the shadow above him as black as the void of space. Glimmer closed his eyes again, his thoughts drifting: the night, the darkness, the presence against which he rested, the smithy Wilim was cleaning, Wilim whose arms danced when he spoke.

Simple Wilim. Why was he *simple?* Wilim's thoughts seemed only to skim the surface of life like a round stone skipping across water. Why was that? He was a good man. Glimmer liked him, even if the man had named him Not a Glimmer of Magic. It had actually been a profound thought for the man, an insight into the possibilities of language. It was too bad he didn't think like other men, too bad he couldn't live his life and not be laughed at by others. Glimmer knew how that felt, although most of the laughing done to him was done by himself.

Like now, he thought muzzily: *you're not dreaming, you're daydreaming.* He laughed comfortably to himself, the laugh as soft as a pillow. The young dream mage slipped from waking-while-dreaming to sleeping-in-a-dream to sleeping-without-dreaming as his body lay in his room upon a pallet, embers glowing ruddy, the ephemeral presence of a tiny dragon dancing on waves of heat rising into the cold stillness of the night.

Chapter 9

"O children of immortality . . ."
Cognitions of the White Donkey

ॐ

Glimmer awoke to cold darkness, the embers of the brazier coals now ash. Pulling his blanket more closely about him, he remembered the events of the night, the dragon, the brazier, dragon-in-the-dream. He reconsidered; perhaps he was remembering the non-events of the night. He had not closed his eyes and dreamed magnificent and lordly realities. In fact, he had fallen asleep while performing his craft, the task of the night—to do nothing! Fallen asleep while dreaming! He sat up in disgust. At least no disasters . . . or at least none that he was aware of. His goal had been innocent enough. Even if he hadn't done what he had set out to do, he would still have done nothing.

He drifted downstairs to break his fast and found the kitchen already occupied by Wilim and an itinerant redsmith who had bartered a room for the night from Bega in exchange for resuscitating the modest smithy in the shed.

"What I want t' know," Wilim was advancing to the sleepy-eyed redsmith, "is how do you know when th' coals are hot 'nough? Is it the color, or do you feel't in th' heat?"

"Eh j'st know, ye see it ee-nuf. I' gits sear'd t' ye, f're ov hearth, f're ov knowin'."

Wilim's brow furrowed with thought. "I'd like you t' show me before y' leave—iron, not your redsmithin'. I'll be usin' blacksmithy more. Or maybe both, yea, that's right."

With those words, he left the kitchen for the wattle stable, the man's energy trailing behind him like a swirl of smoke. Glimmer stood frozen in the doorway, pressed against the scarred wood to create a path for Wilim's exit. The memories of his drifting-to-sleep-within-a-dream-while-sleeping coalesced, and he turned sharply in the doorway and followed Wilim outdoors. Wilim had turned left at the kitchen door and was rounding the tower's stone wall.

"Hey, Wilim," Glimmer shouted at the man's back. The man halted and turned to face the hail.

"Ah, it's ye, young master," the man acknowledged.

"Where are you heading so early and so quickly?"

"T' stable an' smithy."

"To what task?"

"For th' obvious," Wilim responded impatiently, and as Glimmer opened his mouth to question further, the man anticipated him. "I woke this mornin' an' realized best if I knew smithy work. An' if one will smithy, then one must know th' fire." The man met eyes with Glimmer, nodded, and said, "An' now I'm off, thankee fer askin', y'ng master." With a quick tug of his forelock, Wilim turned and strode off, rounding the tower and out of sight.

Never, thought Glimmer, *in all the days I have known Wilim, has he ever truly met my eyes with his own,* only the vacuous stare, the sliding gaze, intelligence casting for a place to rest and never finding it. *Did I do this?* he asked himself. *But what did I do? Nothing with full deliberation.* He chilled at the thought: a wandering of the mind, an idle thought before sleep, and a man's life is changed forever. *What,* he thought, *if I had wondered how much pain simple-minded Wilim could tolerate, more or less than a normal man? Then would some painful catastrophe have occurred to test the chance thought of a dream-sleepy mind?*

He shivered and leaned against the stone wall still cold from the night. The morning sun shone upon him, and he raised his face to the heat and breathed in the warmth. He hadn't succeeded in practicing dream magic. No, he hadn't. He had changed a man—possibly for the good—but without the man's knowledge . . . and without even his own knowledge. He had no more control of his magic than a man asleep controls his horse. Only once had he chosen and created his dream, and that had been at the sanctuary at Madrone when he had opened the building to the morning sun—and even then, how much had been the influence of the Silent Ones, the gentle hands of the gnomes of silence?

Glimmer beat his fist against the wall. He would have to talk to the dragon before something bad happened. Perhaps he should talk to Cabbage-pants, too; he seemed more willing now to talk about subjects beyond cabbage recipes. And what about his master, Alma-Ata? Where was he?

Glimmer thought with a chill, *What if I had thought what a good couple Wilim and Bega would make, if only Bega were not so quick of mind?* He felt sick in his stomach. Now he understood in his heart why dream mages were neither encouraged by the craft nor revered by the populace. *No one wants to fall asleep with the fear of waking to nightmare—not even me.*

With his eerie knack of timing, Alma-Alta returned by mid-meal, striding up the road with purpose, entering the kitchen and calling to Bega for a meal.

"There's no time to lose," he stated as he sat with the others to meal. "Glimmer and I must be off to Delta immediately." His face streaked with sweat and dust, fatigue had reddened Alma-Ata's eyes and roughened his voice.

"What have you learned?" Bega asked, glancing at her daughter with alarm.

"Will you need assistance?" Wilim questioned, a determined look on his face. "I owe you for your kindnesses to me."

The mage met Wilim's eyes, an appraising and frank stare. "You've changed, man, haven't you."

"I feel different."

Alma-Ata gazed steadily into Wilim's open countenance. "You woke up, that's what's happened to you." He stood and slapped the man upon the shoulder. "You were a good man when you were simple, and I'm sure you'll be a better one now." Glancing at Glimmer, he added, "I'll leave you here, Wilim, to help Bega. It's my apprentice who must come with me." Glimmer wondered how his master could be so matter of fact about Wilim's change, and then he realized the man had spent his life in the eye of a storm of magic, watching magic happen around him.

"What is it you've heard?" reiterated the woman.

Alma-Ata smiled. "I've *heard* nothing. I was at Madrone and the

Dragon's Spine when I knew I had to come here and then leave."

"Don't look like a mage nor act like a mage, but 'e sure talks like one," Bega muttered, making a sign for good luck with her hand.

"Dress warmly, apprentice, and bring your bag and blanket. We're off by shank's mare to the sea."

Glimmer cast a glance behind minutes later as Alma-Ata and he hurried down the road to the west. Bega, Elesia, and Wilim stood on the cobbles before the kitchen doorway, watching mage and apprentice off. Wondering what lay ahead, Glimmer lengthened his stride to match the mage's.

"I thought I was supposed to keep it calm," he said, having had quest enough with the gnome.

"I know you've learned the Silence of the Saints, so make your own calm. We're off to the sea."

They walked into the wind until evening light, the breeze not yet promising the salt of the sea. The mage's manner did not invite conversation, yet his few words had given Glimmer ample food for thought. Alma-Ata had been to Madrone and the Dragon's Spine. He knew Glimmer had been taught the Silence of the Saints. What did Alma-Ata know, and how had he learned? Bega was right: one never saw Alma-Ata practicing magic (unless sitting and waiting were his craft, Glimmer amended), yet he surely sounded and acted like a mage. "Don't bother me with trifles!" fairly seemed to emanate from the man. Enigmatic, he was, yet perhaps it came with the territory. If a man knew of fire and others did not, then references to *kindling* and *coals* and even *cooking* would seem mysterious. And perhaps for a mage who gathered magic, to not be distracted was even more important. A sudden thought chilled the young mage. What would happen if he were awakened in the middle of his dream magery? What if, for some reason, Alma-Ata woke him up some night? Glimmer thought and thought, and "Don't bother me with trifles!" seemed a perfectly reasonable perspective for both Glimmer and his master, all things considered.

At full dark, Alma-Ata left the main road and approached a modest farm, their arrival heralded by the barking of a shepherd dog. The mage stopped and allowed the dog to approach him, a blacker shadow in the darkness, the dog's white splashes of fur capturing starlight. The dog nosed the man, and introductions made, the travelers advanced to house and then to the barn to sleep the night.

They sat in darkness in the barn, blankets around their shoulders. Glimmer's stomach growled. *A cold dinner and a cold bed,* he thought. Alma-Ata sat in silence for a moment and then addressed the apprentice.

"I met an interesting man on the road and stayed a fortnight with him at freeman Oghan's orchard, in the hut near the apples—the one in which Oghan himself stays during the picking."

Glimmer listened with interest, wondering whom Alma-Ata would find interesting enough to keep him from his apple circuit, wondering who would be interesting enough to keep the mage in one place for a fortnight.

"His name was Wald," the mage continued. "Of the DeVasiers." At Glimmer's sharp intake of breath, Alma-Ata asked, "Heard of him?"

"And met him," the apprentice responded.

"So Wald told me."

Glimmer pondered for a moment, then asked, "But you said you stayed with him for a fortnight, yet he is less than a week gone from the house. How can that be?"

The mage chuckled to himself. "The man, of course, was the Mage of DeVasier, the great teacher of three hundred years past, the man who brought peace and prosperity to the Outlands—or as they say, the Empire—and whose name even we across the mountains know and respect." The opaque presence of the mage turned to his apprentice. "So, in a sense, the *how* of the question is not key. We'll just say *magic* and leave it at that." He paused and then continued. "You were his first student, and so now you know the Silence of the Saints."

"And you were his second, yes? He said it is an experience which deepens over time."

The mage was silent. Then he responded, "Yes, the saints are known for their silence because they maintain it during activity. And now you and I both have experienced it, sitting with closed eyes." The mage paused again and then spoke softly. "The magic of the saints brought him to you, Glimmer . . . and to me. This is a great thing, a gift to cherish."

"It has given me little control over my dreaming, though."

"*Yet*—or so it seems to you. I saw great change, though, in the two men who traveled with DeVasier." The mage chuckled. "He told me their story. It seems you've had some . . . lack of calmness . . . while I was away. I am heartened to see that the world around you is still ordered by waking and not by dreaming."

"So, those men will not kill DeVasier, you think?"

"Kill him! He taught them the Silence just after me. Don't you realize who those men are, Glimmer?"

"Thieves and butchers."

"You forget your history." Alma-Ata turned to his apprentice, humor in his voice. "Now, come. I know you know this. Who serves and protects Mage DeVasier?"

"All the people of his time! He was greatly revered."

"Come, now, you can give a better answer than *everybody*."

"His schools, his students he taught—" and then Glimmer caught his breath, entranced by his sudden recollection. "The Grey Knights in Silence!"

"Yes," said the mage. "Two men who vowed lifelong silence, two men with no allegiance but to DeVasier, no past, no family that anyone could ever figure—actually, they are brothers, they told me."

"And they spent their lives at DeVasier's side, silent men in plain garb, the Grey Knights, men who wished to blend with the stone walls, to serve and protect their master in silence."

"Which is what we must do in Delta, serve and protect."

"What do you know?"

"Nothing more than that we must go."

"And who told you?"

"Let's just say a bird. Or perhaps the wind."

"Not a fox?"

A chuckle. "A bird this time, a bird in flight—a gull. . . that came to visit Lahad and me."

"You saw Lahad?"

"And taught him the Silence."

"Taught?"

"Yes, hence the fortnight with the DeVasier. We will have time to talk, but now to business. Magic is stirring; that is all I know—that, and that we must rest." Alma-Ata patted his apprentice on the shoulder. "Now let us meditate, and then eat and sleep. In several days we will sleep in a bed in Delta." Glimmer and mage propped themselves against the wattle sides of the farmer's barn and closed their eyes, the stillness of the late fall night blossoming to silence.

The next two days consisted of the steady trudge on road's way to Delta, a downhill course following the River Quill. If it were not for the unanswered questions in Glimmer's mind, he would have enjoyed the excursion. Late fall had finally tipped to early winter, yet even the coolness of the season would not have been enough to dampen the newness of the travel. Glimmer had been to Delta once years before but remembered only the horizon meeting the sea and a sky askew with the insubordinate wings of gulls. Now he was to see the town and bay again, see the variety of sailing ships from different lands, although most ships were those of local fishermen. He had heard sailors and fishermen speaking of their ships and boats, had seen the bustle of the boatwrights along the river, the slipways at right angles to the water filled with fishing boats in the making, older boats being dismembered, their parts recycled by the wrights. The larger ships were built in the port at Knight's Landing, although the coast was not busy with trade, not like the great port cities of the Outlands. Delta and its estuary echoed more to the calls of fish mongers than muazzin from exotic ports.

As they finally neared the river's mouth and the land flattened, the sea grasses grew green with the flavor of salt; sky rimed with the salty wind of the sea. The wind blew cold off the ocean, yet winter in Delta was no colder than autumn in the Olifant's Playground, where frozen winds avalanched off mountainsides and onto the high grasslands.

Glimmer breathed deeply, the sun lowering its shoulders to the horizon, colors deepening, saturated by brushstrokes of tide. It seemed that all day he had walked half a stride behind Alma-Ata, not quite able to catch him, even though Glimmer was the younger of the two. Finally, as the road veered away from the river which had cut a ravine into the plain and bluff before the tidewater crested a few miles ahead, Glimmer trotted a few skipping steps to even his progress with the mage's.

"So, what do we do, and where do we stay?" the apprentice asked.

Alma-Ata halted abruptly in the middle of the dusty road, halted so abruptly that Glimmer continued on a couple of paces before stopping and returning. "What do we do? Wake up, apprentice! Have you learned nothing?" The mage glared at the young man who stared back at him, gaping. "Close your mouth! We assist possibilities. Ask not 'What do we do?' but 'What needs to be done?'" The mage glared again at his assistant, the rich colors of the setting sun delineating the myriad wrinkles in Alma-Ata's face. "Close your mouth! What are you, a frog mage, ready to balance the world on your tongue?"

Then Alma-Ata turned again and strode down the road, Glimmer hustling again to keep up with his urgent pace. The young mage thought, *Either this man knows something I don't or is bitter for reasons I don't understand . . . or both.*

Glimmer increased his pace until he walked beside the man, matching the older man's rhythm stride for stride. They walked in silence for a distance, and then Alma-Ata glanced at Glimmer and grinned a sidelong smile. "We'll be staying at the Sea Apple, young apprentice."

Glimmer snorted. "What kind of apple is a *sea apple*?"

"Not a fruit at all, my boy, but an animal, an animal of the tide pools and coral forests of the sea. A beautiful animal." He smiled again at the young man. "Sometimes called a sea cucumber, my young gardener, but I wouldn't advise eating one. Although some people use them in soup . . . they are also used in soap," and then they dropped down off the bluffs to the town of Delta by the sea.

Alma-Ata was glad to find that his favorite room was free, one with a window looking out to the water. They settled themselves on the room's bed, the window open to the cold air and the distant fire of the setting sun. Closing their eyes, the eternal rhythms of the sea flowed over them, through them. The ocean waves tumbled onto the land, but beyond the breakers, waves swelled from the depths and then settled back to the depths. The tide of Glimmer's thoughts and excitement ebbed as he sat with his mage, sun settling into ocean, awareness finding silence between the storm wrack of thoughts the mind so jealously calls its own.

At a supper of chowder and biscuits, Glimmer said, "So we need to stay awake?" He wondered why his master had asked him to come. Now that Alma-Ata was with him, perhaps the mage feared the potential of nightmare and chaos.

"Be precise in your listening!" the mage snapped, almost nicking Glimmer's fingers with the spoon Alma-Ata used for emphasis. "*Be awake,* not *stay awake.*" The mage muttered, shaking his head. "I don't care if you are awake, dreaming, or sleeping—as long as you—how did DeVasier put it?—do not forget your birthright."

He muttered to himself some more, and then began to sarcastically wave his arms and hands before the apprentice. "See me, I'm doing magic; I'm casting a spell!" He sputtered something that sounded like an obscenity, although Glimmer couldn't understand the language. "Magicians do it all the time: petty mind, petty magic."

"Then what is magic?"

"*Magic*, young mage, is the structure of the entire universe, not just the structure of a spell!" Alma-Ata's wispy beard fairly bristled at the intensity of his words.

The mage's face softened, and then he stood. "I'm washing and then off to bed. We'll see what the morning brings." Frustration bubbled over again, and Alma-Ata shook his fist in Glimmer's face. "This is what I hate the most about magery: having to mind the business of others. All that hocus-pocus is all very well and good, but I'd much rather be pruning trees and racking cider." He then turned and stormed off to the back of the inn to wash, followed by his bemused apprentice. Grumbles drifted back: "expect a hero" . . . "by doing nothing" . . . "nothing doing!"

All Glimmer understood was that his master was shaken out of his normal composure. *I'll do for my master what needs to be done,* he thought. *I'll do nothing, and I'll do it impeccably well.*

They lay together on the bed, sharing its softness for their sleep. In the darkness, the sound of waves broke against the shuttered windows. Glimmer wrapped himself more tightly in his blankets and listened to the snores of the mage. The rhythm of Alma-Ata's breathing lengthened, softened to a sibilance whose ebb and flow managed to match that of the waves on the beach, the beach fluid with the turbid merging of sand and sea. It was a sound so unlike that of the young length of the River Quill that flanked the stone house with its apple tree and garden and dragon-hearth. He imagined the great obsidian eye here at the ocean inn, darkly mirroring the ivory opalescence of the moon in a night sky that glimmered with crystals of sparkling salt.

Glimmer eased himself out of bed, as quiet as thought. To be at the ocean and to sleep away the beauty of it was too much to bear. *Let the mage sleep. He's an old man and needs his rest. I'm not even tired from the trek,* Glimmer thought. *I can sleep when I'm old. Right now, I want to walk on the beach, climb the bluff and look at the town and its lights, look at the ocean and the light of the moon reflecting on rippling waves.*

He slipped through the luminescence of the wall, hanging on points of matter, easing himself quietly down from the second story room to the cobbled street beside the inn.

Delta on the Quill, lapped by ocean, was quiet. *Even dogs and sailors are sleeping,* Glimmer thought. *It seems as if I never even fell asleep, but Alma-Ata and I must have been sleeping longer than I thought,* Glimmer reasoned, and that was when he realized he was awake again within his dreams.

Slipping though the walls of the building to earth seemed so natural, he thought. The moon was now high in the sky, and the sea so real, a greater reality than waking-within-waking. He closed his eyes and still saw the beach and waves breaking moonlight into swales of silver. What need of eyes and the other senses! He could trace them to their source and be aware without needing the extremities of sensation.

The dream mage's awareness extended outward, over the darkling waves and cold fabric of the night, out into the void to where sky and water met, and there he found the fleet, the ships from the south come to fill their holds with riches, however they may—with talk and trade or sword and scream. By dawn they would reach the delta waters; by morning the prows of their longboats would plow the sands of the beach; by mid-morning the ships would be roped to pier and gangplanks, hungry for plunder. Delta had no defense, no troops to ward off such a force. This was the danger that Alma-Ata had felt in his bones, the message of the gulls. These men with their black hatchet beards and crimson cloth would be upon them ere Glimmer awoke from his dream.

And what will Alma-Ata do? Throw apples at the janissaries? And the sailors throw fish?

Walking to the water's edge, Glimmer felt the energy of the sea, a huge watery beast breathing its rolling exhalations onto the shore. The moon above him cast its pale scimitar of light onto Glimmer's uplifted face, cool reflection of the sun, stars distant cousins to the fire hidden by the earth. Huge and terribly beautiful had been the dragon-star as it had stooped to earth like a falcon to its prey! Huge and terrible, its wings outspread and its eyes jewels of fire, its mouth moist with the flames of creation!

Glimmer turned away from the sea and looked upon the sleeping shadow of the town, the sea-grassy bluffs above. He had not awakened the dogs, but by dawn men with crimson robes and sun-bright swords would. But what if they beached to find a totem that advised caution? What if they stormed the shore only to find heralded an even greater storm, huge and terrible in its beauty, with iridescent wings stretched wide to enfold and protect the town?

Glimmer closed his eyes and looked down with the essence of his eyes at the sand. Each particle of sand was a beach unto itself, glowing energy, particles of matter, each upon each an infinite universe within the crescent of sand upon the earth of Delta upon the Quill. The dream mage sank within the myriad universes of sand, mingling the speckled luminescence of his being with the glowing galaxies of each grain. He reached into the flesh of his thigh and pulled forth the glowing essence of the bone, reshaping its molten form to that of a blowpipe, draining the dream-marrow from its core. Sand before and within him began to swirl, dark night whispers of shadow warming at the vortex, warming and glowing, brighter and hotter.

Extend the blowpipe and let the winds flow, winds that blow between planets, the distant fire of suns. A body forms of red hues of molten sand—head and torso; then reach with hands to mold the legs, the talons, the head reptilian with its graceful arch of neck, rear legs strong and spread to hold the weight; lift the mass to the bluff overlooking the distant sea and its horizon, ships beyond the curve of the earth. Plant the body, reared in terrific power to crack and crush. Let moonlight and starlight anneal the mass as you construct the bones of the wings, the tendon and cartilage.

Then rise from the glory hole of fiery, molten glass and leap with your body's dream to the empty-bellied ships beyond the horizon, sailor-warriors asleep except steersmen; fall upon the ships like a falcon upon its prey, snatch gold rings from ears, gold laced round seamen's necks, silver of gorget and greaves, copper breastplates and bronze fittings from ships. Sleeping, all of them, their dreams not your *dream*. All but one! Eyes open, and those eyes see you, know of your presence! Know you for what you are! Like smoke through a lattice, you are gone before more than eyes follow you, perhaps with dream-arms and dream-knives.

Quick as thought, return to the beach and offer metals to the fire. Never mind the ocean's horizon and eyes in the dark dreams of the night. Focus and forge dragon scales of glass with metal connectors; add whispers of metal to the glass to tinge gold and silver and copper; mix with minerals within the sand: verdigris green and amber hues, blues of lapis lazuli and yellow sulfur. Scales hang to ripple with a wind and chime a beautiful music of maim and misery to those with ill intent . . .

And then it stands upon the bluff, ready to flame with rising or setting sun, obsidian eyes like pits of light burning darkly for the death of those who transgress.

Glimmer breathed in the fire and roared a solar flare of flame over the huge glass sea drake fixed upon the bluff, annealing the terrible beauty of the translucent beast to a magical hardness, a diamond-like sharpness, infusing within the glowing glass the mettle of the people of the land between the mountains and the sea, a warning tone to the beauty of the chimes: that peace is not weak, nor is happiness helpless.

The fires began to subside within the mage, his dream cooling, the tide of his passion subsiding. Night sounds returned, sea upon beach and wind among grasses. Glimmer's thoughts turned to mage and apprentice sleeping in a room overlooking the ocean; he stood beside the bed and saw the somnolent forms before him, lay down beside the younger, closed his eyes and became the dreaming mage, the sleeping mage, the young mage sleeping, dreaming with fists clenched around the dream of his defiance, his defense of the land, dream magery drifting to dream and to slumber and then to dawn.

Shouts and exclamations awakened the mage and apprentice, and they threw open the window shutters to find out the cause for the early commotion. The sky at the horizon was still lit with stars, but the dawn lit the white squares of sails approaching delta and town. Biremes, sleek and narrow, the martial ram at the prow, the sail amidships, and the reflection of the dawn upon sharpened weapons—fisherfolk and townsfolk pointed at the approaching fleet, but no sooner did they apprehend the vessels than they would turn to other calls and exclamations and look to the direction of the rising sun. Then they would hood their eyes with a hand or simply stand dumbfounded and stare in round-eyed wonder. Some stood so that they could look to sea and dawn, back and forth, back and forth, sobs and shrieks unnoticed escaping from lips.

"Out of the pan, into the fire," muttered the mage. "Let's go down and see what the hubbub is about—all about, I mean. We already know the half of it," Alma-Ata amended with a nod to the approaching ships, which were already dropping sail and lowering hungry oars to water.

Leaving the inn, they rounded the cobbled street to the rear of the building, and there they saw the sight that even dogs appeared to be ogling. On the bluff above the town, a huge and terrible glass fire drake reared to the height of a three-story building, one story higher than any building in the town. Morning sun illuminated the dragon so that light emanated from it, magnified by the prisms of its flowing, awful beauty. Its graceful neck was arched to such an angle that the sun's beams were captured just where the neck met the narrowing serpent-like head, the beams concentrated to a red ball of glassine fire. The eyes glowed a dark fire, illuminated yet still subterranean. The wings, though, dominated the sky above the bluff—scintillating scales shimmering in wind upon outstretched wings, chiming clear, defiant tones to fly the wild winds.

Glimmer stared at the glass dragon, the sharp reality of it even more indomitable than the dream of it. He felt a fierce pride at having accomplished what he had dearly desired: to dream with intent, without haphazard or disastrous results. His heart swelled as he stared at the sea dragon; then he turned to his master, who was gazing intently at the artifact.

Alma-Ata turned to his apprentice and commented: "A nice piece of work," and then added, "Now, let's off to the wharf. We've more work to do."

Nice, Glimmer thought to himself, *nice? Why not just say "cute"? Alma-Ata couldn't do it, and he wouldn't even compliment me for creating it.*

Alma-Ata had already skirted the building leading to the wharf. As the apprentice followed, behind Glimmer the dragon chimed its thousand songs of defiance, and as the wind picked up from off the sea, like an Aeolian harp, the wind across the wires produced hums and moans, even shrieks, depending on the size of armored dragon scales and supporting wire. Some larger wires produced a vibration heard more in the bones than the ears, a song opening within the body of the perceiver like an aural flower. Dogs began to howl, and cats yowled and spat at the wind.

At the quay, one bireme, shipping its oars, glided up to dock while the other ships held off. Alma-Ata headed for the ship, striding with purpose as townspeople milled about restlessly, their glances to the warship and then back to the glass dragon on the bluff. As the mage met the wharf, a gangplank was lowered and two black-bearded sailors walked it, carrying a small table and two stools. They set table and stools upon the wharf while another sailor who had followed placed two glasses and a bottle. The wharf then emptied of crew, except for the mage and his apprentice. A quiet settled, even the wind and the dragon song stilling to silence.

As Alma-Ata neared the table, a tall man dressed in rich crimson robes descended the gangplank, followed by a younger man. The tall man wore a hatchet-sharp black beard like the sailors, but his was streaked with grey. Down his back lay a long plait of hair. Reaching the table, the man settled on the stool to the seaward side, the young man attending behind. Alma-Ata strode to the empty stool and sat, Glimmer following, his position matching that of the young man opposite. As he stood behind his mage, Glimmer took in the tableau—the man opposite, richly appareled, sitting with an imperial demeanor; behind him, dressed more simply yet still elegant and refined, the young man, his smooth face haughty and arrogant; Alma-Ata sitting across dressed as a common freeman, linsey-woolsey and an old cloak of wool, Glimmer standing behind, wearing clothing one grade above rags.

A slight breeze stirred, and Glimmer could hear the music of the fire drake merging with sounds of the sea. *I created the dragon to stand off these pirates,* he thought, *and here I stand, a beggar apprenticed to a pauper! Or perhaps it is a pauper apprenticed to a beggar because what can Alma-Ata do but beg for mercy?*

The man smoothed the brocade of his jacket, his black, expressionless eyes boring into the eyes of Alma-Ata. "A strangeness, sailing to this port of the apple coast, yes, a strangeness." He paused, gauging the effect of his words. "Last night was a time for anger and then confusion. Men woke to serve their watch and discovered rings, earrings, necklaces gone; men at watch found ropes loose, fittings flown away." The man placed his hand to his belt. "Even I found missing my favorite knife, one with a copper blade. All items of the gentler metals—nothing of iron or steel gone." The man looked beyond the mage to the bluff opposite, the glass dragon glowing in the dawnlight, rampant with wings spread. "And then we reach our destination to find that—" he nodded at the dragon "—singing and chiming its song, something our . . . something not known by people who have visited here before. Strange magic . . . and I know magic, strange and otherwise."

The foreign mage paused, one eyebrow raised in anticipation of Alma-Ata's response, but Alma-Ata said nothing, only sat, his hands in his lap, as reposed as if he were awaiting breakfast at his own table. *Not waiting,* Glimmer thought, *no, not merely waiting—my mage is Gathering.* Glimmer caught the young man opposite . . . *it must be the foreign mage's apprentice,* he thought . . . appraising him with hooded eyes, distain in his countenance. He stiffened, glaring at the young man, and then stiffened in shock. He recognized those eyes!

"I am very good at ciphering magery," the foreign mage continued, "of ciphering the magery inherent within a man. You," he said to Alma-Ata, "are that most elusive of magicians, the mage who practices no magic, but whom magic gathers around. Your apprentice . . ." Here the foreign mage paused, thoughtful, his attention attuned to Glimmer. "I feel no magic whatsoever, yet . . . something hidden, tucked away in another place, out of sight." The foreign mage stared at Glimmer's hands, and then with his own the mage reached for the bottle on the table, taking his time with the cork.

"Some wine?" he asked Alma-Ata. The apple mage lifted his glass, and the foreign mage poured. Alma-Ata watched the foreign mage drink, and then he wet his lips with the wine. "I will tell you," advanced the foreign mage, "I am commanded to conquer or establish trade, whichever is most profitable." He smiled for the first time. "Which do you think I should do?"

Alma-Ata's response surprised Glimmer, and it caused the foreign mage to raise his brows. "Your apprentice needs discipline."

The foreign mage sucked in his breath and then let it out. "You speak at this juncture of my apprentice? . . . And you are correct." Glimmer's eyes, leaving the mages and focusing on the foreign apprentice, noticed the apprentice steel himself to exhibit no emotion, yet the foreign apprentice was not totally successful. A contraction of the chin, Glimmer thought he saw, and perhaps a tightening of the eyes. The richer cloth on the foreign apprentice's back was of no avail to his master's sharp words.

And he does not seem to recognize me, Glimmer thought, *although I wonder how much I gave away when I recognized him.*

Reaching to a pouch at his waist, the foreign mage extracted a deck of scrying cards, shuffled them, and placed half before Alma-Ata, placing the other half before himself. "To aid the conversation."

The foreign mage turned face up a card depicting a mage in white standing beneath a bright yellow sun. "Mage of Mages."

"I met DeVasier," Alma-Ata commented.

"He died three hundred years ago."

Alma-Ata turned face up the image of a man, waist wrapped with simple cloth, sitting cross-legged on a mountaintop, eyes closed and beatific expression on his face. "The Silent Saint. We must define our terms, beginning with *ago*."

"And including *death*," the foreign mage agreed.

Then the conversation between the two men abbreviated to a code that Glimmer could only half follow—and one that he could see the foreign apprentice also barely understood. Each bundle of words was accompanied with the flip of a card, revealing a new figure.

"The Silence of the Saints."

"Wind on Sand."

"The Great Teacher."

"The Dreamer."

"The Mage Beggar-Fool."

"He Who Divines with Stones."

"Yes," Alma-Ata replied, "and I can do it. Beyond space and time, I was graced with the knowledge."

"For him . . . and for me? After all, the apprentice cannot outstrip the master."

"Certainly."

The foreign mage rested his elbows upon the table. "Then it shall be trade. I shall get what is needed." He looked around. "Not everyone recognizes strength of spirit. But then that is why I accompany the ships." He appeared quite satisfied. "And the sea dragon that sings?"

Alma-Ata smiled, gesturing back toward Glimmer. "He is learning discipline, too."

"Ah," was the foreign mage's response, but his apprentice's eyes grew round with comprehension before lapsing back to feigned indifference.

Glimmer and the foreign apprentice mage stared at one another, no love lost. The foreign apprentice's lip curled slightly, and then the apprentice of refined dress returned his gaze to his mage. Again Glimmer compared the finery of the foreign mage to the work clothes that Alma-Ata wore, the fabrics rich in color and texture that adorned the foreign mage, the plain-spun garb of his master, greys of natural fiber and simple browns of common plant dyes.

How can we change the world, how can we protect the world, be uncommon, when we blend in with commonness so much that we disappear? thought Glimmer. *How can we be nobody and still accomplish something?*

Are you then going to proclaim yourself the creator of the glass dragon? a voice within the apprentice questioned. *And how shall the people receive you? Even if they received you well, would that improve their lot or yours?*

And what's wrong with improving my own lot? Glimmer asked himself. Then he imagined the stone dragon speaking, the obsidian eye stripping him of pretense: *And how shall you define "improve"?*

The wind increased, and the singing symphony of the sea drake set dogs to howling again. A chill inched Glimmer's back even as his heart leapt with emotions the music stirred. He watched the sailors on the ship beside the wharf and saw them stir uneasily. Yes, there was magic in the dragon's music, magic to stir the people of the coast to love their land, magic to give pause for those who would covet it. *Nice,* Alma-Ata had described the glass dragon. Glimmer remembered his dream, his hands full of liquid glass, lifting a great ball of it to his chest and carrying it to the cliff, the heat of the red liquid merely warm to his skin.

Not the creation but the act of creating—that was what remained in Glimmer's memory. Even now, the actual glass artifact meant little to him, but the memory of creation flowing through his consciousness and extending to his arms, his hands, and on out into the world—oh! That stirred in his heart like fire dancing on hearthstone.

Mage and mage, apple and foreign, stood, and the foreign mage signaled to the docked warship. A horn belled its tone into the morning air, a flag was raised, and the sailor-warriors on the deck relaxed and looked to the town with the demeanor of sailors expecting leave rather than battle.

"I have a room on the ship, private and quiet—once the crew is granted leave."

"Then I will see you after your midday dinner," Alma-Ata responded.

The foreign mage paused before returning to the ship, stroked his beard thoughtfully, and then commented, "I have never before worked with a Mage Who Gathers. A most subtle and enlightening experience." Gesturing to Alma-Ata's garb, he added, "Not one to fill your coffers, though—mine, but not yours. I would not fancy your magery," to which Alma-Ata replied with a monosyllabic, "Ah," and then turned and strode away on the rough planks back to the solid land, Glimmer following, feeling the eyes of the other apprentice cold upon his back.

Off the wharf and back on land, Alma-Ata turned to his apprentice as Delta's aldermen anxiously hurried to the wharf, still adjusting their robes of office and wiping sleep from their eyes as they vainly attempted to take in both the glass dragon and the foreign fleet simultaneously. "I think we've earned some food, lad. They," he said, nodding to the cluster of elders, "should be able to handle the rest. They're more canny than they look at the moment."

"And what exactly did we accomplish?" the apprentice replied, his lack of understanding making him petulant. "I couldn't follow what went on."

"The mage and his apprentice, you mean?"

"Yes," Glimmer replied, feeling the heat of his frustration rising. "What actually happened there on the wharf?"

"That mage is greedy . . . and crafty. He doesn't know what to make of that glass dragon . . . but he has his suspicions. You see, it was magic beyond his means. He is a diviner, with the fleet to determine the results of actions before they occur." Alma-Ata turned and gazed back at the bireme, the cluster of aldermen standing around the table and stools in uncertainty. "There's going to be trade; the sailors won't sack the town. You did that, son." The apprentice experienced a surge of pride until the mage added, "Or I should say, the sea drake and its magic did."

"But you made some kind of bargain. What was that?"

"It's a truly strange thing, son. The apprentice is, like you, a dream mage."

Glimmer stared at Alma-Ata as they entered the inn and sat to break their fast. A hush fell as they entered the room. Others that were eating covertly glanced at them with circumspect whispers. The apprentice realized that their time with the foreign mage and apprentice on the wharf had not gone unobserved. He sat down, Alma-Ata's words sinking into his awareness.

"I didn't hear any of that in what you said."

Alma-Ata chuckled. "Your counterpart probably didn't either." He shook his head. "That other mage, he must spend a great deal of time around court—likes to glitter like a jewel." He grinned at his apprentice. "Notice I didn't say *glimmer*." Alma-Ata continued. "So I played by his rules, pared away the fat of our words." Alma-Ata stretched out his legs luxuriously. "Wasn't too hard for me. I'm used to silence—he, on the other hand, probably guards his words because of who's listening. A dangerous man, though. Any man backed by swords is dangerous."

Glimmer paused, thinking. Porridge was served, along with hot tea. Glimmer sipped his, almost expecting savory cabbage. He smiled to himself and then asked, "How did you know the apprentice needed discipline . . . and that he was a dream mage? Did the scrying cards tell you?"

"A true seer doesn't need the cards any more than a bird needs walking shoes."

"But the diviner thought them important."

"The world is as we are, boy," Alma-Ata said forcefully. "Best to consider the cards an amusement."

"Why?"

"Because one man sees the Serpent and thinks 'death' while another sees the Snake and says, 'Ah, my garden shall be blessed with snakes and not rodents.'"

"Perhaps the man who sees death is right and not the man who sees a healthy garden."

"It isn't *death* or *garden* that is significant: it is the *perhaps*. Better to use your common sense; better yet to meditate and use your cosmic sense."

"So how did you know the apprentice was a dream mage?"

"Pretty obvious the apprentice thinks he's somebody special. His master may be arrogant but he's got caution—has a good measure of himself. The apprentice, though, seemed arrogant . . . and yet comfortable with the glass dragon, the loss of metal from the ships." The mage scratched his head. "The mage knows enough to see the danger of an arrogant apprentice dream mage."

Glimmer opened his mouth to speak, but Alma-Ata cut him off. "And you're not arrogant. An apprentice, yes, but not arrogant. You've seen the danger, lived it, in and out of your dreams." The mage paused to scrape his porridge bowl and then gulp tea. "I do not fear over-confidence on your part, young apprentice. Rather, I fear intoxication, that you grow intoxicated with your dream, and lose yourself . . . and us . . . in the fantasia of your dreaming."

The two men, mage and apprentice, sat in thoughtful silence. *Perhaps this is why he does not over-praise me,* thought Glimmer. *Perhaps he fears of waking to nightmare. I know I do,* he honestly appraised.

"I saw the apprentice in my dream, during my magic," Glimmer told his master. Alma-Ata sat back, listening, receptive. "All were asleep as I collected metal—*their metal*—to increase the magic's power. All were asleep except the apprentice. His eyes were open, watching."

"I'm sure it was magic worth watching," admitted Alma-Ata.

Glimmer felt an upsurge of affection for his master's fairness. "And so what was your bargain?" he asked, happiness in his voice.

Alma-Ata smiled slightly at his apprentice's improved humor. "I will teach them the Silence of the Saints, what they call the meditation of Wind on Sand."

Surprised, Glimmer asked, "But how can you teach this? You already told me no one in this time knows . . ."

"Until DeVasier taught me how to teach."

"In the two weeks wrapped in the few days that you were with him?"

"Exactly," the mage replied, laughing. "A few days, and each day a few weeks. Something like that. *Time* was somewhat fluid . . . at the time." The mage rose. "Now let us go outside and to the wharf. It is time to teach these foreign mages some discipline."

"And what if it makes them better pirates?"

"It will," Alma-Ata responded, laughing again. "And what is a better pirate?" The mage continued laughing at Glimmer's bemused look. Slapping the apprentice on the shoulder, the mage guided him from the inn. "When a pirate becomes very, very good, we call him a *merchant*."

Alma-Ata threw back his head and roared. Then, wiping tears from his eyes, mage and apprentice continued down the street to the wharf.

As they reached the bireme docked at the wharf, a sailor on board waved them aboard. "You wait here," Alma-Ata commanded, gesturing to the table and chairs still on the wharf, and then mounted the gangplank onto the gently rocking ship.

Glimmer sat down on the stool on which Alma-Ata had sat and rested his elbows on the table. He looked out to sea, the foreign ships sitting sharp and clean in the water like axe blades in a smithy's bucket, their lean lines slicing at the dignity of the older Delta ships, which were stained with hauls of fish and the work of many seasons.

Above, the gulls cried and swooped, searching to snatch a morsel of food from remnants of a meal or swill from a ship's galley, and when a gull did find its treasure, it then had to protect it from the predations of other gulls. The ships in the harbor were like that, filled with men who took from the sea or from one another.

We are like the gulls, he thought, *stealing what we need to live, jealous of our offal, not wanting it yet wanting no one else to possess it, either.* He sighed and closed his eyes and then opened them, hearing footsteps on the gangplank.

The young foreign apprentice walked casually down the gangplank, his tailored black breeches and long crimson coat clean and elegant in the mid-morning light. His beard was sparse with youth but still cut in the squared fashion of the other foreigners. He sat easily on the stool, his knees widespread and his back erect.

"I am here to practice your speech, Applelander," he announced, staring down his nose as Glimmer, "although I have no enthusiasm for learning nuances of ignorance." He paused, considering Glimmer. "Your mage speaks like an educated man. What of you?"

Glimmer stared stonily at the foreign apprentice.

"One might say that I don't want my first impression of your language to leave a rotten taste in my mouth."

At the apprentice's smirk, Glimmer was tempted to say the foreign apprentice could kiss his apple if he wanted a memorable first impression, but his conversations with the stone dragon bade him to hold his tongue. Instead, he countered with, "Every barrel hides a rotten apple," and then added on an inspiration, "just as every dream hides a nightmare." He was pleased to note the stiffening of the foreign apprentice's face.

The young man then let out a breath and admitted to Glimmer, "My master said we should talk . . . until it is my time with your master. You are Glimmer? An interesting name. I am apprentice to Mage Khalil. My name is Ramadi, which means *grey*. Another interesting name, hm? And so, do you speak in some manner other than epigrams?"

"Sure," Glimmer replied, aware of his stubbornness and not caring of its consequences.

"I am interested in the dragon. My master says it is yours . . . perhaps."

Glimmer now saw how the conversation of mages could become so cryptic. "It is difficult to claim . . . that which is the stuff of dreams."

"And yet the focus—and the danger . . ."

"Wind on Sand."

"Ah . . . and yet sand is apt to shift."

"The Wisdom of Stone is contained in each grain of sand."

Ramadi sighed and then confessed, "So I hope . . . and then perhaps I can sleep." He then drew himself up again, pulling round his pride like armor. "Not tonight, though, with that thing"—he motioned at the glass dragon—"moaning all night and the dogs and cats yowling down the moon with it."

"You'd be surprised," Glimmer murmured.

At that moment, Ramadi's mage called from the deck. "Come, apprentice," he said in a voice subdued. The mage stood at the ship's railing, gazing down on the two apprentices. "Come with me, lad," he said, and turned away from the wharf, returning below, his carriage less aggressive than before.

Ramadi turned to the gangplank and then suddenly turned back to the sitting apprentice, his face an ugly tangle of emotion. "I think it was you who saved the town with yon dragon, apprentice. So your town will stay free—free to suffer from moans and clanks of glass. The people will be like dogs, free to howl and moan, free to slink about, tails between legs, furtively glancing over their shoulders. Who will wish now to trade at this port, to sleep to sounds which turn bowels to water, to live here?" The apprentice laughed and then abruptly stopped, his emotions choking even the façade of amusement.

"I saw the amulet you wear at your neck," Glimmer offered placatingly. "It was crafted by dream magery." He added truthfully, "Such focus and attention to detail . . . I could not—"

"Do not mock me!" Ramadi shouted, his face livid with rage. He pointed to the glass sea drake on the bluff. "You created that!"

Ramadi lapsed to silence, staring silently at Glimmer, and then added harshly, "Maybe one day I'll teach you the eternal silence of stones—from the inside out," and added bitterly, "assuming we both live that long." Ramadi's face contorted with acrimony and another emotion—fear, Glimmer realized. "Thief in the night," Ramadi hissed.

As he mounted the gangplank, words left Glimmer's mouth, "Brother in dreams." Ramadi's steps hesitated as the words reached him, and then the apprentice disappeared from view. *We are brothers,* Glimmer thought, even though he had not intended the words. *We both have reason to fear.*

Alone in the silence, Glimmer felt tired. Too many miles had he traveled; too many new experiences had he seen. Too many people had crowded about him, jostling his elbows and bumping as he walked, or staring as he sat and ate. He was too much with the world and the aimless meandering of souls lost in the morass of life. Life was yammering at him and set his teeth on edge. The sun was tilting toward the sea, and Glimmer felt hunger, having missed midday dinner. He was even more hungry, though, for simplicity, for the absolute certainties of the world—the certainty that the sun would sink into the sea as it always had before, the certainties of wind and waves and otters cracking mussels on their stomachs with stones as they floated on the water.

He scooted the stool so that it touched one of the pilings at the sea's edge of the wharf. Off into the distance, the sea became one with the sky, the horizon a haze of misty blues. Glimmer closed his eyes, needing the silence possessed not just by the saints but the silent fabric of the world around him and the essence of the secret world. The sea and the sky and the clouds lulled him, *so peaceful,* he thought, *so right.*

Glimmer stood on the wharf, watching the sleeping body that was his, a body sitting easily on a stool, back leaning against the round piling sunk deep into mud beneath the waters. The young man's eyes were closed, his head tilted slightly to one side, his mouth slightly open, his breathing shallow.

What a beautiful day to take a nap, he thought, *and how efficient, to sleep and work at the same time!*

And then Glimmer was standing beside the glass dragon on the bluff above the town, sun slipping more swiftly toward its briny desire. The sea drake moaned in sepulchral tones, and glass scales whispered in the bated breath of the sea. Dream mage resonated with the music of the dragon's singing, and galaxies danced within his body. He raised his hands, feeling a different vibration, his hands greened and ambered in their spinning, halfway between mountain and sea, waves of grass rich in music bursting from the seed. Seed-joy flowed from his hands, nature creating itself again and again, silence the mother of dynamism and dynamism the father of silence. Touching the sea drake like a fiddler tuning his instrument, Glimmer quelled the calls to war and ill to foes, conjured the harmony of prairie and sea, the diversity of all parts within the whole.

Nice dragon: the dream mage's thoughts slithered sideways. *Nice?* He was sick of that word. *Nice dragon, nice conversation, nice job, nice nap!* Why not give them something to talk about? Why not give them a terrible lizard that sings with a bloody beak!

Wind rose and clouds covered the sun. The glass sea drake screamed like a raptor, stretched its neck to the sky, glass scales metamorphosing to flesh, wings of translucent leather iridescent with dragon's blood. Glimmer stepped back, dropping to his knees and clapping his hands to his ears at the dragon's shriek, his eyes pressed shut as if eyelids could block the sound. The dragon spotted movement and focused its eyes upon the mage, hungry eyes, predator eyes locked to prey. Filling its lungs, the dragon arched its neck and opened its jaws, teeth like daggers, white scimitars of death.

Glimmer opened his eyes and saw nightmare before him. The sea drake was risen, neck reaching high into the sky, wings outstretched like a gigantic cobra's hood. Glass cooled and hardened was once again molten and moving. The mage dodged to his left, but a leathern wing slammed to earth to block his escape. He jerked his head to the right and leaned to flight, but the dragon's other wing slammed the earth before he could even move. Dust choked the air.

Nice dragon, you say, hissed the terror, *and that indeed is one of my aspects. But another is not so nice, no, and you feel it, don't you, as you slip into nightmare, slip into nightmare . . . nightmare . . .*

Glimmer fell to his knees, his eyes locked with the dragon's, his head shifting left and right, shaking yes and no in rhythm to the dragon's hypnotic movements. Then his view was blocked. Gentle hands pressed against his hands, gentle hands pressed against his eyes, and an urgent voice said, "Ally of mine ye are, an' Ally am I to ye. No time for dreamin'," and Cabbage-pants lanced Glimmer's arm with a tiny knife of rainbowed obsidian. "It takes a thorn t' remove a thorn," the gravelly voice added as the nightmare popped like a bubble of molten lava.

The sun was shining as Glimmer tipped forward on his stool and fell to his knees. He grabbed his forearm and pulled back the sleeve. A small puncture bled, red blood on white skin. The pain felt clean and pure after the phantasmagoria of the nightmare.

Frantically, the mage leapt to his feet and raced the length of the dock, through the streets and up the trail to the bluff's crest to confront the dragon. Of glass it was made, glass body and glass scales hung with metal, and the wind sang within it a merciless cry. Hungry it was, and its eyes gleamed with life desiring to somehow move, just one tiny tremor to gain its freedom. That is what it desired more than anything, to fly the briny sky above the sea. Breath in gasps, Glimmer beheld the nightmare, the daymare seeking to crack its chrysalis and feed. He straightened and advanced to the glass reptile, its eyes glaring hungrily at him, advanced and placed his hands against the glass body, warmed by sun or inner fire.

"Rest," he said, "sleep," and *Rest when hunger is sated* coursed his blood, *Sleep when belly is full.* Seed-joy rose within him, through him, and glass acquiesced and slept, dreamt songs of hope resurrected from ashes of annihilation.

To those who watched, the glass dragon shivered in the wind, the pitch of its song reaching to bone and finding favor as a tuning fork sings of resonance. Pitch mellowed, moan mended, and the shining scales and woven wires caught the song of beginnings, the song of all beginnings— first wind to new sailcloth, low tide and virgin sand, fragrant scent from a thousand miles of ocean. Seed-joy sang, and all who heard the song smiled. And at the end of one pier, within one of the foreign ships, a conversation halted. An old man dressed in apple farmer's work clothes turned his head slightly to the shore, felt the change in the song on the wind, felt the change and accepted the magic that surrounded him.

Glimmer finally turned to town and sea, his eyes no longer commanded by the sculpture. The townspeople gazed at the sea dragon, awed and uplifted by its benevolent transformation. The young man sat upon the sand at the sculpture's base, sagged against one of the sea drake's legs. He was drained and yet so relieved, the sound of the wind in the sculpture, the clear notes of the scales a harmonious chiming. He sat and gazed at the ocean and at nothing, and then he closed his eyes and listened to the silence beneath the music.

He opened his eyes after a time, knowing what he had done—remembering the nightmare he had almost loosed. *How many times will it be before I wake to disaster,* he wondered—*have eaten the wrong food or am bit by insect or leery of wind moaning in the ribs of a glass dragon? Or lured by a petty peeve into shadows and then let destruction loose upon the world?* He wept from remorse and relief.

Ally of mine, Glimmer thought, his hand going to the tender spot on his arm. Opening his eyes, he looked around, and there beside him, back against the glass dragon's base, sat Cabbage-pants.

"I ask again. You're one of them, aren't you—one of the Silent Ones."

"An' I answer again: silence an' action are one within the other."

"But you *were* one of them, weren't you . . ."

The gnome considered for a moment, gazing thoughtfully at the glass dragon looming over them. "Aye, there was a time when I was silent."

"And you're from the Dragon's Spine?"

"From many places, all and none." The gnome then stood upon his stocky legs and said, "And to there I best return."

"Are you here in a dream?" Glimmer asked in bemused words, spoken almost to himself.

"Are ye yer dream?" the gnome asked sharply.

"No," was the reply, although Glimmer could not understand the significance of the question.

"If ye are not th' dream, neither are ye th' wakin'. Consider yer place, young apprentice," and then the gnome walked into the grasses lipping the hill, a diminutive image of the apple mage, striding into the distance and then disappearing.

The town was draped in shadow, and in the eastern sky, the brightest stars already adorned the dark velvet of the night. The bluff above Delta still basked in the remembrance of light and reflected a white glow from its pale surface. Where the bluffs rose in a half moon east of the town opposite the sea, the last ruddy rays of the sun illumined an object that gathered the light of the setting sun and was incandescent with a rainbow of solar fires. The winds had increased, whipping waves white with scud. The cold breath of the sea swept the land, and the young apprentice shivered. If he were not the dream and not the waking, certainly neither was he the inertia of sleep. *Then what am I?* From the sea, wind silently touched the young mage, touched and then was gone, was nothing. Silence. Glimmer sat, suspended within poised silence.

"Be patient with magic," he imagined a gravelly voice speaking. "The voice of silence will speak in its own time."

He sighed, then stood and slowly walked down to sea and wharf and stool. Sitting to face the shore, he saw the glass dragon facing out to sea, wings stretched wide as if to embrace the emptiness, as if to envelop ships sailing to port—glass sea drake hardened by the fires of creation, to a longevity equivocal to the lifespan of stars and comets with their tails of frozen, refracted light; a fire dragon of beautiful, predacious intent, singing joyfully in rhythms of wind which are the rhythms of the sea churned by the inexorable spinning of the earth upon its dragon-fletched tail.

The dragon filled itself with light and sang of the forces of nature, of fire and wind and the molten conflagrations of the earth. It stood upon the bluff, poised to leap skyward, casting a last glance to the town on the delta, granting a last and least gift to those who lived at the mouth of the River Quill. Grace it granted to ships with holds filled with fair-weather and friendly intent, transformation to those filled with ill will and storm.

Closing his eyes, Glimmer could still see the terrific awakening of the glass dragon perched above the town, larger than any ship in port. Whether with the imaginative eye of the creator or with the refined sensibilities of the saints, whether with the memory of the maker of the beast a heartbeat from breaking its glass chains, the fiery beauty of the dragon glowed on the pedestal of the young mage's inner sight.

What is the greater danger, sailors with hatchet beards and shining swords, or myself, my magic expanding like lava vomited from the earth? What happens when man and magma meet, when magic and madness merge?

Bootsteps on the gangplank heralded Alma-Ata's descent to the wharf, his chin to his chest as if he looked not just to the placement of his feet but also to the placement of his thoughts. Walking past his apprentice, he silently nodded his head toward the shore, bidding Glimmer to follow. They swept the length of the wharf and up to their room in the inn, gathering their satchels and bedrolls.

"We're off tonight; there's moon enough," the mage murmured and lengthened his stride to a steady rhythm acquired through itinerant years.

The air freshened as they left the town and its effluvia of fishing and trade, although the delta air still retained a stagnant flavor unknown in the wind-swept uplands the Stone Dragon Inn bordered. Glimmer hearkened for rolling grasslands rather than sea grasses patched among white sand. Alma-Ata too seemed invigorated by the freshness of the air, breathing deeply as he strode along the road. The gibbous moon rode the night sky, lighting their way along the ruts and gullies. It was cold but not a debilitating cold, the first days of winter tempered by the presence of the sea.

"An interesting experience, teaching the mage and apprentice," Alma-Ata finally said when they had walked long enough for the wind to wash the town from their sensibilities. Their cloaks were belted around them, hoods covered their heads, and satchels and bedrolls were shouldered one to each side for balance. "Teaching the mage was easy—effortless, as a matter of fact. He is greedy but not wicked." The mage paused as they continued walking, their footsteps in concert upon the moonlit road. "The apprentice, though . . . His need to control was overwhelming. And it wasn't just a need to control . . . more, I think, a need to dominate, to assert his preeminence." He reflected in silence, their footsteps dark echoes upon the earth. "I do not envy his mage. That apprentice will be a tribulation—and a danger—to himself, his mage, to the whole world, perhaps. It depends upon his talent."

Glimmer thought about the mage's words, remembered his conversation with Ramadi, and then replied to Alma-Ata. "He was afraid of nightmares during *dreaming*. He should be; I know I am." The apprentice considered his feelings, his words filtering through recent experience. "Control is important. I don't have it. I didn't plan the sea drake and then fall asleep and do it. I didn't decide to change the song and then doze off to do it. It took place within the dreaming," and because he could not yet speak the ugly facts, he spoke the ugly truth that lay coiled like a viper within him. "I could have done anything, something terrible, just as well."

They continued along the moonlit road which skirted the river, the moon behind them climbing in the night sky. The temperature dropped further, and their breath misted the air as they stopped a moment to rest and catch their breath.

"That was a quick bit of magery you did, lad, changing the dragon's song during your catnap." The mage chuckled a frosty breath. "I felt the glass song of the beast change. It was like a sore spot at the base of the skull that built to a bubble then burst." He chuckled. "It was a blessing to the peace, to goodwill."

Mage and apprentice turned and continued their journey, glad to be moving again in the chill of the night air. They walked nearly a mile, their footsteps rippling the stillness of the night, each immersed in his individual thoughts.

"It is difficult, apprentice, to discuss dream magery," Alma-Ata finally continued, "because so little is known of it. Let us consider, for instance, the slender volume you now possess on dream magery. We know little of the mage, not even his name, yet there is one fact we know for certain: his magical talent, his power, was very weak."

"How do you know this?" Glimmer challenged, pulled from his reverie to defend the slender tome and its dream mage.

"Because all we know of him is from that book. No Slag Hills are credited to his magic; no sickness rises from the earth that he has dreamt. His name is not spat like vomita rising from the stomach. And what is the greatest dream that he discusses, his greatest act?"

"He doesn't talk about his magic like that. But he does discuss changing the latch and hinges of a door from one side to the other. But that was just an example, I think."

"I think not. I think he practiced dream magic only a few times in his life." The mage stopped abruptly and grabbed Glimmer by the shoulders with his hands. The apprentice could see the dark gleam of his master's eyes by moonlight, framed by the shadow of his cowl. "That doesn't matter, though!" the mage exclaimed. He dropped his hands and continued along their route which now wound for a time away from the river, following the off-side of a hill along a route less marshy. "The Dream Mage, we shall call him, was not a great mage, but he was a great scholar. He took his small handful of experiences and came to understand the principles which undergirt them. His gift was not his pathetic talent but his brilliant scholarship."

Glimmer was amazed at Alma-Ata's volubility, not solely because his master rarely spoke much but also because he continued to progress down the road in a distance-eating pace. "What is truly the dream is that we control the events around us, or more precisely, that *we* that seek to control events are isolate and separate from that which surrounds us. It is not that we control the arrow leaving the bow. The forces of nature cause it to leap from the string. The laws of nature structure our sight, our muscles and sinew, even our thoughts. It is not a matter of controlling something else; rather, it is a matter of tracing the intent to its source."

The mage slowed his pace, uncharacteristically placing his arm around Glimmer's shoulders. "The mage does not control the dream, lad. Dreams, by their very nature, are too fluid—dreamlike! Like comes from like. You practice your dream magery—the rest of us live the illusion of our lives—and the magical means of the world gather to weave the reality we dream. For some it is a safe and secure nest, for others a spider's web laced with dew, for some a cage of cold iron bars. Like comes from like."

The mage removed his arm from Glimmer's shoulders, and they continued on their way, side by side, beneath the silence of the moon. In their silent advance, the apprentice finally said, "The foreign apprentice said he'd turn me to stone."

Alma-Ata grunted in response, continuing with his long-shanked stride. "It was very difficult to teach Ramadi because he was not innocent. For him, manipulation is like breathing." Sighing into the silence, the mage continued. "The Silence of the Saints will quiet the foreign apprentice's nerves but not his ambition, or at least not soon. That ambition is a vein of ore that runs deep in him. He is jealous of you, lad—and scared of you because he knows what he would do if he could wield the power you did to turn sand to glass, to remove the jewelry from men sleeping miles at sea."

"It is less power than he thinks."

"And more power than he knows." The mage uttered a final word before lapsing into silence: "Even stones have veins. Beware."

In the early morning hours Glimmer stumbled, nearly asleep on his feet. They lay their satchels beneath the low-spreading branches of a fir tree, the rich scent of evergreen a balm to their weariness. Days more they trudged the road, seeing few travelers and many blackbirds, seeking to make the stone inn. Night and weariness overcame them, and they unrolled their blankets in the portion of Jurgen's Wood that lay between the Twill and the road. Gathering fallen leaves, they placed their blankets upon the rustling russet mattress and then lay within folded blankets, heaping more insulating leaves upon themselves.

After three days of worrying the bone, Glimmer finally asked his master the question that had dogged their footsteps all the way from Delta. "Why did we leave so soon? Was something wrong?" *Do you know what happened when I changed the dragon's song?* his mind asked.

Alma-Ata spoke as silence gathered around them. "We left quickly because our absence will make us seem greater than we are." The apprentice could almost feel the mage's smile in the thick darkness. "Stagery, not magery. Of course, changing the sea drake's song won't hurt any, either, so quick and easy for you the act appears."

As the silence deepened, Glimmer asked, "Why should I beware the foreign apprentice?"

"Because he is clever but not wise."

"But will not Wind on Sand increase his wisdom? Won't it increase mine?"

"Absolutely. The wound has begun to heal for Ramadi, but which will prevail, the healing or the un-healing, I do not know. You are right to desire control. The gnomes began in harmony and sought to bring it to men, yet how many of us neither see nor believe that land and life is anything more than the tough skin of a seed that resists the knife? Press the harder, then curse the knife that slips and slices the hand."

Glimmer's hand touched the sheathed obsidian blade at his belt, and he was glad he wore no metal, was glad that his blade was of the same earth-gift as a gnome was willing to wear. He drifted to a deep sleep, the rustling of his leafy bed fragrant with the abiding wisdom of the earth.

Chapter 10

Nature layered by God's owne hand,
Divinely ordered, cloth and strand.
Earth and water, fire and air,
Space alone, and minde so fair;
That which reasones, and the *my* of mine,
Thus is the nature of all mankinde.

"Divine Song," 7.4

ॐ

Day past first light but still deep in morning found the mage and apprentice leaving the chill, dapple shade of leaf-bare trees and crossing the stone bridge at the Stone Dragon Inn. Sounds greeted them before the sight of the inn met their eyes: a smithy hammer striking iron, a rooster proclaiming his royal heritage, a woman's voice singing a silly song.

Oh, Tommy, oh! Oh, Tommy, ay!
Where 'ave ye gone this pretty day?
Tomcattin', Tomfool, oh, peepin' me Tom,
With days so short and nights so long.

Laying wet clothing upon the stone fencing the garden, Bega was singing to a pile of laundry. She danced with a grey undertunic as a partner and bowed to a patched set of breeches.

"All's well in the world when Bega sings," called out the mage. Glimmer took in smoke rising from the inn's chimney, the pale sun a tepid warmth on the eastern stone walls bright in sunlight. No wind brushed the smallest branches of the trees. He breathed in deeply the prairie smells of the dormant earth, so different from the sea with its movement and its mysteries, each so varied in beauty.

Bega waved happily, continuing to place the wet clothing to dry beneath the sun. A rooster strolled around the side of the inn, pecking the ground for seed. "Let's break our fast together!" Alma-Ata shouted to the woman, who replied, "Day's been up two hour. Ye think we haven't put somethin' in our stomachs yet? We'll sit with ye, though . . . and be hearin' th' news an' tellin' it."

Breakfast for the travelers, however, was not to be a narrative of their adventures. As Alma-Ata and Glimmer sat down in the kitchen to a meal of eggs and biscuits and gravy, Bega sat down with them, along with her daughter. Entering later, after the two travelers had set to their meal, was the stableman, Wilim, a man who now talked little and listened much. He entered unobtrusively, standing near the fireplace in the kitchen as the others sat at the intimate and homey table. He said nothing, sipping at a mug of tea and warming himself by the cooking fire. He watched the others, his eyes fastening on one speaker after the other, sometimes his brow furrowing, sometimes clearing to a look of comprehension.

"Look here, man," Bega finally said, "sit ye down here wi' us—if'n ye don't mind," she amended, shifting her attention to Alma-Ata.

"No, of course not," the mage replied, catching Wilim's eyes with sudden attention and remembrance of when last he had seen him.

Wilim settled tentatively at first and then sat down with sudden decision. Alma-Ata continued to consider the man and finally asked him, his voice soft as if addressing a skittish animal, "Well, man, ye've something to say, a question, mayhap?" Glimmer noted the slip of the mage's speech to the vernacular, the more familiar the words for their commonness.

Wilim cleared his throat and then spoke. "Have ye magicked me, master?"

"Why say ye so?"

Wilim glanced at Bega and then at Elesia. "I've been thinkin' more than usual, tha's all. Been thinkin' deeper and . . . wonderin' about things, noticin' things." He stammered to a halt and then spoke again. "Is't a spell ye've conjured or is't this place? Have ye magicked this place, these stones?"

"Do ye feel somethin' wrong, somethin' dark has 'appened t' ye?" the mage asked in the silence.

"Nay," the man replied, "I don't feel bedeviled 'r anythin'," his words thickening with emotion.

The fire popped and crackled on the hearth, and the light from the small window high on the rounded stone wall cast a feeble light onto those sitting around the small, rough table. Glimmer stared at Wilim, whose eyes no longer stared with a vacant cast, who now sat a part of the group, the center of the group, and understanding the why of it. Silence stretched until the mage murmured, "It's not for me to explain, Wilim—to you, Wilim, and you, too, Bega and Elesia. It is for my apprentice to explain. I'd like to understand, too." The mage turned his thin face to his apprentice and waited.

The sudden attention of all put Glimmer's heart to beating like a rabbit's, and like a rabbit, he wished for a sudden briar patch to lose himself. Wilim's gaze focused even more with determination. "Have ye magicked me?"

Glimmer settled to the words, to the question, feeling more confidence with the direction of the words. He could almost hear the dragon's phrasing as he spoke. "Magic has not been done to you but, rather, awakened within you."

Casting her eyes on Wilim, Bega straightened at the words. "I had not met ye before our move here, but the mage's words rang true with th' first look o' ye: 'A good man for simple things to be done.'"

"There was a pinch inside you, Wilim, a knot, ye might say. I had the thought—wondered—how ye might be if that knot were untied. I should've asked," he apologized.

"Nay, how would I 'ave understood ye, anyway?"

"An' you just thought this, an' it happened?" Elesia asked, more bold than her usual self, awed curiosity overcoming her reticent nature.

"Well," the young mage replied, reticent himself to discuss the circumstances, "a common kindness thought in uncommon circumstances." Glimmer watched a small smile form on Alma-Ata's lips. Glimmer turned to Wilim, the man's direct stare now dimmed with introspection. "When last we spoke," Glimmer nodded to Alma-Ata who silently listened, his face half in dim shadow, "the mage said you woke up. That's all I did—or, rather, all that magic did. There was a knot, and I untied it. You're still going to have to decide what to do with the rope."

"An' ye had no plan to do't?"

"Not a bit of a plan." Glimmer shrugged at the man's dubious expression. "Sometimes the mage seeks the magic; sometimes the magic seeks the mage."

Wilim met the young mage's gaze. "A man shouldna spend his life asleep." His speech slowed and became more formal. "I do not understand th' all of it, but give you my thanks."

"I do not understand the all of it, either," Glimmer replied, "but I am glad to have done no harm."

"If I leave here, will th' magic leave me?"

"No, the magic was in you . . . and always will be."

Wilim looked to Alma-Ata and then to Bega. "If ye don't mind, I think I'll be stayin'."

"And we'll be the better for 't," the elder mage replied. "And later," he added, "let me get a book of smithing for ye." Alma-Ata nodded to the others. "Maybe we can teach ye t' read." A look of wonder and determination filled Wilim's face, his eyes reflecting the dim light of the kitchen.

The adventures at Delta were not told at that sitting. Too much magic close at hand dulled the telling of magic far away. The story did out in bits and pieces over the following fortnight, over breakfast porridge and evening tea and the work of the day. Days and weeks passed, the routine of inn-keeping and self-keeping occupying the cold winter hours. Alma-Ata stayed, as was more his habit during the cold months when winds swept snow from the mountains or frozen mists from the sea. Slowly the minds of those who had stayed at the inn filled with the image of a glass dragon upon a bluff, poised to strike biremes stealthily gliding shoreward in the grey light of early dawn. Bega barked orders to the apprentice with a new degree of moderation, and her daughter observed the young man more intently beneath the thin blonde bangs fringing her eyes. Wilim said his *sires* to Glimmer just as he did to Alma-Ata.

The height of the change, though, was Alma-Ata's remark to Glimmer the day of their return. Alone in the mage's study, Glimmer heard these words from his master: "What you said to Wilim today, lad, those were the words of a mage."

Alma-Ata did not and could not provide his apprentice with that which would tame his inner fires, and the transformation of the sea drake was a memory of a nightmare that haunted Glimmer. The master spent more time with Glimmer, though, spent more time in his study sitting silently with his apprentice, eyes closed in meditation; in either circumstance, the well of uncertainty and despair within Glimmer remained empty of hope, and even apprentice knew enough to accept that a well is filled from deep within, not from the lip by a bucket and a rope. He took his happiness day by day, bucket by bucket, closed his eyes to find silence, and waited for spring, for deep waters to thaw and flow.

Another cloud dampened Glimmer's spirits during this time. Even though he had regularly found time alone to be in the common room before the hearth, no obsidian eye had found him out. To his sleeping quarters he had brought the brazier filled with glowing coals, but no miniature dragon had appeared to laze above the tiny mountain of coals in their brazen sea. He had practiced no dream magic, but then there had been no need. In his bones the young mage knew that dream magic was not a craft to advance by rote drill. Dream magic had this, at least, in common with the magic of Gathering. *Dream until you get it right. Do nothing until you get it right!* Glimmer smiled. He couldn't imagine even the sternest master demanding such things.

Glimmer puzzled over his successes . . . and failures . . . and puzzled over the silence of the stone dragon. The stone dragon had never been exactly friendly—like a lap dog, as the dragon had compared, yet it had never been openly adversarial, either. Its demeanor had been aloof, true—one could say haughty—but according to its nature, not its specific intent. After all, it was a dragon, Glimmer reasoned, and considered itself superior—or of a separate class—to humans. And it was probably—no, certainly—correct, he further considered. So what had happened to the dragon? Had it somehow escaped, or was it sleeping or for some reason hiding? The young mage chuckled to himself. Was it hibernating for the winter?

A fortnight of silence extended, pressing these questions to the fore of Glimmer's mind, and he found no recourse but to gnaw them as a dog gnaws its bone. Alma-Ata, now that winter was full upon them—even past its full, like moon waning from its glut—had taken to staying longer periods in his study, wrapped in blanket and meditating on the Silence of the Saints.

Mage DeVasier gave me the cruelest blow, the young mage thought: he had provided the Mage Who Practiced No Magic the means to transcend the arena where magic was practiced, where *becoming* stilled to *being*. The Mage Who Gathered now practiced the ultimate refinement of his magery: he Gathered nothing. Even with his master beside him, Glimmer still felt alone.

Glimmer threw himself onto his sleeping pallet one evening, his hands still warm from the fire contained within the brass brazier. He gathered blankets and cloak and slid beneath their weight, perfectly willing to hibernate beneath them until spring was wearing snowflowers once again. He closed his eyes and felt the warmth inside himself slowly extend to the warm pocket carved by his body. He closed his eyes and wished the cold away; let it be gone to somewhere, anywhere, beyond the warmth of his body, the soft retention of his life in the warm-aired interstices of the blankets.

He slept, warm within his covers, his breath deepening, his mind sinking deep into silence, the silence from whence mind arises, from which thoughts bubble and rise until they burst fully formed in the conscious mind. He slept and then awoke, hot beneath blankets which had hoarded his body's heat. Throwing off the covers, he found the door in the darkness and then let his feet remember the stone steps which led to the kitchen below and the door and the night outside, night rich with the fragrance of the pollen of spring.

The moon lit his way as he walked down the slope, across the road to the stream, across the stepping stones and to the meadow, a pearl of dew-damp grass beneath the starlit sky. Just as the blackness of the sky is obscured by the handfuls of stars which speckle that darkness, just so the dark shape at the exact center of the meadow was outshone by the pale luminescence of starlight reflected from the leaves of grass. A dark shape lay close to the earth, its viper arrow of a head resting on forelegs. Eyes closed, it could have been a statue for its stillness if the young mage had not known better.

He was dreaming because it was spring that he was dreaming in the latter-day depths of winter. It was warm in the meadow which that afternoon had glittered with frost. Upon the meadow grasses lay a dragon which in reality (if one chose the reality of waking) shared an ethereal existence with the stones of the building across the stream, just up the hill from the meadow.

"I am here, dreaming you," Glimmer said as he stood before the dragon, but he received no answer. Glimmer touched its warm scales, hard individually yet a supple armor in their entirety. *Do dragons die?* he asked himself. All the legends said they could, yet how could a creature with the stone dragon's powers die? How could such a creature live, though? Did it eat, breathe? Did blood pump through its veins? If magic were eternal, then how could an incarnation of magic die? Yet Glimmer's hand told him the dragon did not breathe.

I am dreaming, he thought. *Am I dreaming this dragon to its death? Am I seeing truly, or am I creating this reality? Am I, through dream magery, destroying that which I have created . . . or summoned?*

Even dreaming, Glimmer felt the weight of his ignorance, his ineptitude: world was as he was; if he didn't like it, change it, change himself. Be foolhardy and evolve. He settled himself, sitting on one of the dragon's forelegs, crossing his legs and leaning his back against the dragon's chest. He closed his eyes and sought that silence which saints knew, tired of the business of magic and wishing only silence. He slipped into the river of silence and in that current brushed against a new shore—a dream within a dream, stillness within silence.

And awoke in a far different place, so different that the ocean of Delta was as familiar as the other side of the pallet upon which one of his bodies slept. Glimmer awoke to a landscape of lifeless dust, a landscape pocked and pitted, a landscape of absolute shadow and light; he awoke to a sky black even though he stood in full sunlight, light as jagged as glass shattered in a smithy's forge. In the sky, near the sterile horizon, a blue and green moon defined the curve of the land.

It is not the moon, Glimmer realized—*no, it is not that pearl, luminescent among the diamonds of the stars.* His mind twisted one hundred eighty degrees; he was standing on the moon, staring at the earth. Sunlight would boil his life and shadow freeze it; vacuum would suck blood from his body, except for the magic, the magic that breathed where no breath was to be had.

Bane and salvation, you have come, a familiar mind spoke to Glimmer.

The young mage looked about him and saw only the sterile wasteland—pearl of the heavens, he ironically thought—until he saw that one black shadow behind him was actually the blackness of a cavern entrance. He strode to the entrance, marveling at the lightness of his floating steps, yet saw nothing in the absolute blackness of the interior. In legend, all dragons possessed a lair, filled with treasure. Was this the stone dragon's lair?

You will find no baubles here, the stone dragon's voice murmured in Glimmer's mind, a faint edge of humor tingeing draconic thoughts. *Only my phantasmagorical self. Grope your way to me in darkness. Why deviate from your habitual behavior, young mage?*

Where have you been? Glimmer's voice echoed within his mind.

I have been of two realities. Glimmer could hear weariness in the dragon's voice.

Dragons can grow weary? he asked himself. *You have been here and where else—not at the stone inn. I looked,* Glimmer stated.

Let me be succinct, the dragon responded. *I am dying.*

I thought dragons were eternal. Didn't you say that?

Only wholeness is eternal. I am no longer whole. When you bound me, you bound me to the illusion.

What do you mean?

When you bound me to the stones, that was a great magic, young mage. You sought neither power nor pain even though both were within your reach.

And yet through the binding I am the cause of your . . . What could Glimmer say? Was the dragon dying as they spoke, or was he already spirit? Indeed, had he not intimated that he had always been spirit-in-the-flesh?

Magic has bound the body but not the soul. My body is blessed with mortality . . . to the everlasting chagrin of my immortal soul. Again the young man sensed the weary sigh. *My incorporeal self witnesses my corporeal demise.*

Glimmer tried to understand the dragon, tried to quell his mind's impatience with the dragon's words and ways. He had now entered the cavern, arms outstretched, and groped his way to the dragon's form, arranged as it had been in the meadow (or in the meadow as it was here now, in a deeper dream): head unmoving, resting on forelegs. The young mage mirrored his earlier movements and sat upon a foreleg, leaning back and resting against the dragon's bulk. Before him, the bright dust of the lunar landscape was framed by the blackness of the cave's interior. In the blackness of the star-speckled sky, the earth beckoned its living presence. Glimmer closed his eyes, and still the memory of the earth and its living beauty presented itself to his inner eyes, crocuses poking through snow.

Can I undo what I have done? he asked. *I am tired of magic. Give me spring and the garden and being left alone.*

Not yet, if you wish my eternity.

Then what must I do?

First is being; then being becomes. Aware of itself, the elements of nature are expressed. You must seek the place where the elements converge, taking with you agents of air, water, and earth. There you must unite the elements and in that unity make the duality of body and spirit one.

In spite of himself, Glimmer thought, *Is that all? I was worried it might be hard to do.* He had learned, though. *Could we discuss what I have to do, point by point?* he politely asked, the fiery ball of the sun now edging into the oval window of sky framed by the blackness of the cavern.

You must travel to the place where the elements converge: space, air, fire, water, and earth.

Where is that?

You shall find it. You shall take agents of air, water, and earth with you.

What do you mean by "agents"?

You shall know them.

Why only air, water, and earth? Why not space and fire? There are five elements, not to mention mind, intellect, and sense of self.

Abstract nature is that which we seek to unite and is inherent within the structure. Where there is structure, there is intelligence.

And why only the three elementals?

Space is represented by that which must be made whole again.

And what about fire?

Think about it, young red-headed mage who melts sand to glass and molds the fire drake.

Oh, me.

Indubitably.

The young mage reiterated. *So I go to the place of convergence, bringing along these three "agents," and then what do I do?*

You pour my blood upon the junction point as you speak my true name.

Dragon's blood? I've got to cut you and get your blood?

The dragon's voice had changed in timbre as they spoke, its mental frequency gaining sinew and strength, perhaps even pride. *Look before you, and you shall see your dragon's blood!*

The sun now burned full in the sky, its light creeping into the cave, touching the young mage as he sat upon the forelegs of the dragon. Glimmer felt the dragon stir, and he leapt to his feet, kicking an object as he stood. He stooped and retrieved a crystal glass vial shaped like a dragon, etched and faceted, the viper's head and serpentine neck the glass stopper of the vial. Sunlight poured more deeply into the cavern, and now Glimmer felt the dragon standing behind him. A glance behind saw the dragon, its eyes filled with obsidian light, standing like a mythic reptilian flower drinking the pure light of the sun.

Dragon's blood is dragon's fire. Know this all children of the stars, the dragon keened and then burst into flame. Like a solar flare lifting itself into the black vacuum of space, of the sun yet also separate from it, the stone dragon transformed to fire before the young mage, a burning nuclear conflagration of primal fire.

See me as my first emanation! The words burned in Glimmer's mind. *In the mother tongue speak this first word: fire!* Glimmer stood before the incarnation of the sun, bracing himself against the solar winds of its pure power. *Take now my blood, oh forger of glass baubles! Fill your glass with dragonfire; plunge the crystal into the ore!*

Removing the stopper from the vial, Glimmer plunged vial and hand into the primal fire, yet the fire did not flow. He then unsheathed the obsidian knife and pricked fire with blade formed by fire. Fire flowed, and Glimmer tipped the vial to it, filling the vial with the dragon's fiery blood, then affixing the lid to the vial. The glass vial glowed with the light of the sun, a prismatic miniature of the dragon before him. The mage placed his hand to the flowing blood, and joy recognized bliss, child the mother, the healer healed.

Why do I stand upon this lifeless husk? Let us take to the sky! the dragon sang, stepping to the cavern's entrance. Glimmer sidled to the cavern's wall as the dragon passed, and as it flamed before him, he leapt upon its back, fire rising from where his legs gripped the dragon, fire rising though him until he flamed like the dragon, until they were one sculpted solar flare rising now into the black vacuum of space, leaping across astronomical void, the viper-shaped head of dragon and slender neck pointing like a golden arrow to earth, to the green and blue sphere of living things, to home.

Glimmer's name no longer did justice. Not a Glimmer of Magic a shadow self of times past, *Glimmer* did not describe the being of primal creative energy now riding the serpent: snake eating its own tail now uncurled to arrow-straight dragon flight, sunfire stooping flight, blood flaring eyes of obsidian fire transfixing target with the promise of talons flaming. Earth grew and vision filled; wind began to whip the mage's fiery hair as the dragon's raptor flight plunged earthward, clouds and mountains and upland plains and the grey stone of a house, an upturned, youthful face glimmering in the darkness, elation skewing terrifically to the realization of what was stooping to its strike, the form shrinking back from the fire, one arm shielding eyes from light, mouth open in sound-less scream, the scree of apprehension that nightmare had struck like a snake from its pit, like a falcon to its prey, like a dragon descending with fire upon a child mage's dream conjured without reckoning.

As flame struck its prey, dream dodged like a coney beneath the beak, magic stunned fire to the cool deliberation of grey stone. Glim-mer landed feet first upon the tower stairs descending to the kitchen. He caught his balance against the curved coolness of the wall, arms still flaming flares of sunlight. Light of infinite candles lit the grey stone of the staircase as it curved down to kitchen. Following the stairs, the light that was Glimmer's body stepped outside. A thrush began to sing the dawn, fooled by the false light, dream light—or rather true light from an untoward source. Across the yard, across the road, down the slope to the stream, across the stepping stones to the meadow where a dragon slept as still as stone and a young man dreamt, supported by the unmoving bulk of the dragon, soul of stars. From a pocket in the flames, the fire mage found the glass dragon-shaped vial. Pouring one drop of its con-tents onto the palm of his hand, he slipped the vial into the exact same pocket of the mage sleeping before him. He then reached a fiery hand to the dragon and rubbed the dragon's blood onto the dream-form. Extend-ing the same hand to his own dreaming self, the dream mage within the dream touched a flaming palm to the forehead before him—then closed his flaming eyes and ceased to be.

Silence imploded beneath the silver pearl light of the moon—the dreaming Glimmer stirred, awoke, stood and turned to face the dragon recumbent before him. Dragon's eyes opened and neck rose so that obsidian eyes looked down on the young dream mage.

"I am *Samhita*," the dragon spake and then closed its dark eyes of fire and ceased to be.

Glimmer-of-the-Meadow-Dream stood alone in the silence, the humid night air moist, dew settling on the grasses. He felt his pocket and recognized the hard bulk of the vial. *I am dreaming,* he thought, *but am true to my dream.*

Across the stepping stones, up the slope to the stone inn, through the door and up the tower's stairs to his room; there, on the pallet, beneath a twisted bulk of bedding, lay himself. Temperate was the dream, Glimmer at ease in the evening air. It seemed odd to see the form of himself buried and burrowed, seeking warmth in the bedding. The brazier still glowed its ruddy heat into the cold stone room. Taking the vial from his pocket, he removed the glass stop and poured one drop of liquid fire onto the brazier's coals. Heat and fire surged from the bronze container as he turned to place the vial on a small table next to the sleeping form's pallet.

Turning back to the brazier, a miniature dragon now hovered above the coals, obsidian eyes like two black poppy seeds. The dragon rose above the brazier, its wings beating to the meter of Glimmer's heart. Reaching the height of the young mage's chest, the dragon swooped at him, and as he flew so mage shrank till at their convergence Glimmer caught himself onto the dragon's shoulders. The dragon banked, navigating the room, and aligning with the brazier, miniature dragon and mage flew and merged with the coalfire, burning to a deep sleep.

Glimmer awoke and burrowed up through covers to frigid air. On the low table next to his sleeping pallet sat the crystal vial filled with dragon's blood, glowing dream-like in the early morning chill, delineating the etched scales and lithe body of the glass dragon, tail curled around its torso.

Jumping up, he grabbed the glowing bottle and scrambled down the stairs to the kitchen. No one was there, but beyond the door, the young mage could hear the sound of a lute from the common room. Swinging open the door, he saw Alma-Ata, Wilim, and Bega and daughter Elesia sitting at table with another man, full of beard and dressed in the colorful apparel of a minstrel. Beside the sitting minstrel stood another man, younger, similarly appareled in the blues and ivories that the minstrel guild preferred, colors soothing to the listener, they said. Bard Reis and his apprentice Jukka had returned to the inn, and an impromptu breaking of bread and celebration was in progress. The tableau froze as Glimmer entered, his hair awry and his eyes huge. He was aware of intense scrutiny from all in the silence, glances from his person to the glowing vial in his hand.

Elesia looked at the young bard, back at Glimmer, then back to the bard as she bade, "Please, first sing your song of the wind."

The young minstrel spoke in a full and pleasant voice, "'Tis not a song designed to cheer us, though it will. 'Tis a song to inspire wind, one of the elemental songs." With this he plucked notes from the lute, smiled a welcome to Glimmer, and then began to sing.

> Take these children, seed-drift of the flower;
> Lift them to the heavens, ancient Power
> To caress them, cherish them, carry all
> To the Four Corners, Mother of the World.
> Find them haven to sleep where soil runs deep,
> Where rains timely fall, where Sun is warm.
> Give them stillness that tender roots may find
> Their tilth and strength to blossom from bud.
> Cherish their children, cradle of Power;
> To Four Corners wind-drifted seed to flower.

The listeners seemed to absorb the words like sunlight. Tenseness eased from their expressions, and they nodded gratefully to the minstrel, thanking him with their eyes. Magic was in the air, was glowing in a vial in Glimmer's hand, the worm was turning, but first they willed song to completion.

After a moment, Bega filled a bowl from a pot on the hearth and handed it to Glimmer, who had opened his mouth to speak. "Eat first, then we can talk," the woman urged. "Always in a hurry, ye are, like a prairie gnome chased by grassfire."

Glimmer sat to table and focused on the bowl of porridge before him. The minstrel picked idly at his instrument as he sat perched at the end of the bench beside his master. The others at the table were silent, Alma-Ata staring at the flames of the fire, the others studying their hands or gazing out a window. The silence swallowed the clicking of Glimmer's wooden spoon as he ate his porridge, click-clicking like a mechanical device measuring how many drops of water fill the ocean of time. *It's not an impatient silence,* he thought, *merely one that abides. Each thing to its order.*

Only Elesia stared at him through her eyelashes, her head tipped slightly downward. The young mage saw her eyes and yet did not see them. *It is her way,* he thought, *fluid, like water: seeing the wholeness, seeing the drop of water in a rippling steam.*

Something about her elusive glance reminded him of when Bega and Elesia had first come to the inn. Glimmer had gone to the stream to bathe and had found Elesia there in the water, already at bath. He had arrived openly, with no furtiveness, and moved to turn away and leave in politeness when he noticed something odd—something magical— about the form of the young woman bathing in the pool. At his glance he should have been able to see her entire form, yet somehow, he hadn't. Her long pale hair had seemed to always drift to demurely cover her, or a froth of water or reflection of light had fallen upon her in a manner to clothe her with radiance.

He was reminded of Cabbage-pants reaching into the soil to unearth the weeds, reminded of that blurring of the earth as the gnome magically extricated weed where it had rooted. He was reminded of how the gnome had leaped into the soil like an otter into a stream, that blur of form at home in its medium. That was Elesia in the water, as awkward as a duck on land, hobbling on shortened leg, but graceful in the water—at home.

You shall know them suddenly rang within the young mage's mind, the dragon's words from his dreaming. *I shall know them,* he thought. *And I do!* The young minstrel Jukka, his lute notes and sweet voice charming the air; Elesia, swimming in water that protected and supported her with parental intensity; Cabbage-pants, magical spirit of the earth; himself, dream mage of the fire drake, elements converging to unite the dragon across space to his estranged soul.

Glimmer stared at the bottom of the bowl and then looked up at those who shared the table with him. "I've got it," he said. "I know how to do it and who will help me." He smiled. "I've had this dream before."

Bega, who had opened her mouth to speak, closed it with an audible snap. Then she tossed her head and said with a laugh which caught in her throat, "Just like a mage, always two steps ahead o' everyone else." She glanced at Alma-Ata. "That's what I like 'bout you, mage. You keep yer magic t' yerself—great apples, an' no lightnin'." She rested her eyes then upon Glimmer. "This boy, though . . ."

"This boy," interposed Alma-Ata, "is now a mage, albeit a young one, and as we expect him to act like one, we must treat him as one." Glimmer's master turned to him and said, "Last night, the good people of this inn—guests included," he added, glancing at the minstrels, "experienced something. I believe you should know about this, Glimmer, before we talk about . . . that," Alma-Ata said, glancing at the vial of dragonfire. The mage collected with his eyes those who sat at the table. "Who would like to tell the young mage the events of the night?"

Hitherto silent, Wilim spoke, "Me, if none o' ye mind." When no one intervened, he continued. "We all found ourselves here at sunrise because o' th' dream," he began. The popping of the fire, the addition of a log by Bega, and Wilim's tale of the household riding the nightmare of a flaming dragon unfolded into the silent morning. *They all dreamt my dream,* Glimmer thought, *all experienced at least the last part, the dragon falling from the sky to scorch the earth and heat stone until it burst like pitchy wood within the hearth. And it was not dream but nightmare for them*—the unknown, wild ride into the dark mysteries of the night, a nightmare so real that they awoke and arose, seeking everyday companionship and reassurance.

At Wilim's pause, the dream mage became aware of the silent eyes upon him. "Did you dream this . . . nightmare . . . also?" he asked his master.

"The dream but not the nightmare," responded Alma-Ata. "I witnessed the events but without the terror, as if I were reading a narrative of the event."

"And what do you make of it?"

Alma-Ata smiled. "It was not I doing the making, hm?"

Glimmer sighed, reluctant to tell the full tale before all assembled, reluctant to open to others the intimacies of his dream magery. *That will take the nightmare out of dream and into waking.*

"I too had this dream," he finally conceded. Safe enough to admit that. "And I believe I know its portent." That he did, in fact and deed. "Wilim," he continued, "that magic that woke you up and that magic which causes the fires here to burn so little wood for so much heat—"

"Not so lately," considered the man, "even with th' cold, th' fire 'tis not so magical, as you call it, and a great deal more o' th' *musclical*."

Glimmer's eyebrows rose at the significance of those words. *I am dying,* the dragon had said.

"—Then, at least, we can include the magic down in the delta from which my master and I last fall returned." The young mage studied his hands, forgetting his surroundings, speaking his thoughts. "Even with my master's guidance," and now Glimmer did recognize that guidance— Alma-Ata's craft of Gathering, his wisdom of the need for whole vision— and how it had balanced the chaos of dreams with the evenness of silence, "even with that, my magic was not complete, not . . . impeccable. I have attempted to do good and not evil, to learn—and have learned."

He raised his eyes and addressed those sharing the table. "There is something I must fix, a fabric I must mend, and I must do it where the elements converge." Glimmer felt a profound sense of connectedness with this moment, these people, this place. "I think that here is the place where the elements converge, at the Stone Dragon Inn."

"The elements in balance," whispered Reis with a gesture of his hands, "fire of hearth, song through air, water in soup, shelter in stone, all together in this space."

As the master fell to silence with a slight clearing of hoarseness from his throat, Glimmer affirmed, "Exactly right. I didn't think it would be here"—he glanced around him and to his listeners—"the convergence of the elements, that is."

Silence followed his words, punctuated by the popping of the wood burning in the hearth. The apprentice Jukka broke the silence with, "Pardon the thought, Mage Glimmer," and the young mage blinked at his words, "but I believe my master implied that all elements exist everywhere—are indeed the fabric of creation—and, therefore, all elements do indeed converge here." Jukka glanced questioningly at his master. "Our minds perceive them; we celebrate them with discriminating thoughts and words. Our selves participate in this unity." He plucked thoughtfully a single string upon his lute. The sound vibrated in the silence, filled it, and then slipped again into silence. He smiled self-consciously. "My master has taught me not just chord and verse but also their purpose." He laughed. "At lease, he has contrived."

The assemblage chuckled as the young minstrel continued. "My ears grow red at remembering my learning—and the use they received."

Minstrel Reis listened in silence to the good words of his apprentice, his face content with agreement to Jukka's words. "He speaks for me now," the master whispered, "as my voice as my own mends."

The apprentice minstrel continued for his master. "So this is not the *Convergence of the Elements*, at least not as in lays I have learned. That title is always connected with the ancient volcano in the mountains to the north, the one called the Dragon's Maw. You have heard of it, perhaps?"

Glimmer, staring at the young minstrel, became aware that his jaw had dropped and mouth was hanging open. He closed it, feeling that sudden tension of knowing something to be absolutely true and that energies were already collecting as a presage to action. The Dragon's Maw! What better place to unite a dragon with its soul?

Mage Alma-Ata stood and stretched, then advanced to the hearth and poked at the fire. He placed his hand upon the rounded stone rimming the obsidian set within the mantel, absent-mindedly stroking the water-sculpted smoothness of the stone.

"And you have learned this from . . . a dream?"

Glimmer noticed how carefully the mage had phrased his question. "Yes . . . a dragon spoke these words in my dream."

As Alma-Ata silently considered his apprentice, Wilim spoke. "Is this place far? I would not leave this place," he glanced at Bega and her daughter, "or these good people willingly, but if ye'll be travelin' to this . . . Dragon's Maw . . . an' not stayin' here, I will tread yer steps."

"I will need help," Glimmer disclosed, "but it is not yours I need—or at least not *essentially* yours that I need." He stood also, placing his hand alongside his master's on the cool stone of the mantel. "I believe that my business is not here, and it cannot be anywhere and everywhere, even if the convergence of the elements is the very fabric of the world. I believe the Dragon's Maw to be my destination."

"But ye can't go alone!" Wilim exclaimed.

"No, you are right, but not because of dangers. I cannot travel alone because this task I cannot accomplish alone." *And I do not want to be alone,* thought the young man. The dream mage gave his eyes to all at the table. "With me must travel you, Jukka, and you, Elesia, and also the gnome Cabbage-pants." He turned away from the ordinary popping of the fire in a hearth devoid of life. "Air, water, earth, and fire—we must travel to the Dragon's Maw, at the junction point, the space at which these elements converge."

This information dropped into the center of the assemblage like a stone into water. A gasp from quiet Elesia and a "Not 'n yer life!" from Bega; an "Ah!" from the young minstrel accompanied by, "Wiser heads must consider," from Jukka's master, the minstrel Reis; and, "We canna' deny th' magic," from Wilim: all swirled around the head of the young mage as similar emotions swirled within him. Alma-Ata said nothing, did nothing—simply waited.

"My daughter is not magical," protested Bega.

"There is magic in music," interposed Reis, "yet I will not willy-nilly let my apprentice be off!"

"Where is the Dragon's Maw?" Glimmer said, tossing another stone into choppy waters. "I've heard the name but never seen it on a map. Is it far?"

A pause ensued as Alma-Ata and Reis both began to speak. Then the mage nodded politely to the minstrel, who continued in his whispering voice. "Minstrels are often itinerant souls, and so maps are a part of ministrelry. The Dragon's Maw is not too far from here—oh, a journey, certainly, but not an impossible one."

"I studied geography with my tutor and remember no Dragon's Maw," Glimmer said.

With a slight smile, Alma-Ata said, "Oh, it's there, all right, but its lesser cousin is more famous, at least in popular song. Two volcanoes, the lesser known as . . ."

"Old Smokey," concluded the minstrel Reis.

"We must travel to the top of Old Smokey?"

"You are the one to tell us about any exactitudes," Alma-Ata clarified.

"I don't have any exactitudes—be it on Old Smokey, in the Dragon's Maw, or . . ."

Jukka mused aloud, "One would be *in* a maw, not *on* a maw, therefore the best phrasing—"

"This is no time for versifying," Glimmer said.

"The name changed," Reis lectured in his raspy whisper, "because of a popular folk song—a love ballad. Perhaps you've heard it," and the minstrel hummed a few bars and Jukka strummed a gentle chord on the lute.

Glimmer felt his face redden with sudden anger. "Are you all teasing me? Is that it?" Seeing the shock on their faces, Wilim mouthing a "No" of protestation, Glimmer's anger fizzled to self-mockery.

"I know I'm just a country bumpkin . . ."

Minstrel Reis opened his mouth to protest and then, considering, closed it.

"Never mind," said the young mage with a self-effacing chuckle. "I suppose Old Smokey will be covered with snow this time of year . . ." at which all assembled chuckled.

"And *versifying* is important," justified the younger minstrel. "The Lesser Dragon's Maw is hardly a name worthy of a map."

"An' havin' no plan an' magery go together like fried potatoes an' scrambled eggs," Bega concluded. "Ye might as well be walkin' in yer sleep," a comment which sent a cold finger tracing Glimmer's spine.

The rest of the day centered on convincing Bega that her daughter should be allowed to leave. Convincing Reis consisted of a private talk with Alma-Ata, culminating with the two masters bent over maps, discussing distances and obstacles. Bound for a Delta ship and southern climes for the winter, the redsmith who had taught Wilim the basics of smithing had left his white donkey at the inn. The masters commandeered the donkey for Elesia and for equipment. These were merely details, though. The tide of doubt had turned when Glimmer had placed into a beam of sunlight the vial. Distillate of sun, the gem of light danced within the bottle, flickering the walls with all the colors of purity. For Bega, the deciding factor was the donkey, reassurance for the mother that Elesia had means to travel the distance without discomfort. As Jukka consulted with his master, Glimmer packed his satchel and descended the stairs to the kitchen, which had become the staging area for the dragon quest.

"If a guest comes, I suppose what they lose in service they'll gain in entertainment," muttered Bega, staring at the bundles piled on the table.

"Ye shall dress as a man," she ordered her daughter. "I've done it, an' it may be the savin' o' ye." She stared at Glimmer, standing at the foot of the stairs, satchel in hand. "No sword this time?"

"And someone to protect," he said, glancing at Elesia. "What about a walking staff." He smiled. "Maybe I can borrow your broom."

"A staff is a good idea. Humble enough to keep you from getting' cocky." Bega stared at the young man in silence. "Still best t' run, though."

"What about Elesia? How fast and far can she run?"

"Best for her to just stay atop that donkey an' kick it good. Best all 'round t' be like rabbits in th' grass." With a twinkle in her eye, she added, "Like me t' teach ye a few tricks with th' staff before ye leave?"

"Best for me to just plan on yelling, 'Run!' and then t' take my own advice."

Later that morning, Glimmer, Elesia, and Jukka were sitting at a table near the southern windows of the common room, as far as the room allowed from their usual haunt of hearth and table near the kitchen door. Two tables, empty and barren, sat between the trio and their customary table to the north of the room. This, as Jukka put it, was their chance to find some quiet to "put words to the melody." They had been given a map by Alma-Ata, a scolding by Bega, and had been told by the master bard a cautionary tale involving innocent travelers and duplicitous highwayman with hard eyes who smiled and smiled. Wilim had said nothing, had only curried the white donkey.

As masters of their craft and the most knowledgeable of those at the inn, Alma-Ata and Reis had given the trio of travelers their final instructions.

"It is not for us to order or inform your actions. You know what you have to do, and you know your destination. Be alert and listen not just for sounds and echoes but also for silences. No birds singing can mean as much as a flock in song," Alma-Ata had advised the three as they had stood, their bundles stacked upon the kitchen table. "And remember, doing nothing is sometimes the best way to get something done."

"Jukka, you have been trained not just to sing in the hall but also to survive the travels between halls. Remember, the wise traveler knows not only when to halloo and wave but also when to stand in silence, hidden by tree branch at trail's edge," Reis had added in his hoarse whisper, his face severe with concern. "I let you young ones go with no protest only because magic clearly compels. Sometimes we sing the song; sometimes the song sings us."

And then the three were down the road, Jukka leading the white donkey upon which Elesia sat, Glimmer walking beside Jukka, all wrapped in cloaks to maintain warmth. He looked over his shoulder as the distance lengthened between themselves and the inn—Bega and Wilim standing together watching them off, Alma-Ata and the minstrel Reis standing side by side a few steps advanced, their feet on the road as if they wished to walk with them.

Alma-Ata had told Glimmer not to worry, but the young mage had wondered about the gnome Cabbage-pants. Where was he? His presence had lessened with the coming of winter. He had not been told of the journey, nor had he been told of his part in it. The young mage thrust those doubts aside; let gnomes to their own magic.

Chapter 11

"Magic is acknowledged rather than commanded."
108 Aphorisms of Mage DeVasier

რა

Glimmer's footsteps were muffled by the tall grasses that fringed the frozen track of the road as he, Jukka, and Elesia advanced into the afternoon light. Thoughts circling inward, it seemed to Glimmer that he was always leaving the stone house in late afternoon, a most unreasonable time because darkness would find the travelers before they found lodgings for the night. Air grew thin and hazed as the distance from the inn increased, and still there was no evidence of the gnome. How could Cabbage-pants catch up with his short, bowed legs? Yet the young mage remembered the gnome leaping from Lion's Loft and arriving so quickly at the inn, remembered gentle hands and words at the bluff above Delta. He remembered the fox, Alma-Ata's friend; its winter coat would be so rich and luxuriant, he thought.

He had questioned the gnome about the occurrences at Madrone and Lion's Loft, a long distance covered by a short, stumbling walk in the dark. The gnome's reply had included references to how "*distance*, mind ye, can be measured diff'rent ways" and other comments that the young man had eventually lumped into the category of *gnome magic*.

Glimmer looked to the roadside and saw a jagged fracture of a rotting stump which for a moment appeared to be a gnome, standing statue-like and blank-eyed beside the road. A while later, he was fooled for a moment by a tufted mound of frozen grass that seemed to be Cabbage-pants' head peeking from the frozen soil, two black stones like eyes shining in the wan sunlight. Glimmer sighed and trudged on, his companions Jukka and Elesia (and, in deference to the magic, the white donkey) beside him, brushing away his doubts and worries like cobwebs. He would meet with the gnome when needed and then arrive at the Convergence of the Elements in time to save the stone dragon's life. *Stick to the plan, fried potatoes and scrambled eggs.*

Rounding a turn of the road, before him Glimmer encountered a frost-rimed tree stump which he then recognized as the gnome Cabbage-pants, dressed in winter clothes intricately woven from barks and plant fibers.

"'Tis somethin' to moither a body to travel with menkind, the ways they travel so deliberate an' steady slow," the gnome explained as Glimmer advanced to face him.

The young mage squatted before the gnome, his smile beaming down on the creature's earthy countenance. "Where have you been? I couldn't help worrying that you wouldn't come."

"Wouldn't come?" the gnome indignantly exclaimed. "Wouldn't come?" he complained to Jukka and Elesia, and even the donkey. "Are ye blind? Haven't I been with ya all along? Are ye blind?" The gnome sighed. "Take me hand, Glimmer, an' you too, minstrel. Lass, hold t' the minstrel's hand, an' we'll travel as a gnome does, deep in th' earth streams."

"I think we'd better hold tight," Glimmer commented under his breath to his companions.

Taking the gnome's proffered hand in his, Glimmer felt the road sweep beneath his feet as if he were standing on the moving surface of a river. Trees rushed by him, and the grasses, brown and dry from the winter, rippled in a movement that surrounded Glimmer, movement soundless except for a sense of the flow of particles, a hum of lively existence, a vibrating sense of dynamism. The road ahead twisted and whipped its tail like a cobra fighting a mongoose. After one dizzy look downward at the rushing river of earth beneath his feet, Glimmer kept his eyes locked to the steady horizon or to minstrel and donkey plodding along beside him. Occasionally to his left or right a sudden glimpse of stillness would flash like lightning in darkness, and these flashes of stillness, these placid pools in this river in flood had black, bead-like eyes and mottled flesh of earth tones. The river of earth rushed, yet gnomes, like stones in a mountain stream, were unmoving in the magic of their being as they stood watching the cavalcade pass them by. The kaleidoscope darkened as the mad rush of the earth continued, the bright blur of fire in the sky stretching toward the horizon. Then movement ceased as suddenly as it had begun, and Glimmer, caught off-balance by the suddenness of the transition, teetered and leaned, only keeping himself from stumbling and falling by placing a hand upon Cabbage-pants' head to catch himself.

"Eh! What d'ye think I am? Find yerself a squire's stick! C'llect thyself, young mage, a'for ye embarrass ye'self," grumbled the gnome.

"So this is how I got from Madrone to Lion's Loft? That's how you left the Lion's Loft and got to the inn so quickly?"

"Didn't really leave th' bluff, that time. More like was it left me."

"What do you mean?" Jukka responded, puzzled, his natural curiosity overcoming the vertigo of the experience. "We have traveled. Why, we're at the entrance to the Madrone Sanctuary of Hospitality!" he exclaimed, looking up at a familiar statue sculpted of three figures: Glimmer, with a wide grin on his stone face; Sister Superior, flirtatious, her veined marble hand sliding down Glimmer's back; and the younger Sister, her stone robe slit up the side as she displayed an extravagant excess of leg. "We certainly are here, all right," he concluded, shaking his head and grinning at Glimmer. "How can you say we didn't travel?" the minstrel addressed the gnome. "Master and I just returned from here, and it took us three days' travel and then some."

"'Cuz we didn't. We stood an' did only a bit o' walkin', corr'ct?" As Jukka, Glimmer, and Elesia nodded their heads, Cabbage-pants continued.

> Earth spin through space,
> Gnome ne'vr 'n haste.
> Earth like a top,
> Gnome like a rock."

"So you are saying we didn't move—" Jukka further inquired.

"—but the earth did?" Glimmer completed.

"Is it like that for you all the time, what we experienced?" Elesia asked. "It was wonderful, like swimming with a swift current."

"Nay an' yea, that 't is."

"Well, that tells us a lot," Jukka said, smiling at Elesia.

"Th' earth spins an' we let it."

"And when you head in another direction?" Glimmer asked.

"Why, we . . ." The gnome scratched his head. "What do th' sailors call 't? We *tack* an' slide along the spinnin' of the spine as fine as ye like."

Glimmer considered that for a moment. "Could you teach me?"

The gnome scratched his side and then pulled his ear as he pondered. "That I could. But ye see, I don't know how well I could teach ye. I wouldna want ye to end up in th' middle of the earth, y'know."

Glimmer blinked. "I wouldn't either."

"It may be that the Silent Ones taught ye some, though."

"I don't think so," and then the young mage laughed, "but then, of course, what do I mean by *think*?"

Glimmer looked to the stone pillars, the wrought iron gate, and the over-arching wrought iron filigree which graced the entrance, now each day placed to greet the rising sun. He wanted to enter the building, to see if he had done well with this dreaming, to determine if he had done well by choice, not chance. "Well, I guess we should find rooms. I wonder what will happen because of, you know . . ." Glimmer petered out, nodding to the statue.

"Master Reis and I had a good laugh when we came here last to sing and play . . . sing the winter through, we thought, but other places called," the young minstrel observed, his eyes meeting Elesia's.

"Then they'll know me!"

"I'm sure they will when you when walk through that door," laughed Elesia, glancing pointedly from statue to mage.

"Maybe I should sleep out in the bushes with Cabbage-pants."

"Now yer makin' sense," fussed the gnome. "Iron the first time and still iron. Give me a thicket and a stone knife any day," he declared, slapping his sheath and turning to cross the road. "Are ye with me?"

"No, I'd better face the music. At least I can do that with accompaniment," he added with a nod to the musician. Glimmer stared one more time at the statue of himself grinning like a fool, and he then entered the sanctuary, accompanied by Jukka and Elesia.

"They didn't seem so upset, really," the minstrel said placatingly. That comment sounded a lot like Cabbage-pants' on the gnome's quest: ". . . it prob'bly won't cause ye no injury . . ."

Glimmer sighed as they walked beneath the wrought iron filigree.

"They'll probably enjoy wiping that smile off my face," he muttered. "And the next iron I'll see will probably be straight bars, and I'll be behind them, enjoying a hospitable meal of bread and water in a 'lower guestroom' of the sanctuary!" For all the banter, it was truly the steel in the Sister Superior's blue eyes that fueled his qualms, that implacable resolve to be hospitable.

The travelers advanced up a stone walkway bordered by neatly pruned apple trees, bare-branched in the winter but still neat, the grass beneath the trees bleached by winter's bluster yet raked and free of debris. A sense of orderliness and serenity dominated the environment; here and there on the branches of the miniature apple trees were tied bows of red and green and gold ribbons. As the young mage approached the twin massive wooden doors to the castle, he saw more ribbons tied to the dormant espaliered apple trees framing the entrance, and also small silver bells that rang a merry hello as he approached.

These small touches of joy were new to the entranceway, which Glimmer remembered to be somber and forbidding on his first visit to Madrone. He felt amazement and pride at his choice to invite the morning sun into the gloom of the sanctuary. Even though the act had been spontaneous, there had been more conscious choice to it than to Glimmer's other works of dream magery. He hoped the effects of his choice had benefited the Sisters. He was eager to see.

Opening one of the oaken doors, Glimmer, Jukka, and Elesia, leaving the donkey outside the door, entered the short adjoining hallway and then proceeded straight ahead through two more doors to the Hall of Hospitality, the social and dining room common to all the orders of hospitality, of which the windowed common room of the Stone Dragon Inn was the equivalent. Two Sisters, one young and one perhaps the aged Sister of his first visit, were sweeping the stone floor and glanced up at Glimmer and the others as they entered.

The Sisters smiled and delivered the ritual greeting, "May you rest with us and know the joy of God," but as Glimmer emerged from the shadows of the entranceway and the younger Sister spied his face, she dropped her broom in shock. Glimmer smiled a rueful smile, and then, as fire lit within him to not shrink in weakness, he smiled widely, exactly matching the smile carved in stone on the statue outside.

As the older Sister exited the entrance to tend to the animal outside, the younger Sister exclaimed, "My goodness, 'tis thee!" her voice rising with emotion. "I must tell Sister Superior Lisbeth," and she skittered off, leaving the broom lying on the floor, its handle crossing Glimmer's path like a sword of retribution.

"So far so good," Jukka commented wryly with a smile to Elesia.

Glimmer picked up the broom and swept the small pile of dust to the side, leaning the broom against the wall. He felt hesitant to enter farther into the sanctuary, considering what had happened during his first visit. This was reinforced by the behavior of the young Sister who had just dropped her broom and disappeared into one of the sanctuary's hallways, a young Sister whose face seemed . . . familiar.

The room was large—big enough to hold a hundred individuals at its tables—and lit by high, arched windows on the south and east sides. The tables were hewn from wood and massive, sided by benches obviously crafted by the same hand. Candles sat at each table, unlit now, the room still lit by early evening light flowing through the windows. Glimmer wondered if guests lit the candles themselves as needed or whether the Sisters lit them after their ceremonies of devotion—or perhaps, he thought, their service to their guests was their devotion.

The hall echoed in its silence, but several groups of travelers already sat at tables, one man laughing loudly and slapping another on the back. In another group, a man, a woman, and two small, black-haired children occupied a bench, the boy sitting beside his father and the daughter beside her mother. A relaxed air emanated from the travelers, different than when Glimmer had last observed this room. Then the air had been hushed and the travelers apologetic for the hospitality they had received.

The sound of approaching footsteps preceded the arrival of the Sister-of-the-broom and another Sister. To Glimmer's dismay, he realized it was the stern-faced Sister who, the last time he had visited the sanctuary, had stood by door and dourly blessed the travelers as they had left. It was the Sister Superior of the sanctuary, identified as Sister Lisbeth by the young woman who had fetched her. The older woman's tall and slender form stood head and shoulders above the young Sister before her. The two women walked up to the young mage, the young Sister at the last moment faltering and standing behind Sister Lisbeth.

190

Sister Lisbeth looked Glimmer up and down in silence, gazing first into his face and then nodding slowly. "Well, what do you have to say for yourself?"

"It wasn't my intent . . . or at least not my design—" the young mage began, only to be interrupted by the elder: "Then whose was it?"

"I admit, it was my doing—but not my *deliberate* doing, I swear." Glimmer looked to Elesia and Jukka beside him, seeking support from their presence.

"A mage who magics without deliberation. We must talk further of this. And these two are with you?" she added. Then she asked Jukka, "Where is Master Reis?"

"He stays with Alma-Ata. We travel," the minstrel continued, "with common and urgent purpose."

Jukka's words galvanized the Sister Superior to instruct the other Sister to assist Jukka and Elesia, which left Glimmer standing alone with the sanctuary's head.

In silence the Mother of Hospitality stared at Glimmer, but not in anger, it seemed to Glimmer, not in anger. A small smile lightened her countenance, similar to that mischievous smile which adorned the statue at the sanctuary's entrance.

"Perhaps you had best come to my study and explain," she finally responded. As they had spoken, another Sister, broom in hand, had arrived at the door. "Sister of the Broom, such a coincidence that you arrive here just at this moment," she addressed the woman, which caused Glimmer's eyes to widen and his stiffness to crack into a smile. "You come along, too. I can think of no faster means of communicating to all the Sisters than to have you a party to this conversation." Sister Broom managed to smile, frown, and adopt a gleam of curiosity in her eyes all at the same time. "First, get rid of that pile of dust and then come up to my study," ended Sister Lisbeth as she turned and strode off toward a hallway entrance.

Glimmer jumped at the order and reached for the broom. "Not you, silly boy. You come with me."

As Glimmer followed the Sister Superior down the hallway, he could not help but notice other Sisters stopping to stare at him. He felt his face turning red and had to stop his hand from pulling the hood of his cloak to his head to shadow his face. The Sister's study was a room without a door, its walls lined with books and manuscripts, a large writing table at the center of the room, a window backing the table for light. Sister Superior Lisbeth sat in the chair closest to the window and gestured for Glimmer to sit in the chair on the other side of the table.

I must remember that Jukka, Elesia, and I are here for a purpose, Glimmer thought to himself. *I cannot anger this woman but must appease her.*

The Sister settled herself in her chair and then leaned to Glimmer, her elbows on the table. "I'm not angry," she stated. "Or perhaps I should say, 'We're not angry.'"

The young mage started at her words, feeling as if his mind had been read. Seeking something clever to say, he responded, "You're not?"

"No," Sister Superior continued. "Oh, there were many emotions at first: anger, amazement, joy—or perhaps I should say that these I felt, since I don't read minds and cannot speak for others, although a face often is shaped by thought." Glimmer again felt a flip of his heart at her words. "But after a time, I realized that the statues were the signature of the maker . . . and a message, and we should always listen to those messages which are ours."

Message? Glimmer asked himself.

"And like many mages and perhaps especially young mages—although I have little time for such things—moving the entrance of a stone castle was certainly an attention-getter. Now, you're probably wondering the nature of the message I read in those stone images—once we finally noticed the three figures instead of one that fronted the east entrance rather than the southern," the Sister ironically stated.

Glimmer tested the waters with the thought: *No, I'm not wondering anything.*

"Or perhaps you don't care and simply hope no trouble is coming your way."

Good, she only reads what I send, he thought.

"I don't think that's true, though. You wouldn't have come back to us unless you had some deeper purpose."

The Sister Superior folded her hands before her and closed her eyes. "You need assistance, which we can provide."

Logical, thought Glimmer.

"You have to do something important for someone else," to which he thought: *It's my honest face.* The Sister opened her eyes and smiled wryly. "Although with a face as honest and open as yours, it's difficult to imagine duplicity," she added. "And, believe me; I've spent a lot of time looking at your face—or, rather, a stone version of it."

Glimmer looked into the Sister's eyes and found no duplicity. Grey and white scarves framed a face that had that ageless look some fair-haired women gain with maturity: unlined and serene yet full of wisdom, not at all child-like. The young mage decided mind-reading or not, the Sister's insights were those of wisdom and not magic, *as if wisdom is not rooted in magic, or magic in wisdom,* he amended.

Turning full circle, Glimmer asked, "What was the message?"

"Ah," murmured Sister Lisbeth, smiling, "a man who can hold a train of thought. You *are* magical." With Glimmer's continued attention, she continued, "The message was that we at the sanctuary were so adamantly devoted to hospitality that we had lost our joy and, thus, were no longer hospitable." She leaned back and smiled. "A terrible shock, I can tell you . . . and a lesson—a message, if you will—that opened within me like a flower."

Sister Lisbeth stared at her hands, work-worn yet delicate. "So the sculpture was a message and a gift, yet the real gift was the unexpected joy you left here. I've never heard of that kind of magic, just filling the air with joy."

Glimmer spoke carefully. "I did not create the joy; it always existed within you. I reminded these stones that joy exists . . . pulled back the veil that hid it." Sister Lisbeth raised an eyebrow, and after a pause, Glimmer added, "Something else I also did. Perhaps it was the influence of you Sisters, but I also eased the pain of someone or something here that is very bitter, very angry. Even . . . that . . . deserved seed-joy."

"And may we never forget the joy of God. And those who need it most are those who have it least." The woman's eyes searched those of the mage. "And this . . . what? Thing?"

"I know not what it is. I do not feel its presence now and learned of it only through dream." Glimmer had never felt a more penetrating gaze than the Sister Superior's. "I do not feel its presence now."

"Nor do I . . . yet not death or absence . . . perhaps rest . . ."

Their eyes met across the desktop, and then the Sister spoke as

Glimmer thought, "And so why did I ask you to come to my office?" She smiled as Glimmer's brow furrowed. "It is simple: first, curiosity; second, you helped us, and so how can we help you?"

"That's it?" the young mage asked.

The Sister nodded. "How, why, and our help. We are Sisters of Hospitality," and then waited patiently for Glimmer to respond.

For the dull boy to catch up, he reasoned wryly. A little sweetness hadn't blunted the Sister's edge.

"Well, considering the second question first, I really didn't plan." He shrugged uncomfortably. "Sometimes my magic just *happens,* but I was brought here by the Silent Ones of the Spine to do it." He shrugged again uncomfortably. "Sometimes it is a reaction . . . deeper than a plan or a series of choices. Sometimes my magic organizes itself . . . or accomplishes an intention in its own way." He spoke with sudden conviction and remembrance. "The Silent Ones felt your pain."

Sister Lisbeth leaned forward again, her elbows on the scarred wood of the desk, her chin resting on her hands clasped at the apex of the triangle. "A conspiracy of miraculous happenstance. We thought that we had held our pain . . . privately."

"No," Glimmer said gently. "No pain is truly private . . . and, perhaps, the same is true of joy."

Their conversation advanced, an interplay of speech and thoughtful silence. The room added its stony silence to theirs, and the winter stillness outside was devoid of birdsong or the workaday hubbub of humanity.

"My master's magic is not mine," concluded Glimmer, "but he has helped me find the means to maintain a . . . purity of purpose." He paused, struggling for words. "I have never talked of this before. What I have to do now is not to act in order to accomplish good, but to act from that level of existence from which good arises . . . if that makes sense."

The Sister smiled a beatific smile and raised her hand in blessing. "How fitting that your image graces the statue before our sanctuary. That which you seek is also our goal—to not only do good work but to work from that level of life from which goodness arises." She smiled a smile that matched the coquettish image graven in marble next to Glimmer's. "I could almost kiss you," she murmured, and then chuckled as the young mage blushed.

194

"Your work is now easier?" Glimmer asked, attempting to draw the conversation back to the task before him and his company.

The good Sister smiled again. "Infinitely. Your magic . . . and your master Alma-Ata visited and had . . . a private talk . . . with me. Best to drink from a full cup." They regarded one another for a time in silence. "And now, how can we help you with whatever your task is, O mysterious young mage?"

"Our task is mysterious even to me. All we require of you and the good Sisters is your hospitality until next dawn when we will be on our way.

Sister Lisbeth's eyes widened. "Of course," she murmured. She pressed her hands, palms together, before her. "Forgive me. I fall into old habits. Let us formally know one another. I am Lisbeth, Sister Superior of the Sisters of Hospitality, of the Order of Arguliana, sometimes known as the Order of the Hidden Jewel." She held out her hands to Glimmer, and he reached out to meet her hands, suddenly self-conscious. "And you are Glimmer, devotee of Alma-Ata, the Apple Sage. You are the worker of the magic of Wilim, of the Sea Drake of Delta. You are the loyal friend of the Prince of Cabbage, and you are joy-giver to the Castle of Madrone."

"Somebody's been talking," commented the young mage.

"Minstrels aren't known for their vows of silence. You are already the prominent figure in a number of excellent ballads which a balladeer of our mutual acquaintance has sung to entertain—and to educate—our guests. He never did, however, mention that he not only knew the tale but also knew the grinning face that my granite self seems so fond of." The blood rose in Glimmer's face again.

"Oh, gods."

"'Oh, gods,' indeed," the Sister continued. "It's a good thing our handsome and handy balladeer is already in love. We Sisters are chaste— yet we take no vows of chastity—if you follow the delicacies of my reasoning. And you, young mage, beware. Some young, impetuous Sister might seek to verify in the flesh, shall we say, the statuesque grandeur of your reputation, carved in stone and lauded in song?"

As Glimmer felt once again a hot blush overcome him, the Sister reassured, "Don't worry, I'll protect you. But who's going to watch the watcher, hm?" She laughed as Glimmer found himself squirming in his chair. "Come, let us find the minstrel and his Elesia, and perhaps you won't be our guest long enough to lead us unto temptation—and to put our hospitality to the test."

Sister Lisbeth rose from her desk and swept from the room, a figure of energy and enthusiasm, a flower forever blooming, even in the bleak final days of wintertime. As Glimmer hurried after her retreating figure, wondering about the Sister's references to Jukka and Elesia, it seemed appropriate to him that he followed, two steps behind and one to the side.

"Halloo!" shouted Jukka and Elesia, waving from a table as they made the eating hall.

Sister Lisbeth stopped for an aside to Glimmer before they reached the table, commenting, "You came with the gnome. A vital task this must be for a gnome to elect the journey—and a deep one to need empaths of air and water. And earth . . ." she added thoughtfully. "And fire," she extended, considering the mage's ruddy topknot. "The Convergence of the Elements is your destination," she concluded.

When Glimmer did not respond, a bland expression upon his face, she shrugged. "We can talk later," she suggested, and then both turned to address those whom they had sought, "but remember, we wish to help."

The mage thought, *How can we talk about plans when I don't know what I'm doing?*

The travelers ate their dinner as the sanctuary's honored guests, a sense of lightness and ease existing in the room, so different than Glimmer's last visit. As the meal progressed, Jukka nudged Glimmer and commented, "Have you noticed our table is being served by many more Sisters than the other tables: one Sister to pour water, one Sister for every serving, one Sister to check the salt? It's a good thing we weren't having pasta," observed Jukka, laughing, "or there would have been an opportunity to have a different Sister for every noodle." Then he paused and added thoughtfully, "Maybe that would have been good, though. Then the notorious and mysterious mage could have been fully inspected by one and all." Glimmer did hope that it was a mischievous twitch to the minstrel's mouth that accompanied the comment.

"I am glad you both are here with me," Glimmer said. A short silence followed his confession, and then Jukka said, "How does one say no to a mage brandishing a vial of dragon's blood?" followed by Elesia's comment, "I do it for Wilim and my mother. And it will give my . . . good friend Jukka . . . the chance to use the word *transubstantiation* in a song." Jukka placed his arm around Elesia's shoulder, "So we're in for a song."

Glimmer nodded slowly, understanding why master minstrel and apprentice had returned down icy roads to the Stone Dragon Inn. *To the Convergence of the Elements,* he thought, *converge two hearts.*

After dinner to the encouragement of the guests and Sisters, Jukka uncovered his lute and tuned it as the guests turned expectantly to his table and as Sisters lined the walls, their eyes intent upon the bard. He sang a song that Glimmer had not heard before, a song about a man who loved and admired a woman that he could never attain. The man knew that he was flawed, that he could not understand, that he stood in the shadows and watched others love and live their lives, beyond his understanding, beyond his reach. It was "The Ballad of Wilim and Bega," and it created a tightness in the mage's chest, knowing that he had done one good act in his life, even if it had been done through him and was not truly of his doing, his only contribution a good thought and kind consideration which had catalyzed his knack and the ineluctable laws of nature.

> In silent shadows stands a man
> Who loves the lady as he can.
> Gifts of flowers, words so kind,
> He cannot 'magine nor can find
> Until the magic of the mage
> Mends his mind, unlocks the cage.
>
> Heart of Wilim, his body, soul,
> Favor what his mind does know.
> "Love me, Lady; all I am is yours.
> Un-key my heart so it may soar.
> Love me, Lady; in sun I stand.
> These words I sing to win your hand."

A silence lay upon the guests and good Sisters as the last strains of the lute faded with the minstrel's voice. A hush of whispers rose from the silence as individuals glanced covertly at the table where Glimmer sat, *as many glances falling on me as on the minstrel,* he thought. He was glad when the minstrel stood, shouldered his lute, and extended his hand to Elesia. Glimmer had risen with the minstrel and followed Jukka and Elesia to the doorway.

As Jukka and Glimmer turned to leave for the men's quarters, a figure emerged from a nook behind an archway pillar. As she stepped from shadow, Glimmer beheld the flushed face of the third Sister of the statuary, the one snuggled to Glimmer's marble figure, the Sister who had met him at the door, he realized.

"I have heard that you are leaving. Take me with you. I am Sister Merri," she implored.

"On the way, there may be danger. I cannot risk such a thing," countered Glimmer. She was not needed; already he had the emissaries of the elements and felt unease at any sudden shift in plans already so tentative.

"Take me with you, I say," she cried again, standing before the mage, face to face, her entreating eyes upon the man.

"I cannot, and do not ask again," Glimmer said again, his eyes glancing away from the twin torches of the young Sister's blue eyes. "Do not ask me, please."

"Then take this with thee," responded the Sister, and reaching up, she grabbed his face with both hands and kissed the mage full on the mouth. Then she spun away and disappeared into the evening shadows, a choked sob left behind.

"Gods!" exclaimed the minstrel. "You make writing songs too easy!"

"She's older than me," muttered the mage, feeling the blush for the third time in one day. He remembered the intensity of the woman's kiss. "I'm not ready for such a fire."

Humor seasoned the minstrel's words. "Howsoever ye say, methinks th' fire's ready for ye."

The only reason Glimmer did not blush was because he was already doing so. Like a teapot left too long to flame, he sputtered, the women silent in kindness, respectful and amused. *Her sob,* he thought, *was of a deeper pain than thwarted passion. What pain and why?*

Jukka and Glimmer were led from the common room down the hallway and ascending stairs to their room, Elesia led by another Sister to the women's wing.

As they settled to their beds, Jukka murmured his appreciation.

"How did ye learn to speak with such romance, young mage?" he questioned, and Glimmer's heart swore that he could hear laughter beneath the somber timbre of the minstrel's question.

"'Tis your ballads, ye love-sick fool of a minstrel," he retorted, his face flushing again. "The night lends itself to foolish dreams I have no right to pretend are mine."

"It was well said," responded the minstrel forcefully as they crossed the threshold to his house. "I found no pretending in't."

"Nor I," finished the Sister who had led them to their sleeping quarters, listening from the doorway. "And Merri may well follow ye anyway. Sensitive she is, an' a ghost in th' woods, come from a holding friendly with th' clans of mountain gnomes, far into th' Eagle Talons. Mountain magic—an' ye know what they say . . ."

Glimmer groaned, hoping the question would not come, but Jukka solicitously asked, "What do they say, good Sister?"

"Like attracts like, an' th' magic of th' heart is th' hardest t' deny."

"She will stay," reiterated Glimmer with sudden conviction, "even if I must say it with magery."

"The heart contains its own magery, young master mage," the Sister continued with her own feminine conviction.

"Aye," the minstrel added, "it beats with more'n blood."

"Let's prepare ourselves for an early start," Glimmer growled. "Whatever dawn brings, at least let's meet it without stars in our eyes."

"Ye are the one who gave us the door to meet the sun, an' who swept misery from our halls. What matter a little starlight in thy eyes?" the Sister responded as she gestured her blessing and left.

Cabbage-pants met them at the doorstep the next morning. Glimmer had stopped worrying and wondering about the gnome, leaving Cabbage-pants to his magic and his ways. Jukka strode on strong boots, warmed by cape and warded by a burled walking staff given him by the Sisters. Elesia rode on the white donkey, her cape of grey and white wool with embroidered fringe also a gift of a good Sister's hands.

Cabbage-pants, wearing breeches and tunic of cabbage-leather and cowl of braided cabbage, red and green, mostly wore his magic and a demeanor of increasingly quiet dignity, the farther he removed himself from familiar garden. In the sheath at his waist rode his obsidian knife, gift of the knight-sage Lahad.

The travelers continued on the road north as it skirted the west of the Olifant's Footprint, and then when the lake narrowed again to river, were ferried across on a raft anchored by ropes to each side of the water. Continuing north up the rutted and grass-choked track on the eastern bank of the river, they progressed, Cabbage-pants leading the way, the reins of the donkey tendered to his hand, Glimmer to the left of the mounted lady and Jukka to the right, each with a hand to the blanket-saddle upon which Elesia rode. The sanctuary walls of Madrone had ceased to companion their journey, the grey stone walls replaced by trees to the west which fringed the river and open grass to the east. Across the expanse of the Olifant's Playground, Glimmer could see the low vertebrae of the Dragon's Spine, and the mage thought of his role as ally to the gnome's quest when they had walked the Gnome's Path.

"Wouldn't we travel more quickly by the Gnome's Path?" Jukka ventured.

"I don't think we can walk that road without knowing more than 'When we get there, I'll recognize it,'" Glimmer responded. A cardinal called from the bare branches of a tree, and Jukka imitated back its call. The minstrel's footsteps seemed light, Glimmer thought, as long as Jukka's hand held to the saddle that Elesia rode.

They traveled the trace as it defined the juncture of upland, deciduous forest and grass, the trail following the long, long slope of the saddle of an immense hill that was the demarcation of upland and the meadowlands between the upper and lower branches of the river. Sky lightened to the east, sun breaking over the mountains as Glimmer gazed across the donkey's neck to the expanse of the meadowlands called the Olifant's Playground. He knew at the horizon, or beyond, that as the land rose and rose, the horizon of grass added new horizons with the undulations of the land; eventually the land would drop sheer at the escarpment, the Shield, which had been formed when the tectonic collision of continents ages past had pushed to form the immense face of unassailable escarpment that had imposed its barrier of east to west years before counting, the easy climb of prairie grassland leading to a drop thousands of feet to the Outlands beyond. The travelers were skirting this land to reach deeper into the mysteries of the mountains to the Convergence of the Elements, the land of fire and boiling water, the forge of the gods where liquid stone was bubbled to mountain spires.

Dawn dovetailed to day, and the trace once again began twisting like a snake, whipping its body back and forth, humping its back as the travelers continued plodding ahead foot by foot yet racing along, the land blurring in its spinning, the comic cowl of the gnome ahead continuing its pedestrian plodding, the donkey seemingly half-asleep, the clops of its hooves belling in the silence of the whirring landscape. Elesia's hands whitened as she grasped the front edge of the cinched blanket upon which she sat, and Jukka took his cue from the staid demeanor of the young mage, who mirrored the minstrel's position to the lady.

They continued their way, not minding anything, as one does when walking down a town's street and another matches one's gait, intent on his own business. The travelers kept to their business, step by step, and let the rut of the road keep to its business, twisting and bucking to the roystering of the landscape; and then abruptly the careening journey was ended with the travelers standing before the upstream branching of the river, the smaller branches upstream merging, the river then merrily wending its course downstream through grassland without end, barriers of white-capped mountains distant against blue sky.

Elesia pulled her woolen cloak closer about her. Although they still stood within the rich grasslands of the Olifant's Playground, they stood now on the northern aspect, and the gentle undulating swells of grassland had risen and risen in elevation as they had traveled north willy-nilly.

"I thought you said we couldn't do that," she reminded Glimmer.

"I did say that," Glimmer replied, "but, now that I think about it, Cabbage-pants didn't say anything at the time."

"I canna take ye more, but the Convergence ain't in th' Playground with nothin' but grass, I'll wager," said the gnome with a twinkle in his eye, and then he gestured to two inns, smoke rising straight from stone chimneys into the cloudless sky. "Here's Tuck's Ford, and 'tis step an' step th' rest of th' way." He handed the reins of the donkey to Glimmer, who handed them to Jukka.

"My, an' it's not noontime yet, an' all the way we've traveled!" exclaimed the woman. "No need to be stoppin' here, so much day left." She gazed at the two inns, one on each side of the eastern upper branch of the

Quill a short distance from where both east and west branches merged. "And why is this called Tuck's Ford, and why are there two inns? Surely there're not th' travelers to keep both full?"

She was referring to two identical twin brothers Jukka had described from information given him by Master Reis, two brothers who owned the inns on each side of the river, Tucker residing in the inn on the southeast side of the River Quill and . . . Tucker . . . to the northwest side. Forever competing, each brother would rather pay a guest than have the guest stay at the other brother's inn. Jukka had once observed to his master that he could not see why more people did not populate the Olifant's Playground, considering the Sisters of Hospitality at Madrone and the brothers at Tuck's Ford. His master's reply had been the same as that given to Glimmer by the young man's tutor: the winds, the winds sweeping the valley, winds funneled by the mountains. Better to live in the uplands or the valley, better to live down south than to live in the north and always walk with a lean.

Elesia considered the two log buildings, almost identical, wooden bookends bracketing the river. "So these identical twin brothers are innkeepers in the middle of nowhere on two sides of a river-stream grown so small you can almost spit across?"

Glimmer turned to the woman in amazement. "I think that's the longest sentence I've ever heard you say."

"Stick around," Jukka commented. "She can be a regular bluejay. And," the minstrel added to Elesia, "the brothers are also good at ford scrying."

"How do ye scry a ford?"

"Why, you walk into the water and cross 't, an' if it comes no higher than mid-thigh, then ye've scried a ford." The minstrel began laughing, his face reddening as he held a hand to his chest.

She turned away from the minstrel in mock disgust and asked Glimmer, "Where to from here?"

He pointed to a black bulk of stone that dominated the northern horizon, jutting up into the sky above them and marked fresh with cinder despite the best efforts of water and wind. The cinder cone of the Dragon's Maw jagged the sky, earth and stone blown to tatters that even the ages had not significantly mended. Behind the Maw rose a second, more distant cone.

"Somewhere up there, I believe, we will find the Convergence of the Elements."

"'*Somewhere up there,*' you believe?" sputtered Jukka. "Well, I guess if we don't know where we're going, we don't have to worry about getting lost."

"Ye don' *find* the Convergence," opined the gnome, "ye *recognize* 't."

"As in re-cognize it," furthered the mage. "You remember it with your bones."

"From the looks of the place," muttered the minstrel, "probably lots of bones remember it."

As they started down the graveled incline to the ford, a broad-shouldered man stepped from the inn on their side of the water and waved to the travelers, the blonde hair framing a weathered face so pale it could not be told that blonde was turning to white if not for the thinness of the hair and the redness of the sunburned pate.

"Hail an' weel-met, travelers! Welcome to Tuck's Inn, an' 'tis Tucker hemself 't welcome ye. Will ye be stayin' th' night?" His grin of welcome was genuine, a smile that shone from his entire face and his blue eyes. As Tucker addressed the travelers, across the ford, another man shouted to them. "Ne'vr ye be mindin' that loud talker! Welcome all ye to Tuck's Inn, th' finest victuals and bed o' th' valley! An', master gnome, I've a fine garden harvest fer ye, too, rich in the flavor o' turnips an' carrots, mulched deep from th' frost."

"Any cabbage, say ye?" shouted Cabbage-pants across the ford.

"Green 'r red?"

"The very colors, an' I can see ye're a connoisseur o' the plant, are ye?"

The man on the farther shore was indeed the first Tucker's identical, down to the thinning hair, red pate, and leather straps of suspenders for his breeches.

"Why is't both inns are of the same name?" Elesia shouted, smiling at the novelty of the two brothers.

"Because he stole th' name!" shouted both brothers, simultaneously pointing an accusatory finger at the other.

"Ne'vr mind that ol' gabber across yonder," shouted the nearer brother. "What knows he o' th' cabbage, master gnome! He thinks cabbage a fine plant fer green compost, that he does!" To Cabbage-pants' sputter, he added with a delicious chuckle, "Once did I see'm pull cabbage t' plant a patch o' beans."

"Abominable liar!" shouted the farther brother, shaking his fist. "Don' listen to that forked tongue or ye'll sleep with voles an' rabbits!"

"We are onward," Glimmer shouted over the hubbub of the brothers. "'Tis early yet."

"And perhaps," added the gracious minstrel, "we will spend a night in each of your inns someday to enjoy the hospitality of your words."

"Godspeed!" shouted one and then the other, and then with a glare across the water, each the mirror image of the other, they turned away and entered their respective doorways, both having done their duty and upheld their honor, such as their bickering love considered it.

A diminished track followed each branching of the river which girdled the Dragon's Maw, blue ribbons rising to the cinder. Glimmer stood a moment, the Maw before him, river-streams to his left and right, grassy slopes rising before him to give way at a distance to volcanic stone and sky.

"Left we will go. I agree with Cabbage-pants and do not believe we will find that which we seek at the edge of the Shield. Sky and its emptiness dominates the escarpment and that tipped table of grass," and so they turned to follow the western fork of the River Quill, although if either Tucker had been asked the name of the waters, the "East Tusk" and "West Tusk" of the Olifant would have been their replies.

The wind and cold increased as the travelers ascended the extensive meadowland, bordered east and west by river, defined to the north by the bitter-black slopes of the Dragon's Maw. Glimmer took the lead, donkey following of its own accord, Cabbage-pants now riding the donkey before Elesia, the leather reins in the minstrel's hand as he walked beside the donkey to the windward in an attempt to block wind cutting from the north.

Their day continued with dreary continuity, heads lowered to the icy bite of the wind, feet feeling for a trail dappled with frozen root clumps of grass. To their left and the west, the West Tusk now rippled through a narrow band of meadow, the land beyond rising to deciduous trees devoid of leaves. Beyond, blue in the distance, was the solid darkness of conifers on the mountains. The Dragon's Maw increasingly dominated the landscape, even the meadowland dotted with volcanic effluvia, the slopes of the mountain penciled with grey lines of lava runs, the winter den of snakes and marmots and creatures less likely and more magic.

Volcanoes attract magic like flies to a carcass—or like bees to honey—depending on one's perspective. The wind enjoyed the day, and only Jukka seemed to truly appreciate the cold clarity of the upper meadows of the Olifant's Playground, the lap of the Dragon's Maw. He walked and listened, seeming to hear melodies indiscernible to the ears of the other travelers. At times the minstrel would hear birdsong and would purse his lips and mimic the cry. Glimmer set the pace, the route an unimaginative following of the West Tusk. As afternoon progressed past midday and light began to weaken, their route leaned farther to the west as they closed upon the flanks of the sullen volcano. Space narrowed until they traveled a narrowing valley between the sleeping fire to the east and the sentinels of ice to the west.

As afternoon deepened with the threat of dusk, Glimmer saw the grey serpentine of an ancient lava flow across the narrow meadow to the north. Once lava had flowed and ebbed, and then the outer skin had cooled, leaving the interior hollow. Worn though and fragmented with time and elements, one segment reared from the meadow like a huge, extended rick of hay weathered grey by the elements. An opening darkened the side of the ancient flow where the thinner rock skin had eroded, creating an entrance to a shallow cave.

Handing the reins to Glimmer, Jukka pointed to the black entrance and walked ahead, followed by Cabbage-pants.

"I'd better be th' one to scout yon hole. Those that take to th' earth are better rec'gnized by such as me," said Cabbage-pants. He hurried on bowed legs and caught up with the minstrel, tugging on the minstrel's tunic and speaking to Jukka as the man bent to the gnome. With a nod, the two continued to the cave's entrance, the opening flanked by two tall pines that had fallen in a wind.

Jukka halted a distance from the cave's mouth while the gnome continued to the entrance and peered into the interior gloom while sniffing and snuffing the air. He loosened his obsidian knife in its sheath and cautiously entered the cave. Jukka peered into the opening from where he stood, and Glimmer and Elesia farther down the trail with the donkey silently watched. Then Cabbage-pants exited the cave, a stick extended before him, a large, dormant snake draped over the length of branch.

"Two more, an' then she's clean. I'll be takin' these to another, smaller cave a bit up this flow," he added, disappearing into the small fringe of trees which had seeded in the lee protection of the flow. Twice more he entered the cave and left with his dormant burdens, and then he returned and reentered the cave. "Th' earth is sleepy and not much willin' to talk, but all is well in th' cave—a bit of fire would even liven th' spirits, a remembrance of the fire of their birth, ye might say." Waving a large beckon to the pair with the donkey, the gnome entered the thicket of trees again, searching for firewood.

The cave opening was situated to the lee of the wind. Soon a fire crackled in the entrance of the cave; encircling the blaze were stones that would later be transferred to the back of the cave to warm the travelers while they slept. They ate their travelers' fare of bread and cheese, drinking cabbage tea brewed from water warmed in a cooking pot placed upon the coals.

The cave was too small for standing upright, except for the gnome, the entrance as tall as the roof of the cave, which kept the cave from filling with smoke. Behind the fire, the cave extended in an oval of about ten feet, large enough to sleep the party yet small enough to benefit from the heat of the fire. Jukka planned to picket the donkey before the entrance, thinking that the donkey might even choose to sleep within the entrance, further blocking the cold of the night. The gnome found a small nook at the deepest retreat of the cave, the lava tube providing a vein of fresh air from the porous depths of the earth. He slept on smoothed soil at the entrance to the subterranean depths, "likin' the air," he said, "an' f'rst t' greet any guest from th' deeps," he finished. With that he curled into a ball, almost indistinguishable from the earth. Glimmer wondered if this night he would discover whether or not gnomes snored.

Before the travelers laid themselves in their blankets, wrapped in their cloaks, Glimmer conferred with Jukka and Elesia. "The Elements are all lively here. Can you not feel it?" At their nods, he continued. "I don't yet know the exact place but feel firm in the direction. You, Elesia, how was your day?"

"Following river turned to stream, how could it not go well—in spite of the cold? To follow a river to its birth—this I've never done. The waters are more tender at every turn of the banks. And how is't with you?"

she asked Jukka.

"The air is rarer the higher we climb. And, yes, mage, I feel some difference. The air here is both cold from the mountain peaks and warm from the fire of the earth. It is sprightly, this air. I would not say good or bad—this air tastes of time before such words had value."

"And the Prince of Cabbages has conversed with the earth of this cave, and," here Glimmer jutted with his chin to the cave's entrance, now dark beyond the fire except for the white presence of the donkey, "fire is to our north like the Pole Star in the sky."

"And so . . ." questioned Jukka with a raised brow, the lowering fire mottling his face with shadow.

"And so continue, seeking where all these elements focus, the locus of our intentions."

"That's easy for you to say," commented Jukka, "and here I thought I was the master of rhymes." A snort, followed by a hum, was the sleeping gnome's commentary on the conversation.

"Cabbage-pants is right," observed the mage. "We should be off before sunrise on the morrow."

They slid fire-warmed stone to the back of the cave wall, Elesia nearest the stones, Jukka beside her and Glimmer nearest the cave's entrance. The white donkey was led into the cave, and it stood, a black shadow shouldering out the stars of the night, the donkey's equine scent warm and pungent within the confines of the cave.

Glimmer lay in his traveling clothes, cloaked and blanketed as were the others, his mind certain in its grasp of their journey and its significance, even though the details, the actual steps to be taken were still shrouded and inaccessible to him. He slowly sat upright and moved cautiously in the darkness to the coals still glowing before the entrance. Now behind him, the donkey nuzzled his shoulder as the mage lowered himself to the cave floor, finding stone to lean against at the edge of the entrance. The coals emanated a steadfast radiance, solid and comforting, and the stars now visible from Glimmer's position glittered their own chips of cosmic fire. He closed his eyes, tired as one can tire of teas and juices and yearn for the uncomplicated savor of fresh, pure water. He closed his eyes and began to meditate on the Silence of the Saints, the veil of the busy business of the world sliding from his shoulders. A chamber to house silence he became, and bliss stirred within him, this child of the light.

His head had fallen to his chest, but Glimmer raised it at a sound, raised it and opened his eyes—but nothing was seen but grassland milked to pearl by the moon and the black silhouettes of mountain crags erasing the stars. The sound had been a crying, a woman's cry, but it was not near, not within the range of his ears, not a sound at all but vibrations produced from an emotion, and those vibrations had stirred an empathetic response in the mage, just as vibrations of a tuning fork will evoke a resonance with another nearby. He stood and looked back into the cave, leaning over the sleeping donkey to gaze within. The absolute darkness at the rear of the cave revealed nothing, yet the absolute certainty of his inner vision told him that those within slept quietly, Jukka's arm protectively covering Elesia's shoulders.

Turning again to the entrance, the mage slipped from the cave and followed the trail of his intuition to the meadow below the lava flow, followed the memory of the subtle weeping in the night, heard in the memory of that cry the sadness of the stones of the sanctuary at Madrone; and followed on silent feet, slipping to the path in perfect silence, treading the black and white pearls of moonlight and shadow without falter, spilled like a specter of himself into a night of dreams and the cries of owls and a woman's weeping voice heard before. A tendril of sound, the most fragile tendril of the memory of sound, lingered like moonlight on morning glory, and the mage followed the sound, afoot and then with feet not touching the earth, pulling himself along the tendril of sound, weightless within the warp and woof of his perception; and then the world began spinning past him as he pulled himself along, gnome eyes gazing startled at the human form following their spinning earth-path without gnome to guide.

The tendril of sound thickened, becoming clearer but then without warning fading away to silence—the memory, the song slipping away to nothingness. If one can pause while skiing the slippery slope of magic, the mage now did. He raised his head and extended his senses out to find the living presence his memory was tracking. The mage now smelled rosewater in the air, the small, meaningless vanity of a woman somewhere isolate in her misery—or crying out, not helpless or weak but giving a voice to tenacious emotion, a tendril the mage followed—and now he could taste something tangible in the air, a flower or fragrance that he remembered, someone who had once brushed his lips and left an impression—lips, lips of a woman, the Sister of entreaty—somewhere on the trail, cold and alone and somewhere closer and closer as the world spun and the axis of the moment rotated to a convergence of maiden and mage, Sister and sage. The snaking tendril of convergence coalesced from a phantasm of blurred pearl moonlit montages framed by shadow to a spruce tree, the night-lit black of its blue needle-leaves sweeping the earth, thick and close and private, Glimmer's tendrilled flight ceasing to stillness before the conifer, senses so acute with the magic of the moment that he could hear a woman's breathing, smell her rosewater essence staled with fatigue and journey, remember the taste and touch of her lips.

The spruce grew close to a stream where the water dropped to a pool below, the flow of the stream frozen by the cold, the small waterfall a flowing, frozen sculpture arcing into space and then flowing down to form a frozen pool below, a freezing greater than the temperature warranted. Dark stones wet with black ice framed the stream's course, and the spruce grew thick and green amid the black and white of ice and stone. Senses focused on the scene before him, the Gnome's Path fading to the wintry spectacle. The hollow where the pool lay was sheltered in silence from wind, yet the mage heard a sound, a faint, clear singing, the quiet, crystalline purity of a murmuring, humming melody that captured the elegant essence of the cold in song. Some magical presence focused the cold, intensified it, froze water to cascades of solid ice.

He knelt and parted the spruce's limbs and crawled into the fragrant tent of the tree's canopy of branches. Cold, cold beneath the limbs, wrapped in the grey woolen cloak of her order, her head cowled and tucked as she lay on her side, her warmth curled in upon itself in protection from the cold. Even within the dark tent of the canopy of branches, pale, cold light illuminated Sister Merri, the light emanating from a woman, pale as moonlight, who cradled the Sister's head upon her lap.

The woman glowed in a faint, blue light, her skin a white-tinged-with-blue luminescence. The woman wore a dress seemingly woven of a gauze of ice, a soft shimmer that revealed and concealed simultaneously. Long hair, a translucent white, framed an ageless and ethereal face. Glimmer parted the last branches and entered the presence of the ice naiad, the spirit of the winter stream, who sat upon the blanket of needles and lovingly stroked Sister Merri's hair while singing softly.

"Ah, dream mage, I felt you approach. Have you come to celebrate with me my new sister? Long is the sweet cold, and sweet is my cold sister," the naiad said, her voice like rippling waters.

"I have come to be with my friend."

The naiad looked up to the mage's eyes. "Even at first meeting, you call me your friend. My heart is moved," and the mage felt his heart move, his soul move to meet the naiad's magic. The naiad's head bowed to attend to Sister Merri, but eyes glanced up demurely to consider the mage.

"The Sister is cold," Glimmer managed to say, pulling his attention back to the chill form of Sister Merri.

"Water is the flowing, and the flowing has many forms. Even ice is a flowing," the naiad smiled, raising her arms in a languorous, sensual gesture, "as you see before you now."

"But the woman is not the flowing, not as you."

"Not yet . . ." The naiad bent over the Sister, stroking the cold, pale face. The naiad's hair brushed and covered the woman like a blanket of snow. "But you, dream mage, have also come," the naiad continued. "Shall you be my brother? Ah, but you are not my brother, are you? Perhaps you wish to be something else, to be the fire to my ice? Shall you be my cold fire, my pale fire?"

As the naiad lifted her head and smiled at the mage, he felt the magic of her being—not evil but a magic older than humanity, an elemental magic more ancient than that which breathed and bled and walked upon the earth. Oh, to become that! For the elements to separate, to be clarified, for the water of his being to move with the spirit of stream and waterfall—to sing the song and dance the dance of water flowing! His blood flowed with the desire to flow for eternity by the naiad's side.

The naiad stroked Sister Merri's face that was now attaining a beautiful, pale, translucent luster. "Sing us a dream song, dream mage. Let us share our magic as dream flows, water to ice to vapor." The naiad drank in the mage with her eyes. "I feel the flow of you, the warm summer waters of your blood. Sing to me. Be my winter sun, my cold crystal of light."

Glimmer closed his eyes, remembering the beauty of the sculpted ice of the waterfall, the frozen patterns etched in the ice, the crystalline silence of the air above the frozen stream. He remembered the flow of water in summer, the singing of water as it flowed its course to the sea. He remembered the flow, the journey, the flight of the water; remembered water as white as wings, as white as the whitest flames of fire. Wings, he remembered wings, wings of fire and himself a living flame, a flame riding a dragon of fire down through clouds, the clouds expanding in the fire, thinning to vapor, thinner and thinner, burning to faint excitations expanding in the ether. He had dreamt the dream, lived the dream, was the dream . . .

"Ah!" he heard a gasp and opened his eyes. The naiad sat upright, her spine a lightning rod as she stared upward in wonder and ecstasy, her arms reaching to the mage. She gasped again then and *flowed*, expanded, burst in a sudden explosion of ice to water to steam, the fires of the mage's dream melting the winter cold of the naiad's magic. "Ah!" the naiad gasped and then a fog surrounded the mage, surrounded Glimmer sitting beside a woman sleeping, curled upon a bed of spruce needles.

Sister Merri did not start at the ice naiad's sudden transition to steam, only opened her eyes to see a change in the shadowed blackness before her.

"I knew you would come," she whispered with absolute certainty, her voice slurred with cold. "I was hoping it'd be you and not a blacker shadow. But it was not a blacker shadow I dreamed," she stated, confusion in her voice. "It was a white shadow, a beautiful cold shadow."

"How could you tell it was me now with you?" the mage asked.

"I do not think death, dressed either in black or white, would smell of woodsmoke and . . . well . . . you."

The mage felt moisture on his cheeks, magic lingering in the water vapor. "Come," he said, "I think we should leave before the magic of this place condenses and we get frostbit." Ice can be cold, cold and hard as steel, and the mage wished to leave the naiad to the cold silence of her solitary season.

Glimmer was then again standing in his dream, standing before the spruce, the young woman in his arms, light as bread; and he thought of bread, fresh and fragrant from the oven, and the heat it radiated, so warm to the hands on a cold day; and the woman sighed and cuddled herself closer to him, breathing in deeply and letting out her breath with a sigh before drifting to the stillness of sleep. The spruce whorled, twisting in upon itself, and then was another tree, another place, the Sanctuary of the Madrones, a point before the entrance. Glimmer turned and saw the moonlit statuary across the road, the gate open, the sanctuary doors opening, the woman a loaf of the lightest bread, easy in his hands and arms, an easy walking up path and through door into the echoing silence of the grand hall, up two flights of stairs and down a hall to a door as incorporeal as a moonbeam, a form sleeping in a humble cot, Sister Superior sleeping, her eyes opening to see the mage carrying the woman before her, bathed in moonlight from the room's window.

"She is with you and is well," Sister Lisbeth spoke, and then in his arms the woman woke, eyes on the room, the stones, and said, "Not here, the sadness of the stones grinds me, even now . . ." and sagged again to the mage's chest, the agony of the stones a physical pain.

"She is with me and is well," the mage said to the Sister of the humble cot, repeating Sister Superior's sleep-shadowed murmur. "She knows the sadness of these stones, even beneath the ease I have given them. Here she cannot stay."

Young Sister murmured, words muffled by Glimmer's cloak, "Ye came, an' I knew ye would, my teacher . . ." the words fading again.

"No, Sister Merri, I am not the teacher ye seek." The young mage met eyes with Sister Superior, still within her blankets, and spoke what he knew the woman already understood. "She cannot stay here. I will take her to her true teacher, to Alma-Ata."

Sister Lisbeth acknowledged Glimmer's words with a slow nod. "Will I remember this dream when I awake?" she asked. "And will I believe?"

"It is a true-dream—or perhaps, better said, truth within a dream."

Sister Lisbeth raised herself to one elbow and then spoke: "I have been reading DeVasier's aphorisms. 'Convergence is consciousness,'" but the room was fading, collapsing to a point, the point bleeding into distance, pulling mage once more into the gnome's mad riverstream of travel, the path now a drunken zigzag of momentum, single gnomes standing like stones in the careening, anchoring the points of the tack, the woman sleeping still within his dreaming arms, her face painted with the light of the moon, beautiful ivory to dreaming mage-eyes.

He carried her up the meadow to the lava flow, her form growing more substantial with every step until he reached the cave entrance, his back bowed with the weight of her actual form; her weight now not one of dream-wight, the young man sagging at the cave's entrance to sink within the form of another image of the young mage, an image fading and fading as the dream-mage approached, then vanishing as the dream settled into the night, settling his back against the rough stone of the entrance, the coals still glowing in their ruddy splendor, the woman settling her head against his shoulder, an awkward sprawl of two bodies blurred by shadow, the moon eclipsed by the stone shoulders of the lava flow above and around them.

Glimmer rested his head against the stone behind him, felt himself sink more deeply into silence, and from within that primal silence could suddenly see the interior of the cave as clearly as if it were noontime on a clear day outside in the meadow, sky as blue as the grass is green.

"Come," he said to the sleepers, and Jukka stirred to an elbow and then gently shook Elesia. They stood, Cabbage-pants now beside them, murmuring, "I'll be comin', too."

Dream Mage Glimmer stood, holding the sleeping woman easily, Jukka lifting Elesia into his arms, smiling and tossing her a foot into the air as she squealed, dream-knowledge structuring the logic of the moment. The gnome loosened his knife in its sheath, reached with his hands to grasp minstrel and mage, and then together they whirled within the whorls of the earth, the cabbage gnome calling the tacks, the phantasmagoria of their career increased beyond reason, blur of pearl light and dancing silhouettes, even the eyes of gnomes mere apparitions in the tapestry of their travel until they stood rock solid before the Stone Dragon Inn, the sign's colors blackened by moonlight, the windows like pale, vacant eyes that know no dreams.

They entered the inn through the kitchen door, the gnome holding a taper to coals, and the men carried the women up the stairs to the wooden landing, the door to Alma-Ata's study open and waiting. They entered to find the elder mage sitting on his pallet, cross-legged in meditation.

Opening his eyes, the mage spoke quietly. "So it is time for them to learn the Silence of the Saints? All, of course, except for you," he added, nodding to the gnome. "Your body breathes to its own magic."

"I came f'r th' teas," commented the gnome. "Ladyfolks'll need a special blend o' the cabbage, y' see—"

"Perhaps a later time, my gnomish friend?" suggested Alma-Ata, to which the gnome nodded, slapped his forehead, and left the room muttering to himself and shaking his head.

Elesia stirred for Jukka to let her down, and then Glimmer also slowly placed Sister Merri on her feet, Elesia and Jukka holding her upright as Glimmer massaged the Sister's wrists and hands, seed-joy rejuvenating her. When the two women and Jukka stood before him, Alma-Ata nodded to Glimmer. "Perhaps you will help Cabbage-pants downstairs?" He smiled slightly. "You still have a thing or two to learn about teas."

"And the gnome is just the one to instruct me," muttered Glimmer as he turned to leave the room, first with a look to the three standing before the elder mage.

"Sit," murmured the sitting man to his students, and it began, wholeness and holiness the first instruction, the greatest gift given first.

The young mage descended the stairs, yet as he stepped, the stones rose to meet his feet until at last he moved merely to meet the shuffle of stones, rising or descending, neither seeming a motion, or was it that the mage stood at the apex of both motions, neither progressing or regressing, inclining or declining, movement immaterial to the physiology of the universe, awareness aware of itself. He sat on a stone step and closed his eyes, the shimmer of the world ceasing its celestial calling, light beyond light and night beyond darkness, wholeness and holiness, simplicity, simplicity, simplicity, as simple as a hand touching his shoulder, his master bading him to the door, three others with the master, their eyes shining and their faces joyfully awakened, the kitchen glowing with a replenished fire and Bega hugging her daughter and son-to-be Jukka, Bega hugging Sister Merri as a mother hugs her child. Wilim, standing close to the mother, bowing silently to Glimmer, who bowed back an equal measure.

"You must stay here," Glimmer said to Sister Merri. And as she opened her mouth to protest, he urged, "Stay with your master, with these good people. No stones weep within these walls."

The Sister bowed to him and then kissed him, softly, one cheek and then the other. "I was raised surrounded by mountain stone. These stones," she said, looking about her, "tell me you must go . . . and I must stay. I accept sacred hospitality as it is offered."

Glimmer bowed an equal measure, and gnome loosened his knife in its sheath; then out the door the pilgrims swept, the road whipping down its length like a whale's tail, spume of mountains and cinder cone scud in an ocean of earth, earth-sea wild with the storm of their traveling to a meadow, a cave entrance, the ruddy coals crystalline with ash, dawn lightening the horizon and a white donkey, inquisitive ears pricked forward, its head thrust from the cave entrance.

The sojourners added wood to the fire and heated water for tea. Glimmer closed his eyes but did not sleep; rather, he slipped again into silence, world whirring about him, planets spinning and stars burning yet his awareness steadfast in that essence, that consciousness that lies at the source of thought.

How far Not a Glimmer of Magic has come, he thought. *Even now, I cast no spells, read no potent words from fragile tomes found in the abandoned libraries of the long departed. I do what my master bid me do long ago—or at least it seems long ago. I follow the daily routine given by my master—keep myself rested and in accord with the world around—then act, be it action in waking or dreaming. And now this day next—or even this day since it is past midnight—I will act to save an immortal, a dragon who struck from the sky when I summoned a star, a dragon on whose back I rode as it fell upon a stone house, upon a young dreamer—myself!*

In amazement, he thought of the seasons past and the steps of the journey to this place. He would do this, he thought, and then return home to soon-coming spring, to the garden and long discussions with a certain gnome regarding the various incarnations of cabbage. The weight of the world is great, and he would better bear it with his family at his back.

My family, he thought. *Yes, families are formed in different ways. I shall return to my family.*

Eyes still closed, he heard the susurrus of the donkey's deep breathing as it returned to slumber, envisioned its white silhouette in the feeble light which filtered into the cave, the donkey's neck lowered and one rear leg cocked. Letting out a deep breath, Glimmer, ready to do what needed to be done, opened his eyes.

Jukka and Elesia stood before him, their faces smiling in the pale dawn light. Movement caught his eye, Cabbage-pants exiting to find wood for the fire.

"So," spoke the minstrel, "we finally see your magic, as you have described it—nurturing . . . and awful."

"Boo!" was the mage's sarcastic reply, not moving his limbs which had stiffened with the awkwardness of his prolonged position.

"The mage who led us to the Silence," added Elesia.

Jukka nodded thoughtfully. "I did not know that Alma-Ata taught the Silence of the Saints. All these years, such a secret to keep. And why?"

"Not all these years," Glimmer explained. "The Mage DeVasier taught me and then a few days later—or a few weeks, depending on how the time is reckoned—he met and taught my master not only the practice but also how to teach it."

"DeVasier! But he—" interrupted Jukka.

"Yes, I know—but time and death are apparently not the same for all men."

"And what now?" asked Elesia.

"First, let us greet the dawn."

"Oh, yes!" was the woman's quiet exclamation.

"An' then t' break yer fast," growled the gnome, then adding with a rough smile, "an' some cabbage tea, a cup o' th' essence."

"And the breakfast will be cabbage and porridge, I suppose?" joked Glimmer.

"Yer readin' m' mind, mage," was the reply.

Chapter 12

"To trace magick backe to its beginnings is to trace backe to the essence of magick itselfe. Magick is the arte of actione from the pointe of beginning. Juste as a king or his champione knowes why the armie moves and the pikeman afoote in the block knowes not, the mage actes frome the first impulse of nature and thus knoweth its full power—the oceane, not the wayve.
The Philosophie of Magick

⅓

At the entrance of the cave, they sat on dried grasses gathered the night before. The morning sun rosed the sky and warmed the meadow. They closed their eyes and slipped into silence. The smell of oats and cabbage was their call to action, and even that challenge to diplomacy was met with aplomb . . . and a generous application of honey. Luckily, the cabbage was a flavoring to the porridge and not the major portion. Soon the travelers were on their way, Cabbage-pants leading the donkey once again, the mage at his side listening to the efficacy of cabbage cordial to cure a stomach weak from traveling the hurly-burly snake of the Gnome's Path.

The West Tusk now branched again, and the travelers followed the east fork of the West Tusk which continued to round the shoulder of the Dragon's Maw. The travelers traversed a narrowing valley between two cones, the larger Dragon's Maw to the southeast on their right and the smaller cinder cone of Old Smokey to the northwest. Old Smokey poured its grey-white ashen steam into the blue sky, the volcanic cloud tailing off to the north as wind swept up the valley from the grasslands. As they reached the midpoint between the volcanic mountains, the valley flattened. The river, now a stream, slowed and was dammed and diverted by the work of beavers felling and weaving the aspens of the valley. Small streams and rivulets fed the main stream from both sides of the valley. At length, the travelers came to a section of the valley where old stone had emerged from beneath more recent volcanic flows. Basalt sheeted the mountain; steam rose and rivulets traced their way. Hot springs fanned across the cold stone of late winter. The circular valley was a cup of warmth provided by subterranean fires, an ancient caldera now encroached upon by the two volcanic upstarts rising high above the valley. Air was warmed, some moss still green on southern-facing slabs of stone protruding from the soil. The travelers stopped, out of the wind, surrounded by meadow and aspen and the glimmer of water, blue sky above and earth below, fire cones and the sun between, the sun's rays following the stream up the valley to where the travelers stood.

Glimmer gazed about him, the others captivated by the beauty and stillness of the place with its trill of running water and susurrus of wind in trees and the occasional slap of a beaver's tail upon water mirroring the blue belling of the sky.

"Somewhere here is where need and purpose will converge."

"A place of beauty," said Elesia, followed by the minstrel's, "Worthy of song."

"An' look! Wild cabbage!" shouted the gnome, pointing to a winter-browned mass beside the chipped tooth of a stone. "Th' fruit o' course's gone, but th' root, now . . ."

Glimmer, seeing steam spuming from a split in stone at the cupped valley's northern edge, knew that this place would be the crucible to test the mettle of his magic.

Steam vented from stone split by primal upheaval, and from the base of the pillars issued a stream of scalding water that coursed across a slab of stone to tumble into the stream, so the farther the water coursed across the stone from the split where it emerged, the more it cooled. At one point the slab had split so that a waterfall a man's height fell, showering at the drop-off. A small meadow rose to the east of the stream, the last vestiges of the Olifant's Playground before the meadow narrowed to a boulder-strewn gorge. At the uppermost extent of the meadow's incline, the Dragon's Maw rose above the grasses, a blasted tumble of stone and gnarled conifer merging with the bleached grasses of winter. A cave, formed of slabs of stone mortared by earth and grass, cemented by roots of pine, led onto a narrow beard of grass at the apex of the meadow. Fire, water, earth—and the fourth, air, was revealed as the wind swept the meadow from the mountains, the other three elements emanating from their respective vessels: vented from the earth, pouring from the gorge, shrouded by the earth-cave. Space extended above them in its most obvious form, the blue expanse of the sky.

Glimmer slowly walked across the meadow until he stood at the locus of the elements, beneath the sky like the earth-mother's body: the steam vent at one shoulder of the upper meadow, the earth-cave the other shoulder, one hip the waterfall sheeting to tumble to the stream, and the other hip the open expanse of meadow grass beneath the pale blue sky. He stood at the nexus of this unity of the elements and raised his head to the heavens, the sun warming him with the faintest promise of spring. He felt the unity of the place, all of existence in seed form, the site an earth talisman of elemental forms. He nodded to himself and then pointed to a bower of undergrowth downstream which would provide fuel, fodder, and protection from the wind.

"Let's set camp there."

They cut pine branches and constructed a lean-to in order to keep the wind at bay. Before the structure, they laid their firepit, raising rocks on the outer side so that more heat would be reflected inward toward the primitive shelter. Water was put to boiling in the cooking pot, and a small, brown form hunched before the fire, maintaining the flames while Elesia and Jukka added ingredients to the pot from a wallet filled with provender. Afternoon shadows lengthened, and the company ate lightly: stale bread, cheese, a thin soup, and scalding tea from water boiled in a second flame-blackened pot. Afterwards, they sat around the fire, realizing that approaching evening was not cooling the day as quickly as they had expected. Fire beneath the earth was subtly maintaining the warmth of the area, easing the late winter temperatures.

"What do we do now?" Jukka asked as they stared into the flames.

"We begin, according to our inner voices," Glimmer responded, at once certain of the instruction, even though he had no clear course of action in mind. "We begin with hearts open, seeking to unite that which has been divided."

"My master said that there are greater songs to be sung if only our ears will hear them," the minstrel considered, and then he sang softly, almost to himself.

> We see beyond our eyes
> But blind are to the vision,
> Hear sounds beyond the ear
> But know not how to listen;
> Taste flavor beyond the lips,
> Beyond senses, smell and taste.
> We are greater than ourselves:
> Sing not the song with haste.

As deliberation progressed, a small animal crept to Elesia's side, a brown otter, barely containing its energy, edging slowly to the woman's side and leaning against her thigh. A bird then flew from the nearby trees, a brown and white wood thrush. It fluttered to land on the minstrel's shoulder, raising its open mouth to whistle its flutelike song, trilling to an end: *t-t-olay-oleeeee*. Pleased with itself, it danced on the minstrel's shoulder, preening. Cabbage-pants had sat through the discussion, his eyes half-closed, his body motionless. When a grey badger crept out of the grass and laid its masked head on the gnome's lap, the gnome merely lifted a hand and placed it on the badger's head, softly caressing it.

"Familiars have come," Glimmer said softly. Magic was gathering, and the young man felt both excitement and trepidation. "So it begins: water, air, and earth. But what of fire, which would be mine?"

"Beg pard'n," murmured the gnome, not even opening his eyes. "Fire drake, hm?"

"Er, yes, I suppose so," admitted the young man.

A look and they stood and scanned the area about them. Glimmer did not seek to orchestrate. It was simply a unity of purpose, a letting go to the intuitive kinship of their hearts. *It is,* he realized, *very much like my master's magic of Gathering:* waiting, poised to act, and then something subtle, something small at precisely the right moment.

A world of magic opened before him; he remembered his master standing before an arrogant mage mounted on a horse, one who had mocked the apple-mage's magic, Alma-Ata saying, "You mean for working spells?" and then his master had extended his hands and wiggled his fingers confusedly, mocking arrogance in his own quiet manner. To do nothing and accomplish everything—how could any magic be greater than that?

Elesia frisked with the otter and then stood before the waterfall. She removed her shoes and tested the water with a foot. Smiling, she began to remove her clothes, and then the curious thing happened that Glimmer had seen once before. Steam swirled from the water and coalesced around the woman so that even though she was nude, she wore a pearl gown of mist that maintained her modesty. She stepped into the water, mist forming around her head in a crown, her arms revealed as she moved and cupped the water with a hand, her expression serene, her movements dance-like. The otter splashed with her, swimming round and round, flipping to its back to observe the woman.

The minstrel gazed at the graceful form of Elesia gowned in crystalline mists and then moved to the meadow to where the shoulders of the mountain lay back and opened to the sky. The wood thrush circled as the minstrel thoughtfully found his place, the width of the small meadow separating air from water. The thrush landed on his shoulder and trilled its song. The minstrel pulled a wooden flute from his traveler's bag and began to pipe back to the thrush. Back and forth they trilled, with Jukka voicing the sounds at times, singing without words, sounds pure and primal pouring from him as joyous and selfless as birdsong.

The gnome walked with phlegmatic gait, flanked by badger equally phlegmatic, to the earth-cave's entrance and disappeared without a backward glance, earth knowing its own exultation, as silent and certain as the grave. Bones know their beginnings, and gnomes know the fit of each within the body of the earth. Cave wisdom is gnome wisdom, magic best left to itself.

Glimmer stood alone at the bower's edge. At length he walked the length of the meadow, following the gnome's path until he set his goal for the pillar of steam rising in the moonlit air.

A pillar of stone rose like a needle pointing to the Pole Star. Steam, emanating from a tumbled heap of stone tossed by an earth giant's hand, rose from behind the pillar. The stone was warm to his touch as he placed his hands flat against the stone's wet surface. Warm mist moistened the air and dimmed the brilliance of the stars. Moon was circled by a nimbus of glowing light, and the faint hiss of steam escaping earth rose and fell in rhythms as if the earth's blood could be heard surging in veins of soil and stone.

Glimmer pulled the hood of his cloak over his head and then sat at the base of the pillar, resting his back against the warmth. Next to the earth, the stone was warmer, closer to the fiery heartbeat, and the stone was dry and hot. He slipped his hood back, letting its bundled bulk pillow his head and neck as he leaned against the stone. What could he do with steam except scald himself? Stone as warm as the stone dragon's scaled sides and air as heated as that scorched by dragonfire—what could he do except sit against the pillar and observe the singing minstrel, the dancing water sprite, and the dark eye of the earth-cave?

O remember the fires of the inn and the stone dragon burning a hotter fire than one built from oak split and carried to hearth! Remember guests remarking on the warmth of the fire and how the flame did husband that which it devoured! Fire and fire and fire without end without beginning—within, not without! Fire within and the mother of all conflagration, liquid fire within the glass, dragon's blood within a vial! Glimmer's hand slipped to the pocket within the breast of his cloak and felt the vial obtained dream within dream within dream. Or was all a dream? Or were there no dreams, only an endless dream of realities? He closed his eyes, imagined the seers of ancient reckoning and entered the Silence, his back against the dragon's talon, hand filled with crystal dragon's blood, his consciousness the heatless, smokeless effulgence of the self. O remember the fires of the self and sleep secure in the silence of the saints! Dream of being becoming and of the silence from which the song of life arises.

The mage dreamt not. He arose, awake within his sleep and, somnambulist rimed with magery, walked steadily to the forest that thicketed the slopes surrounding the earth-cave and began collecting wood. He carried the wood to where the meadow began at the pillar's base and laid it on the ground, a narrow strip of wood pointing from the meadow's shingle of detritus to the locus, the convergence of the four elements. Four beings to unite at the meadow's center to save the soul of a dragon!

He walked and collected; he carried and continued to line his compass point of the convergence with wood. All night it would have taken, but the animals of the meadow and mountain came and began to help—squirrel and fox, beaver, even mice. Still it would have taken a night, for how much wood can an animal carry? Gnomes appeared, dressed spruce green and meadow gold, wood bundled high in their arms, glancing not at the young mage sleepwalking his dreamless magic. An automaton, a thrall to his vision, the mage continued his silent collection, the clatter of wood as it fell to its place only emphasizing the silence of the task. The minstrel and the water sprite, no longer their smaller selves but immersed in the elemental truth born and borne deep within their bones, continued water-dance and birdsong elemental with beauty. Gnome and animal laid wood as inexorably as landslide. The elements converged not upon a point but a unity of consciousness.

The mage then turned with sedate steps and stood before the pillar, facing the wood lined to the locus of the elements, to the center. He stood before the pillar, his arms stretched wide and to the sky, awake within his dreaming, having walked to waking. Silence splintered as the mage spoke the ritual words of the Orders of Hospitality: "Be warmed by the hospitality of the hearthstone."

The tableau was a weird and fantastic one: woman sprite in water, player of the pipe in the meadow, phlegmatic gnome an incarnation of earth, mage before a pillar of steam. Otter, wood thrush, badger, and soul-blood of the dragon—before all the stars in the sky and all the grasses of the meadow, the elements were assembled at the convergence. The avenue of wood stretching before the mage was touched by a single drop of dragon's blood as the mage poured from vial to wood, a fiery path igniting, a rising promenade of flame from the incline before the pillar of stone and steam to the apex.

The movement of the actors was almost dance-like, slow and deliberate, movement full of significance and intent. No script was there, nor dramaturge, unless it was nature's tendency to seek equilibrium. Slowly air, water, and earth proceeded along the power line of each element. Air proceeded step by step, each stride expressing its corresponding music. Water glided from its pool, mists gowning the sprite's glory until she lifted her cloak and wrapped herself in its woolen length, a halo of mist still her crown. Gnome advanced with strides as abiding as the earth. All were now equidistant from the apex, as if the four were cardinal points on the circumference of a circle, crossed lines to form equal quarters within space. Silence was matched by stillness, the next act to begin as all creation had begun, dynamism arising from silence.

The flames had died to a ribbon of coals when Glimmer, standing before the glowing coals, awoke outside the dream; and then he realized, integrating the vision before him to his intent, that the bed of coals was a path, his path—that the dream mage, the young mage of red-blonde hair, mage of the dragon of stone with blood like sunfire—would walk open-eyed a concourse of fire to find his purpose at the Convergence of the Elements: not Gnome's Path but Glimmer's Path, his fate and destiny. He could feel the steam-heat like moist breath behind him, curling to wreathe him in moist fire; and he could feel sheaves of dry burning before him evaporating the steam curling to lick his face.

Where is the dream when the mage is waking? Where is the mage when the mind dreams not? Where is the magic of Not a Glimmer of Magic? *It is madness that will maim,* he thought, never a clearer thought within his mind. *I am awake in a nightmare, captured in the crux of my imaginings. Run!* his memory voiced. *Run as fast as you can away from here, or you will burn!*

"Convergence is consciousness," the good Sister's memory reminded him, and the mage stepped one step down the incline, his step matched by the other elements. Heat increased before him, cooled behind him. He burned, but as he burned he healed, seed-joy no less joyous than the burning of the flame. Gone was water afire; he now would dance as the saints of the desert, where blue lakes and gliding waters were but a dream.

Firesteps and flagstones cut from the Gnome's Path; elements converge closer to a point in space as mage-mind settles to a point of consciousness and then collapses upon itself. The vessel of his consciousness, consciousness itself, moves and mage witnesses feet stepping upon coals, fire surging to meet him. A fiery mirror vision of himself rises from the burning red of the coals, eyes and hair and lean cheeks of pale flame. A flaming hand rises, and the mage raises a hand to match that of fire.

"I place fire within your hand," lips of burning light speak in sibilant, crackling tones. Fiery hand flames a red ball of fire and then dies back, fingertips to palm, until fire fades from Glimmer's palm and the flaming apparition collapses into the bed of coals upon which the mage stands.

"Convergence is consciousness" reverberates in his mind, and how can fire deny that upon which it feeds, how can consciousness burn consciousness, how can one hand deny the existence of the other? A gravel of coals glows beneath him as the mage advances step and step to the center of the circle, the convergent elements collapsing to a point, expanding to infinite unity.

Center was met: air, water, earth, and fire now at arm's length, a circle delineating a focus of space, the witness and recipient of all, the vessel to be filled. The mage removed the vial from his cloak and extended it within the circle. The fire within the glass, the dragon's blood like a solar furnace glowed, brighter and brighter until the glass melted, dripping through his fingers to fall sputtering onto the dry meadow grasses. Dragonfire retained its shape, though, serpentine *draco* held within his hand. He knelt, the other elements mirroring his movements, until all were sitting on the wind-blown grasses of winter, stars above pocking the darkness of the sky, dragonfire so bright they could see nothing else, only the mother of all earthly light, all mortal fire.

Mage Glimmer placed the sculpture of fire to the earth before them, and it burned not the grasses, emanated no heat. Heat implies cold; light implies darkness. Now there were no dualities, only oneness, only light beyond lightning, flame beyond fire, blood beyond body, action beyond activity. The halo of mist that crowned water's hair Elesia now lifted with regal hands and held over the burning dragon. Mist condensed and sprinkled in rain upon the dragon of fire. Gnome reached into the earth before him, his hand blurring as he plunged his arm to the elbow, pulling a handful of soil which he crumbled over the burning blood of the dragon, the soil sifting through the primal light; next minstrel leaned into the light, pipe to his lips. He blew through the pipe, and three notes, each solitary and pure, filtered into the air. Fire pulsated, bright beyond vision, expanding and rising above the seated signatories of the elements. Fire rising and the four rising to their feet, Glimmer raised his hands to the dragon of fire above them, wings outstretched, fire's actions matched by air, water, and earth.

"*Samhita,*" the mage articulated, and the name was formed and repeated by the others.

Sound defined the air, and all elements combined in space to incorporate fire-blood to actual dragon, grey scales and obsidian eyes, mouth of fire and teeth moon bright. Wings flapped once, twice, air moved by corporeal strength. Moonlight now lit the milk-white dragon, and stars of fire glittered like white obsidian, the four signatories craning their necks to the massive dragon that dominated the meadow like a raptor hovering over rabbits.

Samhita. Yes, you have done well, young mage.

"Do what you will, dragon. Whole again, I give you your freedom. The immortal should not die."

And how do you define "die"?

"There is more than one definition?"

As many definitions as incarnations of life.

"And how do you define *life*?"

Ah, you are learning, young mage.

An awkward moment ensued. Dragon loomed like a cloud above them, wings flapping as if in habit or out of convention, surely not quickly or deeply enough to lift the dragon's mass, the company below diminished, awed, cowed, exhilarated alternately by the mountain of flesh above.

Finally: "I hear the voice, the dragon's voice, yes?" from Elesia, her words breaking the spell of the moment, the minstrel and Elesia glancing to one another to verify their experience, the gnome spitting on the ground, not with insolence but with haughty equanimity, the mage realizing that which he had craved was now shared with all.

You should take rest, the dragon said, actually nodding its head and then motioning with it to their camp at the meadow's base. *We shall return to the inn together. I will take you. For now, sleep. Mage, sleep and dream some fanciful and impressive means for your return. I shall carry you all—even your donkey,* the dragon commented, amusement in its voice. *Unless, of course, this body becomes too hungry.*

With that, the dragon curled its neck skyward, arched and beat its wings, rising more quickly than wings should allow, breathing a joyful blast of song and fire into the night sky, diminishing to a comet, a star, and then disappearing into the night sky. Late winter silence descended on the high meadow, the faint crunch of feet on frosted grass and ground, breath fogging the night air, the rustle of cloth in the silence.

In the pause of action abated, in the shifting of weight from one foot to the other, the gnome took the initiative, striding on stocky legs toward the company's camp at the base of the meadow. Reaching the rough shelter of cut boughs, the coals of their fire still glowing with warmth, they settled around the fire, Elesia passing out bread and cheese. Silence still dominated the group, the events of the evening too personal to yet discuss and analyze, but small talk arose in quiet tones—the passing of the water gourd, a request for more cheese, the search and placing of a pot of water to heat for cabbage tea. At length the silence turned to fatigue, that draining of energy which comes with the aftermath of great efforts and deeds. They readied themselves for sleep and then, wrapped in their robes and the fire replenished, they retired to their beds of boughs to rest.

Crickets mere frozen promises of song within the soil, the only sounds of the night were liquid sounds of water over stone and wind in tree. Someone turned in sleep; the fire crackled as a bough burned through and settled to coals. Glimmer lay on his back, wide awake, although now he questioned his ability to accurately recognize sleep from waking from dreaming. Had he walked on coals and not his dream-self? Or had his feet never actually touched the coals, upheld by seed-joy and Gnome's Path? Or had his feet burned and healed simultaneously? Had an elemental being of fire incarnated in Glimmer's form and placed fire within the mage's hand—with a fiery version of his own hand? Had the dragon matter-of-factly told him to sleep and perform magic, magic of a precise nature for a specific purpose? He placed his arm over his eyes, seeking relief from the events of the night.

Why do I not feel exhilaration at having achieved what I set out to accomplish? No one is injured; there has been no conflict, no battle.

And yet he felt anxious to be back at the stone inn, to engage in some trivial activity—sweeping the floor of the common room—not thinking of anything, just letting the day flow on its course, just drifting with the minutes until day was ended and he could lie down and sleep. If he were now a mage—and so the dragon had called him—then he was a mage too few in years and experience.

Maybe it gets easier as you get older . . . but then Glimmer remembered Alma-Ata at Delta, furious at the obligation to accomplish magery greater than tending to apple trees. *So much easier to pull weeds, sweat, and complain,* Glimmer thought. *So much better to lie down, to close my eyes and sleep. Lie down and sleep.* Lie down and close his eyes. Close his eyes. Sleep.

Glimmer breathed in deeply the warm, moist summer smells of the meadow across the stream from the Stone Dragon Inn. The stars . . . well . . . *glimmered* in the bowl of the night sky which capped the meadow. The stone dragon was anchored in stillness at the meadow's center, even more timeless than the stars that move with the centuries, the constellations of the sky mutating with their journeys. He raised himself on one elbow, the cold boughs of the upper meadows of the Olifant's Playground no longer his bed; now the soft, lush grasses of summer cushioned the earth.

"So now I'm to build by demand, like a lord's architect?" he demanded.

A mage always responds to the needs of the environment; that is the whole of magery.

"So the drudge who cleans the stable is performing magic?"

Perhaps great magic. Your master, Alma-Ata, is a very great mage, yet he performs no magic, only attracts it—as he attracted you, young mage.

Nonplussed by that answer, Glimmer lapsed into silence. He approached the dragon and placed a hand against the dragon's warm flank. He leaned against the implacable, impossible reality of the dragon and rested his face against its bulk.

"I am glad you are free and whole again, no matter what you do."

And what do you think I shall do?

"Not kill and destroy. That is like stomping on an ant hill—the act of a child, not something that fits you."

The dragon chuckled mental amusement, a small spray of steam escaping the nostrils. *Perhaps I shall surprise you.* The dragon opened one fell eye and arched its neck to consider the mage. *So what do you think I shall do?*

"I think you shall do what you like . . . and like what you do."

And what shall you do?

Glimmer considered for a moment and then replied, "What needs to be done."

And nothing more?

"Oh, I'll think of something else to do—if I have the time, which I think I shall not."

You are learning, young mage.

Glimmer straightened and faced the dragon, who stared down at the mage with eyes like dark stars.

"So now I am to perform some trickery to construct a platform for us to ride as you fly us home? Why don't you just increase your size so that we all can ride on your back? The donkey, of course, you can carry in your talons."

An experience that I am sure it shall cherish.

"Or why not just come along with us? Even if we walk the entire way, having you would ensure our safety and warmth."

Crude but effective.

"So why the whistles and bells?"

Perhaps you can tell me.

Glimmer found himself in no hurry to leave the lush warmth of the summer dream meadow. He sat on the grass before the dragon, leaning back on his arms, his head raised to gaze up at the dragon. *Mother is at home,* he thought with amusement.

"You are free now, so we are of no use to you. However, even though you do not need us, that does not mean you necessarily do not want our company."

A dragon desiring the company of humans?

"Let us say . . . for amusement."

And . . .

"A clever dragon might pose a test, one to measure a mage's vanity, his arrogance."

"Clever" is such a small word.

"Devious?"

Too dark.

"Humungous?"

Excellent . . . for a very large piece of donkey pie.

"Ingenious, inscrutable?"

Never mind. I am satisfied.

"I, too."

Crickets and fireflies and the silent flight of moths. The purling of the stream muted by darkness. Glimmer sat cross-legged before the dragon, the bulk of the dragon like a mountain, and realized that he was not even sure whether or not the dragon *breathed*. He could stand and place his hand to the warm width of the dragon's chest, could feel the heat of the dragon's fire when it breathed fire . . . Now that was an indication that it could take in air and then expel it, but the mage could not tell, could not discern the normal, mortal breathing of the dragon as he could discern the breathing of the white donkey, for instance, were he to stand next to it.

For that matter, though, Glimmer was not sure that he had ever seen the gnome breathing as a human does, in and out without thinking. *Cabbage-pants does snore, though,* the mage thought wryly. *And snoring requires breath. Perhaps I am making this too complicated. Perhaps I should think of their breathing as earth and stone breathe.*

The world is not required to fit the human mold, whether made by mage or common man. To be a mage is to understand that, to *see* with wider and deeper vision, to remove veils and boundaries till one sees to the very beginning of a thing, to know the roots of a thing and not just its distracting leaves and flowers and branches.

"A dragon acts of its own nature. But what is a dragon? What is action, and what is its basis? And what is a dragon's nature, our own nature? What is nature itself, and what are the laws that govern it?" the young man spoke aloud.

The silence of the night stretched to infinity and then collapsed, we who breathe the beneficiaries of this act of creation. The stone dragon inhaled with a subtle sound like that of wind filtering though subterranean caves. Pause stretching to the collapse of silence, and then the sound of wind in trees, as soft and delicate as that of dawn when night air warms and drifts with the rising: Samhita breathed.

Satisfied?

The mage groaned and then growled and stood. *Back to winter,* he thought. To know, at least, the ephemerality of winter was some consolation, as long as one did not mourn the ephemerality of summer. Better to understand that the wheel of the seasons revolved round a hub; better to know the hub, to witness life spin past, to know the center. *It is better,* Glimmer thought, *to ride the dragon than to cower beneath its shadow.*

"I'd better wake up. Time's wasting away."

Time. Ah, that thing, commented the dragon as the mage awoke by closing his eyes, finding the silence-filled interstice between, consciousness witnessing the mage closing his eyes to wake from dreaming.

Chapter 13

"A dreme mage who dremes his magery will die, if fate be mercyful, either bye his dreme or bye the hand of Nature. A dreme mage muste conjure the dreme from its greater realitie, muste shape the dreme frome his owne awarenesse. Entering the dreme and thene leaving it, do not imagyne the mage to be a parte of it, for there lyes the pathe to nightmare and disspaire.

Confessions of a Dreme Mage

එ

Glimmer woke his sleep-drunk companions, all except the gnome, who had gone within the earth-cave—perhaps to sleep, the mage considered. Throwing branches on the coals before their rude shelter, camp was quickly broken, the stone dragon watching, perched in miniature on one burning branch's fork still jutting bleached above the fire. Iridescent were its flanks as fire lapped them, the dragon whipping its tail in the flames, causing sparks to star the pre-dawn sky.

The woman and the minstrel bundled their possessions quickly, casting surreptitious glances at the dragon sporting in the fire like a child in a pond. The dragon arched its back and fell into the coals, fire erupting and fire splashing outward. Elesia stomped out a flicker of fire started from a coal in dried winter grass.

"The dragon's just showing off," muttered the mage. "Ignore it."

"Perhaps he's just glad to be alive."

Yes, mage, perhaps I'm just glad to be alive.

The mage snorted, cinching the pack more securely to the donkey busy rolling its eyes at the dragon's day at the beach. Glimmer led the donkey away from the fire and into the moonlit meadow. The dragon of the campfire arched its neck as it reckoned their departure and then opened its mouth and inhaled the fire, the camp instantly engulfed in darkness merging to moonlight as the eyes of the travelers adjusted to the sudden change.

Mustn't leave the fire burning when we leave, the dragon commented, licking its lips with a narrow, forked tongue.

The dragon grew, larger and larger, and with one jump and flap of its wings, it was beside the travelers. Donkeys are known to whimper, and that is the sound the white donkey emitted, a voiced exhalation of alarm as it bolted for mountains across the river. The dragon casually reached out a taloned claw and secured the donkey, which now voiced its alarm in a loud, complaining bray. The dragon stretching out a hind leg as a stair, Glimmer climbed onto the dragon's back, followed by the others, last of all Cabbage-pants, taciturn and grim-faced.

The stone dragon crouched and then leapt to dawn, its huge wings flapping once, twice, the bulk of itself in the sky, having out-mastered logic and reason. Think of a dragon's wings and its bulk. A dragon flies not like a bird: not through air does a dragon fly but through wholeness. Banking carefully, the travelers clutching gnarled horns of scales along the dragon's back, the route down the Olifant's Tusk and the high valleys of the Olifant's Playground was followed, not at the juggernaut pace one took on the Gnome's Road but like that of an eagle's delicate telepathy with the wind.

Where the north branch of the River Quill gathered together the two tusks of its upper children, the travelers flew above the twin inns of the brothers Tuck. The dragon banked and landed at the midpoint of the two inns, which also happened to be midstream. Holding the white donkey loosely (yet securely, as the donkey discovered as it attempted to bolt), the dragon rested like a huge boulder, the stream swelling on both of its sides, flooding the banks and causing two rowboats pulled onto shore to noisily rattle their bottoms on the gravel beach. The dragon dipped its snout into the water and drank, then raised its head and blew steam into the sky. Where the water had slicked its hide, the grey scales revealed subtle shades of color as varied as the rainbow, just as stones on a rocky shore will discover sudden beauty when wet by the waters from whence they come.

"I wouldn't think you'd like water, being a fire-breather and all," the mage commented.

All elements are my children. Actually I swim quite well. I'd show you, but your . . . donkey . . . would get wet.

"Well, we certainly wouldn't want that," Glimmer returned dryly, observing the white donkey rolling its eyes, its hooves brushing the dancing waters.

The Tuck brothers had exited their inns, their blonde beards jutting and their blue eyes protruding from lean faces. They both were simultaneously slipping their suspenders onto their shoulders, their undershirts half-tucked into their breeches. Their mirrored behavior was made the funnier in that they did it unconsciously, two brothers so much alike trying so hard to be different.

"Tell me, dragon, why did we stop here? Are you fatigued?"

Better not to engage in dragon-baiting, young mage, the dragon responded with a backwards turn of its neck to view his rider. *I wanted to check the baggage before continuing.*

"It'd be me th' draco's talkin' aboot," Cabbage-pants said from tight lips as he slipped off the dragon's bulk and into the water. The dragon calmly extended its tail for the gnome to grasp and then lifted Cabbage-pants to the southern shore. Even from mid-stream, Glimmer could see that the wet gnome's normally earth-toned complexion had paled to shades of tan.

Earth prefers its own element was the dragon's only comment. *And I believe your long-eared companion would also be more comfortable elsewhere.*

"No, I'm fine," Jukka commented with straight-faced aplomb.

Your other long-eared friend, the dragon clarified as the mage raised an eyebrow.

Glimmer looked from one Tuck brother to the other and then asked, "Tucker, any rooms for the night?" The brothers' eyes met across the water, their sensibilities in conflict.

"Ac'ually, I'm cleanin' right now, an' th' place's a mess," ventured one as the other returned, "T'won't be as clean as mine when I'm done an' as ye'll be back p'haps less . . . accompanied . . ." their comments dribbling off to silence as they hitched their shoulders, adjusted their suspenders, and shuffled their feet.

The dragon sighed, steam dribbling from its nostrils. *Familiarity breeds contempt. I have never reconciled myself to the earthy humor you humans embrace. Ah, well . . .* and the dragon hopped to streamside, delivering the donkey to the gnome, who was already regaining his color.

"It's th' Gnome's Road I'll be takin' an' a race to see who gets home f'rst."

"May you find safe haven—good food for your stomach—" said Elesia.

"—and a dry stable for your ass," finished the bard, and then the gnome disappeared, diminishing in a moment down the track and into the distance.

Timed events aren't a dragon's avocation, yet we can't allow gnomes the opportunity to brag—especially cabbage gnomes, as one of my cousins discovered, and the dragon leapt into the sky, the travelers clutching for hold on the hoary scales, their bodies swaying in rhythm to dragon wings while below the brothers Tuck began gesticulating across the water, already debating who had the cleaner inn.

The quickest path to the Stone Dragon Inn was down the valley of the Olifant's Playground, following the course of the upper branch of the River Quill. The dragon swooped over the sanctuary at Madrone, Sisters rushing outside at the halloos, Sister Lisbeth raising one hand in benediction and salute as the dragon dipped its wing, turned, and continued south. The track of a road broadened as they passed east of Ruddy and then saw Red Robin beneath, the route to the inn of stone straight ahead. The dragon flew on toward the inn, road to the west and river to the east beneath them, twin tracks, one a sparkling flow, the other a duller brown in a sea of winter-bleached grass.

Then out of the sea of sameness, variation in color began to occur, the south side of slopes beginning to ripen to green. Sun-warmed even to a slighter degree, this near the sea and down from the mountains, the land had taken the frost-bereft chance to change its winter cloak of grey for one of spring. Just a mixture, a mingling of new sprouting leaves of grass amid the taller derelict stalks of winter had created a mist of green which overlay the drear dormancy of the land.

Lion's Loft lay below, hardly discernible from the air because grass adorned all but the face of the bluff, but as it lay off to the east of the dragon's flight, the naked, grey stones of the bluff's face were visible, like the last castle battlement of some ancient ruin. Jurgen's Wood filled its small valley to the south, and next to the wood across a stone bridge lay the stone inn, still only a bud in the travelers' vision, not the flower of their return, yet there—a destination and a culmination of their adventures.

How certain is the joy, thought Glimmer, *to have a home to which one can return.* Just the knowledge of it, deep and quiet in the mind, was a certain joy, a kind of seed-joy—a constant in all the change.

The terrain surrounding the stone inn was unfamiliar from the air, more cluttered with shapes Glimmer could not identify. The dragon landed to the east of the stone bridge, trees along the river's edge masking the inn except for its slate roof.

Business bids me to leave you here, expressed the dragon.

"Business?"

Your business, mage.

Glimmer felt a prickle at the base of his neck. *The hero comes home to trouble,* he thought. *It never works out the way you imagine.*

Down the dirt road and across the stone bridge advanced the companions, Glimmer in the lead, Jukka and Elesia behind. It was the meadow, the dragon's dream-meadow glimpsed from the bridge, that gave the mage his first premonition. Tents filled the meadow, but such a grab-bag of tents: yurts alongside the black tents of the desert, strange cone-like tents made from skins adorned with paintings of horses, tents for the lady of the castle—and some tents a mixture of styles, a distorted blending.

Dreamlike, Glimmer thought, *that strange, unexpected distortion of dream.*

Warriors walked among the tents, found the stepping stones and crossed the river, moving in the direction of the inn. One warrior felt his way on hands and knees, his face lacking eyes or even the sockets for eyes; the warrior would stop for an instant and jerk his dagger from its sheath, arcing the blade in the air before him. Others danced and others gibbered, a worm's knot of magic skewed, a menagerie of the macabre surging and ebbing to a rhythm, to a heartbeat inaudible yet discernible.

They dance to a melody, thought the mage, *but who sings the song?*

The travelers tightened their ranks, Jukka falling to the rear to be the eyes behind, Glimmer pointing the way, sickened by the grotesque sounds and sights that had invaded the sanity of his home. The road grew crowded at the bridge crossing the river, yet the group crossed the stream without incident, the macabre assembly ignoring the travelers and one another, absorbed in their inner nightmares.

But as the travelers neared the inn, a shadow darkened them and then settled to earth, huge and awesome in beauty and strength. Before them, wings outspread and singing a thousand songs, the sea drake, the glass statue, the dragon of the devouring eyes reared above them; but the dragon's eyes stared only at its maker, eyes hungry and merciless.

Wind rose and wire strands sang a whisper on the breeze. "I have come for you."

"Why?" Glimmer asked.

"Because I can, because another has set me free."

The dragon advanced a singing step forward, and the mage held out a hand to block the advance. "I am your maker."

"And I your un-maker," was a whisper upon the wind.

Voice stilled as the breeze died. All movement held its breath, frozen in possibilities, except one small movement, the flight of an ancient dragon of a different order, a dragonfly darting through sky to land on the mage's outstretched hand. The dragonfly, leaning slightly forward, balanced, and the mage remembered. Glimmer breathed out a breath, sending a small lungful of breeze beneath the insect's wings, and the dragonfly took flight, flew to the glass dragon and landed on a wing. Glass to sand, magic to its elements, consciousness slipping the knot and dream awoken, the dragon sifted through air to earth, sand and bits of metal and wire—terrific beauty returned to original form.

"All is illusion . . ." was whispered in Glimmer's mind, "a song and a dance," and then there was silence.

The travelers warily advanced into the silence. *There was nothing I could do,* thought Glimmer. *And so I did nothing, and it sufficed. Yet the dragon was here by magic, and magic other than mine.*

It was dream magic, and certainty grew in Glimmer's awareness. This was all dream magic, and there was only one other connection to dreams that he knew: Ramadi of the Children of the Sand, the apprentice whom he had met at Delta.

They reached the east entrance to the Stone Dragon Inn, and before the inn was collected a dream turned sour, men grotesquely animal-like: double-armed with sword and antler, sword and tusk, heads of animals on the bodies of men, men of grotesque proportions, the squeals of animals mixed with challenges human-voiced. The eastern doors to the common room, green with paint that Glimmer had applied himself, were thrown open and a table had been set on the cobblestones before the entrance, a table and two chairs. On one of the chairs sat an old man, wrapped in cloak to keep off the chill the afternoon sun could not burn away. Alma-Ata calmly sipped his tea, ignoring the martial posturing of the men-animals milling the yard like livestock at a fair—men-confused animals, animal-confused men. The old mage sat, calmly sipping his tea, adjusting his cloak, waiting, patiently at one with (or patiently ignoring) the phantasmagoria of the moment.

Beside Alma-Ata sat another, Minstrel Reis, lute before him, calmly attentive to his craft. The arrival of the travelers had stirred the grotesquerie to greater agitation; squeals and grunts, sudden thrusts and charges—eruptions of disorder had expanded throughout the malaise. The lutemaster plucked a single note on his instrument, stroked the strings to one chord and then another, caressed lute strings, and a harmony of sound expanded from that center of coherence where hands met music. The sweet sounds of nature flowed from the minstrel at his work, and the mob settled, subsided to greater quiet.

Jukka pulled his bamboo flute from a pocket and sounded a note in harmony with his master's, one note and then a series: the song of the wood thrush from the high meadow. Like birdsong his flute sang, and peace and ease were reaffirmed, ripples in a pond congruent to the mood of nature.

Wilim, grim-faced, brought an additional chair and then escorted Elesia to her mother. Jukka touched Elesia's hand as she left, and then advanced to stand behind his master, bamboo flute to his lips, minstrels mindful to the moment and its obligations.

Glimmer sat, reached out a hand to touch his master's, bowed his head in respect—spoke: "It seems we have unfinished business."

"They came this morning, at dawn—at dawn, the inn's time. Who knows what dream time?" Alma-Ata's voice was laced with weariness yet not weakness. The mage sat his chair as if he sat a throne of invincibility, sat a reality more substantial than wooden chair on cobbled inn courtyard. Action flows from silence and then returns: the apple-mage reached to touch a cup on the table, yet winds of action did not stir the roots of his being.

An angry bellow of a bull erupted in the distance, bellow sheering to human scream. Glimmer said in the lull following the scream, "Even Ramadi, I think, knows not what goes with Ramadi. Have you seen him or his master?"

"No, no one of the wooden ships, no one but these rudderless vessels of dream." The elder mage stared at the menagerie of war that surrounded them. "They have done nothing. Some have found enmity among themselves with much bellowing and bugling, but none have approached us or entered the inn. None have offered harm or even words, good or ill."

Wilim, linen cloth aproning his middle, exited the inn's kitchen door and set a cup of tea on the table before Glimmer. "Some o' the gnome's best," the man related in low tones.

"Cabbage-pants beat us here?"

"Aye," growled the man, "an' was challenged by a roebuck-man at th' bridge, a bad spot fer th' magic, him over water an' not a handful o' earth within reach."

"So what happened?"

Alma-Ata stirred. "He was backed to the bridge's edge by the swordsman who threatened with both sword and antler." The mage chuckled grimly. "Obsidian kept the man-buck at bay, and then the gnome leapt to the side and pricked the warrior's hide as the man-buck bugled and lunged at him."

"But th' white donkey ended th' dispute." Wilim concluded. "Two well-placed hooves at th' end o' a donkey's kick put th' thing in the water."

"No one else entered the dispute," Alma-Ata said. "They are not a company, not an army," he ended thoughtfully. "They have no direction or purpose—they are strangers in a strange dream."

"Sleepwalking," Glimmer responded. "They are not awake, nor are they at fault."

A stir rippled through the sleepwalking grotesques, a ripple stirring the grotesquerie of the dream like cider turning to vinegar, a delta of energy advancing toward the mages. It was a man advancing in a St. Vitus's dance of the macabre—three steps of stalking stealth, two leaps and a stumble, three steps stout of tread and then a nervous skitter. The nightmare rabble parted in silence and then followed with dream-like tread, leaving the dancing apparition an unencumbered space for its staccato shuffling.

Ramadi, dressed in elegant robes of ivory cloth embroidered with silver patterns, his black braid in stark contrast against the cloth, jittered before the mages sitting at their tea. His face quivered and sagged as if it were melting from the heat of his magic. Unstable, volatile, a chaotic misery was his magic, and Ramadi danced to the music of his misery, danced his crazed dance without form—one foot before, one back, two steps to the side, a hop backward and a skittering slide to a stop. Even stopped, he shifted his weight from one foot to the other, his face slipping this way and that like an egg cracked into a hot skillet.

"You have come, such is my magic," were Ramadi's words, but they distorted as he spoke, something to do with his lips or lungs or, perhaps, something to do with the magic itself, magic dream-blighted, magic not only in the dream but also of the dream.

"I have come home, Ramadi, and I am at home. You, however, are barely here. Any wind will sweep you away."

Alma-Ata remained silent, and Glimmer understood that he had no more to say to Ramadi's magic than to dream mage Glimmer's magic— even less, the younger mage considered. Alma-Ata had given Glimmer the foundation upon which to build his stone house, the young mage acknowledged . . . and the elder mage was deep in his own magic . . . doing nothing . . . waiting.

"How goes the Silence of the Saints, Ramadi, dream mage?" Glimmer asked.

"Wind on sand, on sand, wind took it, gone, gone," Ramadi chittered, dancing a hop and a sliding step to the side. "Gone and forgotten," he continued, his eyes focusing in different directions, different visions. "Who wants to know the wind? It knows me, oh, yes . . ."

Glimmer felt a sudden concern for Ramadi, knowing dream was engulfing him, waves of improbability overwhelming sanity. "How can I help you?"

"You can help me by dying!" the foreign mage shouted, his eyes afire and voice booming like doom upon the dying of the day. Alma-Ata calmly sipped at his tea, crossed his legs, and set the cup again onto the table in exactly the same spot from where he had first taken it.

"You are awake, and I am in my magic dreaming," Ramadi gibbered. "Awake," Ramadi said in the voice Glimmer had known in the port of Delta; "Dreaming," the foreign apprentice mage continued, the muscles of his face sagging for want of control, his voice sounding not just from his mouth but from everywhere, in the air and rising from the ground.

"I have you in my hand," Ramadi finished, raising a twitching arm, hand open, palm upward, his fingers clutching and squeezing empty air. "In my power," he added, a smile sliding to grimace. Glimmer didn't want to think about the nightmare of Ramadi's intentions.

Once again, Glimmer asked, "How can I help you, Ramadi? Remember the good conversation we had by the water? It was a good day. Sun was shining, and the day was warm." *Get him remembering the good,* thought Glimmer. *Don't try to push out the chaos; build a structure. Light the candle and where is darkness?*

"Delta and your glass dragon!" shouted the apprentice. "My master and the sailors wouldn't stop talking about it! The disappearance of rings and chains and the voice of the dragon! Well," danced the foreign mage, his hair now burning and his robes blackening, yet he oblivious to the change, the men-animals around him now pointing their muzzles to the sky and bugling and bellowing, "a dragon you shall have!"

He danced two steps back and extended his arms to the sky. "Behold my dragon, apple maggot dressed in rags!" cried Ramadi, his face now undistorted except for an exultation of mad malice and envy.

Glimmer stood and stepped away from the table, distancing himself from his master and the stone inn. On the steps leading to the entrance to the common room, before the green door painted by Glimmer himself were his friends—his family, to use the word in his heart—his master Alma-Ata cocooned in silence, Jukka standing behind Master Reis; on the steps of the inn Elesia and her mother Bega, stout broom-staff grasped in the white-knuckled hands of the mother; Wilim beside Bega, a smithy hammer in his hand; Sister Merri, face pale and fists clenched, yet to the front of the group, eyes targeted; the gnome Cabbage-pants, standing a step below the others and appearing even shorter, obsidian dagger loosened in its sheath and obsidian eyes pointing straight to the heart of the nightmare vision of a mage.

Glimmer's vision of his family sank deep into his heart, yet singular in his mind was his master, sitting calmly at his tea—Alma-Ata, his face composed, his eyes curious and totally fearless, gathering calmness to dispel the chaos. *Thus the archer pulls back the arrow,* Glimmer thought. *No target, no violent flight, no razor-sharp tip, no release—only the pull and then the poised moment, all possibilities in the balance. May I have that poise, that silence.*

A single bird flew in the distant sky toward the inn, approaching from behind Ramadi, a small black dot in the darkening sky, a movement of wings. The dot grew and defined itself: wings and bulk of a body, tail and serpentine neck, viper's head and eyes of obsidian. Ramadi's summoning approached, and the bugling and bellowing and milling of the rabble stilled, Ramadi's arms still aloft, commanding the dragon.

"It comes! See, I command and a dragon comes!" the mage shouted in exhilaration, dancing his dance of chaos.

Glimmer felt a presence and knew that Samhita was hovering behind him, a presence like stillness after wind has blown for days and days, the stillness beneath all wind.

And then the approaching dragon, flown from magician's madness, was above him, hovering its bulk with wings that logic told could not hover. It lowered and landed on the road and lessened its size to that of a hay wagon at harvest heaped with golden hay and pulled by four draft horses. It ambled across the bridge, ignoring the nightmare warriors that scattered and galloped and buck-jumped out of its path.

Behind him, Glimmer felt a settling and knew Samhita was mirroring the other dragon's actions. The two dragon's met, Samhita at Glimmer's side, Ramadi obscured by the bulk of the other dragon.

The dream mage "summoned" me, so I thought I'd come, Ramadi's dragon said. *I place myself at your feet, O progenitor of all dragons, of all that is and ever shall be.*

The stone dragon said nothing, merely stood before the other dragon, silent and still. No dreams or nightmares attached themselves to either dragon, no skittering or gibbering or shifting of the reality that they were. If the dragon before Samhita were a mountain, solid and stable from earth to sky, then Samhita was a mountain range, world extending beyond vision, all the elements embodied in the regal, abiding stillness of posture and eye.

Then Samhita spoke: *This is Glimmer, dream mage who is not dreaming, dream mage who speaks in the First Language when he sings his dreams* and, if obsidian can soften, the dragon receiving Samhita's message softened its gaze and warmly regarded the mage.

Hail, young mage, we meet at last.

Glimmer raised a hand in silent salutation, the reality of the two dragons beyond words.

Ramadi then danced around the dragon's bulk, placing himself before the dragon. "You are in *my* dream!" he chittered and danced. "I summoned you; now obey me and kill the mage. Kill them all!"

In your dream but not of it. Dragons do not dream.

With those words, the dragon launched itself into the air as did the stone dragon. Shrinking in size, they circling one another in joyous flight as they rose into the sky, circling and banking, one following the other, and then they settled onto the peak of the slate roof, side by side.

Dragons preened before the silence of the assembly, oblivious to the stares, sufficient unto themselves. Glimmer's eyes were on the dream mage before him, his gaze conscious of danger, cautious.

And then into the silence, he who had in silence abided spoke. His voice as easy as if he were relaxing after an evening meal, Alma-Ata reasoned: "With malice and envy and weakness—a potent poison you have mixed, Ramadi, and throughout your veins it has seeped."

The apple mage sighed, paused and spoke again, speaking almost to himself. "Who can say how one comes to such a state? How can we blame someone for wanting more when Totality is the essence of life? All of us, we follow our paths, and all paths lead to the same destination. Yet sometimes we lose our way, become frightened and tired and peckish."

The mage's voice gained intensity, its purpose focusing to the nightmare of a man before him. "Weak and sick at heart, we seek to raise ourselves by lowering others. We seek peace and happiness by destroying that of others." His voice grew even louder, and he stood, turned his back to nightmare and addressed the angels of the sun: "Oh, dragons! Forgive us our ways and guide us as best as we will listen." He then turned again to face both apprentice dream mages. "Are you able and shall you listen?"

Glimmer placed palm to palm and saluted his master, receiving his blessing. Then Glimmer dropped to one knee and raised his arms, palms open, to the dream mage before him. His eyes full upon Ramadi, Glimmer saw the foreign mage's face turn slack with inner absorption, the nervous dancing continuing unnoticed by the dancer, eyes protuberant and unfocused, clothing askew—indeed, the whole being of the man canted by his vision—Glimmer saw the danger, the reason dream mages were feared and despised by others.

He saw in Ramadi not an enemy but a mirror and in that mirror he saw an apprentice who, less than a year ago, had furtively climbed through a window into a new life, a new existence, one that had been fraught with danger because of his ignorance. *Still fraught with danger,* he realized.

He had to hold onto his sanity by letting go, become himself by expanding the stream of his life to larger rivers; and he could not do that by making moods or simply by hope or faith. Not that hope or faith increased his dangers; hope and faith increased with the successful navigation of the river.

Words writ upon each particle of life and words unspoken but lively— underlying the stream is the streambed; underlying the road is stone, bones of the earth; underlying the song of life is the silence from which song arises. Mage Alma-Ata was a Mage Who Gathers; he had no magic other than that which existed in the totality of the world. Yet was that not also true of Glimmer himself, of all mages, of all that existed? And did not that which existed outside also exist within? Fill the cup with water and then submerge the cup in ocean. Cup still exists and is still full but is filled with the wide, flowing waters of the ocean—full beyond measure.

Glimmer could not consider Ramadi his enemy because he *was* Ramadi, a man trying to step from unstable boat to stable shore.

"Wake up, Ramadi!" Glimmer stood suddenly and called out into the silence that had fallen over the assemblage when the mages had faced one another, silence defined by Alma-Ata's musings. "Wake up, you are dreaming. Leave the night of your dream. The sun is still shining. Wake up!"

On the stone steps and plaza before the eastern entrance to the inn, beneath the darkening sky, the sky a glory of reds and oranges to the west, those who had traveled this path with Not a Glimmer of Magic joined his entreaty.

Alma-Ata stood and spoke, "Wake up, Ramadi, awake!"

Minstrel Reis stood, and he and Jukka spoke, "Awake, dream mage, sun still shines!" Lute and wooden flute sang their harmony.

Elesia, Sister Merri, Bega, Wilim, Cabbage-pants in his phlegmatic tones—all called into the silence, "Awake, awake, awake from your dream!"

Ramadi moaned like a child deep within a dream. His dream-body turned rigid, tensed with effort. "I cannot!" he cried. *"Blood, blood, let me go!"*

His body contorted, and he reached to the sky, arms and fingers outstretched and straining. Sunfire flaming forth shot from his outstretched hands into the void, energy unleashed and uncontrolled. A sob shook his frame, and now he dropped to one knee, a moan and a curse escaping him. Raising his head, his arms extended in entreaty to Glimmer, but fire escaped them, shot in a solar flare of incandescence at the mage, heat intense beyond experience, and Glimmer's hands rose in denial: *No, not this.*

Fire shaped itself into a flaming dragon's head, open mouth spewing fire, long neck a flare of fire leaping from Ramadi's hands. Dragonfire touched Glimmer's hands, and flesh was reminded of its own fiery nature, fire incarnate that had touched and said, *I place fire within your hand.* Fire surged in the dream, flaring against the upraised hands, slowed to a pace beyond reckoning, then turned back upon itself.

Gnomes travel a road fantastic to human reckoning, so how can one reckon the path fire takes? Curving back, fire touched Glimmer's upraised hands and looped, pouring back upon its path. A glacier may move an inch in a day, and sun denied bides its own time: fire surcharged with such unity of opposites surged from hand to hand with rapacious enmity, carved curves of space shaped by hands shaped by fire. Light beyond reckoning licked Glimmer's hands, yet hands did not burn. Flesh did not char, nor did bones crack and marrow melt. Flame stroked Glimmer's palm, touched and turned back upon itself, yet the sun's caresses pushed at his hands, creation insistent that void shall be filled. The mage leaned to the fire, braced himself against the jet of flaming dragon leaping from the chaos of Ramadi's hands. Slowly Glimmer was forced backward, was straightened by the river of flame and was in danger of being swept from his feet and engulfed.

Sister Merri, who had stood to the fore of the group on the steps, uttered an inarticulate sound, her cry a braided whip of both affirmation and denial, and ran to Glimmer, stood behind him and braced herself against the flame. Fire was deflected by the mage's body, but still she burned, screams of terror and pain swallowed by the roar of the fiery dragon.

The good Sister leaned her body to the mage's, burned lips screaming, "I live to serve, serve because I live!" In her final act she would choose death in service to one who had eased her pain.

Flame curved, reaching the dream mage Ramadi, flame's first tendril brushing the mage of nightmare. He screamed, he screamed and exploded to fire, his atoms released from their dream: disappeared, the tail of the fire serpent still seeking its mouth, snake swallowing itself and then gone, gone.

In silence all gone—Ramadi, fire, rabble of men-animals silenced and all gone, and when the last particle of sunfire had consumed itself, Glimmer and the good Sister also disappeared, eternal evening settling upon the inn, sky darkening, darkening—scuff of footsteps on cobblestones, black slate of the inn's roof peak empty of dragons—gone, all gone.

In the empty silence, Alma-Ata sighed and then stood, bowed and old. He stumbled, and Wilim gained his side and steadied the old man by an arm. Together they entered the inn through the kitchen and made their way to Alma-Ata's study. The others silently followed but went no farther than the kitchen table to sit, Bega continuing to the common room to cater to the half a handful of guests who would be taking a wealth of tales home about the ways of a certain fieldstone inn along a dirt track on the way to nowhere special.

Only the gnome stayed on the flagstone terrace, legs stoutly fixed, his eyes bright points of obsidian, prepared to wait and await, stalwart and silent, needing no other to share his vigil: Ally and Silent One and garden gnome, cabbage-warrior of the one-inch obsidian blade. He also serves who only stands and waits—and gnome stood and waited, as loyal as earth abides.

Glimmer blinked and seemed to hear that blink in the sudden silence and change of scene. He was surrounded by sumptuous tapestries and silks; lamps shone their ruddy light onto a sleeping chamber such as he had never seen. Plastered walls and hanging plants, luscious pillows and bedding wrapped in a snarl like coiled snakes upon the floor. The abruptness of his transition from arcane duel to bed chamber caused him to stumble, for his last action had been to lean against the flaring blast of fire sent him by the foreign mage. He could still smell the burn in the air, the heat which had coated him like an unguent. His eyes still spotted black from the intensity of the light which had arced space to find his hand.

Straightening and stepping to the window to escape the incense-fragrant fire of the lamps, Glimmer heard a soft sound behind him. He turned and saw a mass of smoldering clothing on the floor, a mass that heaved, a moan escaping. Burned and broken by her bravery, Sister Merri of the Order of Hospitality lay on the flagstones. A sob broke from Glimmer as he knelt beside her, staring impotently at the ruin of the woman. A part of him remembered her dash to his back, only a faint peripheral memory, so intense had been the focus of his efforts to survive.

He touched her burnt body, and concern for the woman kindled within him like a seed sprouting. Life poured green from his hands, spilling onto the woman, encasing her in a seed of glowing energy. He closed his eyes and opened to the flowing of life, through him and of him. Green-growing cocooned the woman, and the mage wept for the gift he had been given and for the tragic necessity of its use.

Footsteps approached, quietly hurrying, and a woman, whose rich apparel matched the décor of the room, entered and softly approached the bed. She bent to the silk covers and pulled them back. Gasping with horror, she straightened, her delicate hand to her mouth, and then she screamed in terror and despair. Turning away from that which she had seen, the woman discerned Glimmer crouching in the shadowed edges of the room, a green seed of light on the floor before him, and then she fled the room, screaming foreign words, an obvious summoning of guards.

The bedding pulled back, Glimmer could see a blackened form—Ramadi, he realized. Glimmer picked up Sister Merri's form and carried her, bandaged in green light, to the bed, laying her next to the man. As he approached the bed to see the fire-blackened body, a rattling approach of running footsteps heralded the approach of the summoned guards. Ignoring the approach of heavy feet and creak of armor, Glimmer sat as still as stone at bedside, one hand on Sister Merri and the other on the blackened form of the dream mage Ramadi.

Scanning the room, the guards lowered spears and advanced, mage not moving except to carefully position his hands to those he sought to heal. The guards stopped two paces from Glimmer, their square-cut beards emphasizing the resolution of their countenances; however, they were not willing to skewer a man sitting so still and magical, and therefore stood before him, ready to thrust should he move. The green of seed-joy, so soothing in its presence, healing and nurturing, reassured the guards beyond even their duty; they felt its goodness and allowed the magic to work its way.

Time passed heartbeat by heartbeat. In the silence, Glimmer could hear the breathing of the guards, the creak of leather armor, and then his awareness passed within, falling to two forms, two bodies of light before him. Light of life they were, light radiating and radiant, as eternal as starfire and dragonfire, consciousness structuring a body out of itself so that it might become. One form's fire leapt brightly from the void, light white flecked with red and orange; joy flowed through the mage at the leaping of the light, and with his joy the light burned more brightly, expanding, infinite, white and pure. The other form burned with a blue flame, cool and flickering. And now into the subsiding of the light, he cast a rope of starlight.

Body of light, grasp light becoming, being expressed!

But flames blued and flickered their diminishing, dying dance. As there is a becoming, so there is an unbecoming, a return to being unmoving, stillness more ancient and eternal than breath or heartbeat.

More footsteps in the hallway sounded a path for the young mage's awareness to follow, and then the young woman returned, this time followed by a man familiar to Glimmer, the mage of the foreign ships that had docked at Delta, the place of the magic of the glass dragon singing in the wind.

The foreign mage—*Khalil*, Glimmer remembered—placed himself between the dream mage and the woman, a protective gesture.

"You!" Khalil uttered, seeing Glimmer at the point of the guards' spears.

The woman poured out words, pulling on the sleeves of the man's embroidered robe, repeating the name *Ramadi* over and over. She pulled him to the bed, collapsing into the older man's arms as she again looked at the bodies now encased in the green glowing emanating from Glimmer's hands. The young woman repeated her entreaty, clearly asking for help, and Khalil leaned closer to the bodies, examining them.

He then looked to Glimmer, questions in his eyes. Beside the body lay a stoppered bottle, which the man sniffed and then asked a sharp question to the woman. Another stream of desperate words poured from her, her gestures and tones overwhelmed with frantic guilt. She then turned to Glimmer and shouted, pointing her finger at him in accusing tones.

Seed-joy faltered, a reservoir run dry, and Glimmer, swaying as the light died, would have tipped from the bed except for the supporting hands of the foreign mage. Forcing himself from his swoon, Glimmer looked upon the two forms beside him, saw the good Sister with flesh red as from a severe sunburn, skin no longer blackened. Ramadi, though, still lay twisted and blackened on the bed, his mouth seared open in a rictus of pain.

Sister Merri breathed, the beat of her pulse at the neck steady, but Ramadi, burned within his dream, did not move. "I could heal injury but not death," Glimmer murmured, relief and agony braiding his heart with their mirror emotions. The dream mage looked up at Khalil with tear-streaked eyes. "He died of his own dream."

The foreign mage checked the good Sister of Hospitality resting on the bed and then spoke to the young woman beside him. Gesturing the guards to leave the room, Khalil then spoke to Glimmer. "I have told my daughter to look to the woman. Come, young mage," the foreign mage sighed. "Let us talk."

They walked to an arched opening to a second-floor veranda overlooking an indoor garden below. A slight wind cooled the night air, and the lamp Kahlil carried lit a sitting area enclosed by waist-high walls of rosy stucco, the floor tiled and strewn with pillows. From somewhere within the inner courtyard came the trickle of running water. Placing the lamp upon a small table, the foreign mage sat heavily and gestured for Glimmer to sit.

"This is my daughter Rosheen's room, of the quarters of the court mage—I, Kahlil—of the palace of His Serenity. She has confessed to helping Ramadi this day." He paused, shook his head, and focused on the one question in his mind. "How did he die?"

"He shot a stream of fire at me. I held up my hand, which turned the fire back onto him." The young mage leaned against the stucco and closed his eyes. "We begged him to wake up." He opened his eyes to the shadowed Kahlil. "He said his body would not let him. He came with an army of strange creatures—half-man and half-animal—half-awake and half-asleep or dreaming, according to my master."

"My poor Ramadi!" the foreign mage cried. "Such a small, beautiful ability to dream, growing slowly, especially knowing the sound of Wind on Sand. And then he would think of you."

Their gaze met, and then Kahlil's gaze extended beyond the mage to an object hanging from a bronze wire from a beam above them. It was a wind chime fashioned from glass and metal, too intricate to possibly exist, too fine in its detail—a graceful dragon with iridescent glass wings, scales of a thousand colors, its wings arched, its neck joyfully stretched to the sky. Kahlil removed it from its hook and sat beside Glimmer.

The dragon caught the light of the lamp and was transformed into a thousand hues of red and gold. Its exquisite beauty caused Glimmer to catch his breath, his eyes tearing.

"Such an ability, small but pure, but it was not enough, not quick enough." The glass dragon turned slowly in the faint breeze, singing a song different than the glass fire drake of the delta, casting hues of light more delicate than those of the glass of Glimmer's magic. "And so he drank an elixir of dreamroot, my daughter caring for him this day, aiding my apprentice."

"And the dream slipped its center, and he could not escape," concluded the young mage. "He died within his nightmare."

"Within his own creation."

The glass dragon spun slowly in the breeze and then stretched its wings. Glass and gold transmuted to dragonflesh, and the wind harp opened its eyes, green with specks of gold, and sang its dragonsong, sweet and pure as desert air.

Mourn the man and praise the child. That which is eternal cannot die.

Mage and mage, young and old, stared at the hummingbird of a dragon in wonder, the dragon the same dragon in miniature that Ramadi had summoned at the Stone Dragon Inn.

"My ears hear, but my heart is deaf," said Kahlil.

Let us to your daughter.

Scrambling to his feet, Kahlil aided Glimmer, weak from his ordeal, to where his daughter sat on the bed, beside the two forms, one still and the other eternally still. The daughter stared at the iridescent handful of dragon hovering in the air above the two men. Suddenly it seemed to Glimmer that wings expanded to envelop the two, father and daughter, and then the image ceased.

"He lives!" breathed the daughter, her eyes luminous with tears.

By his eternal soul, said the dragon. *Now take back the beauty created,* and the wind chime once again dangled from the string in Kahlil's hand, yet the dragon still hovered, a living embodiment of the sculpture, before father and daughter.

"And how is Sister Merri?" Glimmer asked the dragon.

"Ask her yourself," the daughter haltingly said before the dragon could respond. "A little have I talked to her."

Sister Merri gazed up at Glimmer with eyes round and tired. "She said," the Sister nodded to Khalil's daughter Rosheen, "that you coated me in green light."

"It was the magic of the gnomes, not me."

"I was in great pain . . . and then I was not."

"Now we can go back home."

Sister Merri smiled slightly and then closed her eyes. The blackened body of Ramadi still lay contorted on the bed, the body now covered by a cape. The Sister turned her head at the sound of the daughter's grieving and saw the daughter, head bowed, one hand tenderly on the body covered by the cape.

"She grieves. Would that I could stay here to serve and ease the pain."

You may, dear Sister, a voice whispered within, heard by all.

"And if I wish to return?"

The dragon, hovering like a hummingbird over the bed, raised a foreleg and said, *Call and I will hear. Such devotion demands its like.*

The good Sister settled to her pillows, content. "Then I shall accept and rejoice in this opportunity to serve." She place a hand tenderly on the weeping Rosheen's arm, and the young woman, gazing into the tenderness of Sister Merri's eyes, lifted the Sister's fire-reddened hand to her own tear-stained cheek, accepting the gift of compassion.

"'And sister and sister shall be sisters.' So states an ancient saying," murmured Khalil.

The dragon then flitted to face Glimmer. *And now, what would you do, mage?*

"What needs to be done," was Glimmer's unthinking response.

Ah, you are learning, said the dragon. *Speak well your good-byes.* Eyes met, hearts beat once, and in the silence between heartbeats, mage and dragon disappeared.

Chapter 14

"Help another and nature will lend a hand."
"Dynamic as a dragon's flight, silent as its wings."
108 Aphorisms of Mage DeVasier

જી

Glimmer lay asleep on his pallet, spring unknown within the stone walls of the tower yet the green mist on the land had run rampant, mist greening to blossom on the hills and vales of the mountains. Glimmer was huddled within his covers this morning, though, huddled against the cold that had stolen down the slopes of the crooked mountains, slipped down the escarpment and onto the uplands, continuing toward the sea its cold way, reminding the land that spring consists of equal parts summer and winter and that the amalgam of the two was not a certainty, that sometimes one superseded the other as ice can exist on a warm day or sun still shine when the world is frozen.

He tossed upon the sea, he staggered upon the deck of a wind-blown ship, he swam in waters torn by storm—he was rocked awake by the strong hand of his master shaking him by his shoulder.

"Wake up, Glimmer. Wake up!" Alma-Ata urged in the pre-dawn light, and the young mage awoke muzzily from a deep sleep. As he sat up, his eyes still closed, his master continued. "Frost this morning, and we've got to do what we can. A whole season of apples to be lost from too much sleep, and then how will you feel when the sun is high?"

Awake now, Glimmer rubbed his eyes and yawned even as he hoisted himself from his covers to slip out of his nightshirt and into his work clothes, choosing a heavier jerkin and his woolen breeches.

"The foothill orchards are not in danger; the trees have not budded yet, but think of the orchards at Tye's Bottom and the south slopes of Cap's Croft; those trees are ablossom and are bound to frost and be lost."

Glimmer fumbled for a candleholder and its stub of candle in the darkness, touching the wick with a finger, the wick springing to flame. In the flickering light, the young mage saw his master, dressed already in work clothes and cloak, worn and functional his attire, his hair awry and his expression earnest.

"It's to the fields and the smudge fires, then," the young man assumed, and at the elder mage's nod, they left the room and landing, Glimmer stopping at the kitchen for a swallow of cold cabbage tea and a mouthful of bread.

They headed south along the road toward Jurgen's Wood and the bottomland orchards of early apples that now were threatened with fog crystallizing to frost, spring buds freezing away the potential of harvest. They walked, the air steaming from their pace as they breathed, and then the orchards hove into view, black shadow arms speckled with white blossoms luminous in the faint light of the stars. Already farmer Tye and his family, wife and seven sons, were among the trees, smudge fires being lit to warm the air, but it would be too little; the frost would be too severe for the buds, the cold too great for the efforts of the family to counteract.

Glimmer could hear the concern in the voices of the family in the hollow below, the frantic frustration in the sudden shout of the father and the helpless determination in reply. *Seven sons are not enough,* the young mage thought, *although seven sons are more than most would have.*

And then he felt a presence behind him, above him, a stirring of wind and form too large for sky to cup in its hand. Sun had not yet broken the horizon, yet the eastern sky behind Glimmer and his master was alive with the ruddiness of dawn, the sky to the west still speckled with stars— a time of transition, a time when the world awoke and began again a new day, possibilities as ripe as summer apples juicy on the branch.

In the sky above Glimmer was a dragon, colored in all possible shades of fire, lit by all the hues of dawn as the sun's curve colored the horizon. With wings that seemed inadequate to lift its weight, the dragon nonetheless hovered in the air, flying upon currents more subtle than those which belled its wings.

The dragon breathed fire into the sky and with its wings pushed fire-warmed air down the sloping land to the hollow. Glimmer's face warmed with the moving air, and he turned to the hollow to see the family staring with wide eyes to the dawning of the day and the dragon in the sky breathing another flare of fire into the sky and winging it to warm the trees in the hollow. One of the sons lifted a hand and shouted a cry of understanding and relief, a frail sound quickly lost beneath the bulk of the dragon.

Glimmer could almost hear the thoughts of the family below: *Is the dragon saving the trees or simply warming us up for breakfast?* As the dragon moved along the cup of the hollow, fire and wing warming air, fog did not turn to frost, and diamonds of water did not form to freeze crop to ruin.

Alma-Ata walked down the slope to converse with farmer Tye, whose black hair was now beaded with fog as he still urged his family to set the smudges; man does not chance his fortunes upon the whim of a dragon, not with smudge pots at hand.

The dragon settled itself at the highest point above the rim of the hollow, its wings spread to fan the air iridescent with the dawning sun behind. All the colors of creation resided in those wings, all the glory of the world for those with eyes to see and the heart to look.

"Why?" asked the mage Glimmer.

Why not?

"Why now and never before?"

"Never" is an absolute.

The young mage looked up at the glory of the dragon beside him and then asked the question, the real question in his mind. "Why you and not Samhita? Do I now have two dragons?"

You never "had" one. The dragon then paused, collecting its thoughts— if dragons do such a thing, more likely a pause for dramatic effect, following the sense of timing which also directed the spinning of galaxies. *Samhita does not "do" but simply is. To come to you was a gift beyond comprehension. Accept it, young mage.*

"And why did you come? Why do I deserve your gift?"

The dragon lit the dawn with fire and then sent it drifting down the slope already warming with the sun's morning rays. Glimmer realized that the dragon was not collecting its thoughts; thoughts were collecting, consciousness was stirring, to be expressed in the fullness of the moment ripening.

Samhita is Being expressed. The dragon gazed down at Glimmer, shy for a moment, or at least unpresuming. *I am Akshare, the way to Knowledge.*

"And what does that mean?"

Samhita is; I am.

"I also am—am I not?"

Indubitably.

Moving away from abstraction, Glimmer asked, "And what shall we do now?"

Below man and dragon, sun bathed the orchard with its warming fire, smudge pots now burning with their warming assistance. Farmer Tye and Alma-Ata stood beside a smudge pot, the mage's attitude one of listening as the farmer spoke and then pointed toward the man and dragon on the hilltop.

Glimmer raised his hand to his master, a simple gesture complex with emotion. Even in the midst of the bustle of Farmer Tye and his family, Alma-Ata seemed surrounded by silence, by serenity.

The dragon then turned to face the sun now fully risen, a ball of cosmic fire on the horizon. The young mage turned with the dragon, both facing the new day, the dragon spreading wings painted by light all the colors of creation. Glimmer lifted his arms and spread wide his hands, fingertips to one side brushing wing. The wing stretched to envelop the young mage, gently lifting him to the dragon's back.

What shall we do now? You have already answered that question, the dragon responded, and then the dragon, mage upon his back, leapt into the pristine fires of the morning sky.

About the Author

Tom Kepler has been a classroom teacher for grades 7-12 for over thirty years.

A teacher of the Transcendental Meditation program, he has taught at Maharishi School of the Age of Enlightenment, Fairfield, Iowa, since the fall of 2005.

His current project, entitled *Dragons of Blood and Stone*, is a sequel to *The Stone Dragon*. To be contacted when the book is released, send an email to tomkeplerwriting12@gmail.com.

Other publications include *Love Ya Like a Sister* (Wise Moon Books, 2010, ISBN 978-0-9842734-1-6) and *Bare Ruined Choirs* (Wise Moon Books, 2009, ISBN 978-0-9842734-0-9). Online publications are listed at his website.

Tom Kepler Writing Online

Website and blog: www.tomkeplerswritingblog.com
Facebook: www.facebook.com/TomKeplerWriting

About Photographer Suzanne Bonnefond

The cover images are of medieval ruins, a monastery for nuns created in 1260 and destroyed around 1790. Suzanne has many beautiful photographs of landscapes and medieval historical sites published online. View her work at Flickr: www.flickr.com/photos/sarvadon. To contact her or to purchase photos, email axzpro@yahoo.fr.